THE VIKING

A Viking Blood and Blade Saga

Peter Gibbons

Copyright © 2025 Peter Gibbons

All rights reserved

The characters and events portrayed in this book are fictitious. Any similarity to real persons, living or dead, is coincidental and not intended by the author.

No part of this book may be reproduced, or stored in a retrieval system, or transmitted in any form or by any means, electronic, mechanical, photocopying, recording, or otherwise, without express written permission of the publisher.

ISBN: 9798281712781

Cover design by: Erelis Design
Library of Congress Control Number: 2018675309
Printed in the United States of America

AUTHOR MAILING LIST

If you enjoy this book, why not join the authors mailing list and receive updates on new books and exciting news. No spam, just information on books. Every sign up will receive a free download of one of Peter Gibbons' historical fiction novels.

https://petermgibbons.com

Farit hefi ek blóðgum brandi

svá at mér benþiðurr fylgði,

ok gjallanda geiri;

gangr var harðr af víkingum.

Gjǫrðum reiðir róstu,

rann eldr of sjǫt manna,

ek lét blóðga búka

í borghliðum sœfask

I have gone with bloody blade

Where the ravens followed,

And with screaming spear;

Vikings fought fiercely.

Raging we gave battle,

Fire ran through men's houses,

I let bloody bodies

Sleep in town gateways

- From the tenth century poet Egil SkallaGrimsson

THE VIKING

By Peter Gibbons

GLOSSARY

Brynjar – Norse word for a coat of chainmail.
Drakkar – A type of Viking warship.
Drengr – A Norse warrior.
Drengskapr – Viking warrior code.
Einherjar – Chosen warriors who have died in battle and are brought to Valhalla by the Valkyrie to feast, fight and prepare for the Ragnarök where they will serve as Odin's army.
Hamingja – Luck, or the personification of a person's luck.
Jörmungandr – The world serpent, unfathomably large and will encircle the earth, eating itself at the end of days, during the Ragnarök where it will battle with Thor.
Nástrǫnd – The afterlife for those guilty of crimes such as oathbreaking, adultery or murder. It is the corpse-shore, with a great hall built from the backs of snakes, where the serpent Níðhöggr gnaws upon the corpses of the dead.
Nágrind – The death fence, the fence surrounding and leading to Niflheim.
Níðhöggr – A serpent or monster who gnaws at

the roots of the great tree Yggdrasil, and also gnaws upon the corpses of the dead at Nástrǫnd.
Nithing – A coward, villain or oathbreaker, not worthy of the glorious afterlife.
Njorth – The Viking sea god.
Norns – Norse goddesses of fate. Three sisters who live beneath the world tree Yggdrasil and weave the tapestry of fate.
Odin – The father of the Viking gods.
Naal binding – Norse style of knotless knitting using a single needle.
Niflheim – Norse frozen hel world.
Ragnarök – The end-of-days battle where the Viking gods will battle Loki and his monster brood.
Skald – Norse poet.
Seax – A short, single-edged sword with the blade angled towards the point.
Seiðr – A type of Norse magic.
Sessrúmnir – The goddess Freya's hall of the slain.
Sheerstrake – The uppermost line of a ship's planking.
Skuld – One of the three Norns who sit at the great ash tree Yggdrasil and decide the fates of men.
Thor – The Viking thunder god.
Thruthvangar – Thor's realm in the afterlife, where he gathers his forces for the day of Ragnarök. Similar to Valhalla.
Týr – The Viking war god.

Valhalla – Odin's great hall, where he gathers dead warriors to fight for him at Ragnarök.
Vik – Part of Viking Age Norway.
Winingas – Long strips of cloth, often wool or linen, worn around the legs as wrappings.
Whale Road – The sea.
Wyrd – Norse/Anglo-Saxon concept of fate or destiny.
Yggdrasil – A giant ash tree which supports the universe and the nine worlds including our world, Midgard.

ONE

For as long as he could remember, Einar had dreamed of becoming a warrior. He had dreamt of shining axe blades, glorious swords, champions, and the clash of iron on stout shields. He had grown up amongst such men; carls, warriors with braided beards, broad shoulders, bright eyes; big men who bristled with reputation and fearsome warrior pride. Rising to the status of a warrior was everything; his only ambition, a dream burning inside his heart like a furnace. Other boys followed in their fathers' footsteps and became apprentice potters, smiths, thatchers, bakers or shipwrights, but Einar only had eyes for the sea. Such men bowed their heads when the carls passed by, when the warrior elite strode through town like heroes with combed beards, tattooed faces, their weapons and arm rings glinting in the sun. But to become such a man, to sail, raid and fight aboard a warship, a young man had to earn his place among the dangerous ones; the killers, and seafarers who risked their lives on the Whale Road.

Einar stared up at the shipmaster, who stood on a raised platform at the ship's stern, one brawny arm resting on the steering oar and another wiping sea haar from his hard, scarred face. Einar skinned his knuckles on the ship's hull as a thunderous wave crashed against the bows and its icy spray whipped his face like a lash. He dragged the bailing bucket through knee-deep bilge water and tossed another bucketful downwind and over the side. His hands, as red as raw meat, shook from the cold as he knelt again to scoop up another bucketful.

"Row!" bellowed One Leg Bolti from the steerboard. "Row, you lazy whoresons, before it's too late!"

Sixty men hauled on long oars cut from stout ash. Those oar blades bit into the ferocious white-capped waves and the warriors grunted, muscled backs stretching, heaving their *drakkar* warship closer to shore. Einar peered over the side as the prow rose above the grey-green swell. He squinted through the crashing water and glimpsed a scrap of dirty yellow sand ahead. Men waited on that beach with painted shields and spear points bristling like a murderous forest.

"Dolgfinnr Dogsblood gathers his warriors," Bolti thundered above the sea's fury and the groan of the ship's timbers. His bulbous eyes fixed on each man aboard the *drakkar* with a maddened stare. He clambered down from the raised steerboard platform and another carl took his place at the steering oar. Bolti's brawny arms hooked around seal hide rigging, his face drawn tightly across his skull. "Dolgfinnr is the bastard who insults our Lord Ragnar with every breath. He broke his oath and defies Ragnar's demands, and we are his punishment. An oathbreaker is a *nithing*, a worm, a criminal who must face our wrath. Ragnar Lothbrok honours us with this task, and we shall show Dolgfinnr and his band of ragged curs what it means to deny Ragnar his dues. So row, row for Ragnar, row for One Leg Bolti, row for your shipmates, and row for the raven banner!"

"Ragnar, Ragnar, Ragnar!" The crew bawled their war cry as one, and Einar squinted up at the triangular banner atop the mast post. A battle standard famed and feared across Midgard, snapping in the furious wind. Ragnar Lothbrok's black raven daubed upon a white background gazed down at the warriors like the eyes of Odin's ravens themselves, and Einar shuddered with fear at the battle to come.

"You, boy?" barked Kraki, the first mate. He glowered at Einar, his bald head wrinkled and daubed with faded tattoos above a rope of braided beard. "Ready the weapons."

Einar nodded, glad to leave the bail bucket in the bilge. Bailing was a constant task on board a warship. Water constantly sloshed over the sheerstrake to swamp the ballast stones and fill the ship's bilge with water made filthy by boots, discarded food, and the dirt of a ship after weeks at sea.

Boy. The word cut Einar like a knife. He was a man, almost. Old enough to wear his first arm ring and hold a spear once he'd earned them. Einar wasn't sure exactly how many summers he had seen. It had been ten, at least, since his mother had died and he remembered it like it was yesterday. He was a boy until he proved himself otherwise, or until a lord took him into his service with solemn oaths. Bolti was the shipmaster of the Waveslicer, a sleek warship, a *drakkar,* in the service of Ragnar Lothbrok, the greatest Northman of them all.

Einar rose from the bilge and clenched his teeth together to stop them from chattering. He ducked beneath the rigging until he came to a barrel lashed to the mast by stout hemp rope. Einar popped the lid off and swept aside the oily fleece cover to reveal magnificently gleaming weapons and armour. Einar pulled out an axe, its bearded blade etched with runes of power, its haft criss-crossed with leather strips for grip. The blade shone like a star beneath the grim sea squall and cauldron-grey sky. One day he would own such an axe; he would row and fight and earn his reputation as a warrior, a carl and *drengr.* But not this day. For now, his duty was to bail the ship and follow Bolti's orders.

"Hurry, lad," growled Kraki. "Get to it or I'll whip the flesh from your bones." He meant the threat, and Einar gathered up an armful of weapons and passed them to their owners.

"Heya," said Sigarr, a stocky warrior with his hair cropped short save for two braids hanging from either side of his face. He nodded thanks to Einar and took one hand from his oar to take his axe and seax and place them beneath his oar bench. He leaned into Einar and smiled to reveal a mouth full of broken teeth. "Today is a war-day, a red-day. A day for Odin and Týr, for the *drengr* to earn their rings." He cackled when Einar gulped and hurried on to the next man.

The prow dipped into a wave trough and Einar lost his balance, clinging to the halyard rope to stop himself from toppling overboard. Sea spray soaked him and he cuffed the saltwater from his eyes with the sleeve of his wool tunic. The prow bore the image of a savage hawk, its beak, talons, and angry eyes fiercely snarling at the shore as the hull crashed through the white-crested breakers. Einar reached into the barrel and pulled out a fleece-wrapped bundle. Unravelling it, he found a sword and a chainmail *brynjar*. The steel shone with lanolin, there to protect the precious metal from the worst of the sea's corrosive bite. The *brynjar* was almost too heavy for Einar to carry, never mind wear whilst fighting. He carried it to Bolti, who hobbled about the deck on his wooden leg, earned after he had lost the lower limb to an enemy's axe long ago.

"Help me with it, lad," Bolti instructed. Einar shook out the *brynjar* coat of mail, which protected its wearer, arrows and all but the mightiest of blades, from neck to knee. Bolti knelt on his good leg and raised his arms so that Einar could pass the sleeves over his hands. Then the shipmaster shrugged it over his shoulders and broad back until it covered his body like the scaly skin of a serpent. Bolti strapped the sword to his belt and drew the shining blade.

"Odin!" Bolti howled at the sky. "Odin All-Father, look how we sail our warship across Ran's furious seas to bring blade and war to our enemies. Grant us battle-luck, make our weapons swift and our enemies slow. Hear me, Odin!"

Einar hurried back to the mast and pulled a sheaf of tied spears from beneath its platform. He untied the leather thong and passed a leaf-bladed spear to each of the crew. Half a dozen men retrieved bows from beneath rowing benches and fresh bowstrings, which they kept coiled beneath their caps or in pouches at their belts to keep them dry.

"Ten more pulls," Kraki said, urging the men onwards, for they could not see the beach. They rowed with their backs facing towards their destination and relied upon Kraki, Bolti, and those not rowing, to keep them on course.

Einar risked another look over the side. The beach was close now, so close he saw an enormous man on a white horse riding along the beach, waving an axe above his head. Dolgfinnr Dogsblood, so called because, as a young child, a wild dog had attacked him. Dolgfinnr had slaughtered the beast, and his father found the boy slathered in the dog's blood. It was a good name, a strong name; a warrior's name. The men on the beach roared and clashed their spears against the iron bosses of their round shields and made a war din to shake the sky.

"How do they know we're coming?" Einar called above the roar of the sea.

"Old Dogsblood is no fool," laughed Sigarr. "No man crosses Ragnar Lothbrok and leaves his shoreline undefended. Look." Sigarr pointed a gnarled finger to the east where a clifftop beacon burned orange through the sea haar and half a dozen fishing boats milled about in the shallows. Dolgfinnr had set the fishing boats to watch for ships coming from the south and set beacons in the high places around his home to warn his warriors of an approaching enemy.

Dolgfinnr had refused to send tribute to Lord Ragnar, which he was duty bound to do as Ragnar's oathman. It was an insult that could not go unpunished. If one vassal refused to pay their dues to Lord Ragnar, others would hear of it, and what sort of lord of the Danes could abide an oathbreaker? The fjords, islands and inlets of Jutland, Kattegat, the Skagerrak and the Vik seethed with Viking warlords and their lustrous dragon ships. Ambitious warriors searched for weakness, sharpened their blades and watched for chances to raid, attack, and win glory, silver and reputation with their brutal daring. There could be no blind eye turned to a broken oath, no place for pity or forgiveness. It was a land of the strong and the ruthless.

"Archers, ready!" Bolti ordered. He hefted a shield from where it hung over the sheerstrake, slipped his hand through the leather strap, and gripped the handle spanning its bowl. More warriors grabbed their shields and followed Bolti, gathering beneath the hawk-carved prow. "Get the banner."

Sigarr lowered the raven banner from the mast and fixed the cloth triangle to a spear stave. He slid its upper edge onto a strip of timber running at a right angle from the spear so that the famous banner flew proudly in any wind and any weather.

Einar's heart pounded at the thrill, at the

surging sea beneath the clinker-built hull, at the battle-fear pulsing from the crew in a fog so thick Einar could have cut it with a knife. He longed to join them, to hold axe and shield and charge into glorious combat beneath Odin's approving gaze. That was the way of the warrior, *drengskapr*, to live and fight with honour. Shale scraped beneath the hull, like the nails of an underwater beast scratching along the keel, that single piece of oak running the ship's length, curved like a woman's hip.

Something thudded into the mast and Einar turned, surprised to see a spear quivering, its steel head half-embedded in the post.

"Bastards can throw like Thor himself," remarked Ravn, a tall warrior with a golden beard.

"Attack!" Bolti hollered, waving his sword above his head. "Over the side! Kill them all, kill, kill! Archers, ready!"

Men leapt over the side with great splashes and waded towards shore. Kraki hefted the anchor stone and tossed it over the side. He collected his axe and hurried to the prow. Kraki paused when he reached the mast and grinned at Einar.

"Say a prayer for me, friend," he said. "Ask Týr to guide my axe and Odin to watch my back. Stay here. One day you will meet your enemies in the shield wall, where men soil themselves and the brave warriors fight. One day, you will hammer your axe into another man's skull before he does the same to you. So watch and learn, watch for the lovers of the battle, the ones who fight in the front line and trade blows with other champions. Watch for the skulkers in the rear ranks who wait until the shield wall breaks to hack at fleeing men and claim glory for their frightened souls. Watch, boy, for soon your time will come."

Kraki laughed and leapt over the side, leaving Einar gaping after him. The six archers took up positions, two in the prow and the rest standing on rowing benches. Their bows sang as arrows flew from the Waveslicer towards the enemy. The warrior at the steerboard leant on the steering oar and the ship banked, bringing her beam athwart the shore so that her wide, shallow belly bobbed on the swell.

Einar darted to the side. Two men helped Bolti hobble through the shallows, his wooden leg in danger of sinking in the soft sand beneath the surf, trapping him, leaving their shipmaster at the mercy of the men he came to kill. Half of the crew made the shield wall where the water lapped at their knees. Heavy shields clanked together. Shields made of linden-wood boards riveted to an iron boss and ringed with a strip of iron, painted in bright colours with snarling war-beasts daubed in red and blue to frighten an enemy. Dolgfinnr's men made the war-music, weapons clashing on shield rims, war horns blaring and gruff voices bellowing their defiance at men who had come across the Whale Road to take their lives.

Dolgfinnr leapt lithely from his white horse and bullied his way into the front rank. He stood taller than his warriors, broad in the shoulder and fierce of face. His men made their own shield wall, shouting as one as their shields overlapped. They wore wolf furs over bare torsos, wild-eyed men with teeth bared and sharp weapons ready to chop, stab, maim, and kill. Einar shivered as hard eyes rose over the shield rims. Most men wore a conical helmet, but the more famous warriors like Dolgfinnr himself wore helmets with horsehair plumes at the crown, nasal protectors and closed cheekpieces.

More of Bolti's men reached the shallows and added their shields to the wall. Archers continued to loose their shafts from the Waveslicer's bow towards the enemy. Einar longed to be amongst the warriors. He wondered how he would fare when the weapons clashed and men faced death beneath Odin's cruel gaze. The fishing boats sculled closer and Einar wondered if it was a trap, if they secreted some of Dolgfinnr's men who would pour from beneath the nets and oars to attack Bolti from the flanks. But as they drew closer, he saw thin faces and drab woollen clothes and realised they were just opportunistic fishermen, waiting to pluck the flotsam of battle from the water. They might grab a dead man's arm ring, an axe, or something else of value which might feed their family for a year or more.

A hail of spears soared from Dolgfinnr's ranks, their points catching the sun for a shimmering moment as they seemed to pause in the air. Then the weapons crashed into Bolti's shield wall with a noise like thunder. Ravn died with an arrow in his eye, blood staining the sea about his corpse, and Einar gasped that the fearsome carl had died so easily, without even swinging his axe. Men closed the gap and overlapped their shields as yet more arrows clattered and slammed into the linden-wood boards.

Dolgfinnr's men came on in an organised line. No glorious charge, just a slow, fearsome advance with shields held firm, each one overlapping the other and blades protruding from the gaps like dragon's teeth. Bolti roared at his men to get out of the water, because to fight in the surf was to fight encumbered and they would need all of their war-skill to defeat the enemy.

Dolgfinnr's men shouted as their feet moved in unison, grunting every time each man's left foot stamped on the wet sand. Bolti's men staggered from the water, clothes heavy and dripping wet. The shield walls paused as both sets of warriors gazed at each other and tried to summon up the courage required to join battle, to close on a man who wanted to heave cold iron into their soft flesh, to rip, tear and rend at their skin, organs, eyes, face and throat until they were dead. Then they charged. The shields came together with an almighty crash, and Einar jumped at the sound of it. His fingernails bit into the sheerstrake and he watched as men hewed at one another across battle lines. Cries of pain joined with shouts of anger and suddenly the surf turned red as men's lifeblood mixed with the froth and churn of the tide.

Battle had joined, blades clashed, and the beach rang with the din of war. Men would die and one side would emerge victorious. The raven banner flew above Bolti's warriors and Einar's heart galloped in his chest, desperate for his shipmates to win, to find glory, and to live.

TWO

Einar dove beneath the rigging as the ship shifted in the water, desperate to keep his eyes on the battle. A spear flew an arm's length from his face and Einar almost fell in the thwarts as he ducked to avoid it. A cry from behind and Einar turned to see one of the archers, a man named Jari, clinging to the rigging as the spear dangled from his chest like a monstrous dandelion bristle. Jari stared at Einar, and a torrent of dark blood slopped from his mouth. He stretched his hand towards Einar, dropping his bow, and then toppled from the rigging to splash into the murky depths. Einar raced after him and hung over the side, but there was no sign of Jari. Just the spear's butt bobbing on the surface and a smear of crimson in the water.

A horn blared, and Einar ran back to the bows. He paused, glancing back to where Jari had fallen. *Should I go after him? I can swim, perhaps I can save him?* But Einar shook his head. What if he leapt after Jari and drowned, or couldn't clamber his way back on board the Waveslicer? He would be left there to die on a distant shore, his corpse bobbing on the swell, his dreams and ambitions forgotten, denied Valhalla for eternity.

On the beach, the shield walls parted to reveal a dozen men lying on the shore amidst rivulets of blood running across the sand, seeping into the tide like gory tendrils. Einar thought again about diving in after Jari, but it was too late now. The archer was dead. There was no *drengskapr* in leaving a shipmate to die. Einar's cheeks flushed, and his stomach churned. *Am I a coward?* Men's voices barked on the shore, but Einar could not make out the words above the waves slapping against the ship's side.

Warriors parted and made two lines, Bolti's men with their backs to the sea and Dolgfinnr's men with theirs landward. Dolgfinnr himself strode out from his ranks, hulking with his blonde hair and face spattered with other men's blood and his axe blade red with death. His wolf-pelted warriors howled and shook their weapons, and Einar trembled as Bolti's men shrank back from their feral fury.

"What's happening?" Einar said, without taking his eyes off the shore.

"They are going to fight," said Orvar, the one

archer still on board, a thin man with a hooked nose and sinewy arms.

"They've been fighting."

"The warriors have, but now Bolti and Dolgfinnr are going to fight to the death."

Einar swallowed hard. "But Dolgfinnr is the champion of the North?"

"One Leg Bolti has fair fame of his own, lad. I've seen him kill three men in single combat."

Bolti limped from his line of shields, his wooden leg holding him back, trailing in the cumbersome sand as he approached his enemy. Dolgfinnr laughed and urged his men backwards with his axe and shield. They shifted, creating a wide space for the men to fight. Bolti carried his sword and shield but seemed slower, crippled, smaller and older than his enemy. Dolgfinnr prowled before Bolti, clashing his axe on his shield rim, looming and malevolent in a shining chainmail *brynjar*. He took off his helmet and cast it aside. Bolti paused for a moment and leaned over to pull his wooden leg from the sand. Einar groaned in fear for his shipmaster.

"What happens if Bolti loses?" he asked.

"He dies. Then, it depends on what they've agreed as the terms of the fight. This isn't a ritual holmgang duel where men lay hazel rods and strict rules apply. This is just a fight to the death on a bloody beach. Maybe Dolgfinnr will let us go, maybe he'll kill us all."

"So why are they fighting? Let the battle decide it."

Orvar shrugged. "If we lose too many men, how can we sail home? If Dolgfinnr loses too many men, he is prey for the next warlord who attacks his beach. It's better this way. Clean. There's reputation in it for the winner."

The two war leaders closed on one another, and Einar winced. He expected Dolgfinnr to shift around Bolti's wooden leg and slash the crippled man down as he struggled in the sand. It would all be over with one swing of the champion's axe. Einar wondered how many men Dolgfinnr must have fought and killed to earn that reputation. Champion of the Northmen. The greatest and most savage warrior of all the men in Denmark, Norway and the lands of the Svear, where the greatest fighters in all Midgard dwelt. How could Bolti stand and fight against such a man?

Dolgfinnr sprang at Bolti. He moved with a quickness belying his vast frame, axe coming about in a wide arc as he danced around to Bolti's weak side, where his wooden leg struggled in the cloying sand. Bolti's shield came up and caught the blow with a ring like the god Völund's mighty hammer crashing against his anvil in Asgard. Then Bolti moved like a serpent, pivoting on his wooden leg so that his sword came about in a vicious arc and sliced open Dolgfinnr's thigh in a spray of blood. Bolti's leg wasn't caught in the sand. He moved lithely now, all speed and savagery on a beach wet from the tide, its sand dark and sturdy. Bolti had feigned slowness, and now he moved with the brutal speed of a killer. His sword stabbed at Dolgfinnr and cracked into his ribs. Dolgfinnr staggered backwards and dropped his shield, clutching at his midriff, but his *brynjar* took the blow and the sword had not pierced his body.

Dolgfinnr grinned and wagged a knowing finger at Bolti. One Leg had come close, his ruse had almost worked. But Bolti perhaps only had that one chance to kill his enemy, to open Dolgfinnr's throat or pierce his heart whilst he reeled in surprise, and Einar's heart pounded in his chest. Dolgfinnr slid a wicked bladed seax from his belt and came on, seax in his left hand and axe in his right. He attacked Bolti with a speed and ferociousness Einar had never seen before. From the time he had first walked, Einar had spent his life practising with axe, spear, shield and bow. That was the life for the son of a warrior, even a dead one. His days were a mix of work, of fetching, carrying, pouring, emptying, washing and wiping, and then the glorious hours of weapons practice. Even in those endless, joyous days of weapon work, he had seen nothing close to Dolgfinnr's speed.

The fight was over in moments. Bolti's shield came up too slowly and Dolgfinnr's seax slid beneath it and sawed at the tendons in Bolti's arm. The shield dropped, and Bolti's sword came up. But it waved at the space where Dolgfinnr had been, and his axe slammed into Bolti's chest with enough force to shatter the interlocked chainmail links, crunch through bone and piece the heart beyond.

"No!" Einar screamed before he could stop himself.

Bolti fell to his knees and dropped his sword. His men took three steps back and a dread silence fell across the beach. Dolgfinnr slid his axe into a loop at his belt, bent, picked up Bolti's sword, and placed it back into the dying man's hand. Bolti clutched it to his bloody chest and fell onto his face. A warrior tossed Dolgfinnr a long-handled war-axe, and he slashed down once, and then picked up Bolti's severed head by the hair. He shouted something to his wolf warriors, and they charged with a savage howl that seemed to shake the very sands.

"Thor's balls," gasped Orvar. "We're dead men!" He turned to the man at the steerboard. "Get the anchor stone up! Now!"

Bolti's men turned and ran into the sea, pursued by Dolgfinnr's wolf men. Warriors dropped their shields to run, all willingness to fight fleeing from them like Bolti's soul had fled to Valhalla. Dolgfinnr's men fell upon them with a barbarous fury, chopping into backs and heads as men struggled in the tide's push and pull.

"We can't just stand here whilst they die," Einar said, desperate to help but unsure of what to do.

"Ready the oars. Gather rope to help the men on board. And get that bloody anchor stone up or I'll cut its line!" Orvar snarled as he busied himself at the oars. "Odin, help us..."

The archer gaped and pointed towards the shore. Einar turned and watched as the raven banner fell and one of Dolgfinnr's men picked it up. The wolf warriors cheered and cavorted with delight amongst the blood-thickened shallows. Ragnar's banner, the banner bearing Odin's sacred raven, had not only fallen, but was seized by the enemy. It was unthinkable. Bolti was dead, and now the raven banner captured. Ragnar was said to be descended from Odin himself, and to lose the banner was beyond defeat, beyond humiliation. It was an insult to the gods, and a cutting blow to Lord Ragnar's reputation.

Einar ran to the side, grabbed a length of seal hide rope and threw it to his shipmates wallowing in the water, desperate to escape the slaughter.

"Keep them back, keep the bastards in the shallow water," called Orvar as he dropped the oar, picked up his bow and loosed arrows at the enemy.

The first warriors reached the ship, water sloshing around their chests, their faces drawn taut by panic. A bald-headed man grabbed hold of Einar's rope and Einar hauled him over the side. The warrior flopped onto the deck like a landed fish, trembling and soaking wet. The ship shifted on the swell and her hull bullied the desperate survivors backwards as the man at the steerboard fought to keep her still. More men reached the ship and Einar helped a dozen clamber over the side.

Fishing boats drew closer to the Waveslicer, emboldened by the slaughter, and the fisherman cast their nets at Bolti's men, catching them and hauling them close to strip them of anything of value, cutting their throats with the sharp knives they used to gut and clean their catch. A figure leapt from the closest boat and dived into the sea. He swam towards the Waveslicer and a toothless man raged on the fishing boat, shaking his fist and yowling like a madman. The figure swam like a salmon and he reached the Waveslicer in a dozen long strokes.

"Take me with you," he shouted up at Einar in strangely-accented Norse. He was a lad of an age with Einar himself, with a fluff of beard on his lip and chin.

The day was already turned upside down with Loki-madness, so Einar tossed him a rope and hauled the young man over the side. Four more warriors reached the Waveslicer, including Sigarr, who embraced Einar after he had helped him climb over the side.

"We have to go," Sigarr panted, thrusting Einar away from him.

"The others…" Einar replied, but as he turned back towards the water, he realised there would be no more survivors.

"They're all gone, lad. Gone. Defeat shames us, but if we don't go now, we shall all die in this place."

"Better that than return to Ragnar without the raven banner," said a warrior with a bloody slash streaming across his cheek.

"Row for your lives and live to fight another day," Sigarr ordered. He lifted men and thrust them at their oar benches. "Live, and we can return and recover the banner and avenge our fallen brothers. But we must row!"

Dolgfinnr's men thrashed in the tide, lashing at any of Bolti's men still in the water. It had been a massacre. More than half their number had perished, and Einar was astonished at the savagery and bloodlust. The Dogsblood himself capered on the beach with Bolti's severed head in one fist and the famous raven banner in the other. Einar had expected glorious combat, shining blades and heroes striding to meet their foes. That was how the skalds described it in the tales he had heard at countless firesides. Instead, the battle was brutal and bloodthirsty. The warriors were like animals, wild-eyed and teeth bared as they cut at one another.

Einar sat down heavily on a rowing bench and grabbed an oar, its ash shaft smooth in his hands. He paused to catch the rowing rhythm as the survivors rowed, and then he joined in. Einar turned the oar blade as it hit the sea and hauled backwards, the muscles across his back stretching. He lifted the blade, turned it, and hauled again. The Waveslicer banked and slowly left the bloody shore behind, a skeleton crew of survivors moving her away from the scene of their humiliating defeat.

"Will they follow?" quivered a voice from the bench next to Einar.

He turned, still in shock from what he had witnessed; he had forgotten about the young man who had jumped from the fishing boat. It was he who had spoken. The young man sat to Einar's left, hauling an oar.

"They'll follow," Sigarr growled. "But we have

the wind and are lighter, and the Waveslicer is faster than a starving weasel. Lower the sail!"

Six men leapt from the benches and worried at the shroud and the reef ties.

"Who are you?" Einar asked the youth.

"Adzo," he replied as they both pulled their oars. "Those bastards took me from my family six moons ago. So I jumped from my master's boat when I thought you might escape that godforsaken place." The young man made a cross sign in front of his chest, and Einar noticed that he wore a small wooden cross on a leather thong around his neck, in the same way Einar and his shipmates wore miniature symbols of their own gods. Einar wore a wooden hammer for Thor, and many men wore symbols to honour Njorth, Ran, Týr, Freyr, Freya, Frigg, or whatever god they prayed to for favour.

"Row if you want to come with us, thrall," snapped Sigarr, using the common term for slave. "Or we'll throw you overboard to join our oar mates' corpses beneath the sea."

The sail fell down the yard and men hurried to tie-off the sheet rope. A southern wind blew into Einar's face and snapped the woollen sail taut. Faded red and white stripes bent under the wind's force and the ship lurched, picking up speed, and Einar sagged against his oar with relief. He hauled the ash shaft through its oar hole and placed it with the rest of the oars on a set of crutches by the bilge.

The dreaded shore retreated behind them, and the survivors of Bolti's crew gathered in the stern. They stared ashen-faced as the golden strip of sand disappeared along with the bodies of the dead.

"My brother is gone," said a warrior in a low voice. He clutched the hammer amulet at his neck and glanced up at the broiling sky where storm clouds gathered to block out the sun. "Thor protect his soul. He was a brave man and just. Take him to Thruthvangar, or see him safely to Valhalla or Sessrúmnir, and tell him to wait for me there. I will care for his wife and child. I swear it, and may Odin cast me down if I break that oath."

"Do we head for home?" asked a man named Refill. He sat on a bench, hands clutched to his thigh, bleeding freely from a deep cut. Another dark patch of crimson showed at the stomach of his jerkin.

"Of course," replied Orvar. "Lord Ragnar must know what happened here."

"Do you think Ragnar will welcome us when we bring news of this defeat?"

"He will not be pleased, but he must know. We went with only one crew and Dolgfinnr had three crews at least on that beach. Dolgfinnr is Ragnar's enemy, and he has grown stronger. A man with three crews could all himself jarl if he wished it. A warlord and no mistake. Bolti and half our crew are dead. Dolgfinnr had one ship last I heard. Now he has three. They have the raven banner. Ragnar will be furious."

"Aye, and who will bear the brunt of that fury? Have you thought about that?"

"What are you saying?"

"We have a ship and half a crew. We can go anywhere we wish. That's all I am saying."

"Enough!" Sigarr shouted. "We shall talk more tonight when the sun has set and we are dry with clear heads. For now, we must get as far as we can from Dolgfinnr and any ship he sends against us."

The Waveslicer ran before the wind, cutting across the Whale Road. The smooth keel and shallow hull sailed on top of the white-tipped waves, cutting through them like a scythe. Bolti was dead, as were Kraki, Ravn, and most of the leading warriors. Sigarr assumed charge and nobody objected. Einar worked the rigging and followed orders as they fled for the rest of that long day. They followed the wind, more concerned with speed and distance than direction. Their home lay south across the Skagerrak strait, deep into the sandy, stony reefs of the Kattegat Sea, at Hrafnborg, where Ragnar Lothbrok's fortress lay.

"Are you a warrior?" asked Adzo as they rowed the ship into the lee of a tiny island on the east coast of the Skagerrak.

"I will be one day," Einar replied.

"Is your father a warrior?"

"He was. He died when I was a child."

"A great warrior?"

"He sailed with a famous champion, a man named Vigmarr Svarti. Vigmarr the Black, a feared shipmaster. He outlived my mother, and before he died, he gave a battle-won golden arm ring to Ragnar Lothbrok to pay for my keep until I grew old enough to join his crews. So it is my destiny to be just like him, to sail and fight as a carl, a warrior of a warship."

"I have heard of Ragnar Lothbrok."

"So you should. He will be king of the Danes one day, and Dolgfinnr broke his oath to Ragnar."

"That's why you came?"

"Aye. You speak our language well, for a Frank." Einar knew thralls in Hrafnborg from Frankia, England, Frisia. He knew Finns and Slavs and peoples from across Midgard, folk captured on raids who spoke foreign tongues.

"I learned quickly. My master bought me from the warrior who captured me. He was cruel. He beat me and made me sleep out in the cold. So I took the first chance I could to run."

"Do you wish to be a warrior? It is hard for a thrall to rise to the rank of carl, to be a free man."

"I want to go home."

"First, we have to live, and then return to Ragnar. If we survive those tests, then perhaps you can go home."

"Am I still a slave, then?"

Einar shrugged. "Only if someone says you are. If you say you are not, and are strong enough to prove it, then you are free. Nobody on this ship has claim to you."

"How do I prove it?"

"You fight."

"I don't know how. Do you?"

Einar chuckled. "You'd better learn, Frank. Better learn fast."

Sigarr steered the ship to within a boat's length of shore and dropped the stone anchor. Normally, the crew would go ashore and spend the night sleeping on dry land, but that night was different. They stayed on board, taking turns at watch.

"We rise and sail with the sun," Sigarr stated. "In two days' time we will be home."

Some men grumbled at that, and Einar sensed their displeasure at the prospect of returning to Lord Ragnar in shame. Einar didn't relish the thought himself. Ragnar was a fierce man. He could be generous and full of laughter, but also baleful, cruel, and violent. The survivors must trust their luck with the gods and seek Ragnar's forgiveness. They were his oathmen, his warriors, dependent on him for silver, food, and shelter. Many of the crew's families lived at Hrafnborg or in the surrounding hills, and losing Ragnar's favour meant finding a new lord and a new home. Their lives were in his hands. He could punish them with death, take their heads or a hand; he could whip their backs raw or give them to the Godis, the holy men, as sacrifices to the gods.

Einar's hands shook as he stowed his oar for the night. He leant over the side and dipped his hand in the sea, its icy chill soothing the welts on his palms. Einar had never rowed so much, nor worked the rigging as hard. His back throbbed and memories of the day's slaughter swirled around his mind like a winter storm. But he was alive. For now.

THREE

Einar chewed on an oatcake and stared up at a clear sky full of bright stars. Spots of twinkling orange light showed settlements to the west. Fires from farms on the mainland and on the scores of islands were dotted throughout that part of the Skagerrak strait, the long stretch of perilous water which split Jutland from Norway's east coast and the west coast of Svear land. It was a Viking waterway, the only way for raiding and trading crews to access Kattegat, the Baltic sea and the wondrous, winding rivers which led daring Northmen south to the lands of the Rus, through wild Khazar horsemen and on to the strange, rich world of Miklagard.

So much had changed that day. Einar had set out from Hrafnborg with the same pride and arrogance as the rest of One Leg Bolti's crew. They were warriors in the service of Ragnar Lothbrok, out on the Whale Road on a fine ship crammed with fighters of stout reputation sent out to represent their lord in a matter of honour. In less time than it took to milk a cow, Einar's dreams of returning to Hrafnborg as part of a victorious crew were as hewn to pieces as Bolti and his crew.

When Bolti had first told Einar he could sail as bail boy on board the warship Waveslicer, his heart had filled with pride. The other Hrafnborg boys who milled about the settlement working chores and dreaming of war had been so jealous that Einar had got into three fights before the Waveslicer set sail. Einar had hoped that this voyage might be his chance to make the leap from boy to warrior. Had Bolti returned victorious, Einar would have asked Lord Ragnar if it was time to honour his father's wish. The wish Einar's father Egil had paid for with a gold arm ring, for Einar to become a carl and a *drengr* aboard one of Ragnar's ships.

How could he ask Ragnar now? Einar would be lucky to keep his head. The lads his age would chortle with glee. They would take their chance to push in front of him in the race to become a fully-fledged warrior. Einar would return to mucking out the horses, feeding pigs, mending thatch, fetching water and firewood for another season. What if Ragnar and the other important men forgot Einar altogether? Was it to be his fate to give up on his warrior's dream and become a farmer instead, or an apprentice thatcher, shipwright or blacksmith? Einar looked to the stars for answers. He gazed up at the great sky formed from the giant Ymir's skull, and the stars formed from sparks from Muspelheim, the first world before creation. There were no answers there, only the gentle lap of the sea and the wind in the rigging.

Refill coughed and groaned where he leant against the hull, his face drawn and ashen. Men had washed his wounds clean with sea water and bound them with clean cloth, but blood still showed in crimson blossoms on the dressings.

"We need to talk," Refill wheezed as he tried to sit upright.

Sigarr strode along the deck and fixed each man with a hard stare. His two long braids had come loose, giving him a dishevelled look, and he flashed a broken-toothed, mirthless smile. "We are going home," he said. "The only matter to discuss is how we do it. Today was a dark day. There's no shirking from it now. We lost. Dolgfinnr Dogsblood didn't become champion of the North by weaving wool and telling riddles by the fireside. He's a killer and his crews are as stout as any I have faced. I stormed that beach and I fought in the front. My shield took a blow from Dolgfinnr himself and it was like being struck by Thor's hammer. I'm not ashamed to say I fought. But we lost, and that's the truth of it. We went up against the greatest warrior in Midgard.

He had more men, three crews at least. We should have brought another two ships, maybe three more, to get the job done properly. We have a tale to tell when we get back to Hrafnborg, and should aim to sail there as soon as we can."

"We have enough food for the journey," said Orvar the archer. "We have oatcakes, dried fish and half a barrel of ale. There's no need to go ashore for supplies."

"That's if we sail straight home," said a warrior with a bulging bruise on the left side of his face. "Stay out of trouble, keep away from the coast. Don't stop. Then we might make it. We could take the long way around, hug the coast, and stay east before we go south. Just in case Dolgfinnr's ships try to head us off. But if we take that long way, we might need more food, and certainly more ale or water."

"If Dolgfinnr catches us, we are dead men," said another. "Did you see him swinging Bolti's head around like it was a basket of eggs?" He touched the amulet at his neck to ward off the ill luck of it all.

"Might be better that way," said Refill. "I wish I had died in the water with my axe in my hand."

"Shut your cheese pipe!" Sigarr shouted, startling Einar. "You are alive, and we are oathbound to fulfil our duty to our lord."

"Alive?" Refill retorted. "Yes, I draw breath. But for how long? Look at me. There's no healer here, no Godi to treat my wounds. How many brothers have we seen die from the wound that does not kill? How many men have we seen wither and die days after battle from the rotting sickness? Or return home missing an arm or a leg and left living on the charity of others for the rest of his days? Where is the *drengskapr* in that? Where is the honour? At least Bolti and the lads died with blades in their hands. They are in Valhalla now drinking ale from curved horns with the slain heroes of old. I envy them! I wish I had died on that beach. Why weren't one of these wounds fatal? What have I done to offend the gods so? Have I not always fought from the front when the shield walls come together? I fought a holmgang in my twentieth year and have killed at least a dozen men in battle. These wounds won't heal. I can feel it. It is my wyrd to rot and die on this ship. I shall wander in Niflheim for all time, until the end of days, denied a glorious afterlife."

The rest of the warriors hoomed in discomfort and looked away at those dark words, for Refill spoke of every warrior's gravest fear. They shifted uncomfortably and reached for their amulets. Men glanced at his wounds and looked away in shame, unable to meet the gaze of a man who lived, who would fall asleep each night in fear until his wounds healed. Every morning he woke, Refill would smell the wounds and hope not to find the rotting stink there, for if he did, his worst fears would come true.

"Do your gods not allow every good man into heaven?" Adzo whispered into Einar's ear.

Einar and the Frank sat beneath the prow whilst the warriors gathered around the mast to talk. Einar had no voice at such a council. He wore no arm rings and could not talk amongst the warriors.

"A warrior who fights well and dies in battle holding his weapon can expect to be taken to Asgard by the Valkyrie, Odin's choosers of the slain. A brave warrior goes either to Odin's hall Valhalla, or Thor's Thruthvangar, or Freya's Sessrúmnir. Did your master teach you nothing of our ways?"

"Just how to speak and how to serve."

"Your god does not honour the brave?"

"My God is the one true God. He is just, a God of peace. He rewards folk who have lived good lives with a place in heaven. What of those who do not die in battle?"

"They go to Niflheim to wander there with the rest of the dead. Where they wait until the Ragnarök."

"The Ragnarök?"

"Enough questions. Let us listen to what they decide." Einar leant closer to the warriors, desperate to learn their decision. There was no time to talk of Adzo's arrogant god, who denied the existence of all others. There were many gods, all men knew that. How could one god put the stars in the sky, rule the seas, the underworld, grant luck, bless one woman with a baby, and take another's life in the crib?

Einar wanted to return home, even if there was a price to pay for losing the raven banner. There was no honour in running from whatever punishment awaited them at Hrafnborg. If he ran now, Einar would run for the rest of his life. If he was to be a *drengr,* then he must not shirk from the warrior's path at the first difficulty. He would not place his dream in peril because he was afraid to face Ragnar's wrath.

"We sail for home," Sigarr said. He whipped a knife from his belt and slammed the blade into the mast. "Straight home. There is no other way." He set his jaw and glowered at the crew.

"I know men who have left one lord to seek another," said Refill. "We have met and fought against masterless men who go from one war to another and fight for pay. Men leave their lords all the time. They leave because their jarl is not a good ring giver, because he has grown old and tired of war. Men seek new lords for many reasons. We have a ship and we have our weapons. Lords in the south and east will pay us well to fight their enemies. Who would not want to bring into their service men who have fought for the great Ragnar Lothbrok? We could become richer than we ever dreamed."

"But always in our hearts, we'd know we are oath breakers. Do you think the gods grant luck to men who run from their duty? Do you think Odin welcomes such into his hall? I am not afraid to die, if that is to be my fate. Nor am I afraid of the lash, nor of the branding iron. If Ragnar decides we deserve punishment, then so be it. But at least my oath will be whole, and I can sail out to fight again with a full heart."

"You are not our captain, nor shipmaster, nor jarl nor lord. Why should we listen to you? Do you think we can just limp into Hrafnborg in our half-crewed ship and Ragnar will meet us with open arms? That he will feast us and forget about the shame we have brought upon his reputation? He might keelhaul you, cut the blood eagle into your back, cut off your manhood, hang you, or give you to the Godis to hang in the sacred tree. What will your honour and your oath be worth when you are screaming beneath his son Ivar's knife? We all saw Ivar the Boneless cut the blood eagle into Jarl Hrorik's back two summers ago. Who can forget how that brave man wailed as Ragnar's son spliced open his back, chipped away his ribs and pulled out his lungs? I can still hear his chisel crack Hrorik's bones. They hauled Hrorik up on ropes so that his ruined back resembled an eagle's wings. When you are all screaming beneath Ivar's knife, it will be too late to wish that you had listened to Refill instead of Sigarr and his hot air."

"Lord Ragnar will give us the chance to redeem our honour. I know it. He is our jarl. I swore on this ring to be his man, and I will never break that oath." Sigarr lifted his arm where four rings twinkled beneath the starlight. He pointed to a silver ring inlaid with runes and kissed it to add weight to his argument.

"Fool! You'll be dead within the week. What use are honour and oaths to a dead man? I say we take the ship and sail to Svear land, find another lord. We can take on men at Hedeby or another trading port and go to war for pay. There you have it. That's what I say. Build a crew, go out into Midgard and get what we deserve. Each of us could be as rich as a Saxon fleece merchant before summer's end. Think of it! Would you not rather go into winter laden down with silver than let Ragnar give you to his blood-mad son?"

"And I say we go home." Sigarr's words came through clenched teeth. Men shifted on their benches, unsure which of the two arguing warriors to follow.

"Home to die, or out onto the Whale Road to earn our fortune? That, to me, is no choice at all." Refill licked his lips and glanced about the crew as if to gauge every man's will. Men exchanged nervous looks, and some even muttered "Aye" in response to his words. "What about you, young Einar Egilsson?" Refill asked, his dark-rimmed eyes boring into Einar. "I fought alongside your father. Egil Brokenaxe was a good man and a fine warrior. He had a wise head on him, there was deep cunning between his ears. Many of us here sailed and fought with your father. Perhaps some of his wisdom passed on to you. So, what do you say we should do?"

Einar swallowed. Every drip of moisture had suddenly fled from his mouth and throat. He sat up straight as a dozen hard men looked to him as if a young warrior's words suddenly carried weight amongst carls. They had earned their reputations across countless battlefields and raging seas, and Einar was yet to be tested in the forge of combat. Refill had used Einar's full name, Egilsson, and that stirred something within him. Most people called him lad or boy, except the other young men of Hrafnborg, who used his first name. It was an honour for Refill to refer to him as Egilsson. But Einar sensed something in Refill's squint-eyed stare. Why ask Einar what he thought? He was the lowest-ranking man on board, save Adzo, who was a runaway thrall. Refill thought he could sway Einar to support his argument, that by mentioning his father, he could sway Einar to his side. The crew were on the edge, delicately balanced between supporting Refill or Sigarr. One voice of support for either side could push the rest over. Refill sensed weakness in Einar, thought that by putting him on the spot, he could pressure the young lad into supporting his desire to flee.

"My father was Ragnar's man," said Einar, balling his fists to keep his voice steady and his chin up. Hard men looked on as he spoke, and he wanted to speak like the man he wanted to be. "He died in battle, as you all know. Before he died, my father bought me a place on Lord Ragnar's crews. He paid Ragnar a good arm ring, a ring won in battle, and Ragnar gave his word that when I was grown, I would pull an oar on one of his *drakkars*. That, I think, is to be my destiny. That is what my father would have wanted. I say we go home and meet whatever fate awaits us there with the courage of *drengrs*."

"Ha! Then you are a fool. Go home then, pup. Run home to Ragnar and see how cruel the gods are to boys with empty heads and hopeful hearts. Before Ragnar beats you to death, remember to ask old Vigmarr Svarti how your father died."

Einar's eyebrows knitted at the insult and the comment about Vigmarr, the famous sea-jarl who had been his father's shipmaster. Men looked surprised at the words, but no one spoke and they stared at Einar to see how he would respond.

"Enough!" Sigarr rumbled.

"You are not in charge here. You don't determine our fate. I am wounded but I might live yet. I don't want to survive these wounds and have your blind loyalty cast me under the Boneless' knife. Throw Sigarr overboard, lads. Be done with this fool and let's be on our way. If we sail south, Dolgfinnr's men await us in the straits, and even if we can sail the Slicer home, what fate awaits us there? Cut this bastard's throat and toss his filthy corpse overboard. Do it!" Refill roared, spittle flying into his beard. "And the bail-boy." He pointed a trembling finger in Einar's direction. "Kill them both and let us sail away as proud, free men. Nobody will know what happened here but us. We can swear an oath never to talk of it again. All Ragnar will know is that he sent Bolti and the Waveslicer out to punish Dolgfinnr Dogsblood and no man returned. He'll punish Dogsblood himself and not give a care about us. He'll think we died in the battle. We can sail so far east no man will know who we are or from whence we came. Kill these two curs now and be done with it!"

"Bastard," Sigarr snarled. He plucked his knife from the mast, took three long steps, and plunged the blade into Refill's heart. Men gasped and fell back. Sigarr wrenched the knife free and a spatter of blood slapped against the hull. He drove the point of his knife into Refill's eye, twisted the blade, and Refill was no more. Einar stood in the prow's shadow and set his feet in case it came to a fight. Sigarr turned on the rest of the crew with the bloody knife in his hand, fat drops of blood dripping from it to splash onto the deck. Einar held his breath, the tension in the air as thick as sea fog.

"Odin's balls!" yelped Orvar, and he scrambled away from the murder, as if the further he moved from Refill's corpse the less real it was.

"We go home. All of us. If any man objects, then say so now and we'll fight. Otherwise, every man does his duty, and that's the end of it." Sigarr waited, shoulder muscles bunched and eyes sparkling in the starlight. "Is there anyone who objects?"

No man answered, and Sigarr nodded. "Help me, boy," he said to Einar, gesturing to Refill's body as he wiped his knife clean on Refill's trews. Einar stepped closer and Sigarr pointed to one of Refill's legs. Sigarr took the other, and they hefted the corpse over the side. Einar strained under the weight of the body, but heaved with every ounce of strength in his muscles. Refill slid over the side and plopped into the night-black sea with a slithering slop.

"Don't sleep tonight," Sigarr warned him. "They might cut our throats in the darkness and follow Refill's plan. So keep your eyes open and a weapon close." Sigarr turned to the mast and grabbed an axe from the weapon's barrel. "Here, take this." He handed Einar the axe. A plain weapon with an unmarked head and a stout shaft wrapped in leather. "It's yours now. Keep it with you always. When we get back to Hrafnborg, I'll speak up for you, make you a man. It's time you took your place. You spoke up for me, lad. I won't forget it."

Sigarr clapped Einar on the shoulder and left him alone with Adzo. Einar stared after him, clutching the axe to his chest as though it were made of gold. His own weapon, an axe to own and wield. Einar's chest swelled with pride. Sigarr barked at the men to prepare the ship for the night. They cast the sailcloth over the deck to make a tent and settled down beneath blankets and fleeces, all avoiding the dark smear of Refill's blood. Sigarr sat against the mast, knife and axe in his lap, and Einar did the same beneath the prow.

Einar stayed awake all night, listening to the sigh of the sea and the wind in the rigging. That day had changed his life; for good or bad, he wasn't yet sure. All Einar knew was that the warp and weft of his life had altered. It was time now to be a man, to make his place in the world and honour his father's reputation. If things had gone differently, it might have been Einar and Sigarr lying on the sea bottom with their throats cut. But Einar was alive, and soon, he would return to Hrafnborg to face Ragnar. Adzo snored quietly beside him, huddled beneath a threadbare blanket. All night he wondered if he made a terrible mistake, if all that awaited him at Hrafnborg was death and torture. Words his father spoke to him as a young child came to Einar in the darkness.

"Live with courage, son. Stand and fight and Odin will reward you with *hamingja*," Egil had said.

Einar needed *hamingja*, luck. It could pass from one deceased relative to another, and Einar prayed to Odin that whatever luck his father had before his death could pass to him now, so that when they came to Hrafnborg and stood before the fearsome Lord Ragnar, that Einar would live and find his destiny as a warrior upon the Whale Road.

FOUR

The Waveslicer reached Hrafnborg four days later. Sigarr became the crew's assumed leader after Refill's death, leading the crew on a ranging journey across the Skagerrak and avoiding Dolgfinnr's hunting ships. They sailed from island to inlet, and cove to fjord, chasing the wind; and when Njorth wasn't with them, the crew rowed for their lives. Einar's muscles ached and his palms were worn bloody by the time the horn blew on Hrafnborg's lookout hill to warn the inhabitants of the ship's arrival. The sound echoed around three hills surrounding Ragnar's fortress as though the god Heimdall had blown the Gjallarhorn to announce the Ragnarök. Meadows and grazing pastures swept down from pine-topped heights to where a sprawling coastal town nestled, fortified by a formidable ditch, bank and stout palisade. Smoke rose in winding tendrils from thatch and earth-topped buildings, and spears and helmets glinted on the walls as warriors came to peer at the returning warship.

"Is it too late to turn back?" asked Adzo as he and Einar rowed towards shore. The Frank glanced over his shoulder at the settlement and then back at Einar.

"Just row. Our fate is in the hands of the gods now," Einar replied. The crew had accepted Adzo without objection because he rowed well and complained little. The survivors spoke few words after Refill's death. They had rowed, worked the rigging, slept and worked again. Sigarr had shared out rations and decided which course they should take, and nobody tried to cut his or Einar's throat in the night.

The horn rang out its sonorous tone and folk gathered in Hrafnborg's harbour to welcome the returning ship home.

"Ship oars," Sigarr called from the steerboard. He leant on the long steering oar as the Waveslicer glided towards shore. Einar lifted his oar, placed it in its crutch, and he caught Sigarr's eye for a moment. A look passed between them, silent but tinged with fear. Einar felt it, just as Sigarr did. Fear. Fear that they had been wrong to go against Refill and had returned to Hrafnborg to face their deaths.

Men met the ship on a long timber jetty and secured her to stout posts with lines of coiled hemp rope. The gathered crowd fell silent.

Nothing but whispers came from the throng of wives, daughters, sons and brothers of those who had ventured out on the Waveslicer. Sigarr was the first to step ashore. He had brushed his clothes clean, tied the bottom of his trews with winingas leg wrappings, combed his hair and beard and cast a russet cloak about his shoulders. The crowd parted as a giant man strode along the jetty towards the ship.

Einar held onto the rigging and watched, breath stalled in his throat, as Sigurd Snake Eye, son of Ragnar Lothbrok, marched along the timber latts with his hard, pale blue eyes fixed on Sigarr. Sigurd wore a shining *brynjar* and a sword at his hip, and his long hair was so blonde it was almost white beneath the early spring sun.

"We have returned, Lord Sigurd," said Sigarr, with his chest puffed out, shoulders back and chin held high.

"So few," Sigurd replied, and he sucked his teeth at the sight of the Waveslicer.

"Dolgfinnr Dogsblood defeated us in a terrible battle, lord. Dolgfinnr slew many of our crew and cut One Leg Bolti's head from his shoulders."

"And yet you survived."

"Barely, Lord Sigurd. We broke free of the fighting to bring word home to you and your father."

"My father is in his hall. You had better bring him the news yourself. You are lucky. He leaves on campaign in three days' time. Another couple of days, and you would have missed him completely." A wry smile played at the corners of Sigurd's mouth.

"Lord Sigurd," Sigarr called after him as Sigurd turned to lead the way to his father's hall.

"Well?" Sigurd turned with his hands on his hips.

"There is another thing. Dolgfinnr captured the raven banner."

Sigurd's pale eyes narrowed. He was a hard man to look at, and Sigarr turned away. Sigurd's left eye bore a strange defect from birth, a dragon shape next to the pale blue iris which gave him his name. Sigurd was a killer, proven in battle and single combat many times, though he was but a few years older than Einar.

"You lost the raven banner? A banner blessed by Odin and imbued with my father's battle-luck? One of our hallowed battle standards, woven by my mother and sisters from fleeces shorn of sheep born here in Hrafnborg?"

"Yes, Lord Sigurd. The banner is lost."

Sigurd shook for a moment and then mastered himself. "Come," he said and waved a hand at Einar and the crew to indicate that they should all attend Ragnar's hall. Einar followed as the survivors stepped off the ship and onto the jetty. The moment Einar's boot touched the damp timbers, his chest burned with fear of how Ragnar would respond to their defeat.

"Who was that?" Adzo asked as they walked through the throng of people staring at them with wide eyes. Women standing on their tiptoes searching for their loved ones, and some wept as they realised a husband or son had not returned. Einar cast his eyes down so as not to meet judging stares or the sorrow of bereft relatives.

"Sigurd Snake Eye, one of Ragnar's sons," Einar replied.

"He looked like a great prince. Should we fear him?"

"Each of Ragnar's sons is fearsome. Sigurd, Ivar the Boneless, Bjorn Ironside, Ubba; every one of them a born warrior. But fear every man you meet here, for each one is a fighter and proven in battle. There aren't many shirkers in Ragnar's crews. Don't speak unless spoken to. Don't look at anyone if you can help it, and whatever you do, don't look at the women. If a man sees you ogling his wife, he'll challenge you to single combat. So keep your eyes down and your teeth together."

They marched through the harbour, past fishermen's nets hung out to dry, barrels of salted cod, haddock and wolfish, and small skiffs dragged up onto the shale shore. Folk stopped at their daily chores to follow the procession inside Hrafnborg's palisade of stout, spiked posts. They crossed the ditch bridge and entered the gate, where men in conical helmets carrying bright spears stared down at them from the fighting platform which ran around the inside of the entire palisade.

Einar marched with his shipmates through the snarl of wattle and daub houses roofed with thatch or earth. Chickens, sad-faced dogs and grubby-haired children ran out of their way and boys peeped at the men from corners or behind hand carts. After being at sea, the stink of animal dung and burning hearth fires filled Einar's nose, and the noise of wailing women followed the crowd.

A line of warriors in helmets carrying brightly-painted shields stood in a line before the hall and they parted to let Sigurd Ragnarsson through. The hall itself was as long as ten houses, with darkened oak timbers supporting a roof shaped like an upturned ship whose upside-down keel hung over two enormous doors. Thatch so fresh it shone like gold covered the hall, and smoke billowed from a roof hole, its grey smudge smearing the clear blue sky.

Oak doors, each as wide as three men, creaked open on sprawling iron hinges forged into intricate whorls and runes. Einar entered the hall. He coughed to clear his throat as the smoke hanging in the high rafters like a cloud sucked all the moisture from him. A fire crackled and spat at the hall's centre, and feasting benches crammed with stony-faced warriors filled the open space. Einar's boots crunched on dry floor-rushes, there to soak up spilled ale and food from the tables. The murmur of men's voices reverberated through the open space, but every man fell silent as Sigurd Snake Eye strode past the hearth fire, its orange glow flickering on the shimmering links of his *brynjar*.

Einar had been in the hall before on special occasions, at feasts, to celebrate the harvest, yule, or great victories when Ragnar invited everyone in Hrafnborg to his hall. Einar and the other boys would push and weave their way through the crowds gathered in the field before the hall and through those mighty doors to cram into the longhouse made hot by hearth fire and the press of people's bodies. Ragnar's stewards and thralls would hand out fresh bread slathered in honey, and frothing ale in wooden cups. One spring, Einar had drunk too much and spent the night vomiting into a bush behind the pig sties. Most celebrations ended up with the town boys fighting in the back alleys. Last yule, Einar had beaten an older boy bloody, and the spring before had his own skull rung by a bigger lad from Ivar's crew.

The atmosphere in the hall was now more akin to an execution than a yule or spring feast. Only warriors sat in Ragnar's hall, imposing men with forbidding faces burned dark by sea winds. Piles of weapons waited outside the oaken doors, as was the custom, for ale and blades do not mix well. Einar saw lips curl as warriors drank in the demeanour of the Waveslicer's survivors, counting their number, and feeling the shame pulsing from them like the call of a war horn. Warriors leant into the man next to them and whispered, and Einar's head shrank down into his shoulders. He wished he had the wings of a bird so that he could fly away to a distant shore.

"You disturb our preparations for war," came a voice, calm and strange. A voice soft yet as hard as forged steel. Einar's shoulders shivered, for it was a voice he had heard many times. The voice of a man who had led thousands of warriors and dozens of ships to raid south, east, and west. The first man to lead raids to far England, where Saxon kings sat on hordes of round silver coins. A man spoken of by poets, skalds and scops at firesides in the same breath as tales of the gods. Ragnar Lothbrok: jarl and warrior, a king in all but name, feared by his enemies and loved by his oathmen.

Einar raised his head. Beyond the hearth fire, Ragnar sat swathed in furs, resting upon an enormous chair set on a raised dais. Two men flanked him, one unbelievably monstrous and baleful with shoulders like shields and a head like a bull, and the other handsome with long shining black hair tied back in a braid, a man of average height and slim build. The big man was Sten Slegyya, the sledgehammer, Ragnar's champion, a brutal and feared warrior. The second man was Ivar the Boneless, Ragnar's son. Rising in fame, Ivar fought with two swords named for Odin's ravens, Hugin and Munin, thought and memory. Einar's mouth was as dry as the bottom of a horse feeder, and the need to piss was almost overwhelming.

"These men are of One Leg Bolti's crew," proclaimed Sigurd Snake Eye, his voice loud, clear and confident.

"Where is Bolti?" asked Ragnar. He leaned forward in his high seat, blue eyes as cold and hard as a frozen lake, his broad face scarred and implacable. He wore his hair in a topknot with the sides of his skull shaved close and his beard braided with iron talismans.

"These men have limped home with a tale of defeat. Bolti is slain and the raven banner lost in battle."

Hundreds of warriors sucked in their breath as one at the news and Einar could feel the hall's great walls closing in upon him, as though he were a mouse in a box.

"Odin Bǫlverkr has a hand in this!" screeched a voice from the below the dais. A diminutive man leapt up from his feasting bench, a bent-backed, gnarled figure whose hair and clothes shook and jangled with miniature animal bones and talismans. Einar bunched his fists to stop his hands from shaking. The man was Ragnar's Godi, his holy man, Kjartan Wolfthinker, beloved of the gods and a master of galdr magic. "Odin bale-worker turned his hand against Bolti. The All-Father who decides men's fates on the battlefield. You should be wary, Lord Ragnar, tread carefully for the one-eye's gaze is upon us!" Kjartan made a sound in the back of his throat and shook his staff, a black length of wood painted and etched with runes of power and hung with feathers and bones. Three Volvas leapt up to caper about him, three young witches with unkempt hair and filthy robes cackling and writhing like dark spirits.

"God help me," Adzo whispered and made the sign of the cross. Einar kicked him hard in the shin. If Wolfthinker saw that Christian sign, Adzo might well lose his head. Adzo stared at Einar with watery eyes and Einar shook his head to warn the young Frank against any further outbursts.

"A sacrifice!" Kjartan howled. "The gods demand a sacrifice to placate their anger. Bolti angered them, or perhaps it was these men who fled the shield wall like frightened milkmaids. A sacrifice! The Aesir demand blood to atone!"

Ragnar rose from his seat and winced as he rolled his shoulders. "Quiet," he growled. Kjartan Wolfthinker made the sign to ward off evil and thrust his groin towards the Waveslicer's crew, before sliding back to his seat close to Ragnar's dais, followed closely by his Volvas. Ragnar inclined his head in a subtle gesture and stepped down, followed by Sten and Ivar. Ragnar walked slowly towards Sigurd and the Waveslicer's crew, who waited beside the hearth. Sweat beaded Einar's forehead. Death was close. He could feel its breath upon his neck like a winter breeze. He closed his eyes for a moment. *Hear me, Odin. Do not take my life before I have found the destiny laid out by my father. Let me live and I will take so many men's souls that your hall will burst with champions.*

Ragnar reached Sigurd and laid a hand upon his shoulder. He leant in close and spoke so softly that Einar couldn't hear. Sigurd nodded and stepped away to sit at a feasting bench. Ragnar gazed upon Sigarr, Einar, and the others, and ran a large hand down the braid of his beard. Sten Slegyya loomed behind him, his head tattooed beneath a topknot of hair. Sten was impossibly huge, making even Ragnar seem small. Ivar seemed like a child beside such men, yet his reputation was hard-earned and every grizzled warrior in the hall feared him as much as the baleful figure of Sten the sledgehammer.

"Tell me, Sigarr," Ragnar drawled, his voice calm and slow. "How is it you returned, yet One Leg Bolti lies dead with half of his crew and my raven banner is lost?"

Sigarr cleared his throat and licked at dry lips. "I did not flee from battle, Lord Ragnar," he said, pausing to cough. "We fought on the beach, but Dolgfinnr had the greater numbers. We faced three crews at least. He slew Bolti in single combat and the day was lost. We fought our way back to the ship to bring you the news of Bolti's death."

Ragnar nodded as if he understood. "How did One Leg Bolti die?"

"With honour and with his axe in hand. But Dolgfinnr cut off his head and held it in his hand as a trophy of war."

"He cut off Bolti's head?"

"Yes, lord."

"How many of my warriors died?"

"Forty men lost their lives attacking Dolgfinnr's shield wall. Each of us here fought bravely but managed to escape with our lives."

"But you left my raven banner behind?"

"We could not retrieve it, Lord Ragnar." Sigarr took a step backwards as Ragnar stepped towards him. A fire blazed in Ragnar's eyes and the muscles in his jaw worked behind his beard.

"That banner is sacred. You should have died rather than leave it in that bastard's hands!" Ragnar erupted in rage, jaw jutting, mouth snarling, voice grown as loud and fearsome as a roaring bear. "Dolgfinnr Dogsblood has my banner. His men piss on it, wipe their arses with it. It festoons his hall to show all in Midgard that Dolgfinnr bested my warriors. That banner symbolises my descent from Odin himself! We weave every raven banner in this very hall! And you snivelling wretches left it in the hands of an oathbreaker, a nithing whose very life insults me."

"Sacrifice them!" yowled Kjartan Wolfthinker from his bench. "Give them to me. Give their souls to me and I shall honour the gods with their blood, screams, and suffering."

Ragnar opened his mouth, but Sten Slegyya grunted over his shoulder and gave the jarl pause. Sten curled his lip in Wolfthinker's direction and leaned towards Ragnar.

"We sail south this week," said Sten. "Frankia and Paris await. We have jarls and their crews ready to meet us on the Whale Road."

"There is ill luck in this," Ragnar replied. "Maybe Kjartan is right. Odin needs to be appeased with blood."

"But to sacrifice these men will leave a nasty taste in our warriors' mouths. We have seen defeat before. Have not you and I retreated in battle?"

"Once or twice when numbers demanded it."

"If our men fear what you will do to them if they survive battle, it will make it harder for them to stand in the shield wall. Remove that fear. Let the warriors march to battle with full hearts. When we attack Paris, we need men willing to scale the city's high walls, not men quaking on their ships, fearing what will happen if the attack fails. It might take four or five assaults to take Paris, four failed attacks and one to break them. Think on that."

Ragnar nodded thoughtfully and inclined his head towards his son, Ivar.

"Both Sten and Kjartan give wise counsel, father," Ivar said. "Break up the crew, for they have suffered a humiliating defeat and brought shame to your reputation. Sacrifice a third of them to appease the gods, take a third of them with you south, and give a third and the Waveslicer to join my ships. I will go north and punish Dolgfinnr Dogsblood with my crews.

I shall recover the raven banner and mount Dolgfinnr's head above this hall as a reminder to those who break their oath to you."

Ragnar's hard eyes swept across the Waveslicer's crew, and when they fell upon Einar, it was as though the younger man stood before a mighty dragon with fiery breath and malevolent fury.

"Ten men go to you, Ivar. Take three ships, but the Waveslicer stays here. The ship is bad luck now. She will be caulked, have a new prow and a new name." Ragnar spoke in a low tone, his speech coming rhythmically like a poem. Men banged their fists on feasting tables to keep time, so that the song and din would wing its way high above to the gods themselves. "Punish Dolgfinnr Dogsblood for me. You take one other man and sacrifice him to augur your voyage. Four more go to Kjartan Wolfthinker to appease Odin All-Father for the loss of the raven banner, for all men know the ravens are Odin's birds. Do not his ravens Hugin and Munin go out into the world and report back to him all the goings on in Midgard? They sing to him of men's thoughts and memories and sit on his shoulders high in Asgard, where the gods make their home. The remaining five sorry nithings shall be enslaved and sold at the slave markets so that all men know that only brave men serve Ragnar Lothbrok. That is my doom, and so it shall be."

"Now drink!" bellowed Sten Slegyya, raising a shovel-like fist into the air. "Drink and feast, for in three days' time, we sail to war, glory, and riches."

The hall erupted in riotous cheers and Einar's heart thumped in his chest like the fists beating Ragnar's tables. The Waveslicer's crew exchanged nervous glances, wondering which of them was to die suffering at Kjartan's hands, which one was to be sacrificed by Ivar. Some would be lucky and join Ragnar's army, and others would now serve Ivar. Sigarr stepped towards Ivar and said something Einar could not hear above the shouting and cheering. Ivar smiled and inclined his head and Einar wondered if now was the time to speak up for himself, to remind Lord Ragnar of the place his father had bought with a battle-won ring. Einar opened his mouth to speak, but the words died in his throat as men with spears tramped into the hall and ushered Bolti's remaining crew out of the hall to wait on the green grass between Ragnar's hall and the houses, stables, and barns between it and the harbour.

"Are we going to die?" asked Adzo as they waited between a circle of helmeted warriors.

"We shall find out soon enough," Einar replied. "Here comes Ivar."

The Boneless marched out of his father's hall

with a green cloak billowing behind him.

"And death comes with him," murmured Orvar.

The men huddled together and fell silent. Einar prayed to Odin again, for he was about to discover if he would live or die.

FIVE

Ivar strolled around the survivors slowly, taking his time, staring thoughtfully at each man, assessing their size and strength, their usefulness and what they might contribute to his warband.

"I fought beside you before, Lord Ivar," said a warrior, raising his hands to plead to the Boneless. "On the shores of Lake Lodoga. You killed a man with your two swords and I stopped a blow aimed at your back with my shield?"

"I remember," said Ivar. "But I did not see you in the front ranks that day, nor in any battles since."

The warrior's mouth flapped open and closed and Ivar continued his stroll around the petrified warriors. He draped an arm around one guard and pointed at a group of men close to Einar. Einar held his breath. Ivar counted four, and the fourth man stood directly to Einar's right.

"Those four go to Kjartan Wolfthinker. Cut them out and take them to him," said Ivar.

The four men shook their heads in disbelief, and the man next to Einar whispered to himself and shook like a leaf. To go to the Godi was to be sacrificed to the gods. It meant pain, death and suffering.

"This man," Ivar pointed to the tallest amongst them, a stout fighter named Gaddi. "Tie him up and send him to my ship. The Windspear is in the harbour. These five," Ivar pointed to Einar, Adzo and three other men, "take to the thrall pens. The rest go to my father."

"Thank you, lord," said Sigarr, amongst those who were to join Ragnar's ranks. "I won't let your father down again. I swear it on my arm rings and my honour."

"Honour? Your honour isn't worth a bucket of piss. Take him to the thrall pens with the others. I'll keelhaul him tomorrow. If he lives, he can join my father's crews. If he dies, then let Njorth take the sacrifice for fair winds and calm seas on our journey north."

Sigarr's head dropped to his chin and three warriors ushered him, Einar and the other four men, towards the slave pens. The pens were little more than a modest barn and fence around a circle of mud where Ragnar held slaves captured during raiding season before selling them at one of the many slave markets like Hedeby or Dublin. The warriors pushed Einar, Adzo and the others inside the fence and closed the gate behind them.

"Please," implored Orvar. He reached and grabbed a warrior's leather breastplate. "I beg you. Take me to Lord Ivar again. I must…"

The warrior pushed him away and clouted his spear shaft across the archer's head with a loud crack. The other warriors guffawed, and they marched away without another word.

"Odin, save us," wailed one man as he chewed his fingernails, watching the warriors' backs retreat into the winding lanes.

Sigarr stumbled towards the slave hovel like a drunken man and slumped down against its walls with his head in his hands.

"I am to be a thrall again," grumbled Adzo, and kicked a lump of soil across the pen.

"I won't let this be my fate," Einar replied. He paced across the pen, mind racing. "I should have spoken up in the hall. A curse on myself for lacking the courage."

"Do you see a way out of this?"

"Like my father said, '*Live with courage, son. Stand and fight, and Odin with reward you with hamingja*'."

Adzo seemed to wake from his morbid resignation and his head snapped back and forth like a bird. "Maybe you are right. Look, we're not locked in here, and that fence is barely waist-high. Our hands and feet are free of fetters. What's stopping us from climbing over that fence in the middle of the night and making a run for it? We could be a half-day's march from here before they even knew we were gone."

"Fools," spat Sigarr. "Every farmstead for miles around is owned by one of Ragnar's warriors. It would take you a week or more before you reached the edge of Ragnar's dominion. They don't need fetters or walls to keep us in. We are here and there is no hope of escape."

"We should have listened to Refill," choked the archer rubbing at the lump on his head. "We'd be in the east now, feasting and fighting for pay. He was right, and you were wrong."

Sigarr slipped into silence at that harsh truth, and Einar sat and rested against the fence. Adzo sat beside him and Einar thought carefully, trying to muster all the cunning in his mind to find a way out of Ragnar's doom. The sun slipped down beyond the horizon, casting Hrafnborg in darkness. Fires lit houses in flickering shades of orange, whilst Ragnar's great hall hummed with the sound of laughter and war stories as the men drank, ate and prepared themselves for war and months away from home.

Einar's life hung in the balance. Once he boarded a slave ship, there was no way back. He could expect iron fetters, and after the auction at the slave block, his new master would brand him, perhaps geld him, and then whisk him away to some Odin-forsaken place in a far corner of Midgard. Einar shuddered at the thought of ploughing fields in the harsh north, or beyond in the frozen eastern mountains.

"They'll keelhaul Sigarr tomorrow," Einar said, staring up wistfully, trying to glimpse the stars between shadowed clouds.

"What will Ivar do to him?" Adzo replied.

"Tie a length of rope about him out on the water and drag him underneath the ship whilst it's sailing."

"Will he live?"

Einar shrugged. "I've never seen it done before. But it was Ivar's suggestion, and Ivar is fond of brutal punishments, so don't expect it to be pleasant."

"I don't care what Sigarr says. We could run for it, you know. Maybe we could take one of those fishing boats in the harbour and sail away? Be free of this place."

"Where would we go? This is my home."

"To Frankia, to my home. My people would welcome you there, and we would be free."

"If we made it. But I'm going to stay." A smile split Einar's face, surprising him as much as it did Adzo. A plan had formed in his mind, like an ornate ship's prow carved from a lump of wood under a carpenter's deft chisel.

"You've got an idea?"

"Maybe. A chance. We'll see tomorrow."

Einar slept little that night. The five men in the slave pen retreated inside the hovel for warmth and Einar dozed in a corner, thoughts churning over what may and may not happen that day as he rolled the dice and gambled for his life. In the deepest night, when men snored, and a fox screamed somewhere in the darkness, a figure came to Einar from the gloaming. It crawled like a troll, creeping through the mud like one of the *huldu* folk, the ancient, hidden ones who lived in the deep forests and high mountains.

"Morning will come swiftly, young Einar," said the shadowy shape. It was Sigarr, and he sat beside Einar, wringing his hands, the whites of his eyes darting about the slave pen in case any wakeful ears listened.

"Are you afraid?" asked Einar.

"They're going to keelhaul me, lad. Of course

I am afraid. I have seen it done, seen men die as their heads bang and scrape against the ship's keel beneath the water. They emerge with battered faces and heads leaking blood. Though I saw one man survive, and hope that shall also be my fate."

"Do you wish we had followed Refill's advice?" Einar whispered those words and turned away, for he had wished it over and over as he pondered how to save his own life.

Sigarr laughed. "No, I do not. Many of our men live and have joined Ragnar's crews. For them, the honourable proved just and true."

"But not for us."

"We are not dead yet, young Einar."

"You believe you will live?"

"If Odin wishes it. If not, then…"

"What of me?"

"Slaves can become freemen. Look at your Frankish friend. He was once a thrall and found his freedom in the chaos of battle."

"And is now a thrall once more."

"True. The gods are fickle. Tomorrow will tell all. You should sleep, lad."

"I cannot. I must find a way to win my freedom."

Morning came with drizzling rain and a chill wind. An old woman brought the prisoners sour ale and two loaves of stale bread to share. They ate huddled in the hovel, men who had once been proud warriors now filthy-faced with frightened eyes, eating bread with dirty fingers. A far cry from the strutting men with combed beards and hair, shining weapons and straight backs they had been less than a week ago.

"Einar?" called a voice as Einar finished his last mouthful of bread. "Are you in there?"

Einar poked his head out of the hovel and sighed as five lads stared back at him from across the fence.

"There he is, see?" exclaimed one boy Einar had grown up with on the lanes of Hrafnborg. "I told you."

"Well, well," jeered the largest of them, Kalf, a big-headed red-haired son of a blacksmith. The boys were all roughly Einar's age, lads he had practised weapons with, and played with as a child. "You went off to sea and thought you'd return a warrior. Look at you now, thrall. I should have you empty my grandmother's shit pail."

The other boys sniggered. Einar wanted to tell them that Sigarr had all but made him a warrior on board the Waveslicer, but in Sigarr's current state, that would only fuel their jests.

"When he's emptied the pail, he can shovel out the midden heap, or milk the cows up in the high pasture," offered another lad.

"Or we could get him a distaff and some wool." More laughter.

"Einar Egilsson, a thrall. What would your dead father think of you now?" mocked Kalf. "Maybe they'll sell you to a boy lover from the east? That'll make your father proud."

Einar stepped out of the hovel. "Come inside the fence and I'll teach you not to say that again, turd."

"Why would I come inside a slave pen? I'm a free man, an apprentice blacksmith. You have no rights here now. No law to protect you. You're nothing, little more than a lump of shit hanging from a sheep's arse."

Anger washed over Einar like a tidal wave. He picked up a clod of mud and threw it at Kalf. The clod struck him on the side of the head and all the laughter stopped.

"Bastard," spat Kalf. "He's nothing but a thrall now. We can beat the daylights out of him and there's nothing anybody will do or care about it. Come on." Kalf put one hand on the fence and leapt inside the pen, followed by the other four boys.

"I'll help you," said Adzo, coming to stand

beside Einar with balled fists.

"No, go inside. Slaves aren't supposed to fight back."

"I know. I have been a thrall before, remember?"

"Stay back, Adzo."

Adzo slipped back into the shadows and Einar stalked out into the muddy pen as Kalf and the four lads made a circle around him.

"He's always been too big for his boots," growled Kalf with a curl of his lip. "Thinks he's better than us because his father was a warrior. Let's work the bastard over, knock his teeth out, so he has to suck the juice from meat for the rest of his miserable thrall's life."

Einar didn't wait for any further insults. He charged, hurling himself at Kalf and driving the blacksmith's son down into the mud. They rolled there, punching and clawing at one another. Einar grabbed a fistful of Kalf's hair and twisted his head away. He clambered on top of his body and crashed a punch into Kalf's nose. A boot kicked Einar hard in the ribs and he fell to his left, rolling away as another foot came to stamp where his head had been. Einar surged to his feet, punched one lad in the stomach and another in the eye. Two boys leapt on Einar, driving him down with a rain of punches hammering into his face and head.

A finger poked deep into Einar's eye and he howled with rage at his misfortune and the dire situation he found himself in, as well as the pain. Einar stamped his boot onto a boy's foot and drove the flat of his hand into another lad's throat. He turned and grabbed the lad behind him by the groin and crashed a headbutt into his face. Something hard hit Einar across the back of the head and he stumbled; the crock of ale hanging from Kalf's hand. Kalf swung it again and Einar caught it, kicked the blacksmith's son in the guts and wrenched the crock from his grip. Einar brought it down with both hands so that it smashed across Kalf's head, and the red-haired boy dropped to the mud.

The sound of laughter and clapping snapped Einar from his rage. He stood covered in filth, chest heaving and bloody knuckles stinging to find Ivar the Boneless watching him from a laneway.

"A fine display," Ivar praised, and strolled to the slave pen. "What is your name, scrapper?"

"Einar."

"I have seen you about Hrafnborg with the other boys. You like to fight?"

"Yes, lord,' panted Einar, the side of his face already beginning to swell up.

"Einar the Brawler, eh? Condemned to the slave pens and still able to best five strapping lads. Perhaps I was hasty in putting you in the pens. There must be a place on my crews for a fighter like you."

Einar's spirit soared, and he stood straighter. This was his chance. Einar's luck had turned. Time slowed, his mind flashing back to every time he had held his tongue or stopped himself from acting when the chance came to move closer to his destiny. "Then set me free, Lord Ivar, and I will swear an oath to fight for you and be your man."

"Careful, brawler. Fighting for me is not like swearing an oath to another sea-jarl or two-ship island warlord." Ivar's smile vanished, his mouth becoming a cruel slash across his face which had changed from handsome to sharp, angled and malevolent in an instant. "My crews go to war without end. Many of my men die in battle. We are first in and last out of any fight. I will be the champion of the Northmen one day, and to get there, my warriors must fight the bad men, the dangerous warriors, men of reputation and war-skill. Is that what you want? Are you ready to cross blades with killers, raiders, slavers, and champions?"

"I'm ready." Einar lied, but he held the gaze of Ivar the Boneless and it was like looking into the eyes of Loki himself. Einar's chest burned with the life-changing moment, as Ivar looked into his very soul.

"Come, then." The easy smile returned, and Ivar rubbed his hands together. "Climb out of there and get yourself cleaned up. Today I am going to keelhaul a man. You can come on board and watch. It might be a tale to tell your children one day."

"This man is my friend, and also a stout fight, Lord Ivar." Einar pointed to Adzo and beckoned to him to come from the slave hovel. "Free him too, lord, and gain two men who will fight for you to the death."

Ivar threw his head back and laughed heartily. "You have some stones on you, Einar the Brawler. Come, then. Bring him with you. Meet us at the harbour before noon."

Ivar marched away and left Einar in the early morning silence. The boys he had fought crawled sway, spitting curses and vowing revenge, and Einar bent over with his hands on his knees. He wanted to vomit, but mastered himself.

"Your luck has changed," said Sigarr, a wry smile splitting his face. "Like I said, if Odin wishes it, we shall both discover our fates today. Who else could have sent Ivar to this place at that very moment?"

"I wish you luck today," Einar said. Sigarr nodded his thanks. The other men destined for the slave markets just stared at Einar with ashen faces and wet eyes. Einar had to leave them. His chance had come, and he had taken it. Each of those former warriors must embrace their own fate. He left the slave pen and took Adzo with him. They hurried around to the rear of a set of long stables on the settlement's western edge, where Einar washed himself clean of mud in a barrel of rainwater.

"You did it!" cheered Adzo, clapping Einar on the back. "I am a free man again. That's twice you have saved me from the slave's collar."

"It's not over yet. I hadn't planned on fighting Kalf and the others. They came to me."

"Praise God for that." Adzo laughed and threw his hands up towards his Christ God's heaven.

"Praise to Odin. My father's *hamingja* had a hand in it. I can feel his luck swaying things in my favour after so much misfortune. My plan was to gain an audience with Jarl Ragnar and remind him of my father's payment."

"You don't still believe…"

"I believe. I will speak with Ragnar, and I will achieve the destiny my father laid out for me. Too long have I waited idly for my fate to come to me. But last night in that slave pit, lying in the darkness with only a lifetime of humiliation and servitude beckoning from the future, I realised I must take what is mine. Ivar has offered me a chance, but my father already bought my future. I must claim that inheritance. My mother and father are dead. I was raised alone in this place, sleeping in the houses of my father's shield brothers, listening as they spoke over and again of my father's greatness and how one day I would follow in his footsteps. There can be no more waiting, no more following. A warrior takes what he wants and wins it on the edge of his axe and point of his spear. This much I have learned since we fought and lost to Dolgfinnr Dogsblood."

"So, how do we do it?"

"First, we go to see Sigarr keelhauled. Then we speak to Jarl Ragnar."

"Why is Ivar called the Boneless?"

"Because he can twist and turn around enemy blades as though there are no bones in his body, like he is a serpent, fearsome and lithe, and no blade is fast enough to score his skin."

"You Vikings and your by-names," Adzo shook his head and chuckled.

"It is an honour for a man to carry such a name. It means he has earned it and has the respect of his shipmates."

"Maybe I should become Adzo the Fearless, or Adzo the Fierce. What of the others in the pens? What will become of them?"

"We must look to our own destinies. Perhaps, Adzo, you shall become a warrior. Can you wield an axe, or spear?"

"No. At home my family were farmers, so I know how to prepare crops, till fields, store grain and tend to animals. I can shear wool from a sheep and shepherd a flock of goats. As a thrall I lifted, carried, cleaned, washed, fished, gutted the catch and slopped out the fishing boats."

"Can you use a bow?"

Adzo grinned. "That I can do. I won an archery tourney once at home. I could hit the stones off a gnat at twenty paces."

They laughed together. "Good. Every crew needs archers and hunters."

The laughter melted away, and Einar washed the remaining dirt from his body and hair. He tied his hair back at the nape of his neck with a scrap of leather and brushed the worst of the filth from his jerkin and trews. Einar was free. Other men would suffer, but nobody had spoken up for Einar when Ragnar and Ivar decided the survivors' fates. He was learning, and he had to watch and learn fast. The world of a Norse warrior was violent and cruel, and Einar realised that if he was going to survive, he had to harden himself like the callus on an oarsman's palm.

A horn blared long and loud from the harbour and Einar blew out his cheeks. It was time to see Sigarr keelhauled, and if he could, Einar would try to talk to Ragnar Lothbrok.

SIX

On a damp morning where steam rose from rain-soaked thatch beneath a cold sun, the folk of Hrafnborg filled the lanes and pathways leading from the heart of the village towards the harbour. They talked excitedly about what might happen on the water that morning, and the air was thick with the smell of cooking pots boiling barley, porridge, and freshly baked bread.

Einar and Adzo hurried, weaving through the throng to get down to the quayside before the crowds became too thick.

"We must be at the front," Einar panted to Adzo as he swerved around a chicken coup and ran through a pen containing three braying goats. "Ivar will forget us unless we present ourselves at his ship."

"Slow down!" cursed a woman carrying a basket of eggs as Einar brushed past her. He dashed across the open ground between the wattle buildings and the edge of Hrafnborg's high palisade where it butted against the sea.

A horn blared for the third time that morning, calling people to witness the spectacle about to unfold in Hrafnborg's bay. Its lilting song floated across the water and up to the crowd streaming from the gates. Einar and Adzo ran through the gate and paused on the hillside, looking down towards the jetties where a dozen warships lay moored against six long timber fingers stretching out into the water. A score more *drakkars, karves*, and *snekke* warships of different sizes lay at anchor off the coast.

"Look," said Adzo, and pointed out to sea. A long ship with a golden hull approached, cutting through a calm sea like a blade. A black sail without adornment or images flew taut and full of wind and a crew busied themselves like ants, hurrying back and forth across deck, pulling at rigging, and preparing the warship for port.

"What ship is that?" asked Einar, grabbing the arm of a man in a wide-brimmed hat and an apron dusted white with flour.

"It's the warship Seaworm," answered the man, and he made the sign to ward off evil. "Vigmarr Svarti's ship and crew."

"The Seaworm," Einar said wistfully.

"Do you know that ship?" asked Adzo.

"It was my father's old ship. He served on

it for many years, and Vigmarr Svarti, Vigmarr the Black, was his jarl. A sea-jarl, a warrior of the Whale Road without land or subjects, only his ship and the most fearsome reputation in Midgard."

Einar beckoned to Adzo, and they pelted down the hillside. Einar avoided the stone pathway thronged with people ambling down towards the water. He hurried down the grassy ridge until he reached the timber planking spanning the waterfront. He dodged around baskets of fish and leapt over fishing nets until he spotted Ivar's Windspear on the leftmost jetty.

Einar stepped on the wooden platform, and a weathered-looking warrior barred his path with a spear.

"Piss off, whelp," he grunted, a gust of his fetid breath washing across Einar's face.

"I'm here to see Lord Ivar," Einar replied.

"I said piss off, or I'll ring your skull and chuck you into the water. Go look after the pigs. Away with you."

Einar gulped. The spear pushed against his chest, and he took a backward step into Adzo. The warrior kept walking, forcing Einar off the jetty towards the crowd. He peered around the man's bulk, searching amongst the other warriors on the jetty. Men clad in leather and iron, with amulets around their necks, braided beards and finely-combed and plaited hair. Gigantic men with tattoos of ravens, wolves, dragons, and twisting whorls on their arms, necks and faces.

A loud guffaw caught Einar's attention, and he spotted Ivar talking to an enormous man with a lantern jaw and a shining bald head.

"Lord Ivar!" Einar shouted.

"I've had enough of you, pup," the warrior growled and he grabbed a fistful of Einar's jerkin and was about to toss him into the water when a cheerful voice piped up.

"Ah! It's the Brawler. Let him through, Rorik," called Ivar, and waved cheerfully for Einar to approach.

Einar winked at Rorik, whose round face flushed as red as a beetroot. He stepped around Rorik, closely followed by Adzo, and they walked carefully along the jetty towards Ivar the Boneless. Einar rolled his shoulders and stepped around the fierce-faced men. Any push or perceived slight might result in a fist in his face, or worse, a challenge to fight. Einar wished he still had the axe Sigarr had rewarded him with onboard the Waveslicer, but they had taken it from him outside Ragnar's hall.

The warriors all watched the warship

Seaworm approach, and they hoomed in appreciation as the black sail came down in one fluid motion, and two banks of oars lowered like the wings of a great flying beast. The dragon prow snarled at the shore, and one of the crew removed it from its stem post.

"Why are they taking off the prow?" asked Adzo.

"So the war-beast doesn't frighten the land spirits, and to show they come in peace," Einar replied.

"War-beast? Land spirits? You Vikings are strange men."

A clipped roar came from the Seaworm and Ivar's warriors nodded with appreciative smiles as the oars dipped as one and rowed the long, beautiful ship towards shore. Einar marvelled at the curve of her hull and the intricately carved dragon's head prow. The water parted before its hull in two perfectly formed waves and sent ripples out across the gently rolling sea. Einar remembered standing on the shore as a tiny child when his father had returned from campaign on that very ship. He recalled the pride and joy as Egil had strode from the Seaworm laden with gold and silver coins with a shining axe at his belt and a smile for his son that could brighten the gloomiest of days.

"Old Vigmarr knows his business," observed

the warrior next to Einar.

"Heya. He's a fine shipmaster all right," another piped up. "Wouldn't want to cross him, though."

"He killed three of his own crew last summer," said a third man.

"That's an old wives' tale. Who told you that, Frani the smith's wife?"

"She still coming to you when her husband works late?"

The warriors sniggered and Einar kept his eyes fixed on the warship Seaworm. She banked, oars coming up as one, as water dripped from each blade like shining jewels in the morning sun. The Seaworm found her mooring with the grace of a landing swan, and every person ashore clapped and called out in admiration. They landed in an empty berth beside Ivar's Windspear, and men tied ropes off to secure the longship. An enormous man stepped ashore, hulking and stooped like one bent with age. A scruffy nest of crow-black hair hid his face, and he wore a black leather breastplate, trews that had once been black but were now faded to grey, black boots, and a black cloak about his wide shoulders. He limped along the jetty with a rolling gait, his thick torso lurching up and down like the sea itself. Men moved out of his way until he came to a stop before Ivar.

"Well met, Jarl Vigmarr," Ivar greeted him with his now familiar smile. "You have returned just in time for war."

Vigmarr Svarti stood up straight, and he was suddenly as tall as the biggest men amongst Ivar's crews. He swept a four-fingered hand through the mess of his hair and cleared it away from his ash-white face. Vigmarr's was a hard face to look upon, as twisted and gnarled as a wind-battered tree, and as flat and rugged as the cruellest crag. The entire left side of his face sagged to one side like a melted candle, mouth and eye pulled down as though by a length of rope. Two great scars ran across his nose and right cheek, and obsidian eyes, without life or shine, stared out like bleak, bottomless pits.

"Ivar," said Vigmarr, his voice low and full of gravel.

"My father sent for you in the spring. Where have you been?"

Vigmarr coughed, and his body seemed to rattle with pain. "Raiding," he replied.

Ivar shrugged, as if the answer were obvious. He paused, waiting for Vigmarr to speak further, but the haggard jarl said nothing. He just stared blankly at Ivar.

"We are about to keelhaul a man who lost the raven banner. Care to join us?"

Vigmarr coughed again, racking coughs that seemed to pain him like knives in his chest. "No," he said eventually.

"My father is in his hall."

Vigmarr's great shaggy head dipped again, and he limped across the jetty without saying another word. Men stepped out of his way, barging into each other to avoid brushing against the man in black. He came close to Einar, and he smelled of brine, tinged with the iron stink of blood. A pitch-black eye flashed at Einar through the matted hair and Einar could not help but flinch. He glimpsed two axes in Vigmarr's belt, and a broken-backed seax hanging from a baldric around his neck. Vigmarr disappeared into the crowd and all eyes swivelled back to Ivar.

"Let's get started," said the Boneless. "We haven't got all day."

The Windspear's crew clambered aboard and prepared the ship to sail. Ivar pointed to Einar and Adzo and whispered something into the bald man's ear.

"You two, follow me," Rorik barked. He stepped on board the long warship and as Einar followed, he tripped on a length of seal hide rope and almost tumbled into Rorik's back. Rorik turned and frowned at them both. "You two are as sorry a pair of green, land-hugging bastards as I've ever seen. Ivar says you will join one of his crews, and I pray to Njorth, Thor and Odin that it's not this one. Just keep out of the way. I'd give you a job, but you'd make pig shit out of it. Just stand by the stern, don't look at anyone, and touch nothing. Any noise out of you and I'll slit your bellies and toss you overboard."

Einar nodded and hastened to the stern.

"Seems like a pleasant fellow," said Adzo in an undertone, and they smirked.

A group of men came from Hrafnborg's gate and the crowd parted to let them pass. Einar spotted Sigarr walking, head bowed, between two spearmen, and strolling before him came Ragnar Lothbrok himself. The great jarl waved and shook the hands of men and women as he passed through the throng. Ragnar came on board the Windspear and greeted every man onboard by name, and even cast a suspicious raised eyebrow in Einar and Adzo's direction. Einar's heartbeat quickened. If Ragnar himself was on board, then this was his chance to approach him and ask about the place his father had bought amongst Ragnar's warriors. Ivar had offered Einar hope, a chance of joining his crews, but it depended on Ivar's whim, and that which was granted could easily be snatched away. An order from Ragnar, an iron decision to honour Egil's wishes, would guarantee Einar's future.

The warriors left Sigarr by the mast, and Ivar's crew took up their oars. The crowds cheered as Ivar bellowed orders and the ship edged slowly away from shore, oarsmen grunting with the effort of getting the longship underway. Her clinker-built timbers creaked and groaned as she moved, each gap between the planks caulked with horsehair and tar to keep the boat as watertight as possible.

Ragnar and Ivar stood by the steerboard whilst Ivar guided the ship further out to sea, and Einar watched him from the prow, where he and Adzo did their best to keep out of the way. A sea wind blew through Einar's hair and he tore his gaze from Ragnar to the warship Seaworm, where men unloaded sacks and barrels. He might never be that close to Ragnar again. The great warrior was only a ship's length away, barely thirty paces. But to do it, Einar had to pass the oarsmen, and Rorik, who shot Einar a murderous look across the deck.

When the Windspear was far enough into deeper waters, but close enough for the crowd ashore to see, Ivar ordered his men to raise their oars. Rorik tied a length of rope around Sigarr's armpits and men unfurled the sail. The warship surged forward as the sail billowed and the people ashore cheered as the Windspear picked up speed so that she cut through the swell like a darting fish.

"Odin protect you, warrior," Ragnar called as Rorik ushered Sigarr to the sheerstrake.

Sigarr peered over the side at the rushing waves and whispered something Einar could not hear.

"God help him," breathed Adzo and made the sign of the cross.

"Will you stop doing that?" hissed Einar.

"What?"

"Making that cursed sign of your nailed god. What do you think will happen if the others see you do it? They might send you to Kjartan Wolfthinker, he'd love a Christ worshipper to sacrifice to the gods."

"I'm only praying for Sigarr. What's so bad about that?"

"Stop with the cross signs. Trust me."

The crew stood around Sigarr and Rorik in a half-circle and men beat their boots against the hull in time to Einar's heartbeat. Rorik pushed Sigarr to the very edge, almost dangling him over the sheerstrake as the warship flew across the bay. Ivar raised his arm and then dropped it. Rorik shoved Sigarr over the side and he disappeared into the sea with a splash lost against the roaring wind in Einar's ears. Men rushed to the ship's opposite bow, where two warriors hauled on the rope tied about Sigarr's shoulders. The warriors continued to stomp their feet, as if to gauge how long Sigarr could hold his breath before he drowned beneath the ship.

The taut rope coiled about the two warriors' feet as they hauled. They paused every two or three pulls as the rope seemed to become snagged and continued hand over hand to pull Sigarr underneath the fast-moving ship. Einar closed his eyes. Sigarr's description of the men he had seen keelhauled convinced Einar that he could hear Sigarr's head thudding against the keel as they dragged him beneath the ship. They hauled him crossways to the ship's direction so that the water's force beneath the ship would twist and turn him like a leaf blowing in a gale.

Einar dashed to the side and squinted into the deep blue depths. It had been too long. Einar had not counted the stomping feet, but he doubted any man could hold his breath much longer. The ship was widest at its central point, flaring out on either side of the mast to give its shallow draught stability.

"He's a goner," crowed one man with glee. "Pay up, lads."

"Smug bastard," growled another and handed over three scraps of hacksilver from a pouch beneath his armpit.

Einar chewed his bottom lip as the waves rolled by. Soon Ivar would bring the ship about and lead her back to shore. If Sigarr hadn't surfaced by then, then he was certainly a dead man. The two burly warriors hauled on the rope again, cheeks blowing at the exertion. Their pulls seemed to speed up and Sigarr's head popped up out of the sea, mouth agape and gasping for air. His head and face were a ruin of matted hair, torn flesh, and sheets of blood flooded from ghastly wounds across the top of his scalp to stain the sea red. Einar pushed through the warriors and leaned over the side, extending his hands towards Sigarr.

Adzo grabbed Einar's waist to hold him steady and Sigarr reached up weakly, his hands trembling and his eyes closed beneath his forehead and cheeks, which had become mashed into balls and ridges of ruined bone. Einar caught his hands and hauled Sigarr towards him.

"Help me!" Einar shouted, and more hands reached over the side until Sigarr flopped over the sheerstrake and landed heavily on deck. He coughed and a bucketful of sea water belched from his mouth in a gushing torrent.

"Give that silver back, Snorri," came a voice behind Einar, and the man who had collected his winnings prematurely grumbled because Sigarr had survived.

"He lives!" Ivar called from the steerboard and waved to the people ashore who cheered.

Einar bent to Sigarr. "You did it," he said. Sigarr's mangled face just lay still as air wheezed from his lungs.

"He might still be breathing," said Adzo, "but I doubt he'll live beyond today. Look, his entire body has been crushed."

Einar saw that Sigarr's chest was misshapen, and his neck bulged on one side. A rough hand cuffed Einar around the head and he fell into the bows.

"What did I say, shitworms?" Rorik snarled. He grabbed a fistful of Adzo's jerkin and flung him across two oar benches towards the prow, and the crew chortled as Einar followed. "Keep out of the bloody way."

The Windspear banked towards shore and the crew furled the sail. They rowed back towards their berth, and the warriors took turns to run the oars. Each man began at the stern and leapt from oar to oar, trying to reach the prow without falling into the water. The folk of Hrafnborg cheered each man and laughed raucously whenever one fell into the water. Einar sat against the prow, feeling hollow. The crew ignored Sigarr, leaving his misshapen body flopping in the bilge as blood seeped from the countless wounds in his skull to stain the ballast stones red. Nobody seemed to care. Ivar and Ragnar laughed as their warriors ran the oars, and it was as if Sigarr didn't exist at all.

The ship drifted into shore and the crowd on the hill melted away, heading east towards some other spectacle which had caught their attention.

"Where are you going?" asked Adzo as Einar moved away from the prow towards the mast. "Wait until everyone has gone, or Rorik, that mountain of baldness, will beat us bloody."

"It's time," Einar replied. He ignored a growl from Rorik and swung beneath a length of rigging. Warriors stepped off the ship and Einar came up from the network of ropes and emerged face to face with Ragnar Lothbrok.

Ragnar paused, surprised to see Einar appear suddenly before him as he was about to leave the Windspear.

"Lord Ragnar," said Einar, and bowed his head.

"Thor's balls, pup, but you are a testy little weasel," said Rorik, lurching towards Einar. But Ragnar raised a finger and the huge man stopped a pace away from Einar, his teeth grinding, seething with rage.

"I saw this lad fight four others this morning," Ivar said. "I have named him Einar the Brawler, and he will join my crews."

"Einar?" repeated Ragnar, his eyes narrowing.

"Yes, lord," said Einar. He squared his shoulders. "I am the son of Egil, once oathsworn to you. A warrior of the warship Seaworm, killed in battle many years ago."

"You are Einar Egilsson?"

"Yes, lord. I was destined for the slave markets until Lord Ivar set me free. Before he died, my father told me he paid you a battle-won arm ring to secure a place for me on one of your ships."

"I remember Egil, and I remember his arm ring."

"You have your place," Ivar said, waving his hand dismissively. "You will pull an oar for me, it is decided."

Ragnar placed a gentle hand on his son's stomach. "I fought beside Egil many times. He was a brave man. Einar will serve on your ships, son, but I want to talk to him first. Follow me, boy."

Einar swallowed and followed Ragnar off the Windspear as he marched towards Hrafnborg, trailed by a dozen warriors. Adzo hurried after him as they strode up the pathway towards the palisade gate. From the top of the hill, Einar glanced towards where the crowd had gathered once the Windspear's grim entertainment had ended. In a shallow dip between two hills, Kjartan Wolfthinker capered amongst a grove of hazel trees. The people of Hrafnborg had gathered about him in a wide circle and swayed from side to side, each moving as one and humming so that they looked like one living being. Wolfthinker shook his black staff and howled at the sky, and his three Volvas cut the throats of the Waveslicer sacrificial prisoners. The crowd raised their hands as blood flowed, and Einar turned away as the Volvas collected the blood in bowls.

He had seen such sacrifices many times. Kjartan Wolfthinker asked the gods to bless Ragnar's war fleet with luck and offered souls in return for their favour. Adzo gasped when he saw the sacrifice, but Einar had no time for the Frank's soft, Christian ways. He was following Ragnar Lothbrok to his hall to receive his inheritance, and it felt as though the whole of Midgard was opening up before him.

SEVEN

"Wait outside," Ragnar instructed his men as they hauled open the doors to his hall. "Just me and the boy."

Einar followed Ragnar inside and his footsteps echoed around the high rafters. The place seemed much larger without hundreds of people crammed inside. The ceiling, darkened by smoke from countless fires, rose high, and the sun shone through the smoke hole to leave a patch of brightness on the hard-packed earthen floor. Ragnar strode to his hearth and warmed his hands on the fire, which his stewards kept alight all year around.

A diminutive man with a thin face hurried from the hall's rear, carrying two cups. He handed one to Ragnar and one to Einar. He was about to scuttle away when Ragnar beckoned him close and whispered something in his ear. The man bowed and hastened away. Einar held the cup of ale and stood by the fire, unable to believe he was standing in Ragnar's hall with the man himself. All his life, Einar had dreamt of this moment, of claiming his father's legacy.

"So, you're Egil's boy?" mused Ragnar. He sighed and shook his head. "Egil was with me from the beginning. My father was a king, did you know that?" Einar remained silent, sensing that the questions were rhetorical. "I left his court with nothing but my ship and my crew, and I've won everything you see around you with my own hands. Egil came with me that day, when we were as young as you are now."

"My father would speak of those days. Of the raids and how you bound other jarls to your service."

"Aye. Long ago. I bound all the jarls of Kattegat to my banner. The world seemed… younger then. Simpler. Now, I am responsible for every soul in Hrafnborg. I must keep my warriors in rings and silver, I must keep their thirst for battle sated. Back then, all I had was monstrous ambition and a quick axe."

"Now you are as a king yourself, lord."

"I could call myself one if I wished. Who would stop me? It is many years since Egil died. You should have come to me sooner. Where have you been?"

"In Hrafnborg, living with friends of my

father. I always had a roof over my head and a bed to sleep in."

"That's because your father was a man of honour. His oath was like oak. That is true wealth, having shipmates and brothers of the shield wall who love you enough to take care of your child when you are gone." Ragnar drained his ale and set the cup down. He stared into the flames for a moment, as if reliving old memories. "We drifted apart, Egil and I, as things grew, as I gained more ships. He ended up on Vigmarr's ship. I should have kept him with me. I remember the day he gave me the arm ring. This arm ring." Ragnar pointed to one of the half a dozen rings of gold and silver on his right wrist and forearm. "He won it in a holmgang. Killed a man down in Vulso, and I was his second. Your mother was pregnant here in Hrafnborg and he made me pledge to keep a place for you."

"He told me of it."

"Now you come to claim it. Which is your right. There is always a need for more warriors, Einar Egilsson."

"Your reputation is unmatched, Lord Ragnar. You have achieved more than any Northman who ever went to sea. I am honoured to enter your service and swear my oath."

"Reputation…" Ragnar's eyes blazed, and the firelight danced on the planes of his face. He spoke wistfully, his voice as soft as a father telling a child a bedtime story. "Odin has favoured me. Wolfthinker says I am descended from the All-Father himself. He says he saw the signs of it in the liver of an eagle sacrifice. Heya… I don't know about that. But I know one thing. There must be battle and war to keep my men in silver and glory. I am their lord, and I must be their ring-giver, their war-maker. I want more, they want more, and so we sail to Frankia and the great city of Paris. After that? There will be another voyage, another campaign. Always more… Many brave men have died so that I could be me. So many. Good men, like Egil."

"Will I serve on Ivar's Windspear, lord?" Einar asked, wincing as he spoke, afraid to bring Ragnar out of his reverie.

Ragnar sniffed and snapped out of his melancholy. He adjusted his belt and cleared his throat. "That is up to Ivar. You will swear your oath to him, not I. He goes to punish Dolgfinnr, bring the dog to heel and retrieve the raven banner. You shall go with him. Fight well, and who knows what the Norns have in store for you? I condemned you to the slave pit, and yet here you are in my hall. Perhaps the Norns weave glory into the weft of your life, boy? Or perhaps those three hags cackle beneath the roots of Yggdrasil, the tree that holds up the nine worlds. They laugh at our dreams and lure us into foolish ambition.

"Ivar has three ships: his Windspear, the Fjordviper, and the Seaworm. Beware the Seaworm and Vigmarr the Black. He fights with an unmatched fury. His crew always has fresh faces, for so many of them die each year. He has an unquenchable thirst for blood. Egil was a Seaworm man and there he met his fate. Perhaps the Norns shall bring you to the Seaworm and complete the cycle." Ragnar pointed to a symbol set on the back of his imposing oaken doors. A great serpent set in a circle so that it ate its own tail. "Like Jormungandr, the world serpent who on the day of Ragnarök will grow so large that he will encircle Midgard and eat himself at the end of days. Perhaps it shall be so."

"Yes, lord." Einar stared at the iron serpent and back at Ragnar, whose face creased with a wicked smile.

"Now. I shall honour Egil's bargain." Ragnar waved to the back of his hall, and his steward came from the shadows. He helped two thralls carry a large pine chest towards the hearth, and Einar looked on, wondering what could be inside.

The stories about Ragnar's brutal savagery are tall tales, he thought. Ragnar seemed amiable, almost friendly. He had made a hard doom on the Waveslicer's survivors, but Ragnar was a great jarl and he must be strong. If not, the wicked men across the sea would smell weakness and attack him like a pack of wolves would an unprotected flock of sheep.

The thralls set the box down with an echoing clang, bowed to Ragnar and hurried from his presence. His steward opened the chest with a loud creak, took their empty cups and backed away.

"A son of Egil will not go to war ill-prepared as long as I draw breath. These weapons belonged to a man in my service who died of the sweating sickness in winter," said Ragnar. He bent and pulled out a stout, hard-baked leather breastplate and handed it to Einar. "This will turn most blades aside until you earn enough fair fame to get yourself a *brynjar*."

"Thank you, lord," said Einar in wonderment. He turned the armour over in his hands and slipped it over his head. It smelled of old sweat and leather, but it felt like wearing gold.

"Here is a helmet. I know many a man killed by a dunt to the head. So wear it always."

Einar took a conical iron helmet from Ragnar. It had a felt cap inside and a nasal protector, and Einar pressed it onto his head, feeling a foot taller.

"Weapons. An axe and seax." Ragnar passed

Einar an axe with a bright blade etched with Odin runes, and an oiled haft criss-crossed with leather. The seax was as long as Einar's forearm with a bone handle. It was single-edged with a wickedly broken back and a point sharp enough to punch through even the hardest armour. Einar's hand curled around the haft and handle, and it was like Odin had handed him weapons forged by Volund, the smith of legend. "Last, a belt to hang them on."

"I thank you for these wondrous gifts, Lord Ragnar."

"Ivar will provide a spear and shield, and then you are ready. There is just one more thing, however."

Einar bowed his head in thanks, unable to believe his luck. He fastened the belt around his waist and hung the axe through a loop on the right side. He slid the seax carefully into a sheath at the rear of his belt, just below the small of his back.

"Here. Now my debt to Egil is settled." Ragnar passed Einar the arm ring paid by his father so long ago. Einar took it and slipped it over his wrist. He examined the fine silver set into a smooth ring of gold. The inlaid silver worked into the shape of a writhing dragon, impossibly intricate and deftly crafted. The ring and war gear were worth a fortune, and Einar was suddenly richer than most men could dream of. "You will swear your oath to Ivar on that ring and wear it forever."

Einar bowed deeply. "Thank you, lord."

"Enough, now. Seek my son and set sail. I have enemies in need of punishment and my fleet to prepare. I hope Odin brings you luck, Einar Egilsson."

Einar left the hall as though in a dream, wandering out of the hall doors until sunlight stung his eyes after the dark interior.

"Excuse me, warrior," said Adzo, looking Einar up and down. "Have you seen my friend, Einar?"

Einar laughed and punched Adzo on the arm. "Can you believe it?" he exclaimed, feeling like a preened cat.

"I see you are ready for battle, Einar the Brawler," said Ivar, strolling towards the hall with his thumbs tucked in his belt, accompanied by his brother Sigurd. "Which is just as well. We leave tomorrow once my ships are loaded and ready to sail. You will both sail on the Seaworm under Vigmarr Svarti's command. Report to him today. You'll find him and his men by the western palisade. Tomorrow, you swear your oath before we leave."

Ivar turned on his heel, draped an arm around his brother, and headed off towards the harbour. Einar shifted his shoulders inside his breastplate, suddenly sweating at the prospect of sailing under the command of a jarl so fearsome as Vigmarr the Black.

"Vigmarr is the terrible-looking man in black who arrived today?" asked Adzo.

"Yes," Einar replied. "He was my father's shipmaster, and they sailed together on the warship Seaworm."

"Seems like you are following in his footsteps."

"Everything is moving fast. Only this morning we were slaves."

"I'll pray to God that our good fortune continues."

"You pray to your god and I'll pray to mine. But do it now, because we must go and face Vigmarr Svarti."

Einar and Adzo made the short journey through the densely-packed wattle and daub buildings inside Hrafnborg's palisade. Folk had returned after the spectacle of Kjartan Wolfthinker's sacrifices in the hazel grove. Some bore smears of blood on their foreheads where Wolfthinker's three Volva witches had blessed them with dead men's blood. Einar and Adzo walked in silence, the shock of Einar's newfound position and the prospect of facing Vigmarr both overwhelming and frightening. Einar's head swam with worry, happiness, and fear. It was almost a relief when he found the Seaworm crew lolling on benches outside a converted horse stable where an elderly woman served pots of ale and hot food.

Men in fur, leather, and wool, wearing naalbinding caps and winingas leg wrappings, sat on milking stools or cut logs drinking ale from wooden cups and eating roasted meat and steaming vegetables. Some huddled together, throwing knucklebones for shards of hacksilver, others sharpened blades with whetstones. Two women glowered at Einar, one thickset, her face tattooed with a raven on each cheek and silver rings in her ears, and the other whip-thin with a face like a hawk. Both women had quivers of goose-feather fletched arrows and unstrung bows resting beside them, and the bulky woman waved a dismissive hand at Einar when she noticed his gaze. Two gnarled-looking men with grey in their beards fed scraps to a thin dog, whilst others gathered around an old man with bright eyes who told a story with darting hand movements.

"I seek Vigmarr Svarti," Einar said to one carl paring his fingernails with a knife.

"Who are you?" returned the warrior, without taking his eyes from his task.

"Einar Egilsson, sent by Ivar Ragnarsson."

"Halvdan!" the warrior shouted suddenly, startling Einar and Adzo. He pointed his knife towards a bull-necked man throwing axes at a block of wood.

The bull-necked man turned, spat, and threw another axe, which turned blade over haft until it sunk into the wood with a loud chop. He walked to the block, yanked his axe free and stalked towards Einar, his face creased by an angry frown.

"What is it?" he growled.

"Lad here wants to see the jarl." The man paring his nails looked up at Einar and curled his lip. "Nobody talks to the jarl without Halvdan the shipmaster knowing about it."

"I seek Vigmarr Svarti," Einar repeated, this time to the bull-necked man who ambled closer, twirling his axe in his hand.

A mirthless smile crept across Halvdan's face. He had hoglike eyes, a close-cropped beard, and a mouth like an upturned half-moon. "You must be Ivar's pup."

Einar flushed with anger at the insult, but held his tongue. He had lived long enough in Hrafnborg to recognise a challenge. A man like Halvdan rose to the rank of shipmaster through bravery and toughness, as well as his ability to sail, navigate by the stars, and organise a crew.

To touch the haft of his axe or show anger at such a man would signal acceptance of Halvdan's challenge, and before he knew it, Einar would find himself fighting for his life. The world of Viking carls was about reputation, respect, honour and understanding the pecking order. A warrior shamed himself by refusing a challenge, allowing his weapons and war gear to rust, or by not taking care of his appearance. So, Einar kept his mouth shut, and Halvdan nodded, a silent understanding passing between them.

"Well, Ivar's pup, you'll find Vigmarr inside. Careful, though. He is no baker or blacksmith to barter with. Old Vigmarr has sent two crews' worth of souls to the afterlife, perhaps more, and he doesn't take kindly to small talk or whelps ruining his quiet time. Run along, try your luck. He might kill you and use your skull for a piss pot, or he might flay the skin from your bones and use it to cover his shield. Or perhaps he will listen to your whining voice and hear what you have to say, pup."

Einar again ignored the barbs and went to the stable. He fought to master his fear and keep it hidden from his face. He sensed Halvdan and the seated warrior sneering behind him and walked on, determined to hold his nerve. Inside the stall, the elderly woman's face was so creased it was like a crumpled hemp shirt, and she gazed at Einar through one beady eye. The building had once contained three horse stalls. Two of its doors were closed and one fully opened so that it had both an inside area to sit and the outdoor area. The wooden construction was damp and spotted with patches of green. An iron brazier burned just inside the door to keep the elderly woman warm. The walls held tattered, rusting horse tack, and old straw covered the floor. Three barrels of ale stood behind the woman, who leaned on a table inside the stall, with dozens of wooden cups stacked around her. The smell of roasted meat and boiling vegetables wafted from somewhere beyond the stall, and Einar's stomach groaned with hunger.

"Ale?" the elderly woman asked, her mouth toothless, lips flapping up towards her nose.

"No," Einar replied.

"Food?"

"I seek Vigmarr."

She looked Einar up and down and cackled. She moved and pointed a crooked finger towards the inside of the stall beyond the barrels where Vigmarr Svarti sat in the murk, warming his hands over another brazier where two chunks of chopped wood burned slowly.

"Wait here," Einar whispered to Adzo. Einar stepped inside the stall and wrinkled his nose at the stink of stale sweat and fried fish. He stood before Vigmarr Svarti, but the massive figure's head was low and hidden by the mop of his unruly hair.

"Lord Vigmarr?" Einar said, calling him lord out of respect because Vigmarr was a sea-jarl and a man of reputation. Vigmarr neither replied nor moved. Einar waited for a few moments, shuffled his feet, and cleared his throat. "Lord Vigmarr?" he repeated, this time louder.

"Ivar sent you?" Vigmarr said, his voice low and tired, as though Einar bored him.

"Yes. He said I am to serve on board the Seaworm. Pull an oar and fight in your crew."

Vigmarr grunted. Einar couldn't tell if it was an agreement to what Ivar had promised, or a *we'll see about that,* response. "Egil's son?"

"Yes, lord."

He coughed and wheezed, his shoulders shuddering slightly, which Einar thought might pass for a laugh with the strange man in black. "Good. You must fight for your place."

"Fight?"

"I have one space and two men. So you'll fight. The winner boards the Seaworm."

"And the loser?"

Vigmarr moved his hair aside with his fingers

and sized up Einar, his scarred, disfigured face shocking to look upon so closely. He shrugged and rolled his eyes as though the answer was obvious. "Fight to the death."

"Is there another way?" Einar had to become a warrior and carl of Ivar's crews, but he could not kill Adzo to do it. The Frank had become his friend over the days and evenings they had spent together following the battle against Dolgfinnr Dogsblood. Adzo was, Einar realised, his only friend in all of Midgard. Perhaps there was no room for friendship in a warrior's world, but Einar knew that achieving his dream by stepping across the corpse of his friend would be an ill-done deed, one that would haunt him forever.

"Kill another Seaworm man. Then we have two places."

Einar had never killed a man. He could fight and had fought countless brawls in Hrafnborg's back streets and alleyways, but to fight with weapons and rip a man's life away was an entirely different thing. "Who must I fight?"

Vigmarr dipped his head so that his hair again covered the nightmare of his face. He waved a hand to dismiss Einar, a hand missing part of a finger. "Halvdan will choose."

Einar's shoulders slumped as he left Vigmarr by his fire. The elderly woman's rheumy eyes followed him out of the stall and she giggled at his nervousness. Adzo stared at him as if waiting for news of what Vigmarr had said, but if Einar stopped walking, he might never pluck up the courage to go to Halvdan and say what must be said. The bull-necked shipmaster was throwing his axes again and Einar crossed the space between the stools and logs upon which the crew sat until he stood before the shipmaster of the warship Seaworm.

"He didn't eat you, then. Well?" asked Halvdan, turning to face Einar after throwing his axe. He was shorter than Einar, but much broader across the chest. Einar looked from Halvdan to the crew, every one of them scarred, tattooed veterans of their voyages across the Whale Road. He wondered if he could ever stand and trade blows with such men, never mind kill one. Einar was tall. He had grown that summer so that he was now a head taller than most of the crew, but he was not broad or thick across the chest, not like a man who had rowed ships across the harshest seas. That work built muscle, and gave a man calloused hands, corded arms and chests, and shoulders like wheels of cheese.

"I am to fight for my place on the crew," Einar stated.

"I can't hear you." Halvdan cocked his head towards Einar and placed his hand behind his ear.

"Vigmarr says I must kill a man to take my place." Einar tried his best to speak with menace.

"You? Kill of one this crew?" Halvdan squeezed Einar's bicep and chuckled. "We fought six times last summer and three more in the winter when most crews stay inside warm by their hearth fires and are safe in bed with their wives. These men have sailed so far north that frost froze in our beards and sea monsters with great black eyes stared at us from the depths. We have sailed so far south down fast and lethal rivers that we have met men with skins burned black by the sun. We have killed men in sea battles, on horseback, men within high stone walls built by giants. Every carl here has killed at least a dozen men, many of us more. Places in Valhalla await us. Seats next to the greatest of heroes where we shall swive all night as the dead champions marvel at stories of our daring and bravery. And you, a pup who brawls in the streets with *nithings* and bakers' sons, are going to kill one of us? Well, I suppose today is as good a day to die as any other." Halvdan laughed and shook his head. "Listen up," he called to the crew. "Listen, you ragged-arsed murderers. Who wants to fight Ivar's pup?"

None of the crew even looked up from their ale. Halvdan turned back to Einar and ran his tongue across his teeth, and for a horrifying moment Einar thought he would have to fight the shipmaster himself, a tough, frightening man who was as hard as seasoned oak. Halvdan clicked his fingers and pointed to a man with his back turned.

"Olvir. You can fight Olvir. Kill him, and you're one of us."

The man named Olvir rose from his stool and drained his cup of ale. He was a short man with wiry, muscled arms bare beneath a sleeveless leather jerkin trimmed with fox fur. He carried an axe at his belt and drew it slowly.

"Why do I have to fight him? There's no reputation in killing a grass-green boy. I've more hair on my arse than he does on his chin," Olvir said, pointing his axe at Einar.

"Four years you've sailed with us, and I've never seen you in the front rank. No use calling yourself a Seaworm man if you hide at the back with the shirkers whilst the warriors do the killing. So fight the pup and earn your place."

Olvir spat and shrugged. "Knives or axes?"

"Holmgang," decided Halvdan. "Hazel rods, shields, seconds, and a judge. Let's do it properly."

"You're in the shit now," said Adzo, appearing at Einar's shoulder. And so he was. Einar was about to fight for his life in his first single combat, a fight held under ancient holmgang duel rules. A fight to the death.

EIGHT

The Seaworm crew left their ale and marched up the hill. They talked and laughed, rubbing their hands with glee at the prospect of some violent entertainment whilst ashore. Vigmarr Svarti limped along behind them, using the haft of a long axe as a walking stick. He walked alone, malevolent with his shaggy mane, black cloak and clothes. Sixty warriors crossed the grazing pastures inland of Hrafnborg's fortifications until Halvdan called a halt beside a babbling stream. The crew made wagers with small coins and shards of hacksilver, and Halvdan the shipmaster cut branches from a hazel tree with his axe, stripped away the leaves and laid the bare branches down to make a fighting square. He paced the size of the square out twice and seemed unhappy with one edge, so he cut a fresh branch, trimmed it, laid it down, and paced the whole thing out again until he was satisfied.

"No point arsing about," he barked when one

of the crew asked him to get on with it. "If something's worth doing, it's worth doing right."

The Seaworm crew stood in groups, stroking their beards, engaged in deep conversation about the square, its size, the location of the stream and anything and everything to do with the duel with professional interest.

"What are the branches for?" asked Adzo.

"Tradition," Einar explained. "A holmgang must take place within the hazel rods or on an eyot in a stream. I am about to fight Olvir inside those branches. This is how we settle disputes amongst our people. The winner has the right of it, and the loser is in the wrong. I once heard of a professional holmgang fighter who would hire himself out to landowners in dispute with their neighbours. The man who hired him would challenge his neighbour over this stretch of pasture, or that stream's watering rights, or over access to a pollarded forest. The neighbour would dispute the claim, there would be a fight, and the professional duellist would win and secure the land for his employer."

"You are a strange folk with your war gods and your rules."

A dozen men came from Hrafnborg carrying shields, and with them came Ivar the Boneless and the towering figure of Sten Slegyya.

"Ragnar said that you have your place on the crew," Adzo whispered in Einar's ear, conscious that the crew was close now. "Why do you have to fight for it?"

"We are Northmen. What do you think would happen if I went whining to Ragnar about it?"

"You could try."

"It is an honour to die in battle, more so to die in a holmgang. No Viking worth his oar would understand a reluctance to fight. It looks like cowardice, and that above all things is abhorrent to our people."

"But you are reluctant to fight?"

"I know. That bastard over there is going to try to kill me with an axe. A big, sharp axe. He's been a Seaworm man for four years. Imagine how many battles he's fought, how many raids he's taken part in? I know Halvdan called him a shirker, but I'd say he's a killer and no mistake. Would you like his axe buried in your chest?"

"No."

"Well, then. Being afraid, and letting men know you are afraid, are two different things. You don't have duels in Frankia?"

"The high lords do, yes. But not churls like my family. If we have a dispute, we go to our lord and he decides."

"Good news is you're to be my second."

"What?"

"Each fighter gets two shields. If my first shield breaks, you hand me the replacement. No need to shit your breeches, though. You won't have to fight."

"Let's get this bloody thing moving," called Sten Slegyya, striding into the fighting square with a huge double-bladed war axe strapped to his back. He was taller than Einar and even the hard men of Vigmarr Svarti's crew kept out of his way. Sten checked the length of the hazel rods by pacing out the square, and Halvdan the shipmaster grinned with satisfaction when Sten adjudged it to be lawful and correct. Halvdan handed one shield to Einar and one to Adzo.

"Good luck, pup," he said. "Watch the blow beneath the shield, the groin-slitter. Don't hesitate. Strike hard and without mercy. Olvir might not be the bravest, but he'll gut you if he can, don't doubt it. He'll slit you from groin to neck and dance in your entrails. So kill him if you want to live."

Einar slipped his arm through the leather strap and grabbed the handle that spanned the hollow inside of the shield's boss. He had trained with such weapons his entire life, like all boys in Hrafnborg, so he was familiar with the weight.

He had fought many times with sticks and shields, but this fight was to the death and the shield was about to be the only thing protecting him from the axe Olvir would try to embed in his head, neck, chest and guts. Einar examined the iron rim and boss, checking that each linden-wood board was secure and sturdy. Once satisfied, Einar rolled his shoulders and let the shield hang at his side.

"He looks angry," observed Adzo, jutting his chin across the square to where Olvir drank from a skin of ale until the liquid ran down his beard. He wasn't much older than Einar, with greasy blonde hair and a sparse beard. Olvir carried an axe and knife at his belt and wore a rusting, conical helmet, and a hemp-padded jerkin over his torso. The muscles in his wiry arms moved over one another as he drank yet more ale before hefting his shield and drawing his axe.

Einar took deep breaths. *I must become angry. I need battle-fury to win this fight.* Einar tried to summon it, but all he felt was the churn of fear in his stomach. "I need to piss," he said.

"You went just a moment ago!"

"Well, I need to go again."

"No time, look."

Sten Slegyya stood at the centre of the fighting square and beckoned both fighters forward. The crew fell silent and gathered close about the square and it closed in around Einar, as though he were in a deep hole. Hoofbeats sounded on the hillside, and Ivar the Boneless rode a dappled mare towards the river, his green cloak streaming in his wake. Hrafnborg's high palisade stood behind him atop the hill with its wild heather sweeping down towards the river. Ivar leapt from his mount and handed the reins to a warrior.

"I heard there was a fight," Ivar remarked cheerfully. The warriors parted so Ivar could take his place at the front. He wore one sword in a scabbard at his waist and another across his back. He approached Einar and clapped him on the back. "Getting started already. Good."

Ivar seemed not to care that Vigmarr was about to make Einar fight for his promised place as a carl. Einar said nothing. There was no way out of the fight now, not now that the rods were laid and Sten and Ivar were there to witness it all. To worm his way out of the fight would look like cowardice, so instead, Einar ran through all the lessons drummed into boys on the training field. *Keep your shield up, wait for the time to strike, circle around to your opponent's weapon hand and strike from that side, hit hard but do not overreach, measure your opponent and attack to kill.*

"By the laws of gods and men," Sten began, shouting so that all present could hear. "We have

gathered here to witness a holmgang between these two warriors." Olvir gnashed his teeth and ran the edge of his axe over the rim of his shield to make a
macabre scraping sound. "This is a fight to the death, with one replacement shield allowed. The victor claims everything the dead man owns. If either man steps out of the fighting square, his life is forfeit. Axes, knives and shields are the only weapons allowed. Does any man here dispute the lawfulness of this fight?" No man among the crew spoke. "Then fight, and may Odin All-Father grant battle-luck to the winner."

Sten stepped out of the square, and Olvir let out a bloodcurdling cry. He banged his axe on his shield's boss twice and came on, shield raised, axe resting on its upper edge. Einar gulped and raised his own shield, suddenly wishing he had taken the one available space Vigmarr had offered on the Seaworm crew and left Adzo to his fate. Einar moved to his left, trying to come about Olvir's unshielded side, his grip sweaty about the haft of his axe.

Olvir charged. Without warning, without circling, without trying to test Einar's defences. He simply whooped with mad joy and charged straight at Einar like a deranged man. Their shields came together with a loud clang, pushing Einar backwards and off balance. Olvir's axe darted towards Einar's face and he stooped just before the sharp blade took his eyes. Einar's heart thundered in his chest and he whirled away, but the axe followed. Einar caught it on the boards of his shield and kept moving.

"He runs like a frightened weasel!" jeered Halvdan, and the crew laughed.

Einar was running, but to stop was to die. Another blow hammered onto his shield, and the blade shattered two boards this time. Einar ripped his shield away and tried to make a stand. Olvir lifted his shield and hammered the edge into Einar's, driving it down, and his axe came around in a lunging sweep. Einar raised his own axe and caught the blow. It sent a numbing ring down his arm, and Einar grimaced. Olvir kicked him in the sternum, driving him back, and spat in disgust.

"If you don't fight, you are going to die!" Adzo called.

Einar caught another axe blow on his shield and Olvir ripped his axe backwards, tearing Einar's shield from his hands.

"Second shield!" Sten Slegyya called.

Olvir lurched at Einar, but Sten appeared like a great tree between them and threw Olvir backwards. He came up snarling but thought better of it as Sten the champion glowered down at him.

"Fight, Einar, fight for your life," Adzo urged as he handed Einar his shield.

Einar gripped the shield and blew out his cheeks. He needed anger and fury if he was going to stand any chance of surviving. Einar closed his eyes for a moment and thought of his mother and father, of the nights he had spent lying in other people's houses wishing they were still alive. He thought of the unfairness of gaining his father's inheritance from Ragnar Lothbrok, only for Vigmarr to force him into this fight.

Something churned in Einar's belly, the fear turning hot and travelling up to his chest like fire. Sten stalked out of the square and Olvir screamed his war cry and charged. He smelled Einar's weakness and seemed to grow stronger, seeing his chance to kill a man untested in battle. Olvir lifted his shield as he charged, as though he meant to drive it into Einar and push him out of the square. Einar hefted his own shield and braced himself for the impact. Olvir suddenly changed direction, his weight shifting from his left to his right foot. The shield strike was a feint, and Olvir's axe whipped below Einar's shield in a wicked strike aimed to chop into his groin.

Einar dropped his shield just in time to catch the blow, but Olvir's shield came over the edge and cracked Einar in the face. He fell backwards, legs giving way, darkness and light flashing before his eyes. Olvir's shield hammered into Einar's back, and he turned just in time to catch Olvir's axe blade with his own. Olvir pressed down, trying to use his body weight to force the axe into Einar's face, and the Seaworm crew roared at the prospect of blood.

The axe pressed closer to Einar's face until it was a fingerbreadth from his eye. He could smell the iron, and a wash of Olvir's sour ale breath covered Einar's nose and mouth. It was now or never. Life or death. Valhalla, or his destiny. A great roar came from deep within Einar. It came as a reflex, unbidden. New strength flooded Einar's limbs, and with it came a new feeling. A powerful surging strength beyond anger. Rage.

Einar let go of his shield and drove the thumb of his left hand deep into Olvir's eye. He felt the liquid squelch, and he dug his nail in hard, twisting until it met something solid. Olvir screamed and rolled away, his eye a bloody pit of ruin. Einar leapt to his feet and reached to the small of his back and drew his seax. With his chest heaving and his teeth clenched, Einar charged at Olvir. The Viking carl retreated as Einar battered his shield with axe and seax blows. No cunning weaponcraft or skill, just brutal rage. Olvir's ruined eye bled freely, and he shook his head to shake off the pain. He dropped to one knee under Einar's assault and Einar kicked the shield's upper rim so that it smashed back into Olvir's face. Einar hooked the beard of his axe around the shield's rim and tore it off Olvir's arm by sheer force.

Olvir scuttled away and drew his knife so that both men faced each other with a weapon in each hand. He whimpered at the terrible eye wound and his weapons trembled at the shock. Einar came on again, axe and seax slashing and swinging in a blur. Olvir tried to parry and move away from the blows, but Einar was fast, faster than he knew he could be, and his seax blade tore through Olvir's chest, through the padded hemp and into the skin beyond. A line of red blood showed through the torn jerkin and Olvir dodged as Einar's axe swept towards his head.

Einar realised he was roaring incoherently and the surrounding crowd shouted support, shaking their fists and baying for blood. Olvir struck with his axe, desperately trying to strike back against Einar's relentless attacks. Einar caught the axe with his own axe blade and he ripped the weapon towards him so that Olvir tottered off balance. Einar crashed a savage headbutt into his enemy's face, battering the rim of his helmet into Olvir's nose, splintering it into a mushy mess.

Olvir's own helmet fell away and Einar sliced the blade of his seax across Olvir's arm; a deep cut, and Einar pressed the blade deeper, sawing it back and forth. Olvir cried out and leapt backwards. His knife fell from his useless left hand and he peered at Einar with his one eye wide and watery and his mouth turned downwards in fear.

Einar beat his axe against his chest and surged after his opponent. He was more alive than he had ever been. Einar was faster and stronger than he thought possible, and though he teetered on the edge of death, Einar had never felt so powerful. Olvir raised his axe to parry Einar's own axe, but the seax came up swiftly, almost too swiftly to see, and its point stabbed into Olvir's soft belly. Einar drove the blade deeper, and Olvir let out a long gasp. Einar ripped his seax free and Olvir dropped to his knees. He held his axe tight and closed his one remaining eye, understanding that death was coming. Einar drew his axe back for the killing blow and Olvir clenched his teeth closed with such fear that his front teeth splintered and broke like a kicked-in door. Einar slammed his axe down on top of Olvir's head without pity or hesitation. Olvir quivered and dropped dead, and the Seaworm crew fell silent, staring at Einar as he wrenched his axe free and held it above him in triumph.

Sten Slegyya strode into the hazel rod square and stepped over Olvir's corpse. "You're a wild one, lad, and no mistake," he said with an appreciative nod. "What's your name, boy?"

"Einar Rosti," Ivar proclaimed before Einar

could reply. "You have it, Einar the Brawler; the battle-fury. I see it in you like a horse breeder watching a prize stallion. Oh, but you're a front-line growler if I ever saw one. What do you think, Sten?"

"We'll see. Everything the dead man owned is yours," Sten said to Einar. "His weapons, silver, his oar. Everything. The fight's over!" he shouted to the crowd. "Einar Rosti won fairly. I'm the judge. If any of you bastards dispute the decision, come forward now and we'll fight." Unsurprisingly, no man came forward to challenge the monstrous warrior.

"You're a carl now, Einar, a warrior in my service," said Ivar. "You must swear your oath to me. Why not do it here at the scene of your first victory? Fighting and winning a holmgang is not common. You have a reputation now. Men will fear crossing you."

The rage left Einar as quickly as it had consumed him, leaving him tired and shaking. Olvir's bloody corpse still lay within the square, and Einar swallowed a mouthful of vomit. *So much blood.* He had taken a life. Olvir would never know a woman again, never marry nor have children, never again experience the joy of a fast ship on a wild sea. He was dead and cold, and Einar was responsible. It was lawful, and the gods encouraged battle, but Einar did not feel glorious.

Ivar waited and so Einar knelt. He placed his left hand over Ragnar's arm ring, raised his right hand, which Ivar took within his own hands. Einar knew the words to say, as did every Norse boy who dreamed of one day becoming a carl and a seaman on board a fearsome warship.

"I, Einar Egilsson, swear by oath on this ring that I will be Ivar Ragnarsson's man. I swear to fight for him and give my life in his defence. I swear never to forget the wealth and gifts provided by him, and to wrest glory from his foemen. I swear not to flee one step from battle and to avenge my lord if he is slain. If I break my oath, may I be accursed of Odin and the Aesir, may I become as yellow as gold and slain by my own weapons."

"You are my man now, Einar." Ivar turned to Adzo. "Your turn."

"Wait," said Einar. He went to Olvir's body, took a copper ring from his wrist, his weapons, and handed them all to his friend Adzo. "These are yours now."

Adzo swore his oath and Ivar clapped them both on the shoulder. He turned to where the Seaworm crew gathered about Vigmarr Svarti.

"You there!" Ivar called, pointing towards the crew.

They turned and looked nervously at Ivar,

even the most hardened amongst them looking fearful.

"You." Ivar pointed to the biggest man in Vigmarr's crew, a stocky, round-bellied man with a sword at his belt and a beaten-looking chainmail *brynjar*. "What did you say?"

"Me, lord?" said the big man, pointing to his own chest.

"You. You said something about me. I heard it."

"I said nothing, Lord Ivar." He looked at Vigmarr and then at his shipmates.

"So I am a liar?"

"No, you are not a liar, Lord Ivar."

"Nithing!" Ivar roared, startling everyone on the riverbank, such was his snap from amiable smiles and oath-taking to sudden, flame-bright anger. "Whoremonger! Son of an addled whore! I heard you whispering like a lickspittle *slyðra*. Draw your weapons!"

A slyðra was a wet lump of shit, an insult meant to cut a warrior to his core. Ivar drew his famous shining swords, Hugin and Munin, holding one in each hand. He twirled them so that the blades caught the late afternoon sun.

"No, Lord Ivar, I didn't…"

"Shitworm! Coward! Nithing!" Ivar advanced, his handsome face now twisted, cruel, and snarling. Men backed away from his anger. The big man looked about him for support, glanced at Vigmarr, who looked away. He was alone, facing Ivar the Boneless' wrath and reluctantly, he drew his axe. He picked up Olvir's second shield and prepared to defend himself. Vigmarr Svarti shuffled backwards away from the man with his limping gait, and Ivar broke into a run. He leapt into the air and brought both swords down hard on the big man's shield. All the former respect and tradition of the hazel rods was forgotten as both men stepped outside the square. The big man huddled behind his shield, but Ivar moved with a litheness and speed Einar had never seen before. Moving like there were no bones in his body, as though he were a deadly serpent or dragon. He twisted around the shield, sliced the edge of one sword across the back of the man's legs. Before the man had fallen to his knees, Ivar's other sword stabbed deep into his back. Ivar ripped both blades free, brought them wide and chopped the big man's head from his shoulders.

The fight had lasted mere moments, and the Seaworm crew hoomed at the shocking speed and ease with which Ivar had dispatched their shipmate.

"A place means a place," Ivar spat, and he kicked the severed head towards Vigmarr Svarti.

Einar had joined the crew of the warship Seaworm as a carl. He was a warrior, and the next day he sailed to war.

NINE

Three ships set sail with the tide. They left Hrafnborg with the pale early morning sun still low in the sky, casting a wan glow across the high pines, a half-light shimmering on a gently swaying sea.

"Pull," called Halvdan the shipmaster from where he stood on the steerboard platform with one hand on the steering oar.

Einar hauled on his oar, conscious that he must keep time with the rest of the Seaworm crew. Ivar's Windspear led the way, with the Seaworm and the Fjordviper following in her wake. Einar had wrapped his meagre belongings in a fleece and stowed the bundle beneath his rowing bench. He had a spare jerkin, his hard-baked leather breastplate, axe, seax, and three silver coins. Einar had sold most of Olvir's possessions for twenty silver coins, small thin discs embedded with a picture of a Saxon king.

Those coins had bought a yew bow and a quiver of arrows for Adzo, warm woollen cloaks, and spare jerkins and trews for them both to wear at sea.

"How can I repay you?" asked Adzo before they had departed.

"You can pay me back when our purses are full of silver," he'd replied.

"What purses?"

The two young men had laughed together until Vigmarr Svarti flashed them a murderous look and ordered his men to depart.

"I hope he doesn't hold it against us," Adzo whispered to Einar as they pulled away from shore.

"What?" Einar asked.

"Vigmarr. I hope he doesn't blame us because Ivar killed his man."

"The last thing we need is for our jarl to be our enemy."

"Just keep our heads down and follow orders until it blows over."

That seemed like the best course of action. They left Hrafnborg to finish what One Leg Bolti had failed to do, to kill Dolgfinnr Dogsblood, and recover the sacred raven banner. Ivar took three crews to do it, three ships each holding between sixty and seventy warriors. Brightly-painted shields lined the sheerstrakes, and prow beasts stood proudly, snarling out at the rolling Whale Road. They rowed through a sea thick with warships. Ragnar Lothbrok's fleet had assembled off Hrafnborg's harbour, dozens of war-jarls and warrior crews answering Ragnar's call, ready to set sail for Frankia and the riches behind Paris' high stone walls.

"Pull," Halvdan called once more to keep time. He set a relaxed pace as the Seaworm eased out into deeper waters. Adzo rowed on the bench next to Einar, and the two young men focussed on keeping time. To make a mistake so early in the voyage would bring punishments, anger from their new shipmates, and the dangers of life at sea. Einar had heard about it during his time on board the Waveslicer. Tales about how men who used the *haf* words, the words no man spoke on board ship for fear of bringing bad luck, or those who fouled rigging, or lost an oar, might have their throats cut in the night and their bodies dumped overboard never to be seen again.

Einar concentrated on his rowing rhythm, trying to blend in and not stand out as the new carl on board ship. To drag his oar, or miss a stroke, was to incur the crew's scorn. Einar already felt their sideways glances, and had heard the tutting as he had taken his oar bench. He had killed one of their shipmates, even if it was a fair fight and not one of Einar's choosing, and Einar understood their anger. If he was going to spend his life pulling an oar on the warship Seaworm, he had to become one of them.

The morning drew on and the men took up a rowing song as Halvdan beat time on a drum stretched tight with animal hide. They sang of Thor and his battles with Loki, the trickster god, and Einar sang along once he picked up the words. The wind whispered through the seal-hide rigging as the Seaworm sliced through the slate-grey water of the Kattegat strait. Her oars rose and fell in a rhythmic dance, and though Einar's back muscles ached and the palms of his hands burned, he kept time, leaning forward, dipping the ash-made oar, hauling it through the water, twisting it as he lifted it from the sea, and repeating the action over and again.

The Seaworm's clinker-built hull and sleek keel, carved from a single piece of oak, crashed through the swell. The mast rose like a spear from the deck with her massive black, square sail furled on the yard, a sail fashioned from the fleeces of seven hundred sheep, woven, treated and painted for an entire year by four Hrafnborg women.

"Sail!" Vigmarr growled as the Seaworm came about north and the wind blew in their favour. The crew cheered for joy, Einar and Adzo shouting along with them, relieved that the strenuous work of rowing was over for now. They lifted their oars from the oar holes and stowed them in crutches running parallel to the deck. The crew hauled on rigging and untied reef lines. The sail flapped loose until Halvdan and the crew hauled on the rigging to harness the wind's full embrace. Ropes creaked under the strain as men tied them off with practised knots, then the sail snapped taut and the Seaworm surged forward like an arrow loosed from a bow.

Einar laughed as the wind blew through his hair, and the sea flew beneath them. He draped an arm around Adzo's shoulder and the Frank punched the air. An older man in a wide-brimmed hat brought around bowls of skyr and skins of ale, which the men shared as they sat on their rowing benches. Einar shovelled the delicious skyr into his mouth using his fingers. It was thick and sour and made from sheep's milk. It was the best meal Einar had ever eaten after a long morning rowing. He took a slurp from an ale skin and handed to Adzo.

"You love the sea," Adzo stated, staring across the water.

"It makes me feel alive," Einar replied. "The speed, the wind. It's like flying."

The crew wore simple jerkins and trews, their armour and weapons safely stowed in barrels or beneath their benches. The Kattegat Sea's waters were famously treacherous, but Seaworm crew were grizzled, seasoned sailors, their ears attuned to the sea's whispers and the creaks and groans of their beloved warship. Einar breathed in a chestful of salty air. The sea rolled by and ahead lay adventure, battle, and everything Einar had dreamed of.

Denmark's coastline hurtled by on the port side; undulating hills, dense pine forests and narrow inlets where warlords and their crews prepared to depart on summer raids. Many such lords this close to Hrafnborg owed their oaths to Ragnar, but further north, the fleet entered islands, coves, and inlets peopled by threatening men, the wild warriors who owed their allegiance to different lords, and an unknown ship to them was as prey to an eagle. Modest settlements dotted the land, golden thatched roofs piercing a canopy of green pine, brush and sloping meadows where folk clung to the coastlines because inland lay hard, cruel land unyielding to crops or cultivation. Smoke curled in thin wisps from countless hearth fires to join a blue sky spotted with thin clouds.

Days passed and hazy outcroppings loomed in the west, in Norway, where the land was more severe, its cliffs rising like the jagged teeth of one of Loki's monster brood. The Seaworm swept past a tiny island where waves crashed against cliffs with relentless fury, sending plumes of spray high into the air where seabirds cawed and dived at the water in search of a meal. Patches of snow clung stubbornly to high peaks and so the fleet sailed northwards in pursuit of the raven banner, and Dolgfinnr Dogsblood.

After days on squall-tossed seas mixed with periods of bright, pale skies and howling winds, the fleet put into a small, pine-topped island with a natural west-facing harbour. The sun waned, and the mast cast a long silhouette across the Seaworm's deck. Halvdan guided the ship close to shore on the ebb tide, and the crew dropped anchor when the keel lightly brushed against the sea bottom. Einar waded ashore with the men, carrying his fleece cloak and bedroll above his head to keep it dry. All three crews made their way ashore, where a narrow shale beach stretched below a gap in the cliffs before the deep forest began.

"I'll get a fire going," grunted a man with blonde hair scraped back from his head in a tight ponytail.

"For a change," jibed another Seaworm man, and the rest chuckled.

"Why is that funny?" Einar asked an older man with an iron-grey beard and lyre under his arm.

"His name is Yngvi the Fire," replied the

old man. "He makes the campfire. Every night. Always has. Can't abide it if another man tries to get a blaze going before him. He stabbed a Svear man once over the right way to start a fire. Once it's lit, he spends every evening staring into the flames, adding twigs and branches. He's obsessed with it. Not a good trait, if you ask me. Fire is Loki's symbol." The old man made the hand sign to ward off evil and sighed as he lay his pack on the shale and carefully placed his lyre down on top of his rolled-up blanket. "I'm Thorkild, who men call Storyteller. Not quite as good as a skald, but hopefully better than your old grannies. I'll tell tales by the fire tonight. You two should come and listen."

Einar introduced himself and thanked the old man, pleased that he would spend the evening alongside the crew rather than sitting alone with Adzo.

"Stop gossiping and gather wood," Halvdan said, kicking a slight, bandy-legged carl up the arse. "Sooner we get camp together, sooner we can eat and sleep."

Einar lay his rolled-up woollen blanket and his fleece cloak close to Thorkild's gear, and watched as Vigmarr came from the sea, limping and rolling like a sea-demon. The ship's bail boy came behind him carrying Vigmarr's bedding and the jarl went to sit alone on a piece of washed-up timber whilst the rest of the crew went to work.

Vigmarr sat alone, staring out at the sea, and every so often, he coughed like a man riddled with disease and cast a glance in Ivar's direction as the Boneless and his men made their own camp further up the beach. Vigmarr's shaggy head spun and stared directly at Einar, as though he sensed his gaze upon him. Einar quickly turned away, though he was sure he saw the big jarl's shoulders shaking with laughter.

"Maybe he has taken a dislike to us," murmured Adzo as they hurried towards the trees in search of firewood.

"Seems like Vigmarr takes a dislike to everyone," replied Einar.

"We'd best be careful then. He is the jarl, after all."

"I wish Ivar had taken us on board the Windspear. There's an ill haze on board the Seaworm, and I can't tell if it's just Vigmarr's bad humour, or that the entire crew is as moody as a one-armed fisherman."

"We're Seaworm men now, and we must make the best of it. But there's no harm in keeping our heads down and our mouths shut."

Einar returned to the beach a short time later with an armful of twigs and branches, and a fistful of moss he had pulled from a pale rock deep within the trees. He found Yngvi the Fire where the beach met the forest, and the blonde-haired man was busy carefully laying out wood in piles. Einar set his wood down and knelt beside him.

"I found kindling," Einar offered, and held out the moss.

Yngvi raised an eyebrow and took the moss from Einar. He pulled it apart, rubbing his fingers through it and sniffing it.

"It's a bit damp," said Yngvi. "But it will do once I get the flame going."

"What do you use?"

Yngvi licked his lips and waved Einar closer. He reached down next to him and lifted a small chest inlaid with a brass clasp. Yngvi opened the clasp as though the box was filled with gold, but all Einar could see inside were yellow wood shavings.

"Taken from a shipwright's workshop," Yngvi breathed, as though he spoke of great seidr or a wyrd woven by a powerful Godi like Kjartan Wolfthinker. "A handful of these will do the trick. Then I feed the fire slowly. You must respect it, see? Put too much in too quick and the fire goes out. Not enough and it dies before it's even come to life. But love it, tend to it like a beautiful woman, and it will keep you warm all night, laddie."

THE VIKING

Einar left Yngvi to his work and went to help men gather boughs and pieces of rock around the fire. Adzo sat with Thorkild Storyteller as he strung his bow, and, as the sun dipped, Halvdan ordered rations to be shared out amongst the men. Einar ate another bowl of skyr, some dried beef, and drank mead from a skin passed around by a willowy man with bandy legs whom men referred to as Fat Garmr, which Einar assumed was a jest because the man was as lean as a wolf in winter.

The fire roared and crackled under Yngvi's tender care and once the evening meal was over the crew gathered about Thorkild, who sat on an upturned log with his lyre resting in the crook of his arm. Einar felt fortunate that he and Adzo sat close to the old man as they sipped on luxurious mead, wearing their fleece cloaks, warming their hands on the blaze as a chill sea wind blew across the island beach. The men talked and laughed as they gathered, pulling cloaks about their shoulders, naal-binding caps on their heads and passing ale skins from hand to hand. Only Vigmarr Svarti sat apart with a tiny fire of his own, still staring out at the sea with a skin of ale and a chunk of pork roasting on a makeshift spit. The men seemed to leave their jarl alone, which suited Einar fine. Vigmarr had stayed at the prow for most of the voyage, only taking brief turns at the steering oar when

Halvdan exchanged signals with the Windspear about which course north they should take. Men fell silent when Vigmarr passed them, his foreboding malevolence like a shadow across men both young and old.

"A clear night," announced Thorkild and the crew fell silent. "The stars shine and the gods are watching. So we need a good tale. Any requests?"

"Tell us the one about the time you and Ragnar spent a winter whoring in Miklagard," called one man, and the rest snickered.

"Every night you ask for that story, Ulfketil Brownlegs. I think perhaps that you are too fond of whores," quipped Thorkild, and the crew guffawed.

"So you would you if your wife looked like his," shouted a warrior, sending the men falling about holding their bellies.

"A tale of the gods, I think. A tale about destiny, perhaps," Thorkild continued.

"Heya," chorused the men, and they huddled close together better to hear Thorkild's tale. The old man leaned forward so that the campfire's flames flickered about the nooks and creases of his wind-burned face, and he played a few haunting notes on his lyre to set the tone.

Einar found himself sitting forwards, as eager as he had been listening to skalds' stories as a child. He pulled his cloak tighter to keep out the cool air tinged with the scent of smoke and the sea.

"Gather close, brothers," Thorkild began, his voice suddenly rich and resonant, singing in the rhythmic pattern skalds used to bring their tales of gods and men to life. "Tonight I shall tell you the lay of Sigurd and the dragon, a saga of valour, worthy of telling in the halls of Valhalla itself."

The crew hoomed in appreciation of Thorkild's choice. Adzo grinned, even though the Frank was a Christian and had no more belief in the Norsemen's gods and legends than Einar had in Adzo's nailed god. The ships lay anchored in the bay, the dark silhouettes of their prows and stern posts themselves looking like dragons resting in the settling darkness.

"Long ago," Thorkild began, as Yngvi added two stout branches to his blaze and sent a shower of embers floating into the air. "In a land where icy fjords cut deep into the highest mountains and the skies were ever grey, lived a brave young warrior named Sigurd. He was the son of Sigmund, a champion and mighty hero of his kingdom, and young Sigurd bore the strength and courage of his sire. Sigurd, however, was destined to be greater still for the Aesir had chosen the young warrior for a task that would test not only his *drengskapr,* but his very soul."

Thorkild paused and strummed his lyre, the weight of foreboding floating with the music and the firelight. Einar took another slug of mead and passed the skin to Adzo.

"Sigurd was born and raised in the court of wise King Hjalprek, and it was there he met the old master blacksmith Regin. This man was no ordinary smith. He was a master of hammer and anvil to rival the mighty Völund himself. Regin harboured a deep secret locked away in the sea chest of his heart. He held a white-hot burning desire for revenge against his brother, Fafnir, a man who had become a dragon.

"Regin and Fafnir were sons of Hreidmar, a powerful dwarf king who lived beneath the high mountains. The king had another son, Ótr, who could transform himself into an otter. Many years before Sigurd's birth, Odin, Loki, and Hœnir accidentally killed Ótr, who was in otter form, during a fateful encounter by a river. The mighty Aesir were unaware of Ótr's true self, and, believing him an otter to be hunted and trapped like any other, skinned poor Ótr and took his pelt. The Dwarven king Hreidmar was distraught at the loss of his son and flew into an inchoate rage. He demanded reparation from the gods, pleading to Odin for justice. To settle the debt, Loki captured the dwarf Andvari and forced him to surrender his famous hoard of gold, including a cursed ring, Andvaranaut, which carried a spell of doom upon whoever possessed it.

"Loki had the vast treasure brought before the king, and Hreidmar, blinded by greed, hungrily accepted, even though the terrible curse of Andvaranaut tainted it. As ever with Loki-gifts, the treasure came with an unseen bite. The allure of the gold sowed discord between Hreidmar's sons. Fafnir, the most formidable and ambitious of the brothers, became consumed with a desire to possess the treasure for himself. Driven mad by his greed, Fafnir murdered King Hreidmar, seized the hoard and fled into the wilderness to guard it and keep the shining gold for him alone.

"As Fafnir brooded over his ill-gotten wealth, his greed and paranoia warped his deepest nature. Gradually, as the seasons turned and he polished his hoard, Fafnir transformed into a dragon, a monstrous embodiment of his insatiable greed and of the ancient curse that plagued the treasure. The dragon Fafnir, monstrous, scaled, fire-breathing and fearsome, became a dreadful guardian of the hoard. He slid and slipped into a remote, impregnable lair, where he guarded his treasure, a greedy murderer and betrayer transformed into a monster who slew any champions who came seeking treasure and glory."

Thorkild paused and took a sip of ale, waiting as the crew exchanged nervous glances and murmured, entranced at the unfolding tale. More than one cast their eyes towards Vigmarr who remained alone, a dark figure huddled, retching and hawking over his fire.

"So it was that Regin, cunning as Loki himself, saw in young Sigurd the instrument of his vengeance. He forged for Sigurd a powerful sword, the likes of which had never been seen. Gram, he named it, a blade of unparalleled sharpness and strength. Regin handed Sigurd the blade, and so convinced the youthful hero to seek out the dragon Fafnir, and reclaim the stolen treasure.

"Sigurd journeyed deep into the forests, up into the loftiest mountains, peaks carved when Midgard was young and frost giants and iotnir roamed the world alongside men, elves and dwarves. He found the dragon's lair, a gloomy and foreboding place where the very ground trembled with the beast's every breath. Sigurd dug a pit along the worn path where Fafnir slithered each day to slake his thirst from a nearby stream, and there Sigurd lay in wait."

The campfire flared as if in response to Thorkild's story, and the men, including Einar, gasped as the flames cast shadows that seemed to mimic the sinuous coils of a dragon.

"When the dragon Fafnir emerged from his lair, his scaly body shimmered like fire in the sunlight. As the beast slithered over the pit, Sigurd struck without hesitation and with all his might. The mighty Gram blade bit deep into the dragon's soft underbelly, and with a roar that shook the mountains and foundations of Yggdrasil, the dragon spouted plumes of fire and thrashed his mighty tail, felling the forest about them as Sigurd ripped the beast's belly open and killed him dead outside his own lair."

The crew exhaled in unison, so gripped were they by Thorkild's tale.

"But the story does not end there, friends. As Fafnir lay dying, he turned, his green eye fixing young Sigurd, his lips parted over venom-dripping fangs. He warned Sigurd of the treasure's awful curse, and the dragon wept as he spoke to Sigurd of the Andvaranaut that would bring ruin to anyone who possessed it. Undeterred by the warning, Sigurd tasted the dragon's blood and, in doing so, gained the ability to understand the speech of birds.

"The birds spoke to Sigurd, whispering to him of Regin the smith's treacherous plan to kill him and claim the hoard for himself. Sigurd took up the treasure, returned to court, and with a heart heavy with betrayal, he slew Regin with his own sword."

Thorkild stood and threw back his cloak so his bone-white arms spread wide above the fire, casting a long shadow against the forest behind him. "And so Sigurd had the treasure and a king's ransom of cursed gold. He rode forth with his newfound wisdom, strength, reputation and wealth, and forever etched his name in the annals of our people until the curse and its wyrd would eventually take his life just as it had Fafnir's."

Thorkild made a deep growling sound in his throat, a warning sound, and his eyes blazed in the firelight. "Remember this tale, my brothers of the axe. Sigurd's legend is not one of a hero's triumph over a terrible dragon. It is a tale of fate, and of the inexorable pull of destiny that not even the bravest of us can escape. The Norns wove that wyrd, the fateful curse through the threads of Sigurd's life, and no man can escape his destiny."

Thorkild sat down and raised his skin of ale as the men sat around him in wonder. "Now," he said, "let us drink to Sigurd, to men's greed, and the battles lying in wait for us across the Whale Road. May his story remind us of our own battles in search of fame and fortune."

The men all drank and then cheered Thorkild, clapping their hands, united in praise for the elderly storyteller. When the cheering died down, men broke away and talked amongst themselves, but Einar and Adzo remained, helping Thorkild lay out his blanket for the night.

"A fine tale," Einar said, warmly.

"One of many, young warrior. One to heed," Thorkild replied.

"Why does Vigmarr sit alone like that?" asked Adzo, and Einar shot him a murderous look. They had only just met Thorkild and the Seaworm crew, and Einar wasn't yet sure who to trust, who to fear, and who, if any, were close to the brooding jarl.

"Funny you should ask." Thorkild wagged a bony finger. "Vigmarr sails his own path. He lives in a world of darkness, always has. The only time I see him happy or content is in battle. He seeks it, longs for blood, craves the clash of arms. He would lead us into the Ragnarök itself in search of combat, for it seems to be the only place he can find peace."

"Peace from what?"

"That is a tale for another day. Now it is time for sleep, for we have much rowing ahead of us before we reach the home of Dolgfinnr. That too is a fight which seems fated, for Ivar dreams of defeating Dolgfinnr and becoming champion of the Northmen. So we have one jarl who desires nothing but war, and another who hungers to be best of not just us, but of all warriors."

"What of the others?" asked Einar. "I have met

you, Halvdan, Ulfketil Brownlegs, Yngvi, but do the others yearn for reputation and blood?"

Thorkild laughed. "No, most are like me, and like your father was when he sailed aboard the Seaworm. When we were young like you, reputation was everything. It shines like the brightest of treasures. But as a man gets older, he realises other things are more important: family, friends, a warm fire. We are warriors and we fight for our lord. He rewards us with rings and silver so that we can feed our wives and children who await us at Hrafnborg. Just as the farmer relies on his crops for food, so we rely on our Lord Ivar. I know every man here, and most can be trusted. I know all but him." Thorkild pointed to a man laying down on a threadbare blanket, a man with short-cropped hair in the style of the southern Franks. "He is a new man, like the two of you. A masterless man who came to Hrafnborg seeking an oar, as many men do who have heard of Lord Ragnar's fame. So we have three new crew members, and we are off to war. It's getting late, and we've a long day at sea tomorrow. Best get some rest, lads."

Einar went to his bedroll and curled up beneath his fleece cloak. He lay on his side staring at Vigmarr and wondered if the jarl had been the same in his father's day. He listened to the tide slop against the shale beach and drifted off to sleep, dreaming of fate, war, and the betrayal of Regin and Fafnir.

TEN

Ivar the Boneless led his three ships north, sailing before the wind. The fleet sped through the Kattegat Sea and into the wider, dangerous Skagerrak straits. Einar spent the days following Halvdan's orders. He rowed when the wind fell away. He tied-off rigging, stowed oars and watched as the surly shipmaster and Vigmarr Svarti stood in the prow watching landmarks and using the sun to navigate their way through the treacherous waters. The three-ship fleet avoided shallows and reefs and hugged the shore until they reached the most northern point of the lands where men called themselves Danes. They spent that night close to the trading port of Skagen at that northern spit of land, but Ivar forbade any of his ships from approaching the town, for fear of his men becoming drunk in one of the many taverns, and ending up fighting with another of the myriad crews who stopped there to trade, rest, or take on supplies before making the journey south to Frankia, the lands of the

Scots, Irish or Saxons.

"We sleep on board ship tonight," Halvdan ordered, stomping along the gap between rowing benches, testing rigging as the sun fell and stars appeared in the growing darkness. "Ulfketil, Styrr, Ginnlaug and Fulk, get the sail rigged for the night. Einar and Adzo, help them and learn how to do it. Rig it tight, I don't want my arse flapping in the wind and rain in the middle of the night."

Einar and Adzo leapt from their rowing benches and helped the others remove the sail from the yard and stretch it over the deck, using the oar crutches and shields to create a tent-like structure which they lashed to the hull using rigging ropes.

"Are we all going to sleep under this?" asked Adzo as he tied-off a rope.

"We'll be nice and warm, eh, Ginnlaug?" said Styrr, a rotund man as broad across the shoulder as Vigmarr and Halvdan, with arms as thick as ham hocks. He wore blue and white-striped trews and a sleeveless leather jerkin. His arms writhed with faded, tattooed whorls and crude images of ships and axes.

"If you come near me tonight…" Ginnlaug replied, her hawk face grimacing with disgust. She touched one hand to a wicked-looking curved dagger in her belt. "…I'll open your plump belly like a barley sausage and spill your guts on the deck."

The others laughed, as did Styrr, but Ginnlaug's face remained stuck in a frown and Einar reminded himself never to cross the mean-faced archer. Ulfketil Brownlegs slipped on a corner of the sail and their laughter turned into uncontrollable fits of giggles as he ended up sitting in a bailing bucket and couldn't free himself.

"Why is he called Brownlegs?" Adzo asked.

Styrr wiped a laughter tear from his cheek and shook his head. "Because he shit himself at sea last year. He had a naughty belly after eating some bad pork. We were in a storm and his fear of Halvdan's anger outweighed his desire to wash himself and change his trews. So he spent the day stinking like a midden heap and with a brown stain down his legs."

Adzo smiled. "I need a name. Einar is now the Brawler. Everybody seems to have a nickname."

"What about Adzo the Frank?" suggested Einar.

"A good name," Styrr shrugged. "But a name is earned in an event worthy of remembering. It isn't a thing a man chooses, others choose it for him. Ivar himself gave young Einar his name. You are from Frankia, are you not, Fulk?"

The new, masterless man who had joined Vigmarr's crew after Ivar's brutal killing at the holmgang, looked up from tying a knot in the rigging.

"I am," he said, his mouth parting to reveal a set of mud-brown, broken teeth. He was swarthy, with lank brown hair above a heavy, unkempt beard. He and Adzo exchanged some words in their own language, but Fulk gave short, unfriendly answers and so Adzo gave up.

"One day I will return to my home," Adzo said wistfully, looking out westwards across the sea.

"Maybe we'll go with you," said Ulfketil. "Bring Ivar, Vigmarr and the crews. I hear the women in Frankia are fair. Is your mother wide-hipped and pretty?" Styrr roared with laughter and earned himself a scowl from Halvdan.

"Hurry up!" Halvdan shouted. "Sounds like a Rus whorehouse over there. Don't make me come over and crack your skulls."

The crew fetched their blankets and huddled together beneath the sail awning. Einar lay down between Adzo and Thorkild, and there were no stories from the old man that night. With so many warriors huddled together, it was warm beneath the sail and men drifted off to sleep as the ship swayed on the swell. The two women amongst the crew, the archers Bersa and Ginnlaug, lay together, and despite Ulfketil's jests, the men respected them as warriors and left the women alone. Men began to snore and Einar's eyelids grew heavy, his body aching and tired after a hard day at sea. He rolled over to shift his position, and as sleep came for him, Einar saw a pair of onyx-black eyes staring at him from across the ship. He told himself it was the night playing tricks on him and drifted off into a deep, dreamless sleep.

The morning began with a light squall blowing in from the east with brisk winds and enough drizzle to soak the ship. Once the rain passed, Vigmarr and Halvdan barked at the crew to re-rig the sail and prepare to get underway. That work was completed rapidly, and before the sun was high in the sky, Ivar's three ships left Denmark's northern tip and tacked across the wide Whale Road of the Skagerrak, stretching from the land of the Danes to the lands of the Norsemen. The Seaworm, Windspear and Fjordviper tacked with the wind, and Einar clung to the rigging as the Seaworm dipped and rose on white-topped waves and the ship passed from sight of land before the crags and island of Norway appeared on the northern horizon.

"Bank west," Vigmarr Svarti bellowed from the prow, pointing towards a clutch of islands to the northwest. Halvdan leant on the steering oar and the crew shifted their position on the ship as it leaned, groaned, and turned on the surging sea. The Windspear and Fjordviper followed, as though their shipmasters already knew their destination.

"Weapons and armour," Vigmarr called as the islands grew closer. He left the prow and limped along the keel, scraping his nest of crow-black hair away from his face and tying it with a scrap of leather. His eyes blazed and the horror of his face shifted and moved like a pot of stew. "We fight today. We raid lands loyal to Dolgfinnr Dogsblood. So prepare your weapons and make ready. An arm ring for the bravest man of the day."

The crew roared their approval at Vigmarr's words.

"I haven't heard the jarl speak so much since we joined the crew," murmured Adzo as he strung his bow and readied his quiver.

"You'll earn your keep today, boys," Fat Garmr declared as he crossed the ship, handing out axes and seaxes from the weapon barrel.

Einar strapped on his belt, slid the axe through its loop, and secured his seax in its sheath at his rear. He pulled on the hard-baked leather breastplate and helmet given to him by Ragnar, and helped Thorkild fasten his own breastplate straps.

"Come, Frank," commanded Bersa, the thickset archer with ravens tattooed on both cheeks. She carried her bow and a quiver of arrows at her waist. "You fight beside Ginnlaug and I today. Do you have a spare bowstring?"

"I'm afraid not," Adzo replied.

"As green as a frog's arse." She spat over the side in disgust, dug into her jerkin and pulled out a spare hemp string which Adzo gratefully tucked into his belt pouch.

"Not there, empty head. Keep it somewhere dry. Wear a cap, or put it inside your clothes. A wet string is as useless as your manhood."

Adzo shrugged. "Good luck today, Einar," he said, grabbing Einar's shoulder.

"May Odin favour us both," Einar replied.

"God, you mean." Adzo winked, grabbed his yew bow and followed the two women towards the steerboard platform.

The Seaworm raced ahead of the Windspear and Fjordviper, her sails full and hull crashing through the breakers to send plumes of freezing cold sea water across the deck. The water stung Einar's eyes and soaked his hair as he helped the crew ready shields and spears.

"Why are we attacking this place?" Einar asked Styrr as the corpulent warrior handed him a spear. "This is not Dolgfinnr's stronghold." Einar remembered the slaughter beside Dogsblood's fortress, and this was not that place.

"Why not?" Styrr answered. "Could be that the jarl of this place is sworn to Dolgfinnr, or that he sent men to fight for him? Could be Lord Ivar has a grudge against the jarl here, or just that Ivar fancies a bit of raiding before we hit Dolgfinnr? Who cares? We are grunts, lad, we follow orders. We're sworn to do Ivar's bidding, and that's what we do. You don't need to ask yourself questions. Just fight who you are told to fight and kill who you are told to kill."

Einar took up his spear and slung a shield over his back.

"Half oars," Vigmarr hollered as the islands loomed. The Seaworm headed for the largest of three islands, a place with a coastal settlement of drab buildings and a modest harbour where two ships lay at anchor.

The crew took out twenty oars and fixed them into their oar holes.

"Lower the sail," Vigmarr ordered, and Einar went to help the crew furl the sail and tie it securely against the yard. "Not you." Einar turned to find Vigmarr Svarti pointing his axe right at him. The scarred, ruined mess of his face, drooping on one side, shifted and he licked his lips. "You fight at the front today, Brawler. Let's see if Ivar's pet can fight where the champions go."

Einar's guts clenched, and he staggered as Halvdan shoved him towards the prow. The island grew close, and the long, low sound of a war horn blared from the settlement. Sun glinted off iron and steel as men gathered on the shore, preparing to defend their homes from Ivar the Boneless and his fleet. A dozen men gathered in the prow's shade, Vigmarr, Halvdan, Styrr, and Yngvi the Fire amongst them.

"Odin!" Vigmarr bawled, shaking his axe at the sky. "Odin All-Father, look at what we do to honour you! Open the gates of Valhalla and prepare your Valkyrie, for we are about to swell your ranks with the glorious dead!"

He turned, gripped Halvdan by his chainmail byrnie and bellowed in his face. Einar's heart quickened, Vigmarr's war fury imbuing them all with excitement, drowning their fear in the will to fight and conquer. Vigmarr hooked one arm around the prow and leant over the side, dragging his axe in the sea to send ripples and spume out over the waves, and Einar thought it was the greatest thing he had ever seen. He wondered at the fear Vigmarr Svarti must stab into the hearts of the waiting warriors ashore as they saw him dangle over the prow with his shining axe.

"Come and fight with Vigmarr!" the jarl roared, and then he turned to Einar, leaning close, his impossibly black eyes gouging into Einar's soul. "Let's see the real you, boy."

Before Einar could react, the ship banked suddenly; the prow turning away from shore and Vigmarr leapt over the side without warning.

"Archers!" Halvdan called, waving his axe towards Adzo, Bersa, and Ginnlaug at the steerboard platform.

"Over the side, lad," said Styrr, axe in one fist and the other hand already on the sheerstrake. "Some of us will die today. Honour the gods with courage." He vaulted into the sea and followed Vigmarr, who waded through the waist-deep water.

Einar clenched his teeth, took three deep breaths, and followed Styrr over the side.

ELEVEN

Einar landed on silt and his feet slipped on the shifting seabed. Icy sea water crashed over him, powerful and dark, and he swallowed a gulp of foul salty water. The shield on his back felt like an anvil as the ocean's strength forced him down so that he was almost lying on the bottom. For a horrifying moment, Einar thought he might drown there in the shallows before the fight had even begun. Boots stomped in the sand around him, clouding the water, and Einar pushed himself upwards with his hands, bringing up his knees and forcing himself out of the sea. He retched and gasped, soaking wet, coughing and half-drowned. An arrow sang close to his face and slapped into the ship's hull and Einar's head spun with the madness, cold and desperation.

Halvdan surged past him with an axe in his fist and Einar followed the bull-necked shipmaster towards shore. Styrr and Yngvi had unslung their shields and clasped them together and Halvdan joined them. Einar unslung his own shield, and when the water was knee-high, he reached them and crashed his shield into Styrr's so they created a four-man shield wall. Arrows whipped into the water around them and one thumped into Einar's shield so forcefully that he nearly fell over.

"Here they come!" Halvdan bellowed.

Einar shook the water from his eyes and gasped as twenty men lined the shore before them, bearded men in leather and iron, with spears and axes and faces twisted with murderous anger. They were men prepared to fight to the death to protect their homes and families, and Einar braced himself for the attack. Vigmarr capered uncaring in front of the shield wall as arrows splashed around him. A spear flew like a lightning bolt from the hand of an enormous red-haired man, and Vigmarr Svarti ducked just in time to send the spear sailing over his head. Another spear flew, and this one Vigmarr caught in his left hand; the sheer skill of it took Einar's breath away. Vigmarr turned at the waist and hurled the spear back with such venom that it threw a bow-legged warrior from his feet.

More Seaworm men joined the shield wall, and a carl named Bjorn shouted and screamed like a madman, stripped to his trews and carrying a huge double-bladed war axe. He joined Vigmarr before the shield wall and the two men lumbered through the dragging surf towards the enemy. Six of the defenders charged at the attackers, two heading for Vigmarr and Bjorn and the rest at the burgeoning shield wall. Vigmarr killed the first man, swaying from a spear thrust and opening the man's throat with a sweep of his axe. Bjorn hit the second attacker with his axe so hard that he almost cleaved his body in two. Gone was the lumbering and hunched Vigmarr; replaced by a giant, quick warrior who dared the foemen to come and fight him.

The attackers thrust their shields at the Seaworm shield wall. A skinny man with a prominent nose raised his axe to slice into Einar's shield and died with an arrow in his open mouth. Adzo and the two women archers loosed arrows into the men and Halvdan broke the shield wall to attack the onrushing enemy. Einar drew his axe and charged forward, stepping over the man with the arrow in his maw. There was blood in the water now, mixed with sand and dead men's voided bowls to turn the sea into a heaving brown slop.

Einar stepped out of the sea and took a spear thrust on his shield. An old man with grey eyes stabbed at him again and Einar batted the spear away with his shield and hefted his axe into the man's chest. He fell, and Einar ripped his weapon free. He looked about him for another foe, but the defenders were retreating. Vigmarr fought with an axe in one hand and a broken spear in the other. He laid about him with Odin's frenzied aggression, stabbing and slashing like a man half his age. Bjorn howled like a wolf and charged towards the village with froth in his beard and his weapons waving.

"After them!" Halvdan ordered, and Einar followed his shipmaster after the enemy. He ran across the beach and leapt up onto a boardwalk. Einar barged coiled fishing nets and baskets out of his way with his shield and paused with his back against a wattle building wall. Einar's chest pounded so hard he thought his heart might leap out of his armour. Water puddled about his boots, and out at sea, warriors streamed from the Seaworm towards shore, lumbering in the tide like drunken men as the waves dragged them backwards and shoved them forwards. The Windspear and the Fjordviper spewed their warriors forth, and Einar saw a flash of Ivar's green cape in a fight on the beach's western end.

Einar adjusted his grip on his shield and charged into the gap between two dwellings, unsure of where he was going. His orders were simple. Kill. So that was what he must do. He reached a corner and turned left, but the abodes were too close together, and soggy thatch hung low from their roofs so that Einar had to stoop to keep moving. The homes closed in, like he was hurrying into a decreasing space. A shiver shook his shoulders, a sudden feeling that someone was following him. Einar turned a corner, shield scraping on a wall and taking a chunk of wattle with it. A baying figure darted from an open door and stabbed at him with a knife. Einar tried to raise his shield, but it jammed stuck between two walls, so he let it go and fell back as the rusted knife blade slashed through the air where his neck had been.

"Bastard," spat the knifeman, a lad of Einar's age, with white-blonde hair and a beardless face. A child wept inside one building, and the knifeman clambered over the shield and tried to lunge at Einar. He caught the blow with his axe, and punched the axe head into the young man's face, opening a gash below his eye. The blonde-haired lad flinched at the pain and Einar kicked him out of his way. He drew his seax and as the blonde man tried to attack again, Einar drove the seax into the gap between his collarbone and neck, twisted the blade and ripped it free. Blood sprayed on wattle, and Einar stepped over the dying man, leaving the chilling sound of the wailing child behind him.

Einar ran around the next bend and found himself in a small village square where a line of warriors stood against Vigmarr's Seaworm men. The jarl fought at the front, his axe rising and falling, and his voice booming over the battle. More men poured from the snarl of alleys and lanes. Fulk, the masterless man who had joined Vigmarr's crew at Hrafnborg, emerged from the alley behind Einar, a bloody axe in his hand, and Einar dreaded to think of those who had died in the snarl of homes. Then Ivar was there, charging towards the thick of the fight with his two swords drawn. Einar followed him into the fray, shouldering past the men who lingered at the rear until he reached the front, where men shoved with shields and hacked with axes, knives and spears. The defenders held their ground, a man in a helmet topped with an eagle's feather at their centre. He had a thick beard twisted into a rope, and wielded a bright sword.

Bjorn died with that sword in his belly and another fell away as the sword blade slashed across his face. Einar had no shield, so he shoved his way forward to stand between Vigmarr and Rorik, and he crouched to stab between their shields with his seax. He killed a man with a thrust to the groin and Vigmarr grinned down at him, his face smudged and speckled with other men's blood. Ivar led his men around the defenders' flank, and suddenly the defenders' shield wall split, and then the fight turned into a slaughter.

"Not that one!" Vigmarr ordered, pointing his axe at the swordsman. Rorik and Halvdan bullied the men away from the man with their shields, and Vigmarr strode towards him. All signs of his limping stoop disappeared. Stood straight, Vigmarr was colossal, and he towered over the enemy leader, dressed all in black, like a demon from Niflheim.

Ivar's crews outnumbered the defenders. Men whooped for joy as they darted into dwellings and lashed at defenders who bravely fought one man against three or four of Ivar's men. Einar stood and watched as Vigmarr and the swordsman circled one another and then charged like two great stags. They clashed in a blur of steel, clanging and grunting as they fought for supremacy. The swordsman overreached with a lunge, and Vigmarr plunged his broken spear into the man's shoulder. He dropped to one knee and Vigmarr rested his axe against the swordsman's throat.

"Go to Odin," Vigmarr panted to the wounded man. "Tell the gods the honour I gave you in death. Tell them that. Do you swear?"

The swordsman clenched his eyes closed and nodded, and Vigmarr killed him swiftly. As the man fell, Vigmarr knelt and made sure he kept hold of his sword before he gave up his last breath. Vigmarr stayed there for a time, and Einar watched him. Hrafnborg men swarmed about the village, emerging from houses carrying anything of value; boxes, iron spits, weapons, food, small barrels of ale, and even goats and sheep. Rorik and Halvdan stood guard as Vigmarr stayed with the dead enemy leader, and it was as though Vigmarr prayed over the corpse. Six times he glanced up at the sky as though he thought he might glimpse Odin's Valkyrie riding down from Valhalla to choose the glorious dead. Eventually, Vigmarr stood and limped away from the swordsman, the crippled, bent-backed jarl once more. He untied his hair and shook it so that it covered his face, and he disappeared behind an earthen-roofed home. Rorik and Halvdan stripped the dead leader of sword, helmet, arm rings, and anything else worth taking.

A woman screamed, and then another. Einar closed his eyes and shivered, sea water still dripping from his clothes and sending a chill deep into his bones. He had no desire to search the homes for spits, cloak pins, and other men's bread. Einar's eyes stung with the weariness of battle, and there was little *drengskapr* to be found in looting. He went to sit on a stool outside a house with painted shutters and watched the crews gorge themselves with plunder. It had been his first raid, his first Viking attack.

I've done well, he thought. Einar had killed and fought and had not stood back whilst other men tried to break the enemy resistance. He had done his part. He sat on the beach as the sun dried his clothes, and he supposed that the blood and bravery made him a warrior, but he did not feel like one. Einar felt the same as before; better armed, perhaps, but the same inside. Men clapped him on the back or ruffled his hair as they went back and forth on the sand and shale. Einar wondered if perhaps that was the beginning of acceptance by the crew, the beginning of his reputation.

Ivar dragged an old man wearing a baggy smock down from the village onto the sand. The crews gathered about him as he threw the old man onto his face, his spindly, mottled legs and arms flailing and his pate shining like an egg.

"Who is that?" asked Adzo, sitting down next to Einar on the sand.

"Must be someone important," Einar shrugged. His muscles ached and he couldn't summon the energy to witness whatever Ivar had planned for his captive.

"Hey!" Adzo called to Fat Garmr as he ambled past. "Who does Ivar have there?"

"The jarl of this shit heap," said Garmr, shaking a beaded necklace he held in his hand to show off his plunder. "Someone says he's Dolgfinnr's uncle, or something like that."

Garmr hurried off to join the crowd. Einar rubbed the dried sea salt from his eyes and face.

Men cheered, but all Einar could see were flashes of Ivar's sword between the press of men.

"I have to gather up some spent arrows," Adzo said, and he left Einar alone.

The day drew on and eventually, the men congregated on the beach and made huge piles of loot. Ivar divided up the piles into three for each of the crews, and then let each ship's leader decide what to share between his men. Vigmarr presented Ivar with the dead leader's sword, which he took, but Einar noticed that the exchange between the two men was frosty and brief. Halvdan shared the loot out between the Seaworm crew and handed Einar three silver coins and an antler-handled eating knife. Halvdan gave Adzo a naal-binding cap and winingas wrappings for his trews.

The crew compared their winnings on the beach whilst the sun was still high in the sky, and then waded back towards their ships full of laughter and joy, despite the wailing of the survivors in that nameless village fallen prey to their wrath. Einar clambered aboard the Seaworm and helped Adzo over the side.

"Someone's left a bloody shield on the beach," said Halvdan. "Palni, go get it."

A squat man with a beard more grey than brown cursed under his breath and jumped back into the sea. The tide had begun to flood and so he had to swim two ships' lengths before he could stand and wade the rest of the way. Palni retrieved the shield and was swimming back to the ship when an archer appeared atop the village's highest rooftop. He loosed an arrow which flew high into the sky, and then dipped with murderous speed to take Palni between the shoulder blades. He floundered in the water, struggling with the shield and the arrow in his back.

"I've seen enough death and suffering for one day," Einar said. He pulled off his breastplate, jerkin, and boots and dived into the water.

TWELVE

Einar swam through the dark sea, his arms powering through the swell in great sweeps, his legs kicking to propel him forward. Palni flailed in the water, clinging to the shield, overwhelmed by fear of drowning. His muffled screams rose and fell with the waves, head sinking and then rising, one arm waving, unable to think clearly enough to let go of the shield and save his own life. Mixed with Palni's death screams came shouts of warning from the Seaworm, but Einar did not pause or look back. He was in the water now, a split-second decision made. To let Palni die now would be humiliating.

Einar reached Palni, and the squat man reached out for him with clawing fingers. Einar had grown up beside the sea, learning to swim in the harbour, and had seen more than one child almost drown as the unpredictable tide pulled and pushed beneath their feet. He tested the depth and found he could stand up, the flooding tide reaching his chest. So he stood up, and without hesitating, he slapped Palni hard across the face to knock the panic out of him. Palni shuddered, the arrow in his shoulder quivering above the waterline.

"I'm going to pull you to the ship," Einar shouted over the waves as Palni stared at him wide-eyed and open-mouthed. "If you thrash about, I'll take the shield and leave you to drown. Understand?"

Palni nodded, so Einar hooked an arm beneath Palni's left armpit and swam towards the Seaworm, hauling Palni with him.

"Let go of the shield," Einar shouted.

"No. I won't die for nothing."

Einar cursed and kicked his legs, pulling the water with his right arm. They moved painfully slowly towards the warship, where men watched from the side, waving them closer, urging Einar to make it.

"I can't make it!" Palni dipped beneath the surface, emerged again, and coughed up a gout of water, his head bobbing beneath the water once more. Einar pulled him closer, shifting his grip so that Palni's chest and head rested against his shoulder and above the churning sea.

"You can," Einar said, "and you will."

The ship rose and fell on the waves, but Einar's strokes became laboured, fatigue making every pull and kick burn like fire. A shipmate tossed a length of rope from the side and it fell agonisingly short. The carl dragged it back and threw it again. This time Einar caught the rope and tied it about Palni's midriff. The crew hauled him towards the Seaworm, and Einar swam, feeling suddenly as light as a feather without Palni's weight holding him back. He reached the ship in twenty long strokes. Adzo and Bersa reached down and grabbed his wrists, hefting him over the side.

Einar flopped on the deck like a caught fish, chest heaving, limbs exhausted.

"That had better be the best shield ever made," Einar choked between gasps.

Adzo laughed. "Well done, Einar."

"You saved him, lad," said Halvdan, his beefy, growling head appearing above Einar and blocking out the sun. "But he's wounded. He's yours to care for now." Halvdan reached down and helped Einar stand. He leaned in close and whispered so that only Einar could hear. "You did well." Einar gaped, but before he could respond, Halvdan pushed him away. "That's enough pissing about, shitworms. Let's get moving. Get the weapons and armour stowed, injured to the steerboard platform. I want a count of how many we've lost or who can't pull an oar. Let's move!"

Praise from Halvdan was like receiving another arm ring, and Einar swelled with pride. He pulled on his clothes and put his axe and seax into the weapon's barrel. Thorkild examined Palni, tutting as he probed the arrow wound with his fingers. Vigmarr Svarti stood beside the steering oar, glowering back at the ravaged village as the crew lowered the sail and Ivar's fleet continued northeast. Einar and Adzo sat on their rowing benches as Fat Garmr handed out the last of the skyr and skins of ale.

"Our first raid," said Einar after swallowing a mouthful of creamy skyr, which had soured slightly but still felt like a piece of Asgard in his mouth.

"I think I may have killed a man," Adzo said. "May God forgive me. I wounded four others with my arrows. Perhaps some of those will die of their wounds."

"Then you did well. We came to kill those men."

"Just because Ivar and Vigmarr order it, does not make it right. Those people lived in peace before we came. Now their menfolk are dead, and I dread to think what happened to the womenfolk."

"They were Northmen, just like us. There were

warriors there, which means they raid, fight and kill. Just like us."

"My God forbids murder. It is a sin. I must pray and ask forgiveness for what I did today."

"A sin? Those men have killed, burned, raped and plundered. That is the life we live; the gods encourage us to fight and make war. Only then can we take our place in the glorious afterlife. Your people do not fight wars?"

"They do. There is always war in Frankia. We had a great king in my grandfather's time. Charles the Great was his name and our empire rivalled that of the Rome folk. He died and his sons made war on each other, and still do."

"So every king, prince, warlord, and warrior are sinners who will not go to your heaven?"

Adzo smiled. "It is not so simple as that. A king is anointed by God and is his voice here on earth. So if we fight for our king against his enemies, then it is not a sin."

"Your nailed god is a strange god. Seems to me like you make the rules up as you go along. Sins are clear for us. If you steal, kill, touch another man's wife, take his land or break your oath, then it is a crime. A man is judged for that crime by his lord. The criminal can pay a weregild, or he suffers death. It is clear."

"Nevertheless. I killed a man today who would

be alive but for my arrow. He might have a wife or children. What is to become of them now?"

"He should have thought of that before he sided with Dolgfinnr Dogsblood against Ragnar Lothbrok. We did as we were told to do. We swore oaths to fight for Ivar, and that's what we did. There is no right and wrong in it. You think too much. Are you going to eat that?" Einar pointed to the handful of skyr on Adzo's wooden plate, and the Frank devoured it before Einar swiped it.

"I am far from home, living amongst your heathen Northmen and your violent gods. One day I will till the soil on my father's land and tell my children of the days when I sailed and fought in the land of the Vikings."

"It's not so long ago you were a thrall. Now you are a free man. You have a bow, that cap, beads, an arm ring. Our *hamingja* runs strong at the moment, luck is with us. Maybe, when enough people have died and we return to Hrafnborg, you might have enough silver to make your way home. You should be thankful to our gods and for our ways. Otherwise, you would be emptying shit pails, or wiping arses, or whatever you did when you were a thrall."

"Thankful? It was Vikings who raided my home and made me a slave."

"And now you have more than you did before. You are sailing on a warship with men of reputation."

"That might be all you want out of life, my friend, but I want more."

"What more is there?"

"Land. A wife. Children."

"A carl has those things. Perhaps not land, but if I gain enough silver, I can buy all the land I want."

"But you don't want that, Einar. You want this. You want to sail this ship, fight enemies, and for your shipmates to respect you."

"That is everything." Einar grinned, and Adzo laughed and shook his head as though he pitied Einar. But Einar had come far. Days ago, all his future held was life as a slave. He had fought his way out of the slave pen, fought single combat, and fought in a raid. Einar was a warrior, just as his father had been before him. He leaned over the side and held out his hand so that the chill sea spray splashed against his rowing calluses. He wondered what more the future could hold. Perhaps one day he could become a champion, or a shipmaster like Halvdan? Some men even rose to become famous sea-jarls like Vigmarr Svarti. Everything seemed possible on the Whale Road.

Einar raised his left hand and caressed the smooth wooden hammer amulet he wore around his neck. Thor's symbol. Most warriors prayed to Odin, for he was the god and ruler of the battlefield, but no man wore his symbol, the Gungnir spear Odin carried into battle, out of fear of the ill luck it might bring. Odin granted men luck on the battlefield, but the All-Father had many names. He was battle-screamer and battle-wolf, but also Bǫlverkr, the betrayer, the bale worker and betrayer of warriors. So men wore Thor's hammer, the strongest of the gods, a warrior himself who battled against frost giants and Loki's monsters. Einar closed his eyes and thanked both Thor and Odin for keeping him alive, and he asked them to watch over the souls of the men he had killed, men who had died so that Einar could have his place on the warship Seaworm. Their faces came to him then quickly, flashing from his memory to the sound of Olvir's shattering teeth. Einar gripped the hammer amulet harder. Those souls must leave him alone. He must not dwell on the men he had killed. Einar served Odin, Thor, Týr and the rest of the Aesir; he served Ivar the Boneless and Ragnar Lothbrok, and they demanded axes, swords, shields, wounds, death, and glory.

A groan of pain snapped Einar from his dreams and he opened his eyes to see Palni writhing and moaning in pain.

"Don't just sit there," chided Thorkild, bent over Palni with a knife in his hand. He beckoned to Einar and Adzo. "Help hold him down."

Einar remembered Halvdan's words. He was responsible for Palni's life and so he hurried across the bilge and joined Ulfketil and Yngvi who had hold of Palni's arms. He lay face down, stripped to the waist, with the arrow jutting from below his shoulder blade.

"Sit on the bastard," grunted Ulfketil Brownlegs, struggling with Palni's left arm. "He's as slippery as a slimy fish."

"Keep him still," Thorkild warned. "I have to cut the arrow out. How can I do that when he's moving around beneath me like your mother last yule?"

"Just do it! Your breath smells like cabbage farts."

They tried not to laugh at Ulfketil, and Einar sat on Palni's legs as Adzo tried to hold his neck down. Thorkild bent low, his short, sharp knife in his hand and his tongue between his teeth as he concentrated on the arrow. He gently probed with the knife's tip and his fingers, trying to see how deep the arrowhead was, and Yngvi stuffed a wooden dowel into Palni's mouth for him to bite down on.

"It's deep," Thorkild muttered. "I'll have to break the shaft and cut it out. Could have ruptured his chest; if so, then he'll die."

Thorkild broke the arrow and Palni bucked,

and then as the old storyteller dug around the wound with his knife, Palni mercifully slipped into unconsciousness. The men let him go and Einar turned away as Thorkild dug about in Palni's back.

"Got it," Thorkild announced, like a man who has caught a fish in a difficult stream. He held up an arrowhead smeared with dark blood and threw it over the side. "Now we try to put him back together and hope for the best. How is his breathing?"

Adzo bent down and put his ear to Palni's mouth. "Short and wheezing," he said.

Thorkild shrugged. "His chest could be burst. We'll see."

"Will he die?" asked Einar.

"If he lives through tonight, then he might make it."

Thorkild washed Palni's back with seawater and wiped the wound clean with a clean cloth. He sewed the hole together with a bone needle threaded with a thin hemp cord, and they set Palni to rest beneath the steerboard platform where five other men lay nursing wounds.

"Right then," Thorkild said, wiping his brow on his sleeve. "Who's next?"

Einar left Thorkild to his work and returned to his duties managing the rigging. The three-ship fleet continued northward, hugging the coast as the sun began to drop. A horn blew from Ivar's Windspear, and the son of Ragnar waved at the Seaworm. Halvdan guided the ship close to the Fjordviper and the Windspear, and men shouted across the bows that Ivar wanted the three ships lashed together.

"What is that?" Adzo pointed across the water to the Windspear's prow where something large and white seemed stuck where the hull curved upwards into the snarling prow beast.

Einar's eyes raked over the thing, leaning over the side to get a closer look. At first, he thought it was a Höfrungr, a water he-goat, one of the dolphins that sometimes chased ships, diving and leaping in the water. But then he noticed arms and legs stretched out, and rope lashing the figure to the ship's keel. "It's a man," said Einar.

"It's the old jarl, Dolgfinnr's uncle," said Fulk with a grin. "A nice surprise for Ivar's enemy when we reach his lands."

Adzo made the sign of the cross and Fulk cackled. Einar shivered at Ivar's cruelty. He had seemed so friendly at Hrafnborg, all good cheer and broad smiles. He had shown Einar kindness, saved him from the slave pen and given Einar a pathway to his destiny. How could that same man tie the naked corpse of an old jarl to his prow for the sea to batter and rend just to spite his enemy?

"Stop gawping and tie the ship off," Halvdan ordered, swinging beneath the rigging and pointing at loose ropes and items men had failed to properly stow beneath their rowing benches.

The Windspear, Fjordviper and Seaworm came softly together, tied with ropes and buffeted with shields so that the hulls didn't clash. Halvdan and the other shipmasters gathered the warriors together and handed out skins of ale, whilst others brought around rations of smoked fish and hard bread. The ships floated within sight of a rocky headland where waves broke against cliffs in clouds of gleaming spume. Einar ate beside Adzo, Bersa, and Ginnlaug and listened as the three archers talked about their bows, the condition of the arrows, and comparing the distances over which they had hit targets during the raid. Einar had that strange sensation of feeling like someone was looking at him, and he turned to find Fulk staring at him from the stern. Fulk half-smiled and looked away. It was the second time Einar had caught the newest member of the Seaworm crew's eye. It was strange, but he shrugged it off and went to check on Palni.

Einar bobbed beneath the halyard rope and shuffled out of the way as men shouted to friends and relatives across the three ships. Men told jokes and shared ale, and three ships lashed together became like a lord's hall afloat, filling the Whale Road with loud voices and laughter. He found Palni sitting up with a tan-coloured cloak about his shoulders. Other men lay close to him, men with bloodstained cloth bandages about their wounds.

"Have you eaten anything?" Einar asked. Palni shook his head slowly. "I'll get you something." Einar went to the mast and took a plate of fish and bread and brought it back to the steerboard platform, beneath which the injured men lay.

"I'm not hungry," Palni said. The words came as a low rasp, and Einar noticed that Palni's chest rose and fell quickly, his breath coming in ragged gasps. His face was pale, almost as blue as a river frozen in winter. Einar lifted a skin of ale and Palni took a sip and coughed. The cough wracked his body as though a knife had stabbed him, and Palni shook his head in protest. "I'm dying," he choked, eyes rolling in his head. "Get me a blade, lad. Don't let me die without a blade."

"You are going to live," Einar said, unsure if he spoke the truth. Halvdan had tasked him with caring for the wounded carl, but looking at the sheen of sweat on Palni's face and the haunted look in his eyes, he wondered if Halvdan hadn't said that to teach Einar a lesson. Should he have left Palni to die in the water? Nobody else had dived in. Einar had acted on instinct. After a day of slaughter, he had not wanted to see another man die. He thought of Jari, the archer who had fallen from Bolti's Waveslicer in these very waters, and how he had left the man to drown. Breath rattled from Palni like a winter wind through window shutters and Einar thought all he had achieved was to prolong Palni's agony. But then the grim shipmaster had rewarded Einar with encouraging words, which were as rare as the goddess Idun's apples of eternal youth.

A war horn sounded from the Windspear and a silence spread across the three ships. Ivar left Palni in peace and returned to Adzo just as Ivar stood up on the Windspear's steerboard platform high in the stern so that everybody could see him.

"The sea is calm tonight and Njorth blesses our voyage with sea-luck," Ivar said, his green cape fluttering around him in the evening breeze. He shouted so that all the carls could hear, his handsome face bright and smiling. "Tomorrow, we attack our enemies. We strike at a man who broke his oath to my father, and all men know an oathbreaker is a nithing. He killed One Leg Bolti, a man many of us knew and loved as a brother of the shield wall. Worse than all of those things, Dolgfinnr Dogsblood has the raven banner. A banner sacred to my family, for we are descendants of Odin himself and for any other man to carry that symbol is an affront to me, to my brothers, to Ragnar and to the All-Father himself. Will you fight with me tomorrow?"

Einar heard a few "heyas" and some men cheered.

"I said, will you fight beside Ivar tomorrow? Will you burnish your reputations bright with the deaths of champions?"

Every man stood and cheered.

"I will kill Dolgfinnr tomorrow and recover the raven banner. I will become the champion of the Northmen, and our names will live on forever, spoken of by the heroes in Valhalla at the mead benches, sung about by skalds across Midgard. Are you ready to have your names live on forever?"

"Aye!" Two hundred voices roared as one, and Einar shouted with them, punching his arm into the air. Adzo did the same, and they clapped one another on the back. Bersa and Ginnlaug grabbed them both and the crews laughed and shouted their defiance at their enemies who tomorrow would feel the wrath of Ivar the Boneless.

THIRTEEN

Ivar's fleet slid from the fog like three serpents, like dragons of the Loki-brood snaking across calm waters with their long, curved keels, painted beast heads and stem posts carved to look like frightening monsters. Einar pulled his oar in time with the crew; long, slow pulls, so quiet that each oar blade made less sound than a fish's tail as it bit into the still waters. Einar wore his breastplate and weapons, as did every man on board the warship Seaworm. Ivar had ordered the carls to rise before the sun and make ready their war gear so that they came at Dolgfinnr Dogsblood ready for war. No man wore armour at sea because to fall overboard wearing chainmail, leather, furs and iron was to sink like a stone into Ran's watery kingdom where the goddess ruled with cruelty and fear over those who drowned in the depths. Einar thanked Njorth for the mist and the calm waters, for just as Ran ruled the deep, the Vanir god Njorth ruled the tide, wind and storms.

Vigmarr Svarti hung over the prow like an animal stalking its prey, waiting with his axe in his hand, his black heart poised to come alive in the maelstrom of blood and battle. One of the injured men huddled beneath the steerboard platform groaned, his voice made louder by the ethereal dawn's half-light and mist.

"Quiet that man or I'll cut his throat and toss the wretch overboard," Vigmarr hissed, his great shaggy head turning like an angered bear.

Palni had survived the night, and had even slept for most of it. Einar had checked on him before sun-up and given the injured warrior a sip of ale and a mouthful of hard, black bread. Palni lived, but his eyes were sunken, his skin thin and blanched, and Einar worried for the wounded warrior's fate. Fat Garmr rushed from his oar bench to quiet the wounded men. He shushed and gathered blankets close about them, warning them of Vigmarr's wrath if they uttered another sound.

The sea haar, the mist about them, was so thick that Einar could barely see the Windspear and the Fjordviper, though he knew they were there. Ivar's orders were simple, and every warrior with a sharpened weapon at his belt knew his job and what must be done if they were to defeat Dolgfinnr Dogsblood. Men rowed with grim faces, helmets pushed tight onto their heads, spears ready at their feet. The wait for battle was worse than the battle itself. When Einar fought, everything became easy. It was life and death. The heightened sense of combat took all thought out of the situation. He just fought. But rowing towards the fight, knowing that axes, brutal warriors, blood and death awaited ashore, turned Einar's guts to water. He had pissed three times already that morning. Three men had vomited over the side as the ships drew closer to their enemy, but none now stirred for fear of exacerbating Vigmarr's ire. Adzo rowed in silence, his bow and quiver ready, his lips drawn tight and knuckles bloodless about his oar.

Water shifted and sloshed to the Seaworm's port and starboard sides as the Windspear and Fjordviper made their move. Einar peered over his shoulder, and a palisade and buildings appeared in faint outlines beyond the mist. Dolgfinnr's fortress. His island lair off Norway's south-eastern coast. Einar turned back and pulled his oar again, memories of that beach as fresh in his mind as the arrow wound in Palni's back, and just as raw. He recalled the terrible slaughter, how Bolti had died and lost his head to Dolgfinnr's axe, how his shipmates had died in the water, butchered in the blood-tinged shallows. Today would be different. Today Ivar the Boneless and Vigmarr Svarti had come to wreak their terrible vengeance upon Bolti's killer, the champion of the Northmen.

"Five more strokes," Halvdan whispered, striding along the deck, the iron rings of his *brynjar* making a shunking sound with each step. "Make them count." Halvdan slid between Einar's oar and the man in front and leaned over the side to check the sea's depth. He seemed satisfied and caught Einar's eye for a moment. Halvdan inclined his head slightly, barely a nod, and Einar did the same. It was the smallest of gestures, but between men, it was everything. It said, fight well today and I trust you. One tiny move of the head, but it said more than a skald could say in an entire night of storytelling. Einar's heart swelled; his back grew stronger and his jaw set firm. If Halvdan trusted him, then perhaps Einar was one of them, a carl, a warrior of the warship Seaworm.

On the third stroke, Adzo, Bersa and Ginnlaug hurried around the mast towards the prow. They carried their strung bows, each with an arrow already nocked, scanning the fort, ready to loose their deadly missiles at any sign of the enemy who might appear on the beach. Another stroke and the men not pulling oars checked the straps on their shields. They adjusted the axes at their belts and took up their spears. On the last stroke, Ulfketil pushed the anchor stone over the side, and it splashed loudly into the sea's glassy surface. Einar reached over the side and slid his oar from its hole. Icy water dripped down its shaft to wet his hands, and he joined the others to stow the long oar in its crutch. Einar slung his shield over his shoulder so its weight rested against his back. He picked up a spear, its ash shaft smooth in his grip, and waited for the order.

Halvdan lifted his hand and paused. The only sounds were the slop of the gentle waves against the hull and the caw of a distant seabird. Ivar had chosen to attack before dawn because the tide was at ebb. The beach was long, left exposed by retreating water as Dolgfinnr's warriors slept behind their high palisade. When Bolti had attacked, Dolgfinnr had been waiting. He had the greater numbers and so had decided to kill his enemies on the beach and in the water rather than waiting for them to assault his walls. Bolti's men hadn't secured enough of a foothold on the beach to make a stand and fought with their backs to the sea. When Dolgfinnr's challenge of single combat had come, it was almost a relief for Bolti's men, if not for the one-legged shipmaster himself.

Today it would be different. Today Einar must assault walls cut from trunks of stout pine, each long stake sunk into deep holes and their tips sharpened to a vicious point. Just like Hrafnborg, Einar knew to expect a ditch and bank before the walls and a fighting platform behind the palisade from which the defenders could hurl spears and rocks, pour boiling water, and rain down arrows on their foes. The prospect of assaulting such a place was enough to make Einar wish he had become a blacksmith's apprentice, a shepherd, or a shipwright's labourer rather than a warrior sworn to fight for Ivar the Boneless.

Einar pushed his helmet over his head. The leather liner stank of sweat and the iron nasal protector was cold as it touched his nose. Vigmarr slid from the prow and plopped into the water, and Halvdan lowered his hand. The crew dropped over both sides to stop the ship from rocking and keeling over, and Einar gasped as his legs sank into the glacial water. He lifted his arms, carrying his spear above his head, and winced as the freezing sea water crept above his waist. The men waded ashore, coming for Dolgfinnr and his warriors like the inglorious dead on the day of the Ragnarök. On that day, the end of days foretold by Odin himself and sang of by skalds beside winter fires, Loki would lead his dread ship Naglfar, made from the nails and toenails of the dead and crewed by the poor souls in Niflheim, and his monster children, as he waged war on Odin, the Aesir and the world of men.

Vigmarr reached the beach first, limping, colossal, with an axe in one hand, a gleaming seax in the other. He came to kill, to slake his inexhaustible thirst for blood and combat with the souls of Dolgfinnr's men. He lived for it. Without battle, Vigmarr was a crippled, scarred husk, like the stump of an ancient tree struck by lightning long ago but existing still as a burned, ravaged reminder of Thor's power. Vigmarr was a creature of war. It defined him, kept him alive and gave his fractured soul succour. Einar's foot slipped on slick, green bladderwrack on the seabed. He cursed, half-fell, and shrugged his shield from his back.

"Shield wall," Halvdan hissed through gritted teeth.

Einar hurried through the surf, his boots squelching on the hard brown sand left by the retreating tide. He glanced to his left and right, where the Windspear and the Fjordviper's crews attacked the beach on its opposite edges. Styrr slapped his shield alongside Einar's, and Fat Garmr locked his on the other side. They stopped until more men joined shields together to make the wall. Einar rested his spear on his shield's iron rim and waited, shivering as the cold sea water chilled his bones. The crew were silent, staring at Vigmarr as his cruel face scanned the jagged palisade for any sign of the enemy, but found none.

"Four men go up the walls," Vigmarr said without looking back at his crew. The beach and fortifications were too quiet. Einar had expected to see at least some guards above the gate or signs of life inside the fortress. Not even a sign of smoke rose from the buildings inside. Even at daybreak, folk would have morning fires ablaze to warm themselves, heat water, or cook their first meal of the day. Men exchanged puzzled glances; warriors who had worked themselves up to face axes, pain, and spear points, instead found only eerie stillness.

Halvdan stepped out of the wall, took four axes from the crew, and tucked them into his thick leather belt. He ran forward, followed by Ulfketil and Yngvi. Einar waited behind his shield, in awe that the three warriors marched willingly towards the high palisade without question and seemingly without fear. He waited for a fourth man to join the three, but no other carl moved from the shield wall. Einar's heart told him to go, to join Halvdan and the others, to show his bravery, but his head told him to stay and remain behind the shield wall. Hundreds of warriors could lie in wait on the fighting platform, crouched behind the spiked stakes, just waiting for four fools to climb up and die. Dolgfinnr himself could be there, the champion of the North with his axe, which had cleft Bolti's head from his shoulders with one clean strike. Dolgfinnr's wolf warriors could be up there, his hearth troop, his hand-picked champions in their wolf furs and battle fury, just waiting with bright axes to begin the slaughter. Words Einar's father had once said sailed into his mind. *A warrior doesn't make a reputation by being timid. The brave ones fight at the front. They do what others fear to do.*

Einar dropped his shield and ran after Halvdan, Yngvi, and Ulfketil towards the palisade. A closed gate and narrow bridge spanned the ditch; a gate with stout iron hinges and no doubt a thick locking-bar on the inside. To smash through that gate required a battering ram, or at worst, a thick tree trunk with which the attackers could smash the gate open. But Vigmarr had no such ram, and so his men had to scale the walls. But four warriors could not capture an entire defensive wall and open its front gate. As Einar's wet boots pounded across the sand, he realised that what Vigmarr really wanted was for his four brave men to poke their heads above the parapet and look inside the defences, to provoke the defenders from wherever they hid behind the walls. War was about trickery and cunning. It was about ambushes, traps, flanking manoeuvres and outwitting men who wished to kill you, and killing them instead. Einar held his breath, expecting a hundred growling Vikings to appear above the spiked timbers.

Halvdan reached the ditch first and paused, his breath rising through the chill dawn air in great clouds as the muscled shipmaster stared up at the palisade. He set off again, taking five quick steps before leaping over the yawning gap. Einar followed. He soared over the gap, which reeked of the foul bog water gathered in its bottom, and landed on the bank covered with coarse beach grass. He grabbed a lump of it and hauled himself upwards until he crested the ditch. The ditch and bank formed the first line of defence from any seaward attack. Einar imagined a line of men waiting atop the walls for an attacking army to blunder into that ditch, where they could kill them with arrows, spears, and rocks, as they tried to clamber up the sides of the steep bank. After that, the attacking army would find itself directly below the walls, where the deathly rain continued from above as they tried to erect ladders and climb the walls. But today, all remained quiet and still.

"How do we climb?' Einar asked, leaning with his back against the palisade. The fear of the fortress's emptiness was now as fearsome as the prospect of its walls filled with enemies. Where were they? Was it a trap? Einar's mouth was dryer than a river in drought.

"Axes, lad," Halvdan ordered. He turned, jumped, and hoisted his axe into one of the wall's pine trunks. He took another axe from his belt and gripped the haft between his teeth, jumped and grabbed the first axe with his right hand. Halvdan hauled himself upwards, boots scrabbling for purchase against the palisade. He took the axe from his mouth in his right hand, swung it high and slammed it into the wall as high as he could reach. He dropped to the ground, puffing with exertion. "Yngvi, you next."

Halvdan bent and made a shelf with his hands. Yngvi stepped on it and Halvdan hauled upwards. Yngvi used the axes to lift himself and thumped his axe in above Halvdan's two. He dropped back to the bank and winked at Einar.

"Over you go, laddie," he said.

Einar rocked backwards, eyes flitting from Halvdan, Ulfketil, and Yngvi.

"A pox on that," Einar retorted. "Odin only knows what's waiting behind that wall."

"Ivar is to the west, and the Fjordviper lads are to the north," said Halvdan. "We attack the walls from all sides. Go up, have a look, and let us know what you see."

"Frigg's tits," Einar cursed. He put his boot in Halvdan's cupped hands and reached for the first axe. Halvdan threw him upward and his breastplate scraped against the palisade as he grabbed the haft. He hauled himself higher and grabbed the second haft. Einar waited, muscles straining. He let go of the first axe and reached for the third, gripping it tightly. He closed his eyes, fearing that when he crested the spiked summit, a spear point would pierce his eyes or throat and kill him dead.

Einar lifted himself, and his right hand made the summit. He scratched for purchase between the roughly-hewn spikes, felt a splinter dig into his finger, and pulled himself up. His teeth gnashed, and he closed his eyes as his head poked over the spiked defences. Nothing happened. No spears, no pain. He opened one eye and scrutinised the sprawling network of wattle houses topped with earthen roofs. A dog stared back at him from where it licked water from a puddle. No defenders were behind the wall, nor any sign of life in the village at all.

"The place is empty," Einar called down. He pulled and used his boots to climb over the top and drop onto the fighting platform. He strolled along the palisade and even waved down to Vigmarr and the Seaworm crew, who lowered their shields and scratched their heads that Einar was alive inside the fortress. At first, Einar thought it was great fun, to have been brave enough to be first over the wall and to find it undefended and himself alive. So he danced a little jig, and a few of the warriors on the beach laughed. Einar waved again and was about to drop inside the fortress and open the gate when his brain started working. The thrill of climbing the wall and surviving gave way to clarity of thought. The town was empty because Dolgfinnr had emptied it. He knew Ivar was coming and had withdrawn his people and his warriors because…

A war horn blared long and loud and its sonorous note shook Einar's bones. It came from the hills around the fortress, sweeping pine forest and brush-covered hills where hundreds of warriors appeared, their spears and axe blades tinged red by the sun rising across the bay.

"Back!" Halvdan shouted from the bank below. "Back to the beach!"

Einar ran across the palisade, back to where he had scaled the walls. Another war horn sounded. With one hand on the wall, he risked a quick look up at the warriors on the hills, and his guts churned as a rain of arrows seemed to float from the forest, rising at first like a flock of thin, deadly birds, and then diving towards the town with murderous speed. He swung down from the wall, grabbing an axe and ripping it free before dropping the rest of the way. Einar landed on the bank and rolled into the ditch, his feet and hands sinking into the foul water. He grimaced and looked up to see Halvdan reaching down to him.

"Quickly!" Halvdan urged. Einar grabbed his arm and clambered out of the ditch. Arrows whistled and thudded into the town and its defences and to Einar's left and right, the crews of the Windspear and Fjordviper streamed across the beach towards their ships.

"Odin, save us," gasped Fat Garmr, his lean arm pointing out to sea. Einar's jaw dropped as more ships than he had ever seen appeared from the fog, which had begun to burn off under the rising sun. Sails filled the horizon; Einar counted a score and then could count no more. He followed the crew back to the shield wall, which had broken up as men fled into the tide towards their ship. A great cheer rose from Einar's left, where warriors charged from the hills, hurtling across the beach towards the crew of the Fjordviper.

Panic washed across the beach like a tidal wave as men ran for their lives. Einar splashed into the water, following his shipmates until a flash of green in the corner of his eye made him pause. Ivar the Boneless ran alone across the beach, away from his own men and towards the charging enemy, a sword in each hand and his green cloak flowing behind him like a horse's mane.

Vigmarr Svarti ran after Einar, hirpling on his bad leg, but with every stride the limp faded away until Vigmarr ran with the speed of a warrior half his age.

"Come on," Halvdan growled beside Einar, both men knee-deep in sea water and within twenty paces of the Seaworm and safety.

"Valhalla beckons."

Halvdan ran to join Vigmarr and Ivar, and Einar went with him. Before climbing the wall, he had left his shield and spear, so Einar drew his axe and seax and sprinted towards the enemy. Dolgfinnr knew they were coming. Perhaps a messenger on a small, swift ship had come from his uncle's village, or perhaps watching boats had seen Ivar's fleet approach. It didn't matter now. What mattered was Dolgfinnr knew, and he had the deep cunning of a starving wolf. He had abandoned his fortress and lured Ivar in for the kill, surrounding the town with his warriors, and a fleet at sea to block their escape. Dolgfinnr's charging men were closest to the Fjordviper's crew, and without protection during their retreat, the crew would die in the water like One Leg Bolti's men.

A dozen Fjordviper men were already fighting, standing bravely behind their shields as Dolgfinnr's men thundered into them with spears and axes. The rest of the crew splashed through the surf, wading towards their ship. On board Ivar's three warships, men hauled up the anchor stones, and those who ran fastest climbed up lowered ropes and prepared oars. Ivar didn't even break stride. He swerved around the Fjordviper shield wall and carved into the enemy with his deadly blades. Vigmarr joined him, tearing into the massed Vikings with a fury and skill Einar had never seen before.

Halvdan and Einar came in behind the two warlords, and Einar swung his axe at a man wearing a helmet and *brynjar*. That man saw the axe coming and shunted Einar with his shield, knocking him backwards onto his arse. Ivar killed a man with a thrust of one sword and skewered the belly of another with his second weapon. Vigmarr hooked his axe over the shield of the man who had barged Einar, and Halvdan slit his throat with a slash of his seax. Blood splashed, men screamed, and the salty air became tinged with the iron stink of blood.

Dolgfinnr's men shrank back from the three implacable warriors, and the Fjordviper men edged slowly back towards the sea. Einar surged to his feet and re-joined the fray. He swayed away from a spear aimed at his face and gutted the man with a cut of his axe.

"I am Ivar the Boneless!" Ivar roared at the enemy. "Who among you is brave enough to fight a Ragnarsson?"

A towering man with wolf fur draped about his shoulders burst from the enemy ranks, eyes bulging and teeth bared. He attacked Ivar with his spear, thrusting and slashing with its tip. Ivar bent under one thrust, and twisted and turned like a leaf in the wind. The spear stabbed into the space where Ivar had been and, in three rapid slashes of his twin swords, the wolf-pelted men fell to the sand, leaking his lifeblood into the tide.

"Get back to the ship," Halvdan urged the Fjordviper crew. "Go!"

They turned and ran into the water. Dolgfinnr Dogsblood's men retreated from Ivar, Vigmarr, Halvdan and Einar, even though they were many and Ivar's men were few, such was their skill and fury, and the shock of witnessing their wolf-pelted warriors cut down so viciously drove fear into enemy hearts.

"Time to go," said Ivar, seeming to emerge from his blood-mad rage. Half of the Fjordviper crew had reached their ship, men who would have surely died had Ivar not led his charge across the beach. "Make for the Seaworm." His cold eyes rested on Einar and, for an instant, a smile played on his lips, and then the four men ran into the sea, pounding through the shallow water towards the warship Seaworm. There was no honour in running from an enemy, no *drengskapr* in fleeing before enemy blades. But as Einar waded through the swell, he did not feel like a coward.

Water thumped and splashed around Einar, and his head shrank into his shoulders as an arrow whistled past his ear. Dolgfinnr's archers were loosing at them from the beach. The Seaworm shifted on the water as her oars bit, the great hull slewing close to Einar and nearly crashing into his skull. A rope flew over the side and Adzo appeared there, waving frantically at Einar to grab it. He did, and moments later he was aboard ship, dropping to the deck at the same time as Vigmarr, Ivar and Halvdan.

"Ivar the Boneless!" called a deep voice from shore. The baleful figure of Dolgfinnr Dogsblood stood before his warriors, his gargantuan war axe held in one hand, and the raven banner in the other. The white triangle flapped in the breeze and Dolgfinnr exaggerated a look up at the famous battle standard. "I have defeated you. I am the champion of the Northmen and you are nothing but an addled whore. I have your father's banner. Dolgfinnr Dogsblood is a better man than Ragnar Lothbrok, or any of his cowardly sons. I am better than you, Ivar, better than Bjorn Ironside, Sigurd Snake Eye, better than Ubba. I am Odin's favourite. You should kneel before me and beg my forgiveness for bringing your ragtag *slyðras* and fat-bellied ships to my shore."

His men shook their weapons in defiance and Ivar peered over the side, knuckles blanched as he gripped the sheerstrake. His soaking cloak hung limp about his shoulders and a cut on his neck bled freely.

"Look how your men die." Dolgfinnr pointed his axe at the Fjordviper. Two scores of Dolgfinnr's men loosed arrows at the ship, hammering it with shaft after shaft so that the crew could not organise their oars to get underway as arrows slapped into their backs, faces, legs and shoulders. Rorik roared like a bear as he wrestled with an oar, and then the big man died with an arrow in his eye, toppling overboard into the rolling sea.

The Seaworm banked as her oars bit, and she began to beat away from the murderous beach.

"Look out there, *nithing*," Dolgfinnr swept his axe out to sea, where the vast fleet grew closer, sails full and beast heads snarling. "Behold the army of Gudrød the Hunter, King of the Vestfold. My ally." Dolgfinnr cupped his ear and waited for Ivar to reply, for warlords took pride in the exchange of insults before and during war. But Ivar could not bring himself to speak. The muscles of his jaw worked beneath his skin, and his eyes burned with a malice, which, if Dolgfinnr had witnessed, he might not have spoken so boastfully.

"Two men to an oar," roared Halvdan, dragging men away from the side where they gaped at the oncoming fleet. "Row for your lives, shitworms!"

Einar found Adzo and sat next to him. Adzo shuffled along his rowing bench and Einar grabbed his oar. Both hauled, as did every man aboard, all but Ivar and Vigmarr, who just stared at their enemies, their thought cages broiling with blood-mad anger. The Windspear, being farthest from the enemy, was already in deeper waters, her shipmaster turning her bows and the sail unfurling from the yard. Einar pulled and pulled and the Seaworm lurched away from the beach, but the Fjordviper floundered under the hail of arrows, and dozens of Dolgfinnr's men waded out towards her. A warm wind blew into Einar's face as Halvdan pulled the steering oar and brought the Seaworm into deep water.

"Sail," Halvdan ordered, and six men leapt up their oars to follow his command. King Gudrød's ships swept about the coast like a flock of birds wheeling in a summer sky, and six of their number peeled away to cut off the Fjordviper's line of retreat. The Seaworm crew faced that unfolding tragedy as they rowed away. Ivar watched it all. He watched as Gudrød the Hunter's ships closed in and Dolgfinnr's men clambered on board the Fjordviper. He watched as the ships came alongside and warriors poured over the side to slaughter Ivar's oathmen.

The Seaworm's black sail spread and immediately billowed with wind. The prow rose in the water and the ship sped away from the carnage, from the slaughter and the defeat. Ivar had failed. Dolgfinnr lived, and the raven banner remained in the hands of Ivar's enemy.

FOURTEEN

The Seaworm and the Windspear ran before the wind, surging out into the Skagerrak's deep waters, the stretch of treacherous water spanning the gap between Norway's east coast and the western lands of the Svear folk. Gudrød the Hunter's ships followed, but only their *drakkars* could keep pace with Ivar's slick warships. The king's larger ships, the vessels carrying great numbers of warriors, were more akin to fat-bellied trading *knarrs* than warships, and those vessels and the smaller *karve* warships soon fell behind. Ivar took the Seaworm's steering oar himself and followed the wind as it changed direction in the late afternoon and banked north west. The king's *drakkars* followed, and Ivar led them towards the myriad islands and hidden fjords which made up the kingdom of Geirstad, the southerly neighbouring kingdom of King Gudrød's kingdom of the Vestfold.

The crew fought with the rigging and Halvdan

showed his mastery of the sea, shifting and altering the rigging, moving the yard and tacking when required to make sure that the Seaworm caught every scrap of wind. It was a silent voyage, tinged with the stain of defeat and the humiliation of running from an enemy they had set out to kill. The Windspear followed, and when the two ships slipped between minute islands set before the narrow entrance to an inland fjord, Halvdan ordered the sail dropped and oars set. Then Ivar guided them towards a network of inconspicuous islands within a large fjord, the crew pulling for their lives until their backs burned and Gudrød's ships disappeared from view.

Einar had never worked so hard. Sweat drenched his jerkin, fatigue shook his muscles, and blisters had burst by the time the sun began to dip. Blood seeped into his oar. The friction of endless rowing had worn through his skin and torn his palms to ribbons. When Ivar finally called the halt, men collapsed on the deck whilst others peered over the side, waiting for any sign of Gudrød the Hunter's ships and their painted prows and shields. The Seaworm and Windspear drifted into an inlet, little more than a scrap of filthy beach strewn with sea debris, rocks, and fallen boughs from the forest behind. Ivar had found an island too trifling to be inhabited, too densely covered with forest for any man to make it his home. They waited there aboard ship, drifting silently, waiting for the tide to ebb, oars at the ready in case the king's fleet should appear suddenly from the south and the chase began again.

Only when the sun touched the horizon and the sea turned black with shadow, did Ivar give the nod that the men could go ashore. They rowed right up to the tiny beach until sand and shale scraped the hull and beached the ships for the night.

"Tide doesn't flood or ebb much in these waters," observed Thorkild as he gathered up his bedding and a warm cloak. "She'll flood in the morning, though, and we'll be afloat again."

"Do we bring the injured ashore?" Einar asked, grabbing his own cloak and blanket from beneath his oar bench.

"Aye, they need rest and a meal as much as we do."

The crew leapt down onto the beach. Einar and Adzo helped Thorkild, Bersa, and Ginnlaug carry the wounded men onto dry land. Yngvi the Fire busied himself with his kindling, flint, and iron, and before long, a blaze burned before the overhanging forest. Five fires sparked up across the little beach, so that the crews of both ships could be warm for the evening. The crews gathered about them and shared a meal of ale, oatcakes and cheese taken from the ship's stores. They sat in the grip of melancholy, thinking of the dead and how close they had come to meeting that fate themselves. Einar remembered capering on the walls of Dolgfinnr's fortress like a fool, and his face flushed with embarrassment.

"I ask Odin to protect my cousin," said a Windspear warrior as the two crews ate in silence. "He sailed on the Fjordviper, and I do not know his fate."

The crews made a hoom in their throats. They were the first words spoken beside the campfire and four other men said the same, that they wished Odin to care for the relatives who had either perished or faced capture on board the lost Fjordviper.

"The body has gone," whispered Adzo, making the sign of the cross and pointing to the Windspear's hull where Ivar had lashed Dolgfinnr's uncle's corpse.

"It won't frighten Dolgfinnr now," Einar replied. "He tricked us and almost killed us. We are now lost in Norway, with the king's fleet pursuing us. The crew must have cut the old man loose at sea."

"They did it to ward off the ill luck, I'd wager," said Styrr quietly. "Before all their *hamingjas* became tainted with it."

"Close your cheese pipe," Halvdan barked, pointing a thick finger at Styrr. "There's no bad luck or will of the gods in this, before all of you gossip like a bunch of fishwives. Dolgfinnr outsmarted us, that's all. He's done it twice. Dolgfinnr met One Leg Bolti on the beach before he could get organised. He knew Bolti would come in a fury and he slaughtered him for his foolishness. We did the same. Believed we were stronger, that Ivar could overcome anything." Halvdan jutted his chin to where Ivar stood beside Vigmarr, his arms folded, glaring at the sea. "We never for a moment thought Dolgfinnr had such deep cunning. He lured us in and punished us for our arrogance."

"I've barely seen those two speak before now," mused Einar, watching as Ivar and Vigmarr Svarti talked alone in the darkness.

"Aye, well, they have to now. No choice. We can't go home with our tails between our legs like whipped dogs. Ivar won't do it. He'd rather die. His brothers and father would ridicule him, destroying his reputation forever. There's grim axe work coming, lads, and no mistake. So best eat heartily and prepare yourselves."

"What about Vigmarr?"

"What about him?"

"Will he want to fight, or return to Hrafnborg

for more ships and more men?"

Halvdan scoffed and shook his head. "What do you think? Have you learned nothing yet?"

"We face the champion of the North, the best fighter amongst men who call themselves Vikings. He has shown himself to be as cunning as a fox, as well as a great war leader. We have two crews left and one crew dead. That's what, a hundred and a half men? Dolgfinnr has broken his oath to Ragnar and allied with King Gudrød of the Vestfold, and he has an army at his back. How can we fight that?"

"I don't know, lad. I know how to sail from Hrafnborg to Frankia, from there to Hedeby or down to Lake Ladoga, and on through the rapids of the River Dnieper to the fine city of Novgorod the Great. I can rig a ship, kill a man, skin a deer and have sired three children. But how we are going to kill Dolgfinnr and recover the raven banner? I do not know."

"But Vigmarr will want to fight. We all know that. Why does he thirst for battle so?"

Halvdan sucked his teeth. "Most of us here are lovers of battle. You have it in you, young Einar the Brawler. You rush to the front when the weapons clash and you have no fear. But Vigmarr is different. Without war, he isn't a man. It's like he isn't alive. It's all he lives for."

"How did he get like that?"

"I've sailed with him for five summers. Others like Thorkild and Palni much longer. He's been like that as long as I've known him. I joined his crew because, after Ragnar and Sten, he's the most feared jarl in Ragnar's forces. No man would fight Vigmarr Svarti willingly, not unless he wants to die. I heard an old timer say once that Vigmarr was different when he was younger, that he had a wife and children. But that was long ago. Since then, he has killed so many men, sent untold souls to Valhalla and Sessrúmnir. But he makes his crew rich. I've never had so much silver as I've had since I joined the Seaworm. I've sold more arm rings than I wear." He jangled his forearms, thick with gold and silver rings. "Thorkild, you've known Vigmarr longer than most. What was he like as a younger man?"

Thorkild grumbled, glanced at Einar, and then stared at the fire. "He wasn't born the way he is now, that's for sure," he said. "But nor did he crawl from some Loki pit or spawn in the land of the frost giants. When a man has seen enough death, killed enough men, it changes him. Vigmarr has been burned, stabbed, and cut. He's taken countless wounds and seen more men die than we can imagine. Perhaps his soul is changed, altered in some way. What if all the blood and terrible blade wounds have addled his mind and turned him into a thing of darkness, a twisted man whose soul only comes alive in the wild fury of battle? But that's enough for now. We've had enough fell news today and ill-tidings. Best leave some things in the past where they belong."

"One thing's for sure," said Styrr after a sup of ale, which left glistening droplets in his beard. "There's two of those poor bastards that won't last the night." He gestured to Palni and the injured warriors who lay with their heads propped up by a coil of rope. Palni's chest rose and fell in rapid breaths and his face was as blue as old cheese.

"I think he's beyond your care now," said Halvdan. "Though you did care for him. More than most would have done."

Einar took that to mean his duty to Palni was over.

"Can he go to your warriors' heaven?" asked Adzo.

"Don't mention that," warned Thorkild, as every man about the fire made the sign to ward off evil and bowed their heads. "All men know it's better to die in battle than of the wound days later."

"But if he had drowned?"

"He would now be in Ran's watery kingdom of the dead. There's not much difference between that hel for the drowned and Niflheim, where souls who do not die gloriously wander until the Ragnarök. That's if you ask me, anyway."

"Enough talk of death and dying," said Halvdan. "We aren't dead yet. Ivar won't give up. You'll see."

Ivar turned sharply, as if he had heard Halvdan's words. He marched towards the campfires, trailed by Vigmarr Svarti and his laboured limping gait. The Boneless strode amongst the warriors and climbed up onto a grassy knoll at the forest's edge. He stood there for a moment, firelight dancing on the sharp planes of his face, cold eyes searching amongst the men sitting beneath him as if he tested their mettle for the war to come, sensing if they were prepared and able for what he would have them do. Vigmarr stood beside him, slipping back into the gloaming like a wraith, his black cloak and crow-like plume becoming one with the darkness so that all that remained was his malignant presence making the air thicker.

"We lost men today," Ivar said, his voice calm. "We lost the Fjordviper and seventy brave carls. Dolgfinnr bested us, out-thought me. He still carries the raven banner in an affront to my family." He paused for a second and shivered, fighting to master himself. "War is about more than the clash of arms. We showed bravery today, none more so than you, Einar Rosti." Ivar slipped a silver ring from his left wrist and tossed it to Einar.

"Thank you, lord," Einar said, catching the ring. He could not hide his surprise or his pleasure at being so honoured. The ring was finely wrought, with three strands of silver twisted and coiled together like rope with an eagle's beak at each end. Einar marvelled at it and slipped it over his wrist so that he now wore a ring on each arm. Some veteran carls only wore one ring, others none, having sold them for whores or ale at distant ports. Men of reputation wore rings thick on their arms as a symbol of their fighting prowess, and for the first time, Einar felt like one of them.

"Bravery without cunning, without planning, is how fools go to war. Dolgfinnr ambushed and trapped us like we were base animals. We cannot go home mired in defeat. I cannot return to my father without the raven banner, the symbol of his and my descent from Odin. We are outnumbered and in a foreign land. So we must fight a different war. We have our bravery, we have warriors worth ten of theirs. We have two of the fastest ships upon the Whale Road and we must use things to our advantage. We will strike like serpents and hunt like wolves. We must find something precious to Dolgfinnr and seize it so that we can bend him to our will. We shall separate his forces and destroy Dolgfinnr and this nithing King Gudrød piecemeal, cutting them down like firewood for winter.

"King Gudrød brought a fleet south from Vestfold, and we are outnumbered. But how long can he keep that fleet and army at sea and away from their homes? Who is going to feed so many warriors? Dolgfinnr's small settlement has grain, and animals enough to feed his own people. There were more than a score of ships in that fleet. That's close to a thousand mouths to feed. I tell you this, men, we shall not return to Hrafnborg until Dolgfinnr Dogsblood is dead, and I have the raven banner in my hand. We shall do it even if it costs every one of us our lives. It begins tomorrow. So prepare yourselves."

"But we could wait for Ragnar's fleet to return from Frankia and attack next summer with our entire army," said a man from the Windspear's crew.

Ivar's head snapped around and his face changed, eyes narrow, jaw tensed, mouth twisted. Vigmarr stepped out of the gloom and every man at the campfires leaned away from him. He limped to the closest fire and brushed his hair back from his face with his hand. He stood close to the flames, warming his hands on the fire, allowing the light to shift and dance across his ravaged face.

"No waiting," Vigmarr rasped, his voice like

a ship's hull dragged over gravel. "No quarter. No mercy. Just war, ruin, and death. My time. Your time. We take fire and blood to Dolgfinnr, and may Odin help his folk when we come." Vigmarr's vast body shook as a wracking cough bent him double. Then he seemed to laugh his strange, silent shoulder-shuddering laugh and more than one man made the sign against evil with a hidden hand.

"Tomorrow, then," said Ivar. "We take the war to land. We can't fight a bigger fleet at sea. A skeleton crew will take the Windspear and Seaworm out to sea and keep away from Gudrød and Dolgfinnr's ships. We fight on foot. Sleep well tonight, men, for you shall need it."

Ivar leapt lightly down from his knoll and stalked towards the Windspear, one hand resting on the sword hilt strapped to his belt. Vigmarr went to sit alone by the sea, and the warriors talked amongst themselves in hushed voices.

"We'll be lucky to survive this war," Adzo whispered. "Ivar will lead us all to our deaths rather than admit defeat."

"And yet he is our lord," Einar snapped, tired of the moaning and complaining. "We swore our oaths to Ivar, and if he leads us to our deaths, then so be it. That is what we swore to do, to follow him into battle no matter what the cost."

Einar stood and left the crew by the fire.

He sat beside Palni and wiped the sweat from his brow with a scrap of cloth. Einar sat and watched as, one by one, the carls fell asleep by the fire. He wore his own fleece cloak and pulled it tight about his shoulders as the night breeze grew cold. The group of wounded men lay still beneath their blankets, each of them close to death, lying in that netherworld between this life and the next. Einar felt wide awake, even after the exhausting rowing and fighting. His mind buzzed with Ivar and Vigmarr's promise of a brutal war to come, and of his own actions that day. He had won another arm ring, which only a week ago had seemed like an impossible dream. Einar had fought beside Ivar and Vigmarr, two men of reputation.

"Water!" yelped Palni, suddenly sitting up straight with his mouth wide open.

"Thor's balls," Einar cried, recovering after almost jumping out of his skin. "Lay down, we don't have water. But here, drink this." Einar took a skin of ale and poured a drizzle into Palni's parched lips.

"Thank you, Egil."

"I am Einar, Egil's son."

"Egil's son? Ah, yes. I remember now." He wheezed and lay back, closing his eyes, his ragged breath making a strange whistling sound.

"Sleep, Palni."

"I remember Egil. We were young together. So long ago."

"You must tell me a story of you and my father when you are well. But for now, save your breath and sleep."

"He was my friend, and Vigmarr too." His head flopped to one side and his voice came only as a faint whisper. "All friends together. Until Vigmarr slew him."

Einar rocked as if slapped. He bent closer to Palni in case he had misheard. "What did you say?"

"The three of us were friends, and Thorkild. Vigmarr killed Egil, cut him down like a dog."

"My father died in battle."

"No…" Palni coughed and thick blood spat from his mouth.

"How did he die?"

"Vigmarr cut his throat… no Valhalla… a cursed act."

"Vigmarr killed my father?"

Palni groaned. Einar shook his shoulder, desperate to hear more, but Palni rolled onto his back and one last gasp escaped his ruined chest as he died. Einar's head swam. He had always believed that his father had died with honour in battle. Einar stood and stumbled to his blanket, walking like a drunkard, head swimming as everything he had ever believed melted like iron in a white-hot forge. He needed to know more, to understand if what Palni had said with his last breath was true. Had Vigmarr killed his father, or was it simply the ramblings of a dying man out of his mind with the rotting sickness? Einar thought about waking Thorkild to ask him, or challenging Vigmarr himself. But if he woke Thorkild, then the rest of the crew would wake and every man of the Seaworm crew would know that Einar believed Vigmarr had killed his father.

Einar returned to Palni and pulled his cloak up, covering his face. He said a prayer to Odin and Freya that they might find room for Palni in the halls of the dead, that they might judge his past deeds rather than by his ignominious death on an unknown beach. If the gods would not accept Palni into their magnificent halls, then he would slip down the nine worlds held up by Yggdrasil, the great tree. He would slip down into Niflheim, the dark hell at the bottom of all nine realms propped up by the tree's huge boughs. Einar held his amulet and hoped that Palni's soul was not now passing through Nágrind, the corpse gate to Niflheim, which was guarded by a terrible hound. He imagined Palni crossing the river, which churned with knives and axes and clashing blocks of ice, and finally over the golden thatched Gjallarbrú bridge into the hel world and its endless darkness. Einar shivered, hoping that would not be his own fate.

He lay back and stared up at the stars as they appeared and disappeared behind fast-moving clouds turned into shifting shadows by the night. If Vigmarr had killed his father, then Einar had to avenge him. It meant the blood feud, that Einar's soul was cursed if he did not seek retribution for his father's slaying. Moments came back to haunt Einar as his eyes became heavy; half-glances from Vigmarr across the deck, comments and looks from other warriors and whispers when they thought Einar could not hear. He tried to remember comments made in the homes of his father's friends when Einar was a boy living under their roofs, of talk when they thought young Einar was asleep. His eyes closed and sleep came, and Einar could not tell if such things were real, or if his mind and memories played tricks on him after the shock of Palni's last words.

Sleep came, unwelcome and fleeting. Einar tossed and turned, eyes stinging with exhaustion, his head shifting over and over the revelation. He woke with a start, lying on his side in the darkness, and opened one eye to see the fire burned out so that it was little more than a pile of glowing ashes. Something moved in the corner of his eye, and Einar lay still. With his one open eye, he looked across the fire and saw it, a figure moving in darkness, crawling like a wolf across a sheep pasture. The figure moved slowly, picking its way through the sleeping warriors. It came in Einar's direction, slinking and sneaking like an evil spirit in the darkness. Einar sat up and grabbed his seax. The figure stopped, and as Einar's eyes became accustomed to the gloom, he saw it was Fulk, the masterless man.

Fulk paused on all fours. He smiled, broken, brown teeth showing in the ragged tangle of his unkempt beard. He picked up a skin of ale and drank from it.

"Where are you going?" Einar said, gripping his seax tight.

"I'm thirsty, that's all," Fulk said, and shook the ale skin as if that proved his point. "No need to get your breeches in a twist, young warrior. Go back to sleep."

Fulk winked and crawled back to his blanket. Einar watched him and lay down, but did not take his eyes off the Frank. Someone had followed him during the raid on Dolgfinnr's uncle's village. He had heard it, sensed it. Now Fulk had tried to sneak up on him in the night. There was no mistaking it. Einar was certain. Fulk was trying to kill him, and Vigmarr Svarti had killed his father.

Just as Einar had thought he had achieved his dream, had become a carl in Ivar's crews rewarded with rings and recognised for his bravery, his world came crashing down like a burned hall. Desire for vengeance kindled in Einar's heart like Yngvi's fires, catching fire until it raged like the brightest blaze. He had to find the truth of it, know exactly what befallen Egil so long ago, leaving Einar alone in the world with no home and nothing but a promise of a place on a Viking crew. If Fulk wanted to kill him, let him come, for Einar was no longer the callow youth he had been at Hrafnborg. He had killed a man in single combat, had sailed the Whale Road, fought in the shield wall, and stood in battle beside the Boneless himself.

Ivar and his crews were in a fight for their lives, and a battle for their honour. They must kill Dolgfinnr Dogsblood and save the raven banner. But Einar had to know if Vigmarr Svarti had killed his father, and if so, then it would be a summer of blood and vengeance.

FIFTEEN

At first light, the crews made a funeral pyre for Palni, and Thorkild spoke solemn words before it. Then, Ivar led his two warships south west. They rowed through the countless islands off Geirstad's coast into a sea squall, where driving rain and blustery wind lashed the ship and crews as though the gods tried to blow them away from their destination. Einar pulled his oar with grim determination. He rowed in silence, using the rhythm to help order his thoughts. Had Vigmarr Svarti killed his father and was Fulk trying to kill him? The answer to the first question lay with Thorkild Storyteller, or with Vigmarr himself. They were the last men aboard who had crewed the warship Seaworm in Egil's day, the only two men who knew the truth. Fulk rowed three benches behind Einar, and he could feel the Frank's eyes boring into his back like daggers. Back at Hrafnborg, Einar would have feared Fulk, would have worried that a grown man, a tested warrior, a masterless man who had journeyed north from his homelands to join a fearsome Viking war-crew, wanted to kill him. But Einar was not in Hrafnborg anymore. He was a warrior himself, with two arm rings and proven in battle. Einar wondered if he should kill Fulk before he tried to strike again, or should he wait until his suspicions were proven? But if he had been asleep last night when Fulk stalked towards him, Einar might have died next to Palni and joined him on his journey to Niflheim.

Rain coursed down Einar's face, stinging his eyes and lips. He tasted sea salt, and his jerkin clung to his back. His hands no longer hurt. Thick calluses ridged his palms, and his back and arm muscles had become accustomed to pulling an oar. Once Ivar and Vigmarr were certain that they had lost the enemy fleet, the Seaworm banked landward, veering towards a gash in the headland where a river led deep into Norway's hinterland. Dolgfinnr's fortress lay further south, but to approach it at sea risked meeting King Gudrød's fleet. Einar guessed the river was somewhere between Geirstad's border with Agder, the country in which Dolgfinnr's lands and fortress lay. The ships put into the river mouth, where they could row along its meanders, beside banks thick with reeds and heavy with silt. The men disembarked, taking their weapons and food supplies ashore.

The men hefted shields and shared out rations

of oatcakes, skins of ale, cheese, hard bread and smoked fish. With morose faces, they watched as skeleton crews of ten men rowed the Seaworm and the Windspear away from the river mouth and out to sea.

"We are stranded here," said Adzo.

"That's the idea," Einar replied, slipping his axe into its belt loop and his seax into its sheath. He wore his hard-baked leather breastplate and a russet cloak, his shield slung across his back and helmet tied to its strap. Einar carried a long spear and a sack containing his rations, spare trews and jerkin, and his wool cloak for sleeping.

"No turning back now, shitworms," said Halvdan cheerfully. "Say goodbye to our precious ship. All that lies before us now is war. There's nowhere to run, no quick escape if things get nasty. Defeat now means death. So get used to it."

Ivar led one hundred and twelve men along the riverbank. He marched with Halvdan and two seasoned warriors from the Windspear's crew. Vigmarr Svarti marched in the rear with Einar and ten men from the Seaworm. Styrr, Ulfketil, Bersa, and Ginnlaug ranged inland, scouting the hills and forest for any signs of settlements, enemies, fortifications, and danger.

"Who is the king of this place?" asked Fat Garmr. He trudged beside Einar and Adzo with his spear resting on his shoulder.

"King Harald Granraude," replied Thorkild. He marched just behind them, and only Vigmarr Svarti was further back in the column. The hulking jarl walked along, limping along all in black, using a spear as a walking stick.

"And Dolgfinnr is his vassal?"

"Dolgfinnr swore allegiance to our Lord Ragnar Lothbrok until he broke his oath and became an ally of King Gudrød. Dolgfinnr seized a portion of coastal land in King Harald's kingdom years ago. He killed its jarl and took the hall and land for himself. Agder is a small kingdom. King Harald's kingdom stretches from the Skagerrak straits inland to a dense forest which separates his land from the kingdom of Rogaland, and Geirstad to the northeast. I have been to Agder before, both raiding and trading. It has wide fjords to sail into, natural harbours, many villages to plunder. So Harald's coastal jarls are Vikings, hard men to control, but good for defending his sea borders. I once sailed up the river Otra with Ragnar, and we visited the king's hall at Kongsham, at the mouth of a glass-still fjord. He has another hall, on an island, but we visited his fjord hall and he seemed like a good man, if a little gentle, for a king amongst the Northmen."

"Gudrød is king of the Vestfold, far north of here. The kingdom of Geirstad lies between

Agder and Vestfold. How can Dolgfinnr hold land in Agder and be allied with the King of Vestfold?"

"All good questions, but alas, I do not have the answers."

"There is a feud," said Fulk in his Frankish accent, so like Adzo's, but harsher, with a lisp and a seemingly always amused tone. "King Gudrød proposed marriage to King Harald's daughter, Åsa. King Harald's refusal insulted and enraged King Gudrød. So now, Gudrød and Harald are enemies."

"How do you know this?" asked Einar, irked by the sound of Fulk's voice.

"I heard the tale on my journey north."

"Where? How is it you ended up at Hrafnborg?" Einar felt Adzo staring at him in surprise. They were the youngest of the crew, and when the warriors talked, Einar and Adzo usually remained quiet unless spoken to. But Einar had fought, wore two arm rings, and he had earned his right to speak.

"I sailed on a merchant's ship across the Kattegat Sea last summer, and I heard the tale from him. He was in Agder last winter, trading pelts for iron."

"How did you end up on a merchant's ship?"

"Too many questions this morning, lad."

"I'm no lad. I'm a carl, just like you."

"Just so." Fulk laughed. "I was sworn to a lord south of the Kattegat strait. We fought a neighbour, and he died. So, the few of us that remained of his hearth troop left his lands seeking new lords. I took a berth on a merchant's ship. Like all men, I had heard of Ragnar Lothbrok's greatness and his hunger for warriors to join his crews. So I came to Hrafnborg."

"Far from Frankia."

"Sounds like Agder is about to be at war," said Thorkild, changing the subject to kill the obvious tension between Einar and Fulk.

"Would two kings really go to war because one refused the other his daughter's hand in marriage?" asked Adzo.

"What does a king, and a warrior for that matter, have but his pride and his honour? King Harald's refusal of King Gudrød's proposal insulted him. What else can he do?"

"Marry another young maiden?"

"If only life were so simple. If a king lets a slight like that go unanswered, how long before men whisper of his weakness? How long before a strong jarl challenges him for the throne? Better to have war on another king's land than within his own kingdom, and between his own oathmen."

"Perhaps King Gudrød could request a killer to kill King Harald?" Einar said. "He could find a killer to slip a dagger into his back in the dark of night, a masterless man perhaps, a man of no honour who would gladly kill for a handful of silver."

Fulk chortled behind him, and Einar balled his fists.

"A knife in the dark is not *drengskapr*," said Thorkild. "King Harald most likely tolerates Dolgfinnr on his lands because there isn't much he can do about it without raising an army to throw him out. We all saw Dolgfinnr's fortress; you climbed its walls, Einar. To attack that place, King Harald would have to raise his entire army, feed them, pay them, and lose most of them in the attempt."

"So he leaves Dolgfinnr alone in exchange for peace."

"That's probably the way of it. Perhaps the king exacts a tribute from Dolgfinnr; silver, fleeces, hides, grain. Who knows?"

Lapsing into silence, the column of warriors followed the river north west before seeking higher ground. The waterway led them into a land of rolling hills and flat, fertile plains. Its hills were modest compared to the heights and cliffs of Denmark, and Ivar led the men up a gentle slope, heavy with wild grasses and hardy shrubs. The day wore on until the crews reached a dense forest of birch trees, with stark white bark shining against dark green ferns and briar, sturdy oaks and slender alders. They made camp on the northern side of a hilltop, in between thick brush, pine, and spruce trees. Yngvi started a fire, and the men made crude shelters from branches, cloaks, and tents of old sailcloth.

A dozen warriors, including the archers Adzo, Bersa, and Ginnlaug, went hunting for deer, wild boar, hares and foxes to make an evening meal. Halvdan organised a scouting party, and Einar was honoured when the shipmaster called his name. He marched with Ivar, Halvdan, Styrr and three of Ivar's trusted carls from the Windspear's crew. Ivar's three men all wore shining chainmail *brynjars*, marking them out as warriors with reputations to fear. Few men could afford the expensive armour made of thousands of interlinked iron rings, and any who wore a *brynjar* to war were fearsome enough to stop others from taking it from them, or paid men to protect their wealth. Ivar's men were the former.

"Radbod, Likbjorn and Skallagrimr," said Styrr, introducing the three men to Einar. "This is Einar the Brawler. He might look young and have a beard as sparse as a Finn's barley field, but he fights like a dog with a wasp in its mouth."

Einar supposed that was high praise from

Styrr in his blue and white trews and tattooed arms.

"Good to have you with us," said Radbod, a grizzled veteran with bear fur about his neck, shoulders, and the rim of his helmet, which he wore despite marching through the forest.

Skallagrimr was a squat, heavily-muscled man twice Einar's age, with a jagged scar running the length of his bald head and a thick black beard reaching almost to his eyes. He inclined his head in greeting, as did Likbjorn, a tall, square-jawed man with a full-faced helmet hanging from his belt and a long-handled war axe strapped to his back.

"What are we looking for?" Einar asked, conscious that he was the youngest in the scouting party, but not wanting to appear like an inexperienced boy in front of such seasoned men.

"A village or farm where we can get supplies," said Styrr.

"Anywhere to burn and destroy," added Radbod.

"We don't know where King Harald's land ends and Dolgfinnr's begins," said Ivar. He came from a clutch of trees, one sword at his belt and one across his back. He wore his black hair pulled back and tied at the nape of his neck. "So we raze it all. Take what we need on the march. Eventually, one of them will come for us."

"What if the king brings his army?" asked Radbod.

Ivar smiled, his amiable friendliness returned despite their dire situation. "If King Harald could quickly and easily raise his army, he would have thrown Dolgfinnr the bastard out long ago. But he lets Dogsblood perch on the edge of his kingdom like a wart on a donkey's balls. If the king sends anybody after us, it will be his hearth troop, the warriors he keeps at his hall and pays to fight for him all year round. Hopefully..." he paused, picked up a spear from the ground and tossed it to Einar, who caught it, "we are in Dolgfinnr's land. If his men come, then they shall die. We'll draw Dolgfinnr out and whittle his forces down until they fear us."

"What of the king's men?"

"What of them?" Ivar raised an eyebrow.

"Do we fight them?"

"Any bastard who stands against us dies. We do not stop until Dolgfinnr is dead and I have the raven banner in my hand. Let's get moving."

Einar marched in between Styrr and Halvdan, his boots crunching through foliage and brush until they reached the hill's summit. He decided to talk to Thorkild at camp that night and find out if what Palni said was true. He had to know. Better to ask Thorkild than confront Vigmarr Svarti without knowing for sure. To confront Vigmarr was to poke a bear sleeping peacefully in its cave. Vigmarr would consider it a challenge, and he would only answer a challenge in one way.

The small warband reached a set of sun-bleached boulders covered in lichen, set in a gap between the trees. The land swept away southwards, sun shining in patches through thick waxen clouds to illuminate tilled fields, grazing pastures and a glistening river running through it all like a coiling serpent. Below them lay a village of three longhouses. Timber buildings with steeply-pitched roofs covered with earth abundant with grass and weeds, so that the houses seemed to have sprouted from the earth like living things. Smoke drifted from the longhouses, seeping through the roofs in small spindles, and a low wooden fence ringed the settlement where chickens and goats roamed freely and four pigs squatted in a pen close to the forest's edge.

"That will do, for starters," said Ivar, pointing down at the small village.

"There might be a handful of warriors down there," cautioned Radbod. "Place like that will be defended. Even if it's just farmers with axes and reaping hooks."

"Nothing you can't handle. I once saw you kill a Rus Druzhina in full armour with your bare hands. A muddy-faced farmer with a broom shouldn't give you too much trouble." Ivar winked and set off down the hillside.

"At least he's cheered up," observed Skallagrimr, slipping his axe from his belt.

"Good," answered Likbjorn, pushing his full-faced helmet over his head. "Normally, when things go bad, Ivar starts killing people. At least there are other people to kill now, not Windspear men."

They hurried down the wood-covered hill and into a set of well-tended fields of barley and rye, and the seven men spread out into a line. Einar carried his spear and followed Ivar's lead as the son of Ragnar whistled a cheerful tune. When they were halfway across a barley field, ten men appeared from the longhouses. Men in drab clothes, some carrying wood axes and knives, and three armed with spears.

"Looks like there will be a fight after all," Ivar said cheerfully.

"What do you want us to do, Lord?" asked Halvdan.

"Kill them, take whatever we can use, and burn the buildings."

"Who are you?" shouted one man, standing

before the village fence. He was middle-aged with a bulging paunch and deep-set blue eyes, wielding a spear.

"I am Ivar the Boneless," Ivar said and drew one of his swords from its scabbard. "Who rules these lands?"

The man shifted his feet and stared at the line of warriors approaching him. "You are Danes?"

"We are. Who rules these lands?" Ivar repeated his question, this time with more severity in his voice and a flick of his shining blade. Patterns of smoke ran up the sword's length, blueish patterns woven into its very being by the blade's smith in his white-hot forge. A man with a sword was a man to fear, a powerful lord or famous warrior. A sword was as expensive as a *brynjar*, and a man with both was a rare sight. To kill a man like Ivar was to become instantly rich, to have enough wealth to buy a dozen villages, perhaps even to buy a ship. But killing Ivar the Boneless was to face a lethal warrior, a swordsman of unequalled skill and speed.

"Jarl Floki Thorvaldsson rules here, lord." He called Ivar lord simply because he looked like one with his armour and weapons.

"Who is king over Jarl Floki's lands?"

"King Harald, I think, Lord."

"Then we've come to the right place." Ivar

smiled at his men.

"If it's food and drink you want, we can give you whatever you need. There doesn't need to be any trouble."

"Ah, but there must." Ivar ran, closing the distance between him and the farmer in five long strides. The farmer lowered his spear, but he was a man used to ploughing fields and tending animals, and Ivar was a brutal killer. Ivar's sword cut the farmer open from belly to chest and before the farmer had fallen to his knees, Styrr, Likbjorn, Skallagrimr and Radbod were scything into the rest of the farmers with skilful brutality. Einar slid his axe back into his belt and followed Halvdan, who marched past the slaughter. They hopped over the fence and strode towards the longhouses. Six women stood holding hands outside the main building, sobbing and staring at Einar with faces pulled taut with fear.

"Go," Einar said. "Run for the hills." Einar had been raised on stories of *drengskapr*, of the warrior's code. Women suffered in war, there was no hiding from that. It had always been so. But Einar couldn't bear to watch what the warriors would do to those women if they were caught. The women just stared at him, too frightened to move, too dumbstruck at the sudden destruction of their peaceful lives to react. So Einar ran at them, roaring like a madman until they fled from him.

"Don't be soft, Brawler," chided Halvdan. He strode towards the closest longhouse and watched the women flee for their lives. "You can't save them all. Best get used to it. Some men see women like that as the spoils of war."

"You don't?'

Halvdan shrugged. "I've a wife at home, lad, and three children to think of. When I tell my boys about my voyages and try to teach them to live with honour, how to be a *drengr*, I don't want my memories clouded by rape and murder. Think on that and live your life how you see fit. It's not for me to tell you what to do, lad."

"What about Jarl Vigmarr?'

"He's a killer. You know that. Never come between Vigmarr and his prey, nor that of the crew. These women are to be pitied, but don't die protecting them. That's the job of their menfolk. This is the world we live in. We must protect our families from the sea-wolves, just as a shepherd protects his flock."

Einar wandered around the village until he found a stable where four horses' heads poked from open stalls. He went to the first, a black gelding, and stroked its long nose.

"We'll give the black one to old Vigmarr Svarti," said Ivar, appearing at Einar's side, his face now stippled with dead men's blood. "Let him loose on the land. Odin help them when Vigmarr goes raiding."

Einar nodded and Ivar left him alone. Everything on the voyage so far fitted in seamlessly with Einar's dreams of becoming a warrior. Sailing aboard the Seaworm, rowing the ship, shield wall battles and daring bravery. He had known raiding was part of that life, but he had only ever thought of shining silver and gold plunder, not of the people who had to die to make the raiders rich. He found Styrr carrying a burning log from one house.

"I'll burn this one," Styrr said. "You check the smaller one for food and ale, then burn it."

Einar did as he was told. He found two hams hanging from the rafters to cure amongst the hearth smoke, and he took them down and carried them outside to where Ivar and the others gathered anything else of value. Then he followed Styrr's lead, took a smouldering log from the fire, and set the building alight. Less than an hour later, he, Radbod and Likbjorn marched, each of them carrying a sack of food on their shoulders, following Ivar, Halvdan, Styrr and Skallagrimr, who rode four horses towards the hillside.

Smoke billowed behind Einar and he left the farmers' corpses behind him. They returned to the crews to find a blazing fire and a comfortable camp made for the night. The men cheered when Ivar handed over the looted supplies, and soon, meat roasted over the fire and ale flowed. Night fell, and Thorkild told a tale of Thor and one of his great battles against the jötnar, the frost giants, in their icy kingdom. The men laughed and clapped as Thorkild used his lyre and his sleekit tones to bring the story to life. Einar heard none of it, however. He watched Thorkild's mouth open and close and his beard quiver as the words poured out, but all Einar could hear was his own mind. *He knows if Vigmarr Svarti killed my father.*

SIXTEEN

"How can you be sure?" asked Adzo. He ran a hand over his mouth and shook his head. Einar had led his friend away from the campfire halfway through Thorkild's tale.

"I can't be sure. That's why I need to ask Thorkild," Einar replied. He had pulled Adzo to one side for advice, to share his problems, hoping Adzo could provide some worthwhile advice.

"What if you ask Thorkild and he tells Vigmarr?"

"I have thought of that."

"Are you sure Fulk was going to kill you? What if he was just getting a drink, like he said?"

"He was sneaking up on me to slit my throat. I could tell by his eyes. You must have seen the way he looks at me? Always staring, always watching."

"I haven't noticed. If you accuse him, he'll be

angry. You'll insult him and Fulk will have to respond. There'll be a fight, Einar. I know how you Norsemen think, and any insult, real or perceived, has to be answered with the axe."

"Fulk is a Frank, like you."

"He might have been born in Frankia, but he thinks like a Viking. Fulk wears a hammer amulet, just like you. He has forsaken God and Christ, and there is a special place in hell for men who abandon the Lord."

Einar stared back at the gathered men, and then at Adzo. "I'm going to ask Thorkild this evening. When he's finished his story, I am going to ask him if Vigmarr killed my father."

"Why not think about it first? You've only just won your place on the crew, the thing you have craved and wanted your entire life. Can you be sure that you can trust Thorkild?"

Einar shrugged. "As much as I trust any other man here."

"You don't know these men. You barely know me. I was enslaved by Vikings and only swam to your boat to use the chaos of battle as my chance to escape. What if I hate Vikings? Or what if I decide to tell Vigmarr and Fulk what you have said this evening? They might fill my purse with silver."

"You don't have a purse."

"I mean, what if?"

"You wouldn't do that to me."

"I wouldn't, that's true. But what's to stop Thorkild from telling Vigmarr?"

"He's an ageing storyteller, and he's shown me nothing but kindness."

"Now he's an ageing storyteller who seems gentle with his grey beard and his soft eyes, but he wasn't always that way. He is a warrior on a Viking *drakkar*. What man survives for as long as he, raiding and fighting wars every summer? He is every bit as lethal and dangerous as any man in the crew. Imagine him ten years ago when he sailed with your father, the two of them raiding and fighting across the Whale Road, them and Vigmarr Svarti making their legend."

"I want to know the truth. I have to know. All my life I have lived with the heartrending sadness of my father's death. I lost both my parents when I was a child. My father's death left me alone, an orphan dependent on the charity of others for food and warmth. I remember his smile, his kindness, his advice and his lessons. But I needed him when I was alone, I needed someone to help with weapons lessons, to talk to me of women and life. Vigmarr stole that from me. He stole that from a child, and I remember the nights laying on a hard floor, sleeping beneath a threadbare blanket with tears rolling down my cheeks. I owe it to that boy, to the child I was. I must have vengeance."

"Have you lost your mind? Vigmarr would slaughter you in your sleep and wear your skin as a cloak! Think upon it, Einar. You are about to risk everything based on the last words of a man whose brain was fuddled with infection and fever."

"If Vigmarr killed my father, it is my duty as his son to avenge his death. How can his soul have peace when his death remains unavenged and his son sails under the command of his killer?"

"I can see you've made up your mind. So you must speak to Thorkild and discover the truth. What will you do about Fulk?"

"Kill him before he kills me? I don't know. Who could have tasked him with my murder, but Vigmarr? Perhaps the jarl suspects I know he killed my father and fears my vengeance? So he took a masterless man on board the Seaworm on the condition that he kill me."

"Careful, Einar. If you confront Thorkild, or worse, challenge Fulk, there can be no going back. Once you draw your weapon, you cannot sheathe it again without bloodshed."

Einar clapped his friend on the shoulder.

"Truly, I did not realise there was such wisdom in this Frankish head of yours."

They laughed together and Adzo playfully punched Einar in the stomach. "You asked for my advice, and now you have it. For what it's worth."

Einar smiled and walked back through the trees towards the campfire where Thorkild's story was coming to an end.

"What are you going to do?" Adzo called after him.

"Ask Thorkild," Einar said over his shoulder.

"Nice to see you took my advice on board, then."

Einar waved at the sarcasm and continued to where the crews clapped and cheered the end of Thorkild's story. Einar wove through the knot of men as they rose from their knees to gather about their own smaller campfires and prepare to bed down for the night.

"A fine tale," Einar said, offering Thorkild an oatcake from his own rations.

"That one is a crowd pleaser," Thorkild said, refusing the oatcake with a polite smile.

"You must know a hundred stories."

"I have learned many over the years. What else is there to do in winter or during the nights on a long voyage than listen to legends and tales of the gods?"

"Very little. You could give up life at sea and make your fortune as a travelling skald."

"The sea calls to us, laddie. You'll find out next time you are ashore. Once you've sailed on a ship such as the Seaworm, she steals a part of you, owns a part of your soul. In your sleep, you'll hear the sigh of the sea and the creaking of hull timbers and long for spring when the ships put out onto the Whale Road. Nothing else matters."

Einar walked with Thorkild to the shelter he had made for the night from a cut of old sailcloth. Einar helped him start a small fire outside his tent.

"Sit, please," Thorkild said, gesturing to a log beside the fire. "It is still a little early for a man my age to lie down. I'll be up for a piss three times before dawn."

"Thank you." Einar sat and warmed his hands on the crackling flames and waited until Thorkild sat down with a wince and a groan.

"Old spear wound in my hip. Hurts like a bastard at night and in winter."

"You have sailed for many summers and seen many things."

"That's true. All the men I knew when I was your age are gone. Either killed in battle and awaiting me in Valhalla, or died of sickness in the long winters. Good men, brave men."

"Do you miss them?"

"Of course. But I do not pity them, for they lived well and accomplished many brave deeds."

'Like my father?"

"Like your father. Egil was a skilled warrior, and a good friend."

"How did he die? I have never heard the full tale of it."

Thorkild reached for a handful of twigs and tossed them into the fire. "He died in battle when you were a boy. We were raiding in the east, I think." He waved a hand, its flesh discoloured with pale spots. "You must have heard of it many times. It was so long ago."

"Palni was on that voyage?"

"He could have been. I miss old Palni. Did you know that he and I once accepted a ransom for a princess in Saxony? It's true. The king himself presented us with a chest brimming with treasure."

"I did not know that. You must have had many adventures together."

"So many. Too many to remember on a chilly night like this."

"Palni spoke to me of my father's death before

he died."

"He was rambling at the end, I hear, talking nonsense. I think I will go to sleep now, after all."

"He told me Vigmarr Svarti killed my father."

Thorkild's head dropped, and his eyes closed tight. "He should not have said that."

"Is it true?"

"He was raving with an infected wound. Banish such thoughts. There is no good to be found picking at old scabs."

"Is it true?"

"Leave it alone." Age fell from Thorkild like an old cloak. He stood with broad shoulders, blazing with anger. "There is nothing to find in the past but trouble."

"He did. Vigmarr killed my father."

"What if he did? Do you feel better knowing it? What good will it do you but to lead you to your death?"

"I will challenge Vigmarr. I must avenge my father."

"Don't be a fool. Forget what you heard. Let old ghosts lie. You cannot face Vigmarr. He would butcher you, lad."

"Like he butchered my father?"

"Do not confront Vigmarr with these

accusations, Einar. I warn you. Never, ever, fight Vigmarr Svarti. He sold his soul a long time ago. Vigmarr is not a man. He was once, maybe. But no more."

"What happened to him?"

"Once, he was like every young warrior. Hungry for reputation. Like you. Like me and Egil. We sailed with Ragnar, and every summer we became more feared. Men knew our names across the Whale Road and we were proud. But Vigmarr wanted more. Always more. He wanted to captain a ship, to be a leader, to be a jarl. Vigmarr wanted everything. He wanted a beautiful wife, wealth, children, power. He could not bear to see other men outstrip his achievements. It ate him up inside until his rage bubbled over like a boiling pot."

"Is that what happened between him and Egil?"

"It's complicated. A tale for another time. You must calm yourself. Do not rush off enraged."

"Was it a fair fight, or did he murder him?"

"Does it matter?"

"Of course it matters! Is my father in Valhalla or Niflheim?"

"I don't want to see you cut down, Einar. Can you understand that? We are at war. Stranded in a foreign land. If we are going to survive, we must be two crews fighting together, united under our leaders. We have to trust the man next to us in the shield wall to protect our left side whilst we strike with axe and spear. If you start dredging up the past, it will do nothing but destroy us. Leave your father in the past where he belongs. Until now, you believed he died in battle. Keep on believing it. Live your life and stay away from Vigmarr."

"Did he kill him?" Einar took a step towards Thorkild, and then caught himself just as his anger was about to explode.

"What's going on here?" said Skallagrimr, shouting from the next tent over. He squinted through the darkness. "Why are you shouting at the Storyteller?"

"It's nothing," Einar said. "Go back to sleep."

Thorkild raised his hand to show that there was no trouble. He came around to Einar and placed his two hands gently on Einar's face.

"We were all young. Ragnar led us across the Whale Road and we did marvellous things. But it was all washed in blood. Silver and reputation built on a mountain of corpses. Egil was Ragnar's man; his advisor, friend, and champion. This was before Sten Slegyya became his right hand. Vigmarr couldn't live with that. He wanted everything Egil had. Hated him already because Egil had a woman and happiness waiting for him at home."

"He killed him?"

Thorkild nodded slowly.

"Murdered him?"

Thorkild nodded again and pressed his forehead onto Einar's. "Leave it alone, Einar. Don't go the same way he did. The Norns have woven this into the weft of your life. Don't let Vigmarr end both your lives."

"Why didn't you avenge him?"

"We talked of it. All the crew wanted to. It was wrong. But Vigmarr is a dangerous man. At first, we planned to strike at him, that one of us would challenge Vigmarr and fight him fairly. Nobody did. Then we spoke of a knife in the night, or a push overboard in a storm. But days turned into weeks, summer to winter. Nobody wanted to stand before the furnace of Vigmarr's wrath. After Egil's death, Vigmarr grew darker, more murderous, living only for blood. Do not judge us, Einar. Men want to live."

"I do not blame you, old one."

"It is one thing fighting an enemy you do not know. It is another to challenge your captain and jarl to fight, of accusing him of a fell deed and questioning his honour. Most men want a quiet life. They want to row, drink, eat, sail and fight. They don't want trouble within their crew. Time just softened the blow of Egil's death. That's the truth of it, a hard truth to swallow, I understand. We just did nothing, and that shame lies on all of us."

"Sleep now, Thorkild."

"Wait," Thorkild grabbed Einar's arm as he turned away. "What will you do?"

"I don't know."

Einar left Thorkild to his bed and his fire and wandered through the camp. Vigmarr had killed his father, and there must be a reckoning. There must be vengeance. The thought of standing and fighting Vigmarr Svarti, however, was terrifying. Einar lay down beneath his wool cloak and thought of trading blows with the gigantic monster. It was like a nightmare, a horror to turn a man's guts to water. He imagined that scarred, disfigured face coming at him, snarling and growling with hate, and the speed and strength of his huge, twisted frame swinging an axe to cut and rend at Einar's chest and face. Einar was not sure he could stand against such a malign force. He tossed and turned beneath his cloak, thoughts tortured by his predicament. Sometime during the night, he drifted off into a sleep filled with memories of his mother and father, and of his father's ghost wandering through Niflheim, wailing for his son to avenge his murder.

SEVENTEEN

Ivar ravaged the countryside of Agder for two weeks. Using the hill camp as a base, he divided the Seaworm and Windspear crews into raiding parties and they ranged across the valleys burning and looting any settlements, villages, or farms, killing as they went. Vigmarr Svarti led a war band mounted on stolen horses. He rode the black gelding Einar had found at the first settlement, and every day Vigmarr rode out with a score of warriors and returned before nightfall with his thirst for blood slaked and his men filthy with the gore of slaughter.

Ivar led a force of sixty men on far-ranging marches in different directions, seeking fortifications and warriors to fight, and to discover how best to advance towards Dolgfinnr's lands. They returned to camp some days empty-handed, and on others carrying captured weapons and supplies.

Einar marched with Halvdan and a dozen carls from the Seaworm crew, including Adzo, Bersa, Ginnlaug, Styrr and Fulk. They hunted in the forests and scavenged from local villages, leading a wain pulled by an old horse which they filled each day with grain, meat, fish, ale, mead and whatever else they could find to keep the army fed. The first days were sickening as Einar picked through the ashes of farms ravaged by Vigmarr and his riders. Luckily, Halvdan had no stomach for murder and from the fourth day, they trekked in the opposite direction to Vigmarr and his horsemen. Adzo and the archers hunted deer and other wild animals, and Einar tried to summon the courage to challenge Vigmarr Svarti. That courage, however, would not come.

On the fifteenth day, Ivar led the entire army south west, leaving the hill camp, and a countryside desolated by their presence. They spent a night camping in the ruin of a pillaged farmhouse, and in the morning Halvdan led his usual warband out searching for food.

"A hundred men need a lot of food," he said simply when Bersa complained of the early start.

They trudged bleary-eyed across a grazing pasture as a red sun peeped over the horizon until they saw a fenced village beside the bend of a wide stream. Halvdan ordered the twelve warriors to spread out as they approached, with

Adzo and the archers taking up positions on either flank. Einar marched on the far left with Adzo. As they came within twenty paces of the village, a group of warriors hurried from the collection of buildings and climbed over its waist-high fence. There were twenty of them, most in padded jerkins or leather breastplates, all carrying spears and shields.

"Looks as though the people have finally decided to defend themselves," said Adzo, taking an arrow from his quiver and setting it to his bowstring. "I thought the jarls and king of this place had surrendered without a fight."

"Give us food and ale and there won't be any trouble," Halvdan called.

"You are the Danes who have been killing people?" replied their leader, a hefty man with an axe in his belt and a conical helmet on his head.

"Just give us the supplies and nobody needs to die."

"Come and take them, Danish scum. We don't bargain with cutthroats."

"You are King Harald's men?"

"We are from Jarl Floki's hearth troop. These are his lands. You should have left when your bellies were full of stolen meat."

Halvdan drew his axe and a long knife from his belt. "We're going to take whatever food is beyond that fence. We won't hurt anybody. You can either stand aside or defend this shithole with your lives."

"You've hurt enough of our people. We've seen the burned-out villages, the dead women and children. We are warriors. It is our duty to protect our jarl's land and his folk. It's time for you to die."

"I wish we had our bloody shields," Halvdan said to his men. "This lot look like field hands dressed up for war, but if they're a local jarl's professional warriors, then they'll know how to use those spears."

"We're outnumbered," said Styrr. He led the wain and horse, but as he spoke, he stroked the horse's long nose and grabbed his axe.

"We'll still kill them."

"I know. I was just saying."

Einar readied his own axe and seax and followed Halvdan's lead as he strode forward, closing the gap between them and the local warriors.

"Spears and shields!" the hefty man shouted, and his men made a shield wall. It was a clumsy thing of different-sized shields held at different angles. Some men rested their spears on their shields' rims, others kept them pointing up in the air.

"Archers," Halvdan growled. "Bunch them up so they can't swing their weapons."

Adzo's bow stave groaned as he lifted the weapon and pulled the string back to his ear. With a thrum, the arrow sped low and fast across the pasture and thumped into the closest shield. Bersa and Ginnlaug loosed arrows from the opposite flank, and the men on either side of the enemy line shuffled closer together. They raised their shields and instinctively moved away from the archers, meaning that every man in the line moved closer together, too close together.

"Charge," Halvdan ordered.

Einar set off at a flat run, keeping pace with the line as more arrows whistled into the enemy's flanks. Their leader shouted at his men to ready their shields, others roared at the man beside them to make room. One warrior dropped his spear after it fouled upon his neighbour's weapon.

"We fight for the Boneless!" Halvdan bellowed as they hurtled towards the shield wall. Einar prepared himself, muscles bunched, axe and seax in each fist. "Hold! Hold!" Halvdan shouted as their charge came within five paces of the enemy shields. Einar stopped still, chest heaving, staring at the fearful men opposite him. It was an attack formation drilled into all boys at Hrafnborg along with a dozen others, each tactic suited for a different battle situation. This one suited a charge without shields, and Einar had practised it hundreds of times since he was a boy.

The enemy tensed behind their shields, spears still at odd angles, many of them stooped low to hide their faces from the sharp weapons coming to hack at them. When the bloodcurdling charge did not come, shields lowered and faces appeared.

"Kill," Halvdan said coldly, cutting through the silence. Moments ago, straps and weapons had jangled and boots had crashed through the grass. Weapons had scraped against wood and iron and men had shouted and called their defiance. The halt brought an eerie silence to the battlefield. Somewhere, a cow lowed, and then Halvdan's gravelly, cruel voice cut through the air like a saw. "Kill all but one."

Einar darted forward and slashed his axe across a man's eyes. The blade scraped across his iron shield rim, sparks flew, and then blood spurted hot and red across the next man's face. Einar jolted the shield with his shoulder to push the screaming, blinded man backwards and he stabbed his seax into the next man's ribs. All along the line, men screamed in anger and in pain, weapons clashed, and men died. Einar was taller than every man in the enemy line, and over the summer, he had grown stronger, broader across his back and shoulders, muscles made strong by the oar and life at sea.

The man with the seax in his ribs howled in pain and died as an arrow thumped into his open mouth. Einar kicked him away and saw movement from the corner of his eye. He raised his axe instinctively and parried a spear thrust. The shield wall had broken, shocked by the halt and then destroyed as the surprised men lowered their guard. The spearman shoved Einar with his shield and took a backward step. Einar turned him, hooking his seax around the shield and dragging it towards the man's spear arm. One of the crew dropped to his knees next to Einar with an axe buried in his chest, but more of the enemy had fallen, leaking their lifeblood onto the lush, green grass. The spearman crouched, bracing his shield with his knee, and he knew how to fight. He was stocky with small angry eyes, and his shield came over the rim and sliced across Einar's breastplate.

The leather armour took the blow. Had Einar not worn the breastplate, that spear point would have cut his chest open like a piece of roast beef. Einar sprang backwards, readying himself in a fighting stance, axe and seax poised, bobbing on the balls of his feet. The stocky man stood and glared at Einar beneath the rim of his helmet. His hearth troop died around him, but he ignored that slaughter and kept his concentration firmly on Einar.

"I'm going to kill you, young pup," he spat. "I'm going to meet my father and brother in Valhalla, but before that I'm going to gut you and dance in your entrails, you stinking child-killer."

Einar wanted to tell the man that he was a *drengr*, who had never and would never kill a child or a defenceless woman. The man's people had suffered Vigmarr's ruthless brutality for no other reason than Ivar had suffered a defeat and his crews passed through this land on their way to confront Dolgfinnr. It was luck, or lack of it, nothing more. This land may have seen peace for a hundred years, may never have suffered raids and slaughter, but for the Norns and their wicked manipulation of men's fates. Dolgfinnr and the Ragnarssons were at war, and the people of Agder suffered because of it.

Those thoughts were fleeting, and there was no time for Einar to plead his case. The man stabbed his spear at Einar, feinted, and slashed the leaf-shaped blade again. Einar swerved, parried air and just brought his seax up in time to stop the spear point from opening his throat. Einar hacked at him, and the man took the blow on his shield so that Einar's axe thumped into the linden-wood and became stuck. He wrenched at the axe haft, but it would not come free. The stocky man pulled his shield away, and a grin split his hard face. His spear slashed at Einar's face, and Einar jerked just in time so that the weapon flashed over his shoulder. The man thought he'd struck the killing blow and had stepped into it, overextending himself, leaving himself off balance. He saw his chance to kill an inexperienced young raider, and now he would die. Einar roared into his face and stabbed the blade of his seax into the spearman's armpit. He twisted the blade savagely and ripped it free.

Anger and hate slipped from the stocky man's face, replaced by a grimace of pain. He dropped his shield and spear and slowly rested on his knees. He clenched his eyes closed, listening to the sound of his brothers dying around him.

"Pick it up," Einar said.

The stocky man opened his eyes. His head tilted as a gush of blood flushed from his wound. He picked up his spear and closed his eyes again. Einar opened his throat with his seax and left the warrior to die, hoping that he would join his father and brother in Odin's hall.

"Finish them," Halvdan said.

Einar put a foot on the dead man's shield and ripped his axe free. The enemy lay bleeding on the grass, some dead and others groaning and gasping in pain. Halvdan held a fistful of the leader's hair, who crouched at Halvdan's feet.

"Take anything of value and put it in the cart," said Halvdan. "This one lives."

Einar and Adzo went among the dead and took spears, shields, knives, and purses with coins and scraps of hacksilver. They collected helmets, belts and two cloaks edged with fur. Villagers watched them from behind the fence, and Einar wondered why the people didn't flee for their lives.

Halvdan shook the enemy leader by his hair and threw him down onto the bloody grass. The hefty man scowled at Halvdan and spat in disgust.

"I let you live today, shitworm," Halvdan growled. He cleaned his axe on the man's cloak and slid it back into the loop at his belt. "Remember that when you hold your wife close, and see my face in the darkness."

"Bastard," the man said. His men, Jarl Floki's hearth troop, were dead about him and he alone lived. Einar stopped to stare at the defeated man, wondering at the mixed feelings of shame and relief. Halvdan had spared him, and he would return to his family and hold them close. But the families of the dead would have nothing but grief, and anger that their husband or father was not the man to return from battle.

"You are going to run back to your jarl like a frightened milkmaid. Tell him to fetch King Harald. My Lord Ivar Ragnarsson, whom men call the Boneless, wishes to speak with him."

Halvdan waved his hand like a father dismissing one of his children. "Be off with you."

The hefty man stood and lumbered away from the battle, trudging with his head bowed.

"Lord Ivar wants to fight King Harald?" asked Einar as the rest piled the looted weapons into the wain.

"Ivar wants to fight everyone," Halvdan replied.

"But why challenge a king when we are here to fight Dolgfinnr?"

Halvdan winked at him. "Ivar has the cunning of a wolf. Think of it as though he has drunk from the waters in Mimir's well, where Odin himself sacrificed an eye to drink and gain all the wisdom in the world. Ivar is clever, and you are an empty-headed shitworm." He beamed and punched Einar on the shoulder. "Just keep fighting well and following orders. Don't think. Just fight. Leave the thinking to Ivar. Take the others and gather the food and ale in that village."

Einar did as he was told. The villagers scattered, finally understanding that they must run for their lives. Einar and Adzo leapt the fence and went from storehouse to longhouse to barn, making piles of cured meat, cheese, bread, wheat and barley. Adzo sidestepped into a small building next to a low-roofed longhouse, and Einar went into the alley between them to check for any hidden stores of ale or mead. He turned around a wattle wall, dipped beneath overhanging grey thatch, and came face to face with Fulk.

"There you are," breathed the Frank, a leer splitting his swarthy face, revealing his splintered, brown teeth.

"What do you want?" asked Einar, hand dropping instinctively to his axe.

"Doing my job, just like you." He carried a long knife in his fist, and the blade twitched as he spoke.

"What job?"

Fulk shrugged. "Gathering supplies, doing my duty."

They held each other's gaze for a moment, Einar sure that the Frank was about to attack him in the tight space between the buildings where nobody could see. Fulk could say a villager had attacked and killed Einar. There would be no crime, no price to be paid, and Fulk could collect his bounty from Vigmarr. If the jarl had paid Fulk to kill Einar. Fulk's eyes narrowed, and then Adzo burst from the building behind Einar.

"I found some mead," he said cheerfully.

Einar took a step back and inclined his head to

see Adzo with his bow over his shoulder and a small cask in his hands.

"What's going on here?" Adzo asked.

"Just going about my work," Fulk purred. He lowered his knife and turned back, stalking away along the narrow walking space.

"He was going to attack me," Einar said.

"Are you sure?"

"If you hadn't come when you did, I could be a corpse now."

"Maybe it was an honest mistake? Maybe he was just searching for supplies?"

"Just like when I caught him creeping up on me that night?"

"Forget it, Einar. Have some of this mead."

Einar refused, and the warband scavenged what food and drink they could find in the village and loaded it into the wain. Halvdan led them back to camp, and Ivar was pleased when Halvdan informed him of the skirmish with Jarl Floki's men.

"Good," Ivar grinned. "Let's see if we can bring this jarl and his king to war. We strike camp tomorrow." He leapt up to stand on a log and held his arms out wide. "Drink and feast tonight, men. Tomorrow we begin our march south towards Dolgfinnr."

The men gathered about campfires and shared skins of ale, and the mead Adzo had found poured like the nectar of the gods. Einar sat and brooded. He drank mead and ate roast pork. The men told stories and drank as darkness fell, but Einar heard none of it. He could not tear his eyes from Vigmarr Svarti, who sat alone by his own fire, eating slowly and gazing into the night. The more Einar drank, the more anger overcame him. Why should he fear the old sea-jarl? Was Einar not a warrior now? After more cups of mead than he could recall, Einar rose to his feet, belched and stumbled towards Vigmarr's fire.

"Stay here, Einar," begged Adzo, grabbing his arm. "You are drunk. Get some sleep before we march tomorrow."

"No," Einar replied, and pulled his arm away.

He reached Vigmarr's fire and stood there, swaying under the influence of too much drink. His mind brimmed with hate as he watched the twisted man in black, certain that Vigmarr had killed his father and set Fulk to kill him. The shaggy head turned, hidden by a curtain of raven-coloured hair. Einar's fists balled, and his stomach lurched. When seated, he had envisioned himself confronting Vigmarr, asking him directly if he had killed his father and challenging him to fight. But now the bravery fell away, sucked out of him like water through a hole in a bucket.

Vigmarr lurched to his feet. He was as tall as Einar, but twice as wide. Vigmarr brushed the hair from his face with his four-fingered hand to reveal the impossibly black eyes and a face as scarred as a ship's hull after a summer at sea. He waited for Einar to speak, those murderous eyes gouging into Einar's very soul. Einar's mouth flapped open, but he couldn't find the right words.

"What?" Vigmarr asked, his voice like the bear's growl.

"My father..." Einar stuttered.

"Careful. Go back to your fire."

"You k..." Einar began, and then Vigmarr's fist crashed into Einar's stomach. It was like being struck by Mjolnir, Thor's mighty hammer, and Einar hurled his guts up and bent double. Vigmarr grabbed a fistful of his hair and twisted it hard. He drove his knee twice into Einar's face, ripped a hank of hair from Einar's head and front-kicked him in the chest. Einar sprawled on the grass, vomit in his beard and blood streaming from his nose into his mouth.

"Go away," Vigmarr said and resumed his seat.

Einar shook his head, embarrassment and anger swirling inside his head like churning butter. He tried to rise but fell back, nose throbbing, head dizzy, skull stinging where Vigmarr had ripped his hair out.

"What were you thinking?" cried Adzo, rushing to Einar's side. He grabbed Einar under the arms and lifted him to his feet.

"Leave me!" Einar said, his thoughts somersaulting, Mead, anger and shame twisted his reason, unable to control himself. He took a step towards Vigmarr, thought better of it, and stumbled away from him. A face looked at him across another campfire, a swarthy face, grinning at him as though he were a fool.

"What are you looking at?" Einar snapped, pointing an unsteady finger at the seated men. They looked at each other and then to where Einar pointed. Fulk shook his head and pointed at himself, silently checking if it was to him Einar had spoken. "Yes, you, masterless man, *slyðra*, assassin!"

"Einar, no!" Adzo tried to pull him back, but Einar shook him off.

"You have tried to kill me, Frank. Tried and failed. Someone's paid you to do it. Well, here I am." Einar pulled open his jerkin to show his bare chest. "Come on, do it."

"You are mistaken," Fulk said. "Kids and ale." He laughed, and the men around laughed nervously.

"Turd! Are you afraid?"

"That's enough now." The smile fell from Fulk's face, and he stood quickly.

"Fight me then. I challenge you. Holmgang. Fight me fairly, not a knife in the night or murder in an alleyway. Let's fight like men."

"Very well. Tomorrow then. Though you may regret it when the drink wears off. I'll kill you, boy."

EIGHTEEN

Einar awoke with a banging headache and an impossibly dry mouth. He searched about him for something to drink, daylight stabbing into his eyes like knives.

"Odin, help me," he whispered and sat up, cradling his head in his hands.

"You will need his help," said Adzo. "You fight Fulk before we march."

"What?" Einar rubbed his eyes, and his actions from the night before came back to him with juddering shock. "Water?"

"Here." Adzo handed him a skin filled with clean water and Einar drank it down. The Frank busied himself taking down the tent and rolling up his cloak. "Get up, we march before mid-morning."

Einar stood and took another long drink. His nose throbbed, and he felt it gingerly. It felt squashed, like a trod-on turnip. "What have I done?"

"Confronted Vigmarr Svarti and found a beating. Then challenged Fulk to a holmgang, which you will fight shortly. Other than that, it was a quiet night."

Einar took another drink. It was impossible to slake his thirst, even if he drank the entire Whale Road. "Can I win?"

"We'll find out. You've been talking of nothing but Fulk and Vigmarr since Palni died, so at least today you will solve one of your problems. Or you'll be dead."

"You are turning into a Northman."

"I am learning. There is no room for pity here. Get yourself ready."

Einar pulled on his breastplate and readied his weapons. He gathered his cloak and rolled his belongings into a pack tied with hemp rope.

"It's time, Einar," said Thorkild Storyteller. He leant against a tree, a look of sorrow on his lined face.

"I'm ready," he replied.

"You were lucky Vigmarr didn't kill you last night."

"If he had, I wonder, would my death go unavenged like my father's?"

"I warned you…"

"You warned to keep out of trouble, to let sleeping dogs lie. Just like you all did years ago. How can I let it lie? How can I carry on as though nothing happened whilst my father's tortured soul wanders in the cold of Niflheim? That man Fulk was set to kill me. He came at me again yesterday. I may have been drunk last night, and confronting Vigmarr was a mistake. But at least I do not shirk from my enemies."

"I am not your enemy."

Einar sighed and rubbed his tired eyes. "I know. I am sorry. I do not blame you. There aren't many who would go up against Vigmarr. You wanted to live, so do we all. You did not kill Egil."

"Are you ready to fight Fulk?"

"Ready as I'll ever be. Though my head hurts like Fenris Wolf himself is trying to gnaw his way out of it."

Thorkild stroked his long moustaches. "The best cure is raw eel and crushed pine nuts. But we have neither of those things here. My mother swore by boiled cabbage and leeks. I can prepare that quickly?"

"Thank you, but no, I don't think my stomach could take it. We'd best get this over with."

"Take this then, for luck." Thorkild fished in

his pouch and took out a silver amulet in the shape of Thor's hammer. "I have carried it with me for years. It might improve your *hamingja*."

Einar took the amulet and tucked it into the pouch at his belt. He followed Thorkild to the heart of the camp, where the hilltop grass was worn away by men's boots, leaving a grey-brown smear between the trees. Fulk waited, sitting on a fallen tree trunk, sharpening his axe with a whetstone.

"Here he is!" cried a cheerful voice, and Ivar strode across the clearing, rubbing his hands together. "Einar the Brawler living up to his name again? I swear, young Einar, you love to fight almost as much as I. Even my brother Bjorn hasn't fought two holmgangs. We have just enough time to get it done before we march."

"Yes, lord," Einar said, unable to find the warrior's pride and bravado Ivar expected.

"Tell me, what did the Frank do to get on your wrong side?"

"He tried to kill me, lord."

"Are you sure?"

"No." Einar signed. He thought he was sure, but now that it came to a fight to the death, he wondered if perhaps Adzo was right, and he had imagined Fulk's attempts to kill him, confused as he was after the revelations about his father's death.

Ivar laughed and clapped Einar on the back. "Kill the bastard anyway. I like you, Einar. Once this is done, we march for Dolgfinnr. There will be plenty of fighting to come. You must stand in battle with me, Einar. When we finally face him, I want you with me when I become the champion of the Northmen."

"Yes, lord." Einar could find no more words. All he could focus on was Fulk and the fight to come.

"Well, may Odin protect you."

Einar marched to the clearing where Halvdan was busy shouting at men to clear out of the way.

"Hurry up, Brownlegs," Halvdan said. "Any branches will do. We don't have all day. Just make the square."

"It should be right," Ulfketil replied. He moved about the clearing with a selection of long branches in his arms, trying to make the right-sized square for the holmgang duel. "There's no hazel up here for a start. The least we can do is make the square the right size."

"I'm ready," said Einar, and he drew his weapons. His headache drifted away and the swelling pain in his face became numb. Einar flexed his right hand around the leather-wrapped axe haft and his left around the seax's bone hilt. It came for him then, the battle joy, the exhilaration of danger which made battle a thing that brave men loved.

"I'm ready," said Fulk. He rose from his seat and lifted his knife and axe to prove it.

"How many shields?" said Ulfketil Brownlegs, still pacing out his square.

"No shields," Einar replied.

"What? We can't have a holmgang with no shields. Next you'll be saying no seconds and no quarter."

"No seconds and no quarter." Quarter gave the losing man a chance to back out of the fight after a wound, or if the man felt he was in danger of death. He could admit wrong in whatever insult or feud had led to the fight, and the victor would have the right to be compensated in wergild payment. Einar wanted no payment.

"No seconds and no quarter," agreed Fulk. His dark hair hung lank about his face and he rolled his slim shoulders to loosen the muscles, preparing himself for the knife work to come.

"What is the insult here?" asked Halvdan, striding across the square to put himself between the two enemies.

Fulk pointed his axe at Einar. "Ask the drunken pup who can't hold his ale."

"This man has tried to kill me twice," Einar

shouted so that every man in camp could hear. "I believe another set him upon that task with promise of silver in the event of my death. He is a masterless man, only recently sworn an oath to our Lord Ivar. So I challenge this man to fight in the open, before he stabs me in the back like the nithing he is."

"I swore my oath the same day as you," said Fulk, still calm.

"Backstabber!" shouted a carl as the men gathered to watch the fight.

"Nithing," called another.

"Arrogant young bastard," a man called at Einar.

"All right, all right," Halvdan said, waving at everyone to calm down. "Sounds like there's bad blood. Let's get it done so we can move out. By the laws of gods and men, we are gathered here to witness a holmgang between these two warriors. This is a fight to the death, without shields or seconds. The victor claims everything the dead man owns. If either man steps out of the fighting square, his life is forfeit. Axes, knives and seaxes are the only weapons allowed. Does any man here dispute the lawfulness of this fight?"

Nobody spoke. Fulk prowled back and forth behind Halvdan like a beast, his chest heaving and his face contorted with anger. Battle-joy still pumped through Einar's veins, and he was ready. He had been afraid during his first holmgang. He had killed Olvir back in Hrafnborg, but he had been lucky that day, fighting for his life as a frightened boy. But he was a boy no longer.

"Fight!" Halvdan called and stepped out of the circle.

Einar attacked. He surged forward, slashing and stabbing with his weapons, moving on his front foot as he had always been taught. Fulk parried and dodged each strike, their axe hafts banging together as axes whirled and swung with deadly skill. Einar poured all of his sorrow into each strike, all the fury of his father's murder into every blow.

"Who paid you to kill me?" Einar said as their axes locked together and they struggled, wrenching at each other's weapons with brute force.

"Fool," Fulk hissed through his broken teeth.

Einar kicked him in the groin and crashed a knee into Fulk's face. It had been a summer of war, and Einar had fought more since returning to Hrafnborg as a survivor on board the Waveslicer than most men would in a lifetime. One thing he had learned amongst the blood and death was that many Viking warriors possessed skill at arms, but what separated the lovers of battle from the rest was vicious savagery. Einar had that gift, granted to him by a stolen life, by years sleeping under other men's roofs, by a lifetime spent without a mother or father. He was a child of Ragnar Lothbrok's seaside fortress, raised to the axe, born to kill and sail and send men to Odin's hall. He understood in that moment as Fulk staggered away from him that it was time to let the boy inside him die, and become Einar Rosti, Einar the Brawler, carl and warrior of the warship Seaworm.

Fulk stood and spat a gobbet of blood. "Come and die, turd," he taunted, and twirled his axe. The crowd laughed and whooped at the trick, but Einar set his feet. All fear washed away, gone and left behind with the worries and ambitions of a boy.

"Who paid you to kill me?" Einar asked, voice calm, jaw set, eyes cold.

"Whelp!" Fulk charged at Einar, his face contorted with anger, weapons swinging. He was a killer, a man who had made his way from Frankia, paid to fight by any lord in need of men, lords at war. He was like a maggot, seeking wounds and blood to live in and grow fat.

The axe blade hummed towards Einar's face and he swayed backwards, feeling the wind of it in his eyes. He lifted his seax and blocked Fulk's stabbing knife with a loud clang, and stepped forward and crashed his forehead into Fulk's face with a sickening crunch. Bone and gristle mashed beneath his head and Fulk jerked away. Einar kicked him in the ribs and sliced his seax across the Frank's back.

The crowd winced as one and covered their mouths with their hands. One side of Fulk's face had turned instantly blue, his eye closed, and the cheekbone shattered. The cut on his back bled copiously, and Einar waited.

"You can't kill me!" Fulk seethed, gingerly touching his face. "You're just a pup. I was fighting men when you were still at your mother's tit."

"Who paid you to kill me?"

The question sent Fulk into an even wilder rage and he ran towards Einar, axe and knife swinging towards Einar's body. He parried every blow. Fulk twisted, swung again, and Einar danced out of the way. As he turned, he sliced his axe across Fulk's shoulder, kicked out the back of his knee and stabbed him twice in the side, shallow bursts with the tip of his seax. Fulk fell on his front and crawled away, leaving a red smear in the dirt.

"Who paid you to kill me?" Einar repeated.

"Just kill the bastard," shouted a warrior in the crowd. Einar ignored him.

Fulk got to his feet and set himself again, his

face pale and his eyes desperate. He lumbered towards Einar and roared, swinging his axe overhand. It was a feint, and his long knife came up in a wicked strike aimed to gut Einar beneath the rim of his breastplate. Einar saw it coming and simply stepped backwards so that Fulk stumbled towards him. Einar brought his axe down hard on Fulk's forearm, hearing bones break. Fulk dropped his knife, his left arm now hanging uselessly at his side.

"Who paid you to kill me?"

Fulk grimaced through his ruined face. He swung his axe, tired and desperate, the crazed swing a man might make after a night of too much ale. Einar stepped and slammed his axe haft into Fulk's weapon, using all the strength in his tall, muscular frame to rip the axe from Fulk's hand. It flew across the fighting square and landed at Fat Garmr's feet. Einar stabbed his seax into Fulk's thigh and twisted the blade, tearing through muscle and flesh. The watching warriors groaned.

"Put the bastard out of his misery," a man called from the crowd.

"Who paid you to kill me?" Einar asked. Fulk staggered away from him again, torn, bloody, and dying.

"Somebody help me!" Fulk gasped. "I concede. Einar is the winner. I give up. Stop the fight."

"The fight's not over," Einar replied. "Garmr, give him his axe."

"The fight's over," said Halvdan and stepped into the square.

"Nothing is over!" Einar roared, the sound of his voice startling the men around him. "Stay out of it, Halvdan."

The bull-necked shipmaster stared at Einar for a moment, and Einar could not tell if the look on his face was one of respect or understanding, but he raised two hands and backed out of the holmgang square.

"Give him his axe."

Fat Garmr picked up Fulk's axe and carried it to him. The Frank took it and laughed, strings of bloody mucus drooling from his mouth into his greasy beard.

"You Norsemen are a pox!" he said, turning and almost falling, waving his axe at the crowd. "Nothing but murderers and rapers. Hell awaits you all."

Einar stalked across the fighting square, and before Fulk could raise his axe, he stabbed his seax deep into the Frank's guts. Fulk hissed and dropped his axe, his good hand clasped about Einar's wrist.

"Who paid you to kill me?" Einar said again.

Fulk shook his head and began to weep. Einar twisted the blade savagely.

"Who paid you to kill me?"

Fulk cried out in pain, tears streaming down his ruined face. Something hit Fulk with the sound of a cleaver chopping meat and he fell away from Einar and crumpled to the dirt with an axe buried in the back of his skull.

"Fight's over," said Vigmarr Svarti. He limped into the holmgang square, black cloak swirling around him like bats' wings. He bent and yanked his axe from Fulk's head. Vigmarr paused, hunched as he was with his crooked body. He inclined his head towards Einar as if waiting for a challenge, as if waiting for him to protest. Einar looked to Halvdan, who marched into the square.

"Fight's over," Halvdan repeated. "Einar won. Anybody disagree?" Nobody spoke; the carls just melted away. "Good. Ready your gear. We march within the hour."

Einar stared at Vigmarr Svarti's broad back as it waddled away from the holmgang square. His blood was up, fresh from defeating Fulk and killing a man whom Einar believed wanted to take his life. His hands flexed around axe and seax, instruments of pain and death. He could challenge Vigmarr there and then, strike him down and avenge his father's tortured soul. But to challenge the gnarled sea-jarl was to look into the eyes of death itself, to challenge something born of Loki. But it had to be done. The fight between him and Vigmarr seemed to grow more inevitable each day, growing, metastasising, pressing down on Einar and taking over his every thought.

He took a step towards Vigmarr, but a smiling face appeared suddenly before him and broke Einar's concentration.

"Victor of two holmgangs," said Ivar, grasping Einar's shoulders and looking up into his eyes. "Einar the Brawler, a man of reputation. March with me today. Your enemy is dead. Enjoy the victory."

Einar nodded slowly and walked to where Adzo waited with their gear.

"You'll be a famous man soon," Adzo remarked, shifting his bow from his left shoulder to his right. "If you keep killing people."

"He needed killing," Einar replied. "Better him than me."

"Aren't you going to claim his possessions?"

"I want nothing belonging to him."

"Fair enough. I thought for a moment there that you were going to attack Vigmarr."

"I was."

"Are you mad?"

"Look at where we are, Adzo. Look at the men around you. Our very lives are built around our prowess as warriors, our adherence to *drengskapr,* our pride and reputation."

"Everyone's moving, so let's go. Just try not to kill anybody else today if you can? Or challenge the most fearsome man in the army to single combat. Can you do that?"

Einar managed a fleeting grin. "I can try."

They left the hillside camp, and Einar marched in the vanguard. He and Adzo walked alongside Ivar, Radbod, Skallagrimr, and Likbjorn. Vigmarr and his riders ranged ahead of the column, checking for enemy scouts. The sea-jarl sent riders back to Ivar throughout the day with descriptions of the land ahead on their journey south, letting Ivar know if there were trees, hills, rivers, forests or settlements that might disrupt the march or provide a place to camp.

"I took these for you," said Skallagrimr, Ivar's friend. As they crossed a shallow valley beneath a sea-coloured sky, the warrior handed Einar an arm ring and a purse containing scraps of hacksilver.

"You keep them," Einar said.

"You won them with your axe. Take them or you risk angering the gods." Skallagrimr was a middle-aged man, squat and muscled. A fuzz of sparse hair covered his head and hair grew like a pelt on his arms, chest and back. "The gods urge us to combat. Odin will need us on the last day, when the Ragnarök begins, and Fenris Wolf comes for him, when Jormungandr tries to swallow the world. Odin, Thor and Freya will need hard men on that day. Do not shy away from battle, or regret taking a man's life. There is no wrong in it. We are not hand-wringing worshippers of the nailed god."

"Thank you, then." Einar took the ring and purse.

"The men respect you now. Have you noticed?"

Einar thought about that for a moment, and realised that warriors had begun to move out of his way when he walked through a crowd, that even the most weathered veterans inclined their heads to him in respect.

"I suppose so."

"You're one of us now," Ivar called over his shoulder. "A champion, a front rank growler, and a Ragnarsson warrior."

"A rider, Lord Ivar," said Radbod, pointing ahead.

A man on a dappled mare galloped across the open grassland and reined in, his horse throwing up great clumps of earth as it stopped and turned.

"Enemies, Lord Ivar," the rider said, pointing south. His lathered horse whickered and stomped on the ferns and heather. "Hundreds of them. Mustering beyond that rise."

"We are too far north for it to be Dolgfinnr. What banner do they fly?" asked Ivar.

"A white horse, lord."

"Must be the jarl come to fight at last. Hopefully, it's King Harald."

"Why do we want to fight King Harald when Dolgfinnr is our enemy?" Einar asked Skallagrimr.

"Leave the thinking to Ivar. We just do the fighting. You'll get used to it," Skallagrimr said.

Ivar marched his six-score warriors to the banks of a fast-flowing river, where one hundred warriors waited to do battle.

NINETEEN

Ivar's army left their supplies and belongings in the shade of a sprawling oak tree, and the son of Ragnar formed his men into four ranks and wheeled them around so that they marched towards the enemy with the sun at their backs. Einar wore his helmet, carried his shield and spear and wore his axe and seax belted at his waist. Adzo formed up on the left flank with Bersa, Ginnlaug, and the rest of the archers. Einar marched in the front rank alongside Radbod, Skallagrimr, Likbjorn and the rest of Ivar's picked champions, whilst Halvdan took up position directly behind him with Fat Garmr, Ulfketil Brownlegs, Styrr, Thorkild and the rest of the Seaworm crew. Vigmarr Svarti and his dread riders took the right flank, the side closest to the river.

"Vigmarr's there because he'll hold that flank until the end of days," Skallagrimr remarked.

"The enemy will attack on that side?" asked

Einar.

"This is your first shield wall fight?"

"Of this size, yes."

"They'll try to push us into the river, or attack that side and try to break through. If they can get behind us, we are all dead men. But we won't just stand here like cows waiting to be milked. Our archers will force them to shift towards the river, huddle them up like sheep."

"I've seen that done before."

"Hopefully these sons of whores don't want to fight all day," grumbled Likbjorn. He marched without a shield, holding his double-bladed, long-handled war axe in both hands. He wore the cheekpieces of his full-faced helmet closed so that he looked like a demon from Niflheim.

"You don't want to kill them?" asked Einar.

"I want to dance on their bones. But we are stranded in this place. Our ships are out on the Whale Road somewhere. Their numbers match our own. If we lose too many men, how can we fight Dolgfinnr and his wolf warriors? We shall need as many carls as possible when we face the champion of the North. It makes no sense to lose half our army here fighting over a midden heap beside a river. I don't even know what this place is called."

"Middenborg," said Radbod, and the warriors

guffawed.

"Turdtown," suggested another.

"Kingdom of the piss-donkeys," said a third and even Einar laughed.

Ivar strode before them whistling an oarsmen's song, both swords drawn and resting on his shoulders as though he was strolling to a summer fayre rather than to war. Four colossal men marched out of the enemy line and waited in the space between the two armies.

"Radbod, Likbjorn, Skallagrimr, come with me," Ivar called. "Einar, you can come along, too."

"Where are we going?" asked Einar, leaning into Skallagrimr so that Ivar wouldn't hear.

"To pick a fight. Jarls and sea-lords like to do this before a battle. Exchange insults and have a bit of a pissing contest, perhaps even negotiate a peaceful settlement."

"So there's a chance we might not have to fight after all?"

Skallagrimr laughed. "You should know Ivar by now. There'll be a fight all right."

Ivar beckoned to the right flank with his sword, and the five men waited as Vigmarr Svarti limped across the field. He carried his shield and used a spear as a walking stick, just as Einar had seen him do before. Vigmarr joined Ivar, and the two leaders led the small company towards where the enemy leaders waited ahead of their massed ranks. One of those men wore a shining chainmail *brynjar* and a helmet from which a pale horsehair plume flowed in the wind. He wore a red cape, calf-length leather boots, and a fleece-lined scabbard with a magnificent-looking sword resting at his hip. He was, Einar thought, the greatest-looking warrior he had ever seen. The other men wore leather and fur, and carried axes and spears. They scowled as Einar and the rest drew close.

"Fine day for it," Ivar remarked, swords still resting on his shoulders.

"Remove this rabble from my land," ordered the finely-dressed warrior.

"And you are?"

"Jarl Floki. Everything you see from that horizon to the next belongs to me. You have looted and raided enough. Where are your ships, pirate?"

"I am Ivar Ragnarsson, as I am sure you are aware. Where is King Harald?"

"On his way with an even larger army. So leave your weapons and crawl back into whatever crevice you slipped out of, before we dung the fields with your blood."

"Tut, tut. If your little king is really on his

way with a grand army, then why are you here? Surely it would make more sense to wait for him, no? Why bring the weaklings behind you to fight if your king is coming to save you? Your men tremble with fear. They are terrified. I can see it in their eyes. You and your *slyðras* leave the field, and we shall let you retreat with your lives."

"You are nothing but a pirate. A turd dropped from the arse of a goat."

"And you are a stinking piece of dogshit. Should we fight, you and I, before our armies?" Ivar lowered one sword and the hard-looking warriors behind Floki bristled, lurching forward with blades in their fists. "Settle this battle like warriors."

Floki smiled. "I don't need to face you. My army will crush yours like worms beneath our boots."

"Just as I thought. All that fancy armour, shining metal and expensive weapons are all for show. You are a coward and your men know it."

"Bastard." Floki turned on his heel and waved to his men. They hurried towards their ranks. A moment later, shields banged together and a forest of spears lowered to rest on shield rims as Floki's men prepared for battle.

"Looks like they want to fight, then," said Ivar, turning to Einar, Vigmarr and the rest.

"We might lose a third of our warriors in this fight, lord," said Likbjorn, shifting the grip on his long-handled war axe.

"We need all our warriors when we face Dolgfinnr. Don't worry. This will be over quickly. Rich Floki over there is an inland jarl. The bad men, the raiding jarls and warlords who hold their halls, harbours and river mouths around Agder's coast, protect his lands. He looks magnificent in his armour, and his men look fierce with their shining spears and new shields. Look at our shields, scored and battered by blades. Floki's shields might have been newly-crafted this morning. Prepare to form the swine head on me. The *Svinfylking*, the boar's snout. I shall lead, the rest of you form up behind me."

"Yes, lord," Einar and the rest said as one, except Vigmarr Svarti, who said nothing. He limped away on his spear and Einar followed Ivar towards the crews.

"March twenty paces," Ivar called to them over his shoulder. "Then form up. We'll break them quickly and the bastards will run for their lives. After that, we've a clear march towards Dolgfinnr."

"Unless they hold us," grumbled Likbjorn. "Lose a score of men in this piss-stinking backwater and we are done for."

Ivar called to Halvdan, and the shipmaster roared at the men, using his spear to bully them into the familiar *Svinfylking* formation.

"What's happening?" asked Adzo. He came loping from the flank with his bow in one hand and a white-feathered arrow in the other.

"We form the boar's snout and charge," Einar replied.

"Boar's snout?"

"Whilst you were helping your father plough fields and reap barley in Frankia, we grew up learning how to fight. We make the boar's snout when we want to break an army quickly. Ivar takes the lead, making the point of the snout. Two men line up behind him, four behind them and so on. Ivar and the champions take up the leading ranks, and they punch into the enemy shield wall and keep on charging until we break their lines in two. If it works, we break them with that first charge."

"And if it fails?"

"If they hold us, then Ivar and the men in the front will die, outnumbered and hacked to pieces by enemy blades."

"Then God help us. For if Ivar and the hardiest of us die, then we shall surely all die in this place."

"Then let's hope Odin is with us today, and not your peace-loving god."

Adzo shook his head and followed Bersa, Ginnlaug and the rest of the archers who took up position at the rear.

"Einar," Halvdan called, beckoning to Einar with his spear. "You fight beside me today, in the third rank."

Einar followed Halvdan, striding through one hundred and twenty warriors tightening leather straps, hefting shields, and preparing for battle. Some looked skyward and whispered prayers to Odin, Thor, Týr, Freyr, or whichever god they believed would bring them luck. Others took a last chance to piss beside the river, or to drink ale to slake the thirst that always came before battle. Einar rested his shield against his leg and adjusted his leather breastplate to lower the neck. He made sure his axe and seax were secure, and then hefted his shield. His head sweated beneath the leather liner inside his helmet, but he was ready.

"Advance," Ivar called, and drew his two swords. He lifted one and pointed at the enemy, and his warriors shouted their battle cries.

"Who do we fight for?" Halvdan called.

"Ivar, Ivar, Ivar!" six-score voices roared in unison.

"Then let's see you do it!"

Men beat their spears upon their shields to make the war music, one hard drum for every step of their left boot. The enemy remained in place, shields and spear points glinting in the sun. Einar saw Jarl Floki's horsehair plume in the third rank and knew at that moment that Ivar was right. Floki was no lover of war. He was a rich man's son, a man born to wealth and expected inheritance with an army of warriors to protect him. Amongst the Vikings, the hunters and killers, only the strong ruled. A weak man would find himself challenged and butchered by stronger men. Floki was no Viking; inland he had never faced the fearsome sight of dragon ships bearing down upon his home bristling with blades and bearded growlers.

The army moved forward, still in ranks, and Einar counted his paces. Ten paces and he rolled his shoulders, fifteen paces and he felt the buzz ripple through the men, the quickening, the readiness and apprehension of battle. Death was close, Odin watching, his Valkyrie poised to swoop down and take the souls of the glorious dead to Valhalla. Eighteen paces and he shifted his hand on the ash spear shaft, palm sweaty, breathing deeply, preparing himself for the clash of blades.

"*Svinfylking!*" Ivar roared at twenty paces,

and the Seaworm and Windspear crews swiftly hurried into the boar's snout formation. Shields and spears banged and boots pounded upon the grass. Men grunted and iron clanked as warriors took up positions. Excitement warmed his belly and Einar took his place with Halvdan in a rank of eight, behind Radbod, Skallagrimr, and two other champions. Vigmarr Svarti and Likbjorn took their places behind Ivar so that the triangular boar's snout took shape, like a spear point ready to cut the enemy ranks open.

The Boneless broke into a jog at the formation's apex and a ripple of fear ran across the enemy ranks like a gust of wind. Their spears shook and their shield wall shifted as the warriors at the centre realised that Ivar and his hardest warriors charged at them, their intent to hack and cut at them, to slaughter and maim until their ranks gave way. Arrows soared overhead as Adzo and the archers loosed their shafts over the charging boar's snout. Their arrows slammed into the heart of Jarl Floki's ranks. A man shrieked as an arrow thunked into his face, and the rest raised their shields to fend off the murderous missiles. Spears flew from the enemy ranks, but Ivar's men batted them away with their shields and ten paces out, Ivar sprinted at them.

Einar and the other picked champions of the first ranks kept pace. Einar charged, his shield held high, brushing against Radbod to keep the formation tight. Men growled like animals. Some called to Odin and shouted in anger.

"Kill, Skalla," Skallagrimr said to himself, mumbling and shaking his head, working himself up into madness. "Kill them. Kill them all. Live. Kill. Live. Kill."

Einar set his jaw, determined to make sure his place amongst the foremost warriors was justified. He fought beside the champions, the picked men, the warriors Ivar trusted to fight to the death with savagery and war-skill. Enemy faces showed above their shields; blonde beards, brown and blue eyes, leather and iron helmets, frightened and angry faces, scars, huge fists grasping sharp weapons. Einar realised he was roaring, shouting at the top of his voice along with the other warriors as they did what they must to summon the bravery and will to charge into a hundred men bent on taking their lives.

Enemy faces grew closer as Einar's boots raced across the field and then, in a crash of steel upon wood, a splash of blood and a scream of pain, Ivar was upon them.

"Keep it tight!" Halvdan bellowed, encouraging the men to keep their formation in place. If the *Svinfylking* worked, they would cut deep into the enemy, and if a man broke formation, if he lagged behind, if the enemy could yank or pull him out of formation, that man would find himself hacked to death beneath a welter of blades.

Suddenly the air about Einar filled with the crack and clamour of weapons. His shield smashed into an enemy's and Einar's size drove that man backwards. There was no time to strike with his spear. Einar simply tucked his head in tight to his shoulders and kept his shield high. A face slashed by Ivar's sword flashed past Einar, eye and nose cut open in a horror of blood and bone. Einar pressed forward, and within five strides, they were deep inside the enemy ranks.

"We have the whoresons," Halvdan said, but Einar could see nothing but Radbod's greying hair and his fur-lined broad back in front of him. The charge slowed and Einar stumbled forwards, Radbod disappearing so that suddenly all Einar could see before him was the river and an open meadow. He turned and found chaos. The *Svinfylking* had worked and Ivar's charge had punched all the way through Jarl Floki's ranks, carving his army in two. Ivar and the other front rankers had spun and begun to hack into Floki's rear rankers, and Einar joined them.

A frightened-faced man held his shield too high, and Einar opened his calf muscle with a jab of his spear. The shield came down and Einar pushed his spear point into the man's throat. Shouting to his left caught Einar's attention, where Floki and his men finally understood what they should have done the moment Ivar and his men charged their ranks. They had used their spears to trip the sixth line in the *Svinfylking*, taking their legs from under them as men blinded by their shields and the press of warriors about them could do nothing but fall into the men in front of them. The seventh rank tumbled over the sixth and Einar understood that if he did not charge to the aid of those tumbling men, Ivar's charge, which had seemed so decisive, could turn to ruin in an instant.

"Halvdan!" Einar shouted, but did not wait for the shipmaster. He plunged his spear into the guts of a foe and let go of the weapon. Einar drew his axe and charged into the enemy with his shield. Something heavy thumped that shield and a bearded axe hooked over its rim. Einar let it go, hurling himself towards the enemy who had hacked into the mess of fallen warriors. The men on the ground floundered, tangled by spears, shields and the flailing limbs of their comrades as the enemy chopped at them with axes and spears. Einar grabbed a man by the back of his breastplate and hauled him away. An enormous warrior with a bushy black beard killed a Seaworm man with a wickedly-curved knife and Einar cracked his axe across that man's skull.

A shining figure reared in front of Einar, a man

in a gleaming *brynjar* and helmet, wielding a bright sword in his hand. It was Jarl Floki, sword clean and unmarked by battle. Einar swung his axe at the jarl, but he stepped backwards, almost falling into his own men. Einar followed him and swung his axe at full stretch. The jarl tried to dodge the blow, but the press of men held him in place and Einar's axe blade cut open his neck and cheek. It was a shallow cut, the blade at the extremity of its reach, but such a cut to the face bleeds terribly and in a heartbeat, the jarl's armour became soaked with crimson.

Ivar and Halvdan appeared, cutting and slashing at the enemy and Likbjorn leapt over two falling warriors and swung his huge war axe with such ferocity that it cleft a man almost in two. The horror of that wound and the injury to Jarl Floki sent the enemy into panic and rout. They fled the field, scampering like frightened dogs from the stink of blood and voided bowels and the screams of dying men. Einar rushed to the fallen warriors, standing before them with his axe ready like a wolf defending its cubs. Jarl Floki himself ran like a hare across the battlefield. He hitched up the skirts of his magnificent *brynjar* to run faster, and his horsehair-plumed helmet toppled from his head, only to be hastily scooped up by one of his warriors.

"Let them go," Ivar ordered, resting his hands

on his knees. "It's over."

"Let's kill the bastards," Radbod gasped, his face dotted with blood and his eyes wild. "Destroy them, so they are finished forever."

"I said leave them. Let them run to their king. We advance on Dolgfinnr."

Later, Einar sat on the riverbank and watched a hundred enemy warriors run over a distant hillock. The sound of rushing water dulled the groans of the wounded, and Einar washed his weapons and breastplate.

"Look what I found," said Adzo, sitting down heavily beside Einar with a loud sigh. He held up a fine bronze arm ring, which he slipped over his wrist.

"You are wealthy now," Einar said with a half-smile.

"And we are alive."

"How many did we lose?"

Adzo looked back towards the battlefield. "Five, I think. Eight more gravely injured."

Einar nodded slowly. He realised he had taken a cut to the back of his hand and he washed it in the cool water, allowing the river to flow over his skin.

"What's wrong with you?" Adzo asked. "We

won."

"I was just wondering where the dead have gone. If they are in Valhalla."

"Be happy, Einar. You were picked to fight at the front today, with the most respected men amongst both crews."

"I know, and I am thankful for Odin's luck." He stood and took Adzo's arm in the warrior's grip. Over Adzo's shoulder, Einar saw Vigmarr Svarti going amongst the enemy fallen, cutting their throats with his long knife. Moving like a demon, hunched and all in black. Two men sprang up from amongst the fallen, enemy warriors who had feigned injury to avoid the slaughter. They saw a bent cripple before them and they circled him with axes in the fists. They saw a chance to kill one of the enemy before fleeing for their lives, but those men were mistaken. The understanding of what they faced dawned on them as Vigmarr straightened and flicked the black cascade of hair from his face. They gaped at the ruin of Vigmarr's scars and the horror of his impossibly black eyes, and their feral snarls turned into fearful grimaces. Vigmarr's left hand shot out, and he grabbed a fistful of the closest man's hair. Vigmarr stabbed him twice in the stomach, with so much strength in the blow that he lifted the warrior from his feet. The man fell to his knees and Vigmarr Svarti yanked his head back by the hair, and scalped him. He sawed his knife across the man's scalp until the hair and flesh came free, and then kicked the screaming enemy to the grass. He turned and showed his grisly prize to the second man, who tried to turn and flee. Vigmarr let him run four paces then slowly drew his axe. He threw the weapon underhand, so that it flew low, turning in the air before it took the running warrior in the back. He fell writhing like a hamstrung pig until Vigmarr descended on him, falling upon the stricken man like a black fog. The curved knife rose and fell. Screams and blood came from the dying man, and Einar looked away.

Some warriors made the sign to ward off evil, and others just stared at Vigmarr, the man every warrior in the army feared. He was like something from a nightmare, like one of the *huldu* folk, the hidden folk, the dark elves, Thurs trolls, and dwarves who dwelt in the mountains, forests and beside ancient stone circles and for whom folk left butter, cheese and bread beside sacred stones to appease the wickedness. Such offerings were always taken, and people left them to stop the Loki creatures from stealing children, from laming sheep, blighting crops, or worse, sneaking through windows to steal a maiden's virtue. How could any man stand before Vigmarr Svarti and not tremble with fear?

"Look there!" called a warrior, pointing his spear to the north. Einar turned.

"Lord God preserve us," gasped Adzo and made the sign of the cross, and he was right to ask for the nailed god's help, for a new army appeared over a rise, marching towards the river. A new army to fight, hundreds of them marching towards the opposite bank to finish what Jarl Floki had started.

TWENTY

Ivar ran to the riverbank, joined by a stream of his warriors. The crews were still bloody and wearied from fighting Jarl Floki's men and now faced the prospect of fighting an even larger force. Einar's shoulders burned from battle, and the thrill of combat had drifted away, leaving him drained. Other men's blood dried in dark flakes upon his hands and breastplate, and now a force twice the size of Jarl Floki's army approached the river. A dozen of the enemy came on horseback and a forest of spears wavered above the advancing warriors. A shrill war horn blared to let Odin know men came to do battle in his honour.

"Frigg's tits," muttered a man behind Einar.

"Who is it?" asked Ulfketil Brownlegs, standing next to Einar with a looted pair of boots in his hand.

"Can't be more of the bastards we've just beaten," said Fat Garmr. "They went that way.

Look, though, some of them are joining the new enemy." He pointed a bony arm downriver where scores of Jarl Floki's men splashed through the water and clambered up the far bank.

"It's King Harald Granraude," said Ivar. He clapped Far Garmr so hard on the back that the thin man almost fell into the river. "He arrived sooner than I expected. Very well."

A warrior beside the Boneless bent and washed his spear in the water.

"No, no," said Ivar. "Leave the blood on the blades and the battle filth on your armour. I want them to see us, to understand who we are."

"There must be two hundred men in that shield wall," said Radbod, craning his neck to peer through the reeds and brush across the river. "We can't fight again today, lord. They outnumber us two to one."

Radbod fell short of suggesting they should retreat. Ivar kept his gaze firmly on the approaching army. "Form the men up behind me in three ranks. Shields and spears ready."

Radbod grinned and nodded, as though he had suddenly found a way inside Ivar's cunning mind. "We'll kill the sheep humpers as they wade through the river. They'll never make it up the bank. Numbers won't matter when they're dying in the water."

Einar wasn't so sure. Ivar loved to fight, and he was as unpredictable as a starving weasel. King Harald's men could charge through the water and pin Ivar's centre in the river, then the king of Agder would send men around their flank to take Ivar's rear. King Harald believed the Norns had woven a weft of victory into the thread of his life, and now he approached with a formidable force. Einar took off his helmet and ran a hand through his wet hair, soaked with sweat beneath the leather liner. He didn't relish the thought of dying beside an unknown river in a battle men would never hear of. His corpse would rot beside the rippling river and nobody would know he had ever existed.

"If we are going to die here on this riverbank," Einar said, as much to himself as the men around him, "then let's die as hard as we can. Let's kill so many of these whoresons that Odin All-Father will have to open the gates of Valhalla for us."

A few of the warriors hoomed in agreement, but more shifted uncomfortably. Even if they won the day and beat this new army into surrender, fighting two hundred warriors would cost the crews many lives. Too many lives. Einar saw a grim future, of fifty men fighting their way across to Agder, dragging another thirty injured carls with them. Every farm, village, and man with a blade would dog their journey to the coast, attacking in the darkness, ambushing the column in forests until the survivors finally reached the coast. Even if they made it that far, Einar did not know how Ivar planned to find the Seaworm and Windspear. The two ships were out there sailing the Skagerrak with skeleton crews and could be between any of the countless islands off Norway's south-east coast, or perhaps they had encountered danger and returned to Hrafnborg. All Einar could do was trust Ivar, and as his oathman he must follow his lord, even if it meant marching to his death.

Halvdan and Skallagrimr harried the men into formation, and Einar took his place in the first rank between Likbjorn and Styrr.

"Look at Brownlegs," said Styrr, nudging Einar with his elbow.

Einar watched as Ulfketil tried to put on his new boots. They were supple brown leather, far better than his own worn pair. Yngvi the Fire crept up behind Ulfketil and pushed him into the river, sending the army into fits of laughter. Ulfketil tried to haul himself out and slipped four times on the muddy bank before Yngvi finally helped his shipmate out of the water.

"Lost one of the bloody boots," Ulfketil moaned, staring sadly at the water with one bare foot.

"Form up, empty head," Halvdan growled. "All of you, get in line unless you want your heads dunted."

The warriors hefted their shields and spears and gathered into battle formation whilst Ivar waited beside the river. Three riders came from the enemy ranks. The leader rode a white stallion, its mane and tail shining like a full moon on a frosty night. He wore a helmet chased with gold and silver, inset with a golden crown. His long beard was the colour of a new fire, plaited into two thick ropes. Two riders flanked him, one carrying a battle standard depicting an antlered stag, the second a haggard man with his head shaved bald and a gold-tipped war horn in his hand.

"Harald Granraude," said Styrr wistfully. Granraude meant red-bearded, and the king cut a magnificent figure on his prancing white horse. He wore a long red cloak and as he came close to the river, the king turned his horse in a full circle in an elaborate show of horsemanship.

"Will he fight?" asked Einar. To fight two hundred men so soon after charging Jarl Floki's army seemed like suicide, even for warriors who fought for Ivar the Boneless.

"I hope not. I'm too hungry to fight again."

The king rode his white horse up and down the riverbank whilst his standard bearers sneered at Ivar from across the rover. After two passes along the length of the Seaworm and

Windspear crews, Harald reined in opposite Ivar and drew an ivory-hilted sword from his red scabbard.

"I am Harald Granraude, King of Agder," he called in a deep, sonorous voice. "You trespass on my land."

"I am Ivar Ragnarsson," said Ivar, and then yawned elaborately like a man waiting for the tide to change.

"I have heard of you, Ivar the Boneless."

"In which case you have the upper hand, for I have heard nothing of your exploits. I have just routed one of your jarls. He ran from battle like a frightened child, whimpering like a coward. Some of his men join your rabble, I see." He gestured downriver to the men climbing from the river to swell Harald's ranks.

Harald's face flushed. "Why are you here, and where are your ships? We don't get raiders this far inland."

"I am no raider. We have a common enemy, I believe."

Harald's horse became skittish, and he stroked its neck to calm the beast. "What enemy?"

"Dolgfinnr Dogsblood, who once swore an oath to my father, Ragnar Lothbrok. He has broken that oath and sworn fealty to Gudrød the Hunter, king of the Vestfold."

"Gudrød is known to me. But what has your enmity with Dolgfinnr to do with you slaughtering my people?"

"I came to fight Dolgfinnr, but Gudrød ambushed me after bringing a great fleet into your waters."

Harald glanced at his two warriors and then returned his gaze to Ivar. "There is a feud between Gudrød and I."

"I heard. You refused his proposal of marriage to your daughter."

"I did. Gudrød is not worthy of my daughter."

"Now he returns with an army and has allied with Dolgfinnr Dogsblood, and soon you will find yourself under attack. You, I believe, need warriors. Not piss-weasels like Jarl Floki and his ragged band of pretend warriors. Real fighting men. You need true *drengrs*. Killers, men who can stand and trade blows with Dolgfinnr and Gudrød."

Harald's horse skittered again, and the king sawed on its reins to keep the stallion under control. "You have butchered my people and fed off the uncertainty of war. You want to put my people to the sword when we face an enemy on our shores?"

"I came for Dolgfinnr and find myself in your lands. I have two crews of the most fearsome men on the Whale Road. Ask Jarl Floki, or his men whom we sent to flight without even breaking sweat. My enemy is also your enemy. I don't want to be in your kingdom, King Harald. I want to kill Dolgfinnr Dogsblood, a man who broke his oath to my father and who squats on the edge of your kingdom like shit clinging to a goat's arse. He is not your vassal, and nor have you his oath. We should talk, instead of killing each other."

"Then let's talk. Bring a dozen of your men and I shall do the same. No more. We'll meet beside that oak tree yonder. I warn you though, Ivar the Boneless, if I suspect any tricks, or if any of your men try to cross the river, you shall all die here today."

"Good. I think I might have put my shoulder out killing so many of Jarl Floki's men. A rest is welcome. But your threat works both ways, King Harald. I'll meet you beneath the oak tree, but if you try to deceive me or outflank my men then I will show you something you have never seen before. I will visit such a slaughter on your warriors that I will cripple your kingdom for a generation. Then, when I am done with your warriors, I will loose my men on your people, but not gentle like before. I will give them free rein and soak your land with blood and tears."

The king wheeled his horse around and cantered away from the river. Ivar stared after him, hands on his hips, lost in the depths of his own cunning.

"Get some rest, men," Ivar said, eventually. He strode from the riverbank and rubbed his hands together like an excited wool merchant. "We might be here for a while whilst I talk to the king."

An hour later Einar crossed the river with Ivar, Halvdan, Styrr, Thorkild, Radbod, Vigmarr, Skallagrimr, Yngvi the Fire, Fat Garmr and four of Ivar's largest warriors. They waded through a shallow ford, stepping across slick rocks until they reached the far side where King Harald's men waited. Ivar smiled cheerfully at the sour-faced warriors, strapping men all in *brynjars*, carrying long spears and shields painted with the king's stag emblem. King Harald himself stood beneath the boughs of a sprawling oak tree, sipping ale from a wooden cup. He wore his war finery, and beside him stood a shamefaced Jarl Floki, and the most beautiful woman Einar had ever seen.

"She looks like Freya," whispered Styrr. He brushed down his striped trews and sucked his belly in. "Come from Asgard to walk amongst us."

Einar struggled to find words to agree with his shipmate. A golden-haired woman of astonishing beauty stood beside King Harald.

She was young, of an age with Einar, with bright blue eyes the colour of fjord ice. A silver circlet adorned her brow, and she wore a long, flowing leaf-green gown. Her startling eyes shone from a pale face with a wide mouth framed by cherry-red lips. It was hard to look at her, almost painful to learn that such a woman could exist in the world. Her eyes flicked to Einar, as though she felt him staring at her, and Einar turned away. His face flushed red and his neck became hot. He stared instead at the ground, for to look into her eyes again was as terrifying as meeting the gaze of Fafnir the dragon. She was terrible to look upon, not because she was threatening or stern, but because of her impossible beauty.

"Ivar Ragnarsson," King Harald said. He gestured to the young woman, and then to Ivar. "I present my daughter, Princess Åsa Haraldsdottir."

"My lady," said Ivar, and bowed low. "Please excuse my unpresentable appearance. I have spent the best part of a week killing your father's warriors and today besting Jarl Floki here, whom I commend on his uncanny speed of flight."

"Lord Ivar," said Princess Åsa, and she smiled at his arrogance.

"Floki's defeat is a topic for another day," said the king, and Floki bowed his head in shame. "There is ale for your men and food. Let them rest whilst we talk of our mutual enemies."

A man with a lop-sided jaw led Einar and the rest of Einar's dozen to where three slaves waited with jugs of ale, cuts of cold meat, cheese and bread.

"Why bring a princess to war?" wondered Styrr, holding his stomach as it groaned like a sad bear. "May Freya help her if she falls into enemy hands."

"Perhaps he wants to show her off?" Einar replied.

"To the likes of us?"

"True. To Ivar, maybe?"

"If I had a daughter who looked like that, I wouldn't leave her at home either. Every bastard in King Harald's hall is probably trying to hump her. Is that pork?" Styrr pointed at a slab of meat, and a thrall woman nodded and held the food out in both hands.

Einar took some bread and cheese and stepped back from King Harald's dozen champions, who growled and frowned as Ivar's men noisily helped themselves to food and drink.

"Never step away from them," warned Skallagrimr, without taking his eyes from Harald's men. "Stand your ground." He, Radbod, and Likbjorn returned King Harald's warriors' hard stares, whilst Vigmarr Svarti took some food and ale and sat alone.

Einar had no interest in exchanging angry looks with men he had never met before. Each one was immense, scarred and clearly a warrior to fear, but so were Ivar's men, and Einar was hungry. So, he ate and drank cool ale whilst Ivar, the king and the princess, talked beside the oak tree.

"Seems like Ivar knew what he was doing all along," said Styrr through a mouthful of food. "Everybody complained, not to Ivar's face, obviously. But quietly, on the march or at night, we all grumbled, wondering why we traipsed through Agder when we should be killing Dolgfinnr and going after the raven banner. But Ivar knew."

"Do you think he planned this?"

Styrr's head jerked back, and he frowned. "Of course he did. Soon enough, we'll have a king fighting at our side."

"If he did, then he's as crafty as everybody believes." Einar wasn't so sure. It seemed like luck more than cleverness. Ivar had come ashore and sent the ships away. That gave the men no choice but to fight for their lives, for there was no way out of enemy lands without the Seaworm and the Windspear. Then he had taken the long road to Dolgfinnr's fortress, coming at it from the rear rather than marching directly towards the stronghold. That was good sense. King Gudrød's fleet and Dolgfinnr's warriors searched for Ivar, undoubtedly hunting for him across the Skagerrak strait, so to approach by land was the safest option. But to stumble across a king with a shared hatred of Ivar's enemy was lucky. But a warrior needed luck, especially Odin's luck.

"Ivar has plans within plans inside his head, working over each other like the coils of Jormungandr, and just as slippery."

The men finished their food and before the sun had shifted across the oak tree, Ivar and King Harald took each other's forearms in the warrior's grip, and Ivar bowed deeply to Princess Åsa. Ivar strolled towards his men with a gleam in his eye and accepted a chunk of bread from a thrall. Ivar took a bite, looked Harald's dozen warriors up and down admiringly, and washed his food down with a mouthful of ale. Einar and the rest waited with open mouths for him to finish and tell them what he and the king had agreed.

"We are going to join forces with King Harald," Ivar said at last, taking a morsel of cheese and popping it into his mouth. "He is going to follow the river and march south to his hall. We shall follow, looping around those hills so that we protect his column's flank on the march. We shall come close to Dolgfinnr's lands, and there's a chance that the Dogsblood will have men out searching for us. If we find them, they die. We shall reach King Harald's hall two days after the king's men. Then, we march together against Dolgfinnr and Gudrød the Hunter. To seal the deal, Harald will take four hostages from my crews, and I will take four from his. Vigmarr and Likbjorn will go, and then two more...." Ivar scratched his chin and used his tongue to move bits of cheese from between his teeth.

"The pup," said Vigmarr Svarti, surprising everyone. He rarely spoke, and the sound of his voice was as grating as chewing old rope. Vigmarr brushed the mane of hair away from his face with his hand, and those dead, pitch-black eyes rested on Einar. "And his Frank. Last in, first out."

"Seems fair," Ivar replied. "Einar, you and Adzo are our most recent recruits. Other than Fulk, whom you killed. So you two will accompany Vigmarr and Likbjorn."

"Have you chosen, Lord Ivar?" said King Harald, striding towards them with his thumbs tucked into his belt.

"I have. Four of my best. Have you picked your men?"

Harald pointed to four of his growlers, whose angry faces didn't shift an inch when their king picked them out to accompany Ivar as hostages. "These are champions amongst my warriors, every one of them a seasoned veteran with reputation."

"That's settled then."

Ivar took the king's hand again and Harald introduced Ivar to the four men who would march with him as hostages.

"Unlucky, Einar," murmured Styrr. He sucked his teeth and shook his head.

"Why unlucky? All I'm going to do is march with the king instead of our crews. There'll probably be a feast at Harald's hall before you arrive. Then we go after Dolgfinnr. What's so bad about that?"

"You're a hostage. Don't you know what that means?"

"That if either Ivar or Harald break their agreement to join forces, the hostages will pay the price."

"Exactly. If Ivar doesn't show up at King Harald's hall two days after you get there, you poor bastards will have your throats cut."

"Why would Ivar break his word?"

"Maybe he won't." Styrr walked away and then laughed as Einar hurried after him, looking for clarity. "Keep your trews on. He won't break his word. I was just yanking your oar."

"You there!" Ivar shouted suddenly. Every

person beside the oak tree stopped and stared at the Boneless. Ivar took six quick steps until he came face to face with the largest man in King Harald's retinue. He was a full head taller than Ivar and as wide as a ship's hull. The warrior wore a *brynjar* edged with fox fur, carried a sword in a
fleece-lined scabbard and wore miniature iron trinkets braided into his beard. He frowned down as Ivar squared up to him. "You said something. Do you mock me?"

The warrior's mouth twisted with uncertainty, but he held his ground and looked to his king for guidance. King Harald's new ally challenged him openly, putting the warrior in an impossible situation. Back down, and he lost face in front of his sword-brothers, but insult Ivar and he risked his lord's wrath. "I did not mock you," the warrior said in a slow voice.

"First you mocked me, now you say I'm a liar? Don't look at him, look at me!" Ivar's jovial voice had gone, replaced by the flint-hard voice of a killer. His eyes blazed, and his handsome face grew as flat and hard as the cruellest cliff in the harshest sea. Einar had seen the same situation at Hrafnborg after his holmgang against Olvir. Then, Ivar had challenged and killed a warrior for nothing, and Einar recognised the terrifying gleam of madness in his eyes.

"I said nothing," said the warrior, but his hand

shifted to the pommel of his sword, and in an instant, Ivar kicked him hard in the stomach driving the warrior backwards.

In a flash, Ivar drew his two swords, Hugin and Munin, and everybody took five steps back, even the king.

"Lord Ivar..." King Harald began, but Ivar snarled at him, warning the red-bearded king to silence.

The rest of Harald's men drew their weapons, and so did Einar and Ivar's men; in a heartbeat, a peaceful negotiation threatened to boil over into slaughter. Ivar turned in a circle with his two swords levelled, a cruel smile splitting his face, his eyes shining like opals.

"This man mocked me, and I am Ivar the Boneless. No man mocks Ivar unless he is ready to fight for his life. Draw your sword, *slyðra,* come and fight with Ivar." Ivar was shouting now, roaring like a madman and Princess Åsa stepped behind her father. "I'll fight you all, every one of you turds. One at a time or all at once. Doesn't matter."

King Harald's warriors licked their lips and exchanged nervous glances, unsure what to make of the slight man with the two swords who threatened them all like he was the most fearsome man in Midgard. Einar supposed that some or all of them had heard of Ivar the

Boneless and his famous father and brothers, but he doubted they had ever seen a man fight with such skill and savagery.

"I'll fight you," said the warrior in fur as he got to his feet, rising from where Ivar had kicked him to the ground. "What kind of man makes peace and then starts a fight?"

"Draw your sword." Ivar twirled Hugin and Munin, the twin blades flashing around him like lightning hurled by Thor. He moved with the blades, shifting on the balls of his feet like a dancer.

"I am Jarrold Kjartansson," said the warrior, and he drew his sword, holding the hilt in two hands.

Ivar stopped his display and came to rest with one sword held above his head, pointing towards Jarrold like a spear, and the other held low and crosswise to his body. Jarrold set his jaw and came at Einar. He led with his right foot and slashed overhand at Ivar, keeping his guard high and cutting from left to right. Ivar parried some of those cuts and danced around the rest. Jarrold's breathing grew heavy, and he paused his attack, waiting with his sword held before him. Ivar surged at him, swords moving with impossible speed. Jarrold parried one cut with the edge of his sword, but Ivar's blade scraped down its length until it reached the guard. Ivar twisted his wrist and Jarrold grimaced as his wrist jerked at a terrible angle.

Ivar turned, driving the point of his second sword into Jarrold's chest with such force that it punched through the *brynjar*'s chainmail links. The sword pushed deep into Jarrold's body and he gaped at the blade tearing into his chest. Ivar ripped the sword free with an awful sucking sound and Jarrold slumped to his knees as a gush of blood pulsed from the wound to soak his armour.

"Keep hold of it," Ivar stated, gesturing to the sword in Jarrold's right hand.

Jarrold's hand trembled, the bones in his wrist ruined by Ivar's skill. Jarrold opened his mouth and dark blood seeped into his beard. With a flick of his arm, Ivar plunged his sword down into Jarrold's mouth so that the blade pierced into Jarrold's throat and body. He let go of the sword and turned to Harald, pointing his second bloody sword at the king.

"We have an agreement," Ivar said, his voice cool and calm. "We have exchanged hostages and our bargain still holds. Leave now and take my four men with you. But if you betray me, king or not, I will return with my brothers and put your kingdom to the sword. When I reach your hall, King Harald, I want to see my men safe and your army ready to march. Otherwise, you bring down the wrath of the Boneless and the raven banner upon your house and your people, and that can only be tempered with blood."

King Harald just gawped at the sudden terrifying display. He bowed his head once to confirm that their agreement still stood, but said nothing to challenge Ivar's shocking savagery. Ivar gripped his blade and tore it from Jarrold's quivering body, leaving him to bleed and die in front of his king. Einar turned away from the corpse, and Ivar's fiercely unpredictable rage. He was to be a hostage now, his life in the hands of King Harald and Ivar's agreement. Worse, he was to go to King Harald's hall with Vigmarr Svarti. Harald's men hurried to the king, too stunned to do anything about their dead comrade.

Einar watched Vigmarr limp towards the river, and for a moment, the enormous sea-jarl paused and inclined his head in Einar's direction. Einar shuddered. Why had Vigmarr nominated him and Adzo? If he already knew Einar suspected him of killing his father, then Vigmarr would surely come for him. He imagined that scarred face, those eyes dark like the pit of Niflheim, attacking him, and Einar knew then that the reckoning must come. He must face Vigmarr Svarti. Einar must stand and challenge the man who had killed his father.

"Good luck," said Styrr, and he clapped Einar on the back before following Ivar and the rest across the river. War was coming; King Gudrød the Hunter and Dolgfinnr Dogsblood loomed out of the Skagerrak with a fleet and an army of seasoned warriors. Ivar would face them, and all Einar could see in his future were axes, spears, swords, revenge and the murderous blood feud.

TWENTY-ONE

On the morning of the fourth day since leaving Jarl Floki's lands, King Harald led his army into his coastal home on Tromoya island. The king had three homes: a summer hall set further inland from which he would hunt, feast, and receive important guests, a winter hall in Agder's north where his family spent winters in the deep snow, and Tromoya. Tromoya served as the king's war capital, the home of his warships and warriors. The marching column woke early that morning after a chilly night spent sleeping in the open and arrived at Tromoya as a bright but cold sun hung high in the ice-blue sky.

A sea breeze tinged with salt blew through Einar's hair, and the distant cry of seabirds stirred his love of the sea and lifted his spirits. Einar and Adzo marched on either side of Likbjorn, the tall warrior striding on rangy legs with his long, double-bladed war axe strapped to his back. Vigmarr Svarti shuffled and limped along behind them, alone, grunting and sniffing like a ferocious beast. Einar had spent three nights camping close to Vigmarr, unbearably close. Einar had lain down beneath his woollen cloak, holding his seax close to his chest. He lay awake, listening to men snoring and shifting sleeping positions around him. Whilst they slept beneath the stars, Einar had stared at the lump of Vigmarr's sleeping form, like a demon from the pit, malevolence pulsing from him even as he slept. Einar lay awake late each night, his mind telling him to crawl across the sleeping men and cut the sea-jarl's throat. He agonised over it, wrestling with his conscience.

Fulk would have cut my throat without pause or regret, he told himself. *Vigmarr would gut me and use my skull as a drinking cup.*

But his heart told him it couldn't end like that.

The feud and revenge for his father's death couldn't end with a knife in the dark. It was almost as though the gods sent that message to Einar in the starlight, warning him that murdering Vigmarr would not be the action of a *drengr* and would not free Egil's soul from Niflheim. When Einar struck at Vigmarr, it must be to his face, a fight with honour, so that Vigmarr knew the son avenged the father. Only then could Egil leave the dark, cold horror of Niflheim and rise to take his place amongst the honourable dead in Valhalla, Thruthvangar or Sessrúmnir. So, Einar stayed his hand and approached Tromoya, eyes stinging with tiredness, the sound of Vigmarr's boots scuffing upon the road jarring in Einar's head with every step.

Shields clattered against spears and axe hafts as seventy warriors approached the island on the well-trodden approach path, with deep wagon ruts and sleeping beggars on each side. More than half of King Harald's army had departed in crews and family groups as the column marched through Agder. They returned to their own farms and halls with the king's thanks, ready to march again whenever Harald summoned them. Tromoya's fortifications appeared across the narrow land bridge, leading to the low island perched as it was on the edge of King Harald's kingdom. The island faced the Skagerrak, the waterway where Vikings roamed and warships prowled, sea-wolves in search of prey and plunder. An archipelago of four hundred islands stretched across the Skagerrak strait, protecting the trade and war routes south to the Baltic, to the wide rivers leading south to the wonders of Miklagard and the mysterious east with its coins, silks, and slave markets. Every island was home to a jarl and his sons and their hearth troop of warriors; every man with an axe and a shield who craved battle and reputation, who must seek combat and glory to earn the favour of Odin, and his bloodthirsty Aesir.

A thick timber palisade ran around the entirety of King Harald's settlement. It protected his longhouse hall, barns, byres, stables, barley and wheat stores, and wattle and daub houses topped with greyed thatch. Warriors walked along the fighting platform of that high palisade, its sharpened stakes pointing at the sky like dragon's teeth. The walls offered protection from any landward threat, but more importantly, from the seaborne invaders and raiders who might launch an attack along the island's rocky shores. Guard towers stood at regular intervals along the wall, manned by helmeted warriors whose eyes scanned the rolling Whale Road for any sign of the greedy sea-wolves and their sleek warships.

"I wonder what the women are like here?" asked Adzo. He brushed his hair quickly with a bone comb and placed his naal-binding cap on his head.

"Too handsome and honourable to steal a kiss with a Frank like you," answered Likbjorn with a half-smile.

"Can you smell that?" asked Einar. His stomach grumbled as the smell of smoking fish and roasting meat wafted on the sea breeze.

"I could eat a scabby horse," said Likbjorn, and Einar laughed.

They neared the entrance and a warrior high on the walls blew two long notes on a war horn to announce the king's arrival. Massive wooden gates swung open on thick leather hinges and the smell of food faded, replaced by the town stink of shit and smoke. The king led his men through the gate on his white horse, flanked by his exquisite daughter, and the folk inside the town, clad simply in wool tunics and dyed cloaks, stopped their work and bowed their heads. They kept their heads down as the warriors marched past.

Warriors peeled off to greet their wives and families, and frightened-faced women peeked at the men through wooden shutters, fearful that their husband or son might have lost his life in battle. The path to the king's hall wound through wood and wattle buildings with thatch reeking of damp and rot, and a boy used a switch to usher three goats out of the warriors' path. A smithy rang with the rhythmic clanging of hammer on anvil. Einar's stomach rolled over again as they passed a house from which the scent of freshly baked bread drifted to make him salivate. Children huddled in lanes and pathways, marvelling and pointing at the warriors in their war finery.

By the time they reached the king's hall, only the hostages and a dozen men remained with the king and his daughter. Intricate carvings adorned its sides and door lintels, and carved wooden statues of Odin, Thor, Frigg, and Freyr stood upon a grass courtyard, their wide, painted eyes staring at Einar, making him so uncomfortable that he reached for his hammer amulet for comfort. The thatched hall roof rose steeply, designed to shed the weight of winter snow, and its peak featured a carved dragon's head, snarling and painted in white, green and blue.

Stewards and thralls peeled out of the hall, rushing to help the king and his men with their horses and weapons. The thralls, clad in undyed wool, offered bread and ale to the warriors, and Einar took a chunk of dark bread and a clay mug of ale. An Agder warrior with blonde hair worn in two long braids spoke to King Harald and then approached Einar and the other hostages.

"My name is Farbauti Ketilsson," he said. He wore a *brynjar*, carried two axes at his belt and wore an auburn-coloured cloak about his shoulders. His face was vulpine and bladelike, with a pointed chin and sharp nose between brown eyes. "You will attend a feast in King Harald's hall tomorrow night, in honour of our agreement with Ivar the Boneless and our return to Tromoya. I will show you to your quarters."

Farbauti led the four hostages to a poky room set between the longhouse and its accompanying stables. Thralls hurriedly prepared four pallet beds filled with straw, set a table and chairs, and added logs to the hearth.

"I thought hostages were supposed to be treated with respect?" grumbled Likbjorn, cocking an eyebrow at their meagre lodgings. "It reeks of piss in here."

"I can put you in the stables instead if you prefer the stink of horseshit?" said Farbauti. "I'll send a steward for you when it's time for the feast. Thralls will bring you water to drink and to wash yourselves with, and some food."

"Thank you, Farbauti Ketilsson," said Einar, doing his best to be respectful.

"What are we supposed to do until tomorrow night?" asked Likbjorn. He unslung his axe and rested it against the wall.

"You are hostages, so you must do nothing. You can walk around the island. There is a tavern of sorts on the eastern side, and a smithy, if you want a fresh edge put on your weapons before we fight Dolgfinnr and King Gudrød. But keep out of trouble."

"Unless trouble finds us," Likbjorn winked and Farbauti frowned.

"Keep out of trouble, like I said. And hope that your Lord Ivar keeps his side of the bargain, or your heads will adorn the gable of my lord's hall."

Einar, Adzo and Likbjorn spent the rest of

that day in the local tavern, where Einar drank enough golden-tasting mead that he could not remember returning to their lodgings until Adzo reminded him the following morning how they had to carry him home. All three men nursed sore heads for much of the second day, though they took Farbauti's advice and had the smith put fresh edges on their axes and seaxes. Vigmarr kept to himself. He spent most of those two days standing atop the palisade, gazing out at the Whale Road like it was his long-lost lover. Einar let him be, content to be distracted from his feud with the haggard sea-jarl.

Evening drew in on the second day and Einar washed himself, brushed his hair, beard and clothes clean, donning his cloak and leather breastplate. A mean-faced steward led the hostages to King Harald's hall. Inside, the longhouse was filled with feasting benches and warriors in leather, iron and wool. Fresh rushes covered the floor to soak up spilled food and ale, and hunting dogs padded between the benches in search of scraps of meat. A fire burned at one end where a pig roasted on an iron spit, and the king's thralls hurried about the smoky room, filling cups with frothing ale and fetching platters of steamed vegetables, roasted meat, fish, cheese, butter and bread to the tables. The men in the hall whispered and talked behind their hands as Vigmarr Svarti stalked amongst them all in black, his veil of raven-coloured hair hiding the ruin of his face.

Farbauti led the hostages to a place of honour close to King Harald's high seat, and once the four men were seated, the King stood and raised two hands to quieten the hall crammed with his oathmen, merchants, wealthy farmers and all the men and women of power come to celebrate with their king. Harald Granraude wore his hair loose, combed to a sheen, his red beard in a thick braid hanging upon his chest. He wore a rich tunic of deep garnet, embroidered with gold thread and a heavy cloak of silver fur draped over his shoulders.

"Welcome, warriors and noble folk of Agder," Harald announced, his warm voice filling the hall. "It is an honour to feast with you on this evening where we have four honoured guests. These are warriors and champions in the service of Ivar Ragnarsson, whom men call the Boneless. Ivar is our ally, and will fight alongside us against those who would come with fire and sword to disrupt our peaceful lives. So welcome them, as we drink and eat together and celebrate this alliance between our people and warriors from across the Whale Road."

Every person in the hall cheered their king's words, voices and banging fists echoing around the high, smoky rafters. Harald held up a horn, toasted his guests, and took a long drink. Einar and the three hostages raised their cups and drank to the king, and Einar smiled as a thrall filled their table with food.

"Better than the slave pen at Hrafnborg," murmured Adzo, nudging Einar in the ribs as they sat on their bench.

"Hard to believe a king honours us so," Einar replied. He grabbed cuts of steaming meat and a chunk of warm bread whilst a thrall woman filled his cup with mead.

"I'm surprised you can stomach that after all the mead you supped last night."

"Best cure is the hair of the dog that bit you, or so they say, lads," said Likbjorn, and drained his own cup.

Folk settled into the feast, and the rumble of talking and laughing filled the hall. Flickering hearth light mixed with rush-lights mounted on the walls cast the feast in a warm glow. Vigmarr Svarti ate noisily. Every time a steward or thrall passed him, the sea-jarl grabbed platters of fermented fish, venison, wild berries, bowls of creamy butter and ever more loaves of bread folded and plaited into clever shapes. Likbjorn told them stories of Ivar's voyages and wars and fierce battles fought on foreign shores. He tried to include Vigmarr in those tales, describing how Vigmarr had been first over the wall in an attack on this city or that fortress, of how the Seaworm had sailed up narrow rivers to fight treacherous foes, but Vigmarr barely acknowledged Likbjorn's words, save for a well-timed belch whenever Likbjorn paused to drink.

"Another toast!" called King Harald, swaying slightly as he stood, cheeks flushed red with too much mead. "To my cherished daughter, my delightful Princess Åsa, whose hand is courted by every prince and king from Halogaland to Ireland. And to you, the fine warriors and men who stand before me today." He paused and took a long drink from his horn, the mead running into his beard and down onto his fine robes. "I offer my deepest gratitude for your oaths and your service. Your bravery and strength make Agder the great kingdom it is, and together we stand strong, like Nargrind, the gates of Niflheim itself. Let us toast together and ask for the favour of Njorth, the mighty god whose patronage has brought such blessings to my people. Njorth, fount of wisdom, provider of abundant crops, full catches of fish and a fair wind in the sails, continue to bless us with luck." Harald tipped the rest of his mead onto the floor as a libation to the god, and his guests did the same.

One of Harald's dogs licked the mead Einar poured onto the floor rushes, and as he sat down, he stroked the animal's coarse fur. The evening wore on and the feast gradually gave way to song and dance. A skald took up position by the fire and told a tale of the *Ynglingsaga,* the tale of Odin and the first kings of the Northmen. Men listened and whooped for joy, and banged tables with their fists in the right places as the silver-bearded skald filled the hall with stories of gods and heroes, of triumphs and tragedies and stirred the hearts of all who listened. Mead flowed like a river into the sea, and before long the warmth of the fire and the lull of the skald mixed with the mead's potency so that men began to fall asleep at their benches, or stumble from the hall with their wives to find their beds.

Einar stood and placed a hand on his full belly. He left Adzo and Likbjorn in deep conversation about the merits of Frankish steel over Norse blades, Likbjorn refusing to concede what all men knew, that Frankish smiths were far superior. Einar strolled out of the hall doors and into a night where the fresh air cleared his head. He walked up a set of timber steps onto the high palisade where the moon hung high in the sky, its silvery light casting a soft light over Tromoya, shimmering on the rolling sea. He wondered how far Ivar and the crews were from the island stronghold, and hoped Ivar would appear tomorrow as promised, for he did not wish to lose his head to Farbauti's axe.

The sea sighed against Tromoya's cliffs and Einar stared out across the water. Something caught his eye, a shape moving out in the darkness, shifting like a great sea serpent rolling over the whitecaps. Einar leaned on the palisade, wondering if he had glimpsed one of Loki's sea monsters or if his drunken eyes deceived him. A voice drifted across the water, a man's voice shouting out at sea, followed by another. Einar turned to his right, where a sentry rested against the wall beside an iron brazier crackling with three burning logs in its grate.

"Heya," Einar called to the sentry. The man didn't move. He stood with his head bowed, leaning on his spear. "Heya!" Einar called, louder this time.

"Thor's balls," cursed the sentry, snapping awake and dropping his spear. He picked it up and glowered at Einar, then saw his breastplate and arm rings and cleared his throat. "My apologies, lord. I was resting my eyes." He called Einar lord because he carried wealth at his wrists and wore armour.

"Can you see anything out there?" Einar pointed out into the darkness and the warrior squinted and stared out to sea.

"No, all I see is… wait… what's that?" he leaned in, throwing his cloak back over one shoulder and pointing with his spear.

Einar looked back to the water and inhaled sharply. A dragon appeared from the gloom, a snarling head and beating wings swooping from the sea. But not wings. Oars. Another dragon appeared next to the first, and another. Warships came from the darkness, and bearded men with hard faces stared out at Tromoya in the moonlight.

"Warships. Enemies," the guard gasped. "It's King Gudrød. I recognise his boats."

The warrior picked up two pieces of pitted, dark iron and clanged them together. "Enemies! To arms!" he bellowed.

More ships came from the night, and still more, until a fleet stretched as far as Einar could see. King Gudrød had come for vengeance. He came to settle the feud that started when King Harald refused his proposal of marriage. War had come to Tromoya and Einar ran from the palisade as King Harald's warriors woke from their drunken stupor to man the walls. A war horn blared from the Whale Road, and hundreds of warriors cheered and bayed like beasts. The sea-wolves had come for King Harald, with ships, blades and furious anger.

TWENTY-TWO

Horns blared to warn King Harald's people of their enemies' attack. Women shrieked in alarm, and Einar ran through Tromoya's streets, searching frantically for his crewmates. Men flowed from the king's hall, stumbling, trying to overcome their drunkenness and seek weapons and family. Einar found no sign of his crewmates at the hall, so he pelted to their quarters and found Adzo emerging from its low door with his bow and a quiver of arrows, and Likbjorn brandishing his double-bladed war axe.

"We're under attack," Einar said between gasps, out of breath from his frantic search. "It's King Gudrød the Hunter and his fleet."

"We know, lad. Is Dolgfinnr with them?" asked Likbjorn.

"I could not see," Einar replied. "But King Gudrød seeks his revenge upon King Harald."

"It's not our fight," said Adzo, his head turning

towards the landward gate. "Harald should not have refused the Hunter's proposal. It was an insult to refuse a king."

"Don't even think of it, lad," Likbjorn growled. "We're here and we fight. If that bastard Dolgfinnr is with them, then I'll kill him if I can. End this bloody voyage once and for all. We are here representing Lord Ivar, and we do not flee."

"Where's Vigmarr?"

"Out there somewhere in the chaos. We'll find him where the battle rages hardest. Come."

Likbjorn led them through a maelstrom of warriors scurrying in all directions throughout the fortress. Men carried shields, running with armfuls of spears for their comrades. They carried sheaves of arrows and hurried to their positions upon Tromoya's defences. Mothers and wives led children and old folk towards King Harald's hall to seek safety behind its gate. Einar, Likbjorn and Adzo reached the sea-facing palisade to find it already thronged with warriors, but the three Hrafnborg men forced their way up the steps to the fighting platform. A cool wind hit Einar's face and snatched his breath away as he looked down upon dozens of King Gudrød's warships making landfall in the small coves and beaches amongst the rocks and jagged cliffs.

"There," said Likbjorn. He pointed his axe to

four ships with their hulls driven high onto a shale beach-head. Men poured from the bows, men in wolf pelts carrying shields daubed in red and white. They howled like lunatics with axes and spears in their fists. "Dolgfinnr's men. Bastard flies the raven banner."

Einar peered through the crush of shouting warriors, men in helmets and leather with spears bristling above them, glinting in the moonlight. He saw him then, Dolgfinnr Dogsblood himself, huge and baleful, with his blonde hair flowing beneath a full-faced helmet. He charged like his men, with his torso bare save for a wolf's pelt about his broad shoulders. Behind him, a tall man carried Ragnar Lothbrok's raven banner, the famous white triangle flying high and proud. Rage pulsed from Likbjorn like flames, and Einar felt it too, the insult to Ragnar and his fair fame stabbing at him like a spear.

Adzo nocked an arrow to his bow and loosed it from the wall. Its white feathers crackled in the night air, and the missile swooped down and took a wolf warrior square in the chest, knocking him from his ship and into the rolling surf. More of Dolgfinnr's men swarmed across the beach and tossed ropes tied to axe hafts at King Harald's high walls. They climbed up the ropes like ants marching on a hot day. Some ropes fell away as the defenders cut them loose, but there were not enough Tromoya men on the walls to keep Dolgfinnr's men back.

"Bastards," Likbjorn growled. "Our fight is with the Dogsblood. Come." Likbjorn hastened down the ladder towards where Dolgfinnr's men tried to scale the walls.

"I'll stay here," Adzo said. "I can do more with my bow here than over there." He nocked another arrow and loosed it towards the attacking ships. More archers joined him and their bows thrummed like deathly wind chimes.

Einar left him and followed Likbjorn down the ladder. They dashed through the snarl of houses and barns, and Einar drew his sword and seax. The sound of metal and wood clashing melded with the shouts and screams of warriors as King Gudrød's men stormed the walls, and the battle for Tromoya began. Einar saw no sign of the king or his retinue as he and Likbjorn reached the far section of walls. He saw only townsfolk carrying spears, knives, reaping hooks and whatever else they could find to defend their families from the attacking enemy.

"To the walls," Likbjorn commanded. He raced through the townsfolk to the palisade where already men in wolf pelts clambered over the sharpened timbers, axes swinging and blood spraying. A Tromoya man fell screaming from the walls, clutching at his face split open by an axe blade. A huge wolf warrior fought there, laying about him with an axe in each hand, keeping the defenders at bay, stopping them from cutting the ropes so that more of the attackers could swarm over the walls.

Likbjorn leapt up the stairway towards the fighting platform, and Einar followed. A wolf warrior lunged at Likbjorn with his axe, but he dropped and rolled beneath the blade. Einar caught the axe with his seax and slammed his own axe into the wolf warrior's chest. Likbjorn rose lithely and came face to face with the huge wolf warrior and his twin axes. Likbjorn feinted low and cracked the haft of his long axe into the enemy's face. He stumbled backwards and Einar ripped his own weapon free of the dying wolf man. A face appeared above the parapet and Einar raked his seax across the eyes and thunked his axe into a thick seal-hide rope.

"Fight!" Einar roared at the Tromoya townspeople around him. They were petrified men, standing back from the blood and death, wanting to protect their families but shocked by the terrible violence and horrific wounds made by axe and seax. More wolf warriors appeared at the wall, and Einar cut and chopped at their hands and faces. "Cut the ropes, cut the ropes!" he urged the Tromoya men. Three men darted forward and sawed at the ropes with their knives and crude weapons. A fourth reached the wall just as a wolf warrior appeared. He yowled like a beast and swung his axe over the wall, hooking its bearded blade into the Tromoya man's tunic, and hauled him over the side.

Einar darted in and slit the axeman's throat with his seax, but still, more came, furious faces coming over the walls, climbing fresh ropes. Two more Tromoya men died and Einar hurtled from one rope to the next, hacking at the enemy with his
bloodstained weapons. He looked to Likbjorn just in time to see the square-jawed champion hew the head from his enemy's shoulders with his axe. "Kill!" Likbjorn bawled, and his double-bladed axe hummed about the walls, its butterfly-shaped blade singing its death song as it tore into Dolgfinnr's men. Six axes came over the palisade at once, their edges biting into the timber, ropes tied to their hafts. Einar went to cut the first, but an enemy leapt over the wall in front of him. He kicked Einar away and jabbed at him with a knife. The rusty blade scored Einar's breastplate, and he stared down, appalled for a heartbeat at the horrific wound that foul blade would have made in his chest but for his armour. The knife came at him again and Einar swayed backwards and disembowelled the wolf man with a sweep of his seax. His attacker groaned and fell to his knees, desperately trying to keep his insides from falling out.

"Get back, we can't hold the wall," Likbjorn

panted. He grabbed Einar by the shoulder. Ten wolf men now stood on the fighting platform with butchered Tromoya townsfolk at their feet. Battle raged along the wall as King Gudrød brought his war fury to King Harald Granraude. "Fall back to the king's hall, defend the people there."

There was no way Einar and Likbjorn could hold the wall alone, so Einar made for the steps. He reached the bottom, ears ringing with the howls and screeches of wolf men, and he turned to check that Likbjorn followed. The tall warrior paused on the stairs, eyes fixed on the parapet, his hard eyes narrowed.

"We must go," Einar called to him. The odds were impossible and they needed to find the king and his warriors if they were to stand any chance of defending Tromoya.

"Dolgfinnr," Likbjorn growled, and he hefted his war axe. Dolgfinnr Dogsblood appeared on the fighting platform, gargantuan and wrathful with his blonde hair and helmet. The raven banner snapped and fluttered in the wind behind him, and Einar remembered that cruel face. It seemed like an age ago, that day when One Leg Bolti had died beneath Dolgfinnr's axe. Einar shuddered at the memory of Bolti's severed head and the slaughter in the sea. Einar had been a boy then, naïve and unknowing. It felt like a hundred years ago, like he had been a different person watching fearfully from the Waveslicer's bows as men fought and died in the water.

Einar bent and picked up a discarded spear. He hooked his axe in his belt and threw the spear towards the fighting platform. The spear flew like an arrow and slammed into the warrior standing behind Dolgfinnr; the man holding the raven banner. The banner plummeted and Dolgfinnr's gaze lit upon Einar.

"Kill that one!" Dolgfinnr barked, and his men swarmed towards the stairs. They swept up the banner and charged in a howling fury. Three of them leapt from the walls, obeying their master, hurrying to slay Einar at Dolgfinnr's command. The first man landed heavily, and Einar did not wait for him to recover. He ran forward three steps and cracked his axe blade across the man's skull, splattering its insides across the palisade walls. A second man landed and grimaced as his ankle gave way. Still, the wolf warrior rose, his spear gripped in two hands. He jabbed his weapon and Einar sprang backwards just as the third man landed and came up with a bloodied axe in his fist.

The two enemy warriors spread out, coming at Einar from either side. To wait was to die; to pause and let fear overtake his thoughts would mean his end. So Einar charged at the spearman. He bowed beneath a high thrust and sliced his seax across the spearman's thigh, sending him sprawling on the ground. The second warrior was already moving, leaping over the first, axe swinging and face contorted into a rictus of hate. He was a short man, wiry with corded muscle, and Einar stepped into his jump. He caught the smaller man in the air and slammed him viciously into the wall. The wolf warrior snapped his teeth at Einar, trying to bite his nose, so Einar butted him brutally in the face. They broke, axes clashing together with a reverberating clang. The wolf warrior tried to knee Einar in the groin, but Einar kicked out his standing leg. The warrior fell and Einar's seax punched into his throat and took his life in a gush of fiery blood.

Einar staggered away from the carnage, shoulders burning with fatigue, his mind shocked by the savage bloodshed. The spearman, on his knees, tried to grab Einar's leg, but he clubbed the warrior twice across the head with his axe haft. Enemy warriors streamed down the palisade stairs and Likbjorn hewed at their legs with his axe. He cut at them, standing his ground halfway down the stairs leading from the fighting platform to the ground inside Tromoya's fortifications. He cut the legs from two men and the rest leapt back, baying in front of Likbjorn like feral animals.

"Dolgfinnr Dogsblood!" Likbjorn called across the throng of warriors, which grew thicker as more of them flooded across the now undefended section of wall. "I am Likbjorn Hjalmarsson. Oathman of Ivar Ragnarsson. Come and fight if you have the courage."

Dolgfinnr smiled and drew his axe and long knife. He thrust through his wolf warriors, and they parted for him as though he was the alpha and they were his pack. The walls around Tromoya throbbed with the din of battle as the men of Tromoya fought to keep the raiders out, but as Dolgfinnr reached the stairs, Einar saw three points along the seaward defences where King Gudrød's men teemed over the walls onto undefended sections of the walls. They clambered over the tall wooden stakes and leapt over the bodies of slaughtered defenders, and it could only be a matter of time before the town fell to its enemies.

"Go, Einar!" Likbjorn called over his shoulder. "Find the king and the princess. Protect them if you can."

"No! I'll stand and fight with you to the death." There was no *drengskapr* in running and retreating.

"Tell Ivar and the rest how I died. Tell Thorkild, and I'll save a place for you all in Valhalla."

Dolgfinnr leapt down the first three steps and before Likbjorn could raise his axe, Dolgfinnr kicked him roughly in the chest and sent him spreadeagled down the stairs. Enemy warriors crept down behind their jarl, blood dripping from their axe blades, murder shining in their brutish eyes. Even if Likbjorn defeated Dolgfinnr, there was no way he could survive against so many enemies. Einar flexed his hands around his weapons. He was ready to fight, ready to die as a *drengr* and he felt no fear.

A great roar went up from the walls, and Einar saw a figure there fighting alone as King Harald's men fled from the fighting platform. A figure in black, a monstrous man hewing at his enemies, slaughtering attackers with skill and fury beyond most men. It was Vigmarr Svarti, revelling in the bloodletting, coming alive in the clash of warriors, and Einar could not die beside Likbjorn. He could not leave Midgard and leave his father's soul unavenged. So he turned and fled towards the buildings and streets, and behind him, weapons crashed and clanged together.

Einar paused, turning at a corner between two buildings. Likbjorn and Dolgfinnr twisted and danced like heroes from legend, their blades singing, two champions trading blows beneath the moonlight. Dolgfinnr's bare torso shone with sweat and the muscles on his arms and shoulders moved like the tide. He fought with axe and knife, whilst Likbjorn swung his double-bladed war axe as though it weighed no more than a twig. Each man lunged, parried, cut, and thrust for twenty heartbeats, weapons shifting with skill and poise. Likbjorn's axe passed Dolgfinnr's guard, and for a dazzling moment, Einar thought his crew mate had won. But Dolgfinnr's head jerked backwards and the butterfly-shaped edge sliced across his nose and cheek in a spray of blood.

Dolgfinnr roared, and he trapped Likbjorn's axe with the beard of his own weapon. His knife sliced across Likbjorn's left arm, and then stabbed deep into his stomach, punching through the links of his *brynjar.*

"No," Einar whispered to himself.

Dolgfinnr turned to his men and raised his axe. They howled and cavorted like dervishes, bounding down the stairs and circling about Likbjorn as he sank to his knees. Dolgfinnr took the raven banner from one of his men, hawked, and spat on the sacred sigil. Einar closed his eyes in horror, knowing what that insult meant to a proud man like Likbjorn. Dolgfinnr threw the raven battle standard back at his man and set his feet, staring at Likbjorn with a look of triumph upon his ruthless face. His axe swung and Likbjorn fell, so Einar turned and hurtled through the narrow pathways towards King Harald's hall to make his last stand.

TWENTY-THREE

Einar raced through Tromoya, his boots splashing in mud as low-hanging thatch brushed against his head. He turned right between a stable and a cow byre and found two of King Gudrød's men, their axes bloody and eyes hungry. He turned back and ran left, bobbing beneath an open window shutter. His foot slipped in horse shit and Einar slewed sideways into a wide street leading to King Harald's hall. Men fought there in narrow but deep shield walls. King Harald's antlered stag standard flew behind his warriors as the king's carls protected their families inside his hall.

Einar skirted around the settlement, aiming to circle King Gudrød's men and join King Harald's shield wall. Fire crackled across dry thatch as Einar ran, and the further east he went, more buildings burned until the flames became like an inferno. The heat was overpowering, so much so that Einar went north, running back towards the wall and the shield wall battle where King Harald and his hearth troop made their defence. A goat ran across his path, its coat aflame, and Einar shielded his eyes from the furnace. Figures moved at the corner of his eye, and Einar hid with his back against the wall as four wolf warriors jogged after the goat. They passed Einar without noticing his presence and he continued on, trying to avoid the fire and skirting around the battle's flank.

"Einar!" cried a familiar voice, and Einar turned to see Adzo loping through a crossroads. "Thank the lord I've found you! I feared the worst."

"Likbjorn is dead," Einar panted. "Come, we must help the king."

Soot smeared Adzo's face and his quiver was empty of arrows, and the two friends hurried to join the fight. The sound of clashing weapons came from around a corner. A man screamed and Einar turned right around a wattle wall to find Vigmarr Svarti fighting three of King Gudrød's men. Vigmarr moved like something from beyond the realm of Midgard, his axe and knife slashing with impossible speed for a man who limped and shuffled like a cripple. Within moments, the three men lay dead or dying as Vigmarr lopped at them between two burning buildings.

An enemy warrior came at Vigmarr, charging from behind a building with his axe raised. Vigmarr parried the axe and grabbed the warrior by his leather breastplate. He swung the smaller man around and tossed him against a wall like a sack of grain. The warrior slumped and Vigmarr Svarti fell upon him like a savage beast, chopping with his axe and seax, spattering the wall with blood and filth. Einar's chest clenched, imagining the man as his father, hewn to death beneath Vigmarr's blades. It weighed heavy upon his shoulders, the need for vengeance like an anchor stone upon his back. There was nobody to see what happened there in the alley. No Seaworm men other than Vigmarr, Adzo and Einar. There would never be a better time to confront his father's killer. No consequences, no punishment from Ivar. All he had to do was face Vigmarr Svarti, brutal killer and murderer, who no man could stand against without terrifying fear.

Vigmarr sensed Einar and Adzo's presence and turned, the firelight illuminating the shadows and scars of his war-ravaged face, a wicked smile playing at the corner of his twisted mouth.

"You want to kill old Vigmarr?" he crooned. Vigmarr held his axe and knife wide, as if to invite Einar to attack him. Blood dripped from his hair and gore smeared his blades.

"Did you kill my father?" Einar shouted above the din of battle, struggling to keep the emotion from his voice. Flames crackled across thatch and wall, heat searing his face as Tromoya burned around him.

"I killed him. Enjoyed it, too."

"Why?"

"Many men died so that I could become Vigmarr Svarti, sea-jarl. I was not always thus, but fate makes men what they are. Egil had to die. He was in my way."

"Did he die with honour?"

Vigmarr's shoulders shook in his cruel wheeze of a laugh. "No, pup. He pissed himself when I cut his throat and pushed him overboard. A *nithing* and a coward."

The words cut deep, rocking Einar back on his heels. The thought of his father suffering so, that the last thing Egil had felt was fear, the last thing he saw was Vigmarr's jet-black eyes, consumed him. A memory came of his father laughing and playing with him when Einar was a boy. A fat tear rolled down Einar's cheek.

"Bastard," Einar hissed, and he lifted his weapons to face his father's killer.

"No, Einar," Adzo pleaded. His bow creaked, and the Frank reached for an arrow, only to find his quiver empty.

Vigmarr's arm snapped forward and his axe whipped across the short space, droplets of blood flying from its blade as it turned head over haft. Einar followed its flight, and the axe slammed into Adzo's chest, throwing him from his feet.

"No!" Einar bellowed. He ran to Adzo, but Vigmarr Svarti was already moving. As Einar bent to look into Adzo's dying eyes, Vigmarr smashed into him, his bulk driving Einar backwards and the two men crashed through a burning wattle wall and landed on the floor of a building aflame. Einar rolled with Vigmarr, winded and trying to breathe, suffocating beneath his enemy's bulk and the fact that his father's killer had now killed his friend, and was about to kill him too.

Vigmarr's hand clawed at Einar's face, jagged fingernails digging into his cheek, groping for his eye. It was a huge hand, sweating and strong, and it pushed Einar's skull into the hard-packed earthen floor. Something pressed into Einar's ribs; Vigmarr's knife stabbing into his leather breastplate, but the armour took the pressure and stopped the point from cutting Einar open. The fingernails scratched Einar's face, scrabbling at his eye socket, and Einar twisted his head away.

"Die," Vigmarr hissed, the sound like the

terrible hiss of Jormungandr, the world serpent coming for Thor at the end of days.

The ceiling above them collapsed in a great crash of burning thatch and roof timbers. Einar knew if he did not move, he would die and join his father's ghost wandering in Niflheim's frosty darkness, unavenged and forgotten like dust in the wind. He roared and bucked like a beast. Anger flooded his limbs with strength, rage gave him breath and Einar flung Vigmarr's Svarti's bulk from him and he surged to his feet.

"I am Einar the Brawler," Einar shouted above the crackle and crash of the roaring fire all about them. "Son of Egil." He set his feet and readied his weapons. He was taller than Vigmarr and just as broad across the shoulder. He was a killer and a warrior. Einar was a Viking, and vengeance was his.

Vigmarr Svarti kicked a flaming clump of thatch at Einar and dashed towards the opening in the wall. Einar shielded his face from the blaze and followed. He slashed his axe at Vigmarr's back, but the sea-jarl leapt through the broken wattle and grabbed his axe from Adzo's chest. He turned and stood, a grin splitting his nightmarish face.

"Your friend's dead. You're next," he crowed.

Einar attacked him, his axe and seax moving with all the fluidity and skill ingrained into his arms by a lifetime of practice. Vigmarr held him, blocking with axe and knife, bobbing and weaving like a man half his age. He came up inside Einar's axe and crashed a savage headbutt into Einar's nose, engulfing him in darkness. Einar felt himself falling, felt Vigmarr's knife slice across his forearm like a whip.

Fight, son, said his father's voice in his head. *Fight and live.*

"Just a pup," Vigmarr sneered. "You don't have what it takes to beat me. You're just a…"

Einar snapped himself from the darkness and kicked Vigmarr hard in the groin. He stabbed the point of his seax three times, quick jabs into Vigmarr's shoulder as he bent double. Einar darted away as Vigmarr's knife came around. He crashed his knee into Vigmarr's face and then stabbed him twice in the back. Vigmarr bellowed, a sound to frighten the Loki brood themselves, and it was as though the very roots of Midgard shook. Einar let that terrible howl fuel his rage rather than ignite fear. The boy inside him was dead, and the man, the Viking carl, swung his axe and the blade caught Vigmarr on the jaw, shearing away his chin and teeth to leave an appalling, grisly wound. Vigmarr dropped to his knees, trembling, obsidian eyes wide like black pools. Einar stepped towards his enemy and cut his weapons away.

"You die without a blade. Go to Niflheim and pass my father as he rises to Valhalla," Einar said. He opened Vigmarr Svarti's throat and watched him die. The most fearsome man Einar had ever seen, the monster who had killed his father, bled and died at his feet. It did not feel like a victory; Einar just felt relief. He wanted to sit and rest, to be somewhere else. Adzo and Likbjorn were dead. He was the only man from Ivar's crews left alive in Tromoya, surrounded by a battle for King Harald's survival. But it was not his fight.

A young warrior bearing King Gudrød's colours burst around the corner with a bloody spear in his fist. His eyes flickered from Einar to the corpses beside him. Einar took a step towards the warrior. The fight was not over. Einar was a *drengr*, a warrior in the service of Ivar the Boneless and he must help Ivar's new ally King Harald if he could. The warrior took one look at the blood and gore bespattered across Einar's breastplate and weapons, then turned and fled.

Einar staggered away from his dead enemy, and from Adzo's corpse. His head rang with the weight of it all, but he hurried through the lanes, pulled toward the sound of battle. Men burst from kicked-in doors carrying silver and gold trinkets, furs and food. Einar strode through them and those men ignored him, enemy warriors untouched by battle with sheathed blades and unbloodied hands. A fat man with a straggly beard and a shining bald head lurched from an open door, dragging a woman behind him by her hair. She wailed and screamed, nose bloody and dress ripped. Einar caved the straggle-bearded man's skull in with his axe and barked at the woman to go and hide. He emerged behind King Harald's hall and ran about its gable. Women and children peeked at him through the shutters, watching as their town burned and enemy warriors sacked their homes.

The last survivors of King Harald's hearth troop fought in front of their lord's hall. Fifteen men locked together in a shield wall, comrades dead or dying beside them. Harald Granraude himself fought amid his warriors, his red beard and flashing sword marking him out amongst the spears and shields. Farbauti Ketilsson fought beside him and killed an enemy with a well-timed spear thrust. Dozens of King Gudrød's men swirled in the open ground before King Harald's hall, the bravest amongst them trading blows with King Harald's men, but most hanging back, shouting their defiance but reluctant to fight Harald's champions now that the battle was all but over. The men defending Harald's hall were his last, those who had fought their way back from the walls and through the town to make a last stand. Only the strong remained, only the most savage, skilled *drengrs* marked with dead men's blood and notches on their blades.

Einar picked up a fallen man's shield and pushed his way into Harald's shield wall. Farbauti shuffled aside to let him in and nodded his thanks. The warrior bore a jagged cut on his cheek and a deep gash at his shoulder where the links of his chainmail *brynjar* had shattered beneath an enemy blade. A towering man with long moustaches came at Einar with his spear. He spat and shouted in furious rage, but Einar batted the spear aside with his axe and Farbauti drove his own spear into the enemy warrior's maw, killing him instantly. All along the shield wall, men cut and thrust against the best of King Gudrød's men and Einar killed two warriors, his strength renewed by the passion with which Farbauti and his shield-brothers fought for the king.

A horn blared in two short blasts, and King Gudrød's men fell back. Bone-chilling howling rippled across Tromoya, and Dolgfinnr Dogsblood's men came from the streets in their furs like a wolf pack. They ignored King Harald's men and instead attacked the flanks of King Harald's hall, hurling themselves at the walls, using their axes to climb up the thatch like beasts possessed. The women and children inside the hall screamed and wailed in terror and King Harald's shield wall broke.

"Hold!" Einar called as men peeled away,

dashing to meet Dolgfinnr's wolf warriors.

"My Siggi is inside," Farbauti replied, sorrow drawing at the corners of his mouth, fear in the brave warrior's eyes. "My wife. My love."

Farbauti left his king and ran towards the hall to save his wife from Dolgfinnr Dogsblood and his wolf warriors. King Harald gaped as his hearth troop deserted him, and he did the only thing he could. He charged with them. Einar followed, cutting down a wolf warrior with his seax and smashing another to the ground with his shield. Farbauti killed two foes, dragging them from the thatch and stabbing at their struggling bodies with his spear. A woman screamed through an open window and Farbauti threw his spear into the darkness and leapt in after it. Einar followed, jumping through the smashed open wooden shutters and landing on the hard-packed earthen floor.

Wolf warriors dropped from roof thatch and open window holes. They cut and hacked at the crowded groups of terrified women and children. They killed without remorse or pity and Einar had never seen such reckless brutality, even amongst hardened Viking carls. Farbauti fought before a cowering blonde-haired woman, protecting her with his axe. Farbauti cut down three enemies and Einar ran to help him, but before he could get there, a fourth drove his spear through Farbauti's stomach. Einar killed that man with a sweep of his axe. Einar stood before Farbauti's wife, fending off the surging mass of enemy warriors with his weapons, desperate to save her from the feral attackers.

A knife sawed across his shoulder and another sliced across his thigh, but Einar fought on. A gasp behind him made Einar spin, and he sank to his knees to find Farbauti's wife lying dead in a pool of her own blood. Too much death, too much suffering. All strength and will to fight drained from Einar like water from a holed bucket.

"Look at me!" came a loud roar, a bellow which bounced around the rafters as though it came from Asgard itself.

Dolgfinnr Dogsblood stood on King Harald's high platform. A woman knelt beside him, and he held a fistful of her golden hair. It was Princess Åsa Haraldsdottir.

"Throw down your weapons or the princess dies," Dolgfinnr growled, a look of triumph on his iron-hard face. Men stopped fighting, poised with weapons still raised, unsure what to do next. "I'll kill her, Harald, but first I'll tie her to a feasting bench and every one of my men tup her whilst you watch. You've lost. Tell your men to throw down their arms and she won't suffer."

King Harald's shoulders slumped. He sagged visibly, as though the gods had sucked the very life from his body. He dropped his sword, and it clattered to the floor, the sound tolling his defeat. Harald's surviving warriors also threw down their weapons, and a grim silence fell across the blood-filled hall.

Heavy boots tramped through the open doors, King Gudrød striding through the hall with his warriors streaming behind him. He paused before King Harald and slapped him hard across the face.

"I honoured you," he spat. "Gave you the respect of one king to another. I asked for your daughter's hand, gave you gifts and came in peace. You refused me like a man might chase a dog begging for scraps from his door." He cast his arms about the hall, pointing at dead women and children and then at the princess. "All of this is your doing. You could be at my wedding now, sitting in a place of honour as our two kingdoms joined in marriage. Instead, you wade in the blood of your people, and I'm going to marry the bitch, anyway."

King Gudrød plunged his sword into King Harald's chest and left the blade quivering in his enemy's body. He strode to the high platform and took Princess Åsa from Dolgfinnr and dragged her away as her father watched and died in his own hall.

"It's over," King Gudrød called, waving a

hand dismissively. "Burn it all. We sail for the Vestfold."

King Gudrød's men led the survivors out into the space between King Harald's hall and the rest of the settlement. They left them kneeling whilst King Harald's hall burned. Within an hour, Dolgfinnr and Harald left Tromoya a burning ruin, and Einar hurried through the flames with the other survivors. Men and women dragged the injured and infirm from buildings and barns and they ran from Tromoya island, across the land bridge where they watched King Harald's town burn and collapse in towers of flame.

Einar sat on the grass as the Tromoya folk wailed for their lost loved ones and the tragedy that had befallen their king. Einar was numb, his body cut by enemy weapons and his heart hardened by the death of both friends and enemies. King Gudrød and Dolgfinnr sailed away from the destruction and the fires burned all day and deep into the night until a weary sleep finally enveloped Einar into a dreamless slumber.

Then in the morning, Ivar came.

TWENTY-FOUR

Twenty of King Harald's warriors survived the attack on Tromoya. Five were from King Harald's hearth troop. They were brave men who had stood where the fighting was most fierce and suffered stab wounds, and gashes to their faces, shoulders and limbs. The rest were little more than armed townsfolk, men who had fought to protect their families and lost. They stood with two-score women, children and old folk, all survivors with soot-darkened faces who had searched at first light that morning through the smouldering ashes for any scraps remaining of their old lives. Warriors had recovered weapons, armour, and shields, and a warrior with two missing teeth laid a *brynjar* at Einar's feet.

"Take it. You earned it," he said, and wiped soot from his eyes. He wore a torn and bloody *brynjar* and was missing half his left ear. "I saw you fight for our king. The mail coat belonged to my brother. He would want a warrior to have it."

It was early morning, and the sun sat red and fat above the sea. Einar felt empty, like a ship drifting unmanned across the Whale Road. The gap-toothed warrior waited for Einar to accept his gift, but Einar could find no words. His hands trembled and he could not stop them. The battle for Tromoya had been visceral and bloody, beyond anything Einar had imagined a battle could be. The skalds did not sing of screaming women dragged from their homes, of slaughtered babies, butchered grandmothers or corpses shrunken by fire. Adzo and Likbjorn were in that smouldering mass somewhere, their bodies lying unhonoured beneath charred timbers and layers of ash. It would be impossible to find them now. Their bodies would be indistinguishable from the rest. Einar was certain that Likbjorn was in Valhalla, for he had fought like a hero of legend, and Einar hoped Adzo rested in the halls of his own nailed god.

Einar opened his mouth to thank the gap-toothed man, but no sound would emerge. So he nodded instead, and that was enough recognition between men who had fought through the horror of King Harald's demise. Boots tramping upon gravel caught Einar's attention, many boots crunching upon the well-worn road leading to Tromoya island.

"Your lord is here," the gap-toothed warrior said bitterly. "We could have done with his warriors yesterday."

Einar rose to his feet, his bones weary from battle and his eyes gritty from sleeping in the open. Men bearing shields daubed with the Ragnarsson raven marched along the road, a cloud of dust rising about them like dirty fog staining the pine forest and hills as they descended from the heights towards what had once been King Harald's home. A ripple of alarm and a rumble of surprised voices rose from the marching column as Ivar's men gazed upon the smouldering ruins of their ally's fortress. A dozen mounted men led the column, and two of those cantered towards Einar and the tattered huddle of survivors. The leading rider wore a green cloak and Einar stiffened as he recognised Ivar and Halvdan approaching.

"Einar, is that you?" Ivar called, reining his horse in before Einar and the gaggle of survivors.

"Yes, lord," Einar replied, realising that his own face, hair and clothes were grimy with soot, crusted blood and the filth of battle. Cuts, bruises and gashes suddenly throbbed and stung, countless miniscule nicks and bigger wounds to his flesh which thus far he had not noticed amongst the dark mist which had clouded his mind since King Gudrød and Dolgfinnr had sailed away. The four hostages Ivar had taken from King Harald ran from the marching column, hurrying to the survivors to seek news of loved ones.

"What in Thor's name happened?"

"Dolgfinnr and Gudrød came," Einar said, his throat so parched that his voice came as a thin croak.

"Dolgfinnr was here?"

"He was. King Gudrød killed King Harald and took his daughter."

"The blood feud."

"The blood feud," Einar echoed sadly. He stiffened and squared his shoulders, suddenly aware that the marching column grew closer. Einar should have washed the muck from his body, weapons, and armour. A carl did not present so dishevelled an appearance, especially if he bore the stain of defeat. So Einar raised his chin and stood with a warrior's pride. The marks and dirt upon him were hard-earned in battle, and he would not be ashamed of them. It had not been his battle to lose, but the spectacle of King Harald's death and the slaughter of his people had struck at the core of Einar's being.

"Is this all that remains of the king's men?"

"This is it."

"Vigmarr? Likbjorn and the archer?"

"Dead, lord."

Ivar leaned over his horse's neck and shook his head. "Truly, I believed nothing could kill Vigmarr Svarti."

"Dolgfinnr slew Likbjorn. They fought together, and Likbjorn's axe cut a wound in Dolgfinnr's face that the Dogsblood will wear forever."

"Likbjorn was a stout fighter, and we shall miss his axe."

"As Likbjorn died, Dolgfinnr spat upon the raven banner. That was the last thing Likbjorn saw before he died."

Ivar shuddered and slipped down from his horse. A familiar look darkened his handsome face. "Dolgfinnr spat on the raven banner?"

"Yes, lord."

"And he made Likbjorn watch?"

"Yes, lord."

Ivar's head twitched to one side, and he ground his teeth so that the muscles in his face moved beneath his beard. He gazed across Tromoya's ruins and out towards the shimmering Whale Road.

"Your man fought as hard as the best of our men, lord," said the gap-toothed warrior, and again handed Einar the *brynjar*, which he took absent-mindedly, worried that Ivar would ask him more about Vigmarr's death.

"I do not doubt it," Ivar said. He paused for a moment, clenching his eyes so tightly that the skin around them creased like ripples on a fjord as he fought to master his rage. "I came here to join my men to King Harald's and end this cursed war." He spoke wistfully and a sad smile turned down the corners of his mouth. The red sun glowed upon the polished links of his *brynjar* and he looked every inch the great warrior lord. "The Norns are ever cruel to men of ambition. They cackle at our dreams beneath the roots of Yggdrasil and weave desolation, sorrow and regret into the warp and weft of our lives. Urðr, Verðandi, and Skuld, they are called, and their names all point to what men will be, want to be, and shall be." He placed a hand on Einar's shoulder. "A man must be the master of his own wyrd. He must decide his own fate. When I met you, you were to become a thrall, and you fought your way out of that slave pen. Now you have arm rings, a *brynjar*, reputation, and fine weapons. You have luck, Einar, *hamingja*. A warrior needs *hamingja*."

"What can we do now, lord?" Einar asked.

"Halvdan, Skallagrimr, Radbod, Thorkild," Ivar called over his shoulder. He waited for them to join him and then walked slowly up a bracken-filled hill so that he could look out upon the sea. Ivar beckoned for Einar to join them. "Our ally is dead, and we are alone again."

"King Gudrød has Harald's daughter and will make her his queen," said Radbod. The fur he wore around his neck and shoulders ruffled in the sea breeze.

"King Harald paid the price for his insult," said Thorkild. "That was his fate. But will King Gudrød fight on now that his thirst for the blood feud is slaked?"

"He won't fight any more," said Ivar. "He'll take his princess home and bed her. She'll be fat with child before winter."

"What of Dolgfinnr?'

Skallagrimr sniffed and ran a thick hand across his bald head. "Most likely he thinks us gone," he said. "How long would you search for an enemy in the vastness of the Whale Road? He can't know we came inland. He sought us out in the Skagerrak and no doubt fishermen and merchant ships fed him news of the Seaworm and Windspear's passing."

"But we don't know either for sure," said Halvdan. "Dolgfinnr and King Gudrød could be at Dolgfinnr's fortress now drinking ale to celebrate their victory. They could know we planned to join with King Harald and are at this very moment laughing at our misfortune."

"King Gudrød is gone," Einar said. "His fight

here is over."

"How can you be sure?"

Einar shrugged. "Just a feeling. He lost men in the fight for Tromoya. He had to scale defended walls, fight his way through the town and battle King Harald's hearth troop before the hall. I was there. I saw." He pointed to the survivors huddled by the roadside. "A few of those men are of Harald's hearth troop. Each of them fought like ten men. Both King Gudrød and Dolgfinnr lost many warriors to take this place."

"Einar is right," said Ivar. "How long had King Gudrød been away from his home in the Vestfold? A month or more? Dolgfinnr cannot feed his ally for long, so many men would eat through his stores in no time. They could raid and steal food, like we all do on campaign, but he can't do it to Dolgfinnr's people. Besides, his men are rich now with the silver and women looted from Tromoya. Gudrød will sail home. He won't want to lose any more men fighting someone else's war. Dolgfinnr believes he has won. He cares not where we are or what we plan."

"What do we plan?"

The gleam had returned to Ivar's eyes, and he smiled with his usual easy confidence. "If King Gudrød the Hunter has returned to the Vestfold, then Dolgfinnr is alone again. If what Einar says about the fight for Tromoya is true, then many of his men died or were wounded in the assault. He had three crews, perhaps two hundred men? There will be less of the whoresons now."

"You want to attack?" asked Halvdan, rolling his bull neck.

"Oh, the gods are watching you, Ivar Ragnarsson," Thorkild Storyteller said, and he raised his gnarled pale fingers to the heavens. "There is ruthless guile in that skull of yours. Odin cunning, war cunning."

"I might have an idea," Ivar said with a wink. "But first we need to find our ships."

Ivar hurried down the hill, trailed by Halvdan, Skallagrimr, and Radbod. Einar remained on the heights with Thorkild.

"Vigmarr is dead?" said the old storyteller.

"He is," Einar replied.

Thorkild caressed his long moustaches with his bony fingers. "Did you slay him?"

"We fought whilst Tromoya burned. He killed Adzo, and many of the enemy. But yes, I killed him."

"Then old Egil is avenged and his soul has peace at last."

"I pray the gods see fit to take my father to their halls, just as I pray that Vigmarr Svarti wanders like a *nithing* wraith in the frozen hel of

Niflheim."

"Perhaps he does. But you have come far, young Einar. Few men in the crews are as tall as you, and you have grown thicker in the chest. Rowing and fighting have made a carl of you."

Einar opened the leather pouch at his belt and took out a silver hammer amulet on its leather thong. "You gave me this. You said it would strengthen my *hamingja*, and so it has. I return it to you now with thanks, and to say that the air is clear between us, Thorkild. I don't blame you for not avenging Egil all those years ago. Even I could not summon the courage to challenge Vigmarr Svarti; the fight was thrust upon me."

"He was a frightening man. You keep the amulet. I have little need of luck at my age. I welcome death in battle. A carl has no wish to die of old age, drooling and pissing the bed, reliant on other men's charity. You keep it. Luck is for the young."

Einar pulled the old wooden trinket from around his neck, and fixed the silver Mjolnir hammer amulet there instead. Perhaps Thor had brought him battle-luck. Einar had not felt the touch of the gods when he had fought for his life as Tromoya burned, only a desire to kill and to live.

"Look at you, lad!" shouted Styrr, striding up the hill with his blue and white trews flapping in the wind and his tattooed arms stretched wide in greeting. "I shouldn't call you lad anymore. You look fearsome. Should I be afraid of you?"

"Never, friend," Einar replied with a grin. "Do you have any food to share?"

"Ha! Does a horse piss where she pleases? Yngvi, get a fire going and we'll cook up some food."

"By the gods, Einar," called Ulfketil Brownlegs, striding beside Styrr. "I wagered a handful of hacksilver with Fat Garmr that you'd die in there as a hostage." He tripped on a stone and fell on his face, and Einar chuckled despite his melancholy.

"I almost did," he replied.

"But you came out of the shit pit smelling of roses. That *brynjar* looks like Frankish work to me," said Styrr.

"Did you come across any of Dolgfinnr's scouts on your journey?"

"No. Seems like Dogsblood does not know we've marched about his flank. Ivar is as mad as a stung troll, so Odin help Dolgfinnr when he catches up with him. We marched here and met no trouble on the road. All the trouble was here, I see. Shame that Harald's daughter was taken like that."

"Why, did you think you stood a chance with

her?" asked Ulfketil, rubbing at his bruised nose. "Fancied making a proposal, did you?"

"More of a chance than a man who shit in his own trews."

"A fat man with tattoos so faded they look like manure smeared up your arms. There's more silver under my granny's milk churn than there is in your purse. What sort of husband would you make?"

"Your granny's milk churn has half the silver in Hrafnborg beneath it. The old hag is the best whore in the village…" Ulfketil chased Styrr around the group of men and they all laughed together whilst Yngvi found somewhere sheltered to make a fire. Bersa and Ginnlaug took their bows into the forest and hunted game to make a meal for the crew whilst Einar sluiced the blood and ash from himself in the shallows beside Tromoya island.

It took a week to find the Seaworm and Windspear. Ivar sent men scouting up and down the coastline, asking sea merchants and fishermen for any sign of his ships. Einar and the rest of the army camped beside the ruins of Tromoya until an evening where a crescent moon lit up a sky full of stars, when Ivar's *drakkar* warships came about the headland under sail, and Ivar's warriors cheered with joy to see the glorious ships approach.

"Thor's balls, but I long for the sea," sighed Styrr that evening as they sat beside a campfire.

"Thorkild?" asked Ginnlaug, her hawk-sharp face smiling at the sight of the warships. "Tell us the story of Skíðblaðnir."

"A fine tale. Tell it to us whilst we dream of the Whale Road, which we have missed more than the embrace of our wives back home."

"Speak for yourself," said Yngvi the Fire.

Thorkild took out his lyre and the men of both crews gathered around the fire as they watched their precious ships come about Tromoya. Einar's heart lightened to see the Seaworm; the feeling of desolation after Adzo and Likbjorn's deaths had lifted in the company of his shipmates. It had been a week of hunting and healing, and Thorkild had asked him for the story of Tromoya's fall, which the old storyteller planned to turn into a song.

"Lend me your ears, brave warriors of the sea," Thorkild proclaimed, strumming a tune on his lyre as he spoke. "Gather close, and let us speak of Skíðblaðnir, the finest ship ever crafted by the hands of gods and men."

The crew leaned closer; the fire lighting up their weary faces, as eager to hear the tale as they were to ride the Whale Road once more.

"In the realm of Asgard, where Odin and

his children dwell in their golden halls, there once lived the sons of Ivaldi, a race of master craftsmen. Their knowledge stretched far beyond the ken of mortals, and one day long ago, Loki sought out their skill." The storyteller made the hand sign to ward off evil, the firelight flickering over his fingers. "At Loki's behest, the sons of Ivaldi made truly wondrous gifts for his brother and sister gods as atonement after one of Loki's tricks almost brought them all to ruin.

"For Freyr, the god of fertility and prosperity, Loki entreated the sons of Ivaldi to craft a ship of pure brilliance, a vessel to sail the cosmos with the grace of a swan upon a glass lake. The sons of Ivaldi crafted Skíðblaðnir with great cunning, its hull hewn from the sacred wood of Yggdrasil. Each plank was enchanted, riven with spells that ensured Skíðblaðnir would always harness the swiftest wind. Its sails were spun from the light of the rising sun, and they caught the breeze as a gull soars on the air, carrying Freyr wherever he willed." The old storyteller's voice rose and fell like the waves as he described the mighty ship, mesmerising the crew with his words.

"Freyr used Skíðblaðnir to breathe life into barren lands. With it, he sailed across the nine worlds, bestowing light and rain, ensuring bountiful harvests and the flourishing of all living things. Legend holds that wherever Skíðblaðnir docked, the land would thrive, and the hearts of its people would brim over with joy. But the sons of Ivaldi did not create Skíðblaðnir for Freyr alone. It symbolised the bond between the gods and the craftsmen, a hymn to the prosperity of creation when driven by kindredship. The ship embodied the harmony of the divine order, reminding the gods of their responsibilities to the worlds they ruled. Skíðblaðnir was a marvel to behold," Thorkild continued. "Though mighty enough to carry all the gods and their steeds, it could be folded like cloth and gathered into a pouch when its voyage ended. It was a vessel of magic, its sails full-bellied with fair winds, guiding it faithfully to shore."

Einar watched Ivar as Thorkild wove his tale. The Boneless stood alone, wrapped in his green cloak, staring out at his two sleek warships. Thorkild strummed his lyre and spoke of Freyr, Loki, Odin, and Thor, and Ivar's eyes caught the starlight as his cunning mind devised a plan to bring Dolgfinnr Dogsblood to his knees. It had been a summer of blood, of riding the seas and becoming a warrior. Now it was time for Ivar the Boneless to wreak his brutal revenge upon Dolgfinnr and his wolf warriors. As Einar watched his lord, he was ready to follow Ivar into the hel gate of Nargrind itself, if that's what it took to kill Dolgfinnr Dogsblood. He would never forget how the wolf warriors had swarmed over

King Harald's hall; the memories of those wolf-pelted killers and how they had struck at women and children and soaked Harald's longhouse with blood was enough to harden any man's heart. Einar stood and went to Ivar, something he would never have done at the start of the summer, but things were different now.

"Einar," Ivar said, turning in surprise as Einar's boots crunched on a rotten twig.

"I can go if I am disturbing you, lord?" Einar said.

"Stay. Thorkild tells a good tale, does he not?"

"He does, lord. Were you thinking of Dolgfinnr?"

"I was. He is the champion of the North, and I must face him if I am to fulfil my destiny."

"Your destiny?" Einar pulled his own cloak closer about his shoulders, wondering how any man could believe he was destined to be the best, the most feared, the champion of the most warlike people in Midgard.

Ivar flashed a wide smile at Einar. "It is my wyrd, my fate to be the champion of all the Vikings. How else can my reputation outshine my father's? He is Ragnar Lothbrok, the man who sailed further west than any Northman has ever gone before. Raider of cities, most feared jarl anywhere across Denmark, Norway, or amongst the Svear. Any of the sea-wolves, the wicked men lurking across the Skagerrak, Kattegat or the Vik, hide their ships and cower when they see the raven banner. My brothers have shining reputations of their own. Who has not heard of Bjorn Ironside, Sigurd Snake Eye, or Ubba?"

"Does your reputation have to outstrip that of your father and brothers?"

"Of course!" Ivar cocked an eyebrow at Einar as though he were a madman. "When we die, if we are lucky, we ascend to Valhalla or any of the glorious halls in Asgard. Nothing remains of us here but the reputation we leave. Who remembers the farmer, the potter, or the smith? Who remembers the warriors who died on battlefields a hundred years ago? Such men are lost in the winds of time. It is as though they never existed. Men will remember Ragnar until the sun dims and Loki rouses his monster brood on the day of the Ragnarök. Men remember great deeds, bravery, accomplishments beyond the dreams of normal men. I want what all warriors and jarls want, but I want it more. So I must face Dolgfinnr, even though I know he could kill me, just as he has killed countless warriors he has faced in battle. I must stand before him as he hews at me with his axe, as he tries to cut me open and piss on my dead heart. So I must harden myself to that task, Einar. I must be as cold as frost in the land of the Finns, and as hard as Frankish steel. Dolgfinnr is strong, brutal, and fearsome. But I have skill, I fight with two swords which is almost unknown. I have speed, and I have worked on my skill and speed with weapons from the time I could first lift a practice sword. That must be enough. Perhaps one day a man will then come for me, a warrior who is more skilled and faster than I. Such is fate. But first I must face Dolgfinnr and become the champion of the North."

"It is not easy to face your greatest enemy."

"You faced Vigmarr, no?"

"I faced him, lord." Einar stiffened, a flush of panic rushing down his neck, worried that Ivar might challenge him for killing a sea-jarl in his father's service. "How do you know?"

Ivar laughed. "I just know. Vigmarr has fought countless battles, killed, burned, pillaged and destroyed for many years. It was not his destiny to die in battle. I would not have liked to face Vigmarr. He was a fearsome man."

"What if he had killed your father?"

"Then I would have ripped his life away with my swords and kept his skull as a drinking cup. What happened at Tromoya can stay beneath its ashes. If there was a blood feud between you, let it rest."

"Can we defeat Dolgfinnr and his wolf

warriors? I have seen them fight. I was there as they crushed King Harald's men."

"We have to. We fight and win or we die. Do you think Dolgfinnr and his wolves will spare us if we surrender? That is not the world we live in, Einar. I come to kill Dolgfinnr and recover my father's banner. I will succeed and become champion or die trying. As will you all, for you are my oath men. The best any survivors could hope for is to be enslaved, to become a thrall. Which is surely worse than death. So we must defeat Dolgfinnr. Win, or die."

Vengeance and war beckoned, the dreaded shield wall where the champions fought and lesser men voided their bowels in terror, and in that furious clash of weapons, Einar was ready to kill his enemies, and if necessary, to die and join the heroes in Valhalla.

TWENTY-FIVE

Two days later, Einar rowed the warship Seaworm towards Dolgfinnr Dogsblood's stronghold. Einar hauled on the smooth ash shaft of his oar and the long, curved keel of the ship sliced through the swell. These were familiar waters, the same waters Einar had sailed with One Leg Bolti, Kraki, and Sigarr aboard the Waveslicer when that summer was fresh and Einar was still a young man. He could not recognise himself in the boy he was, in the hopes and dreams of an orphan dreaming of glory and the life of a warrior. Einar was a man now, a carl who had sailed, raided, killed and fought dangerous men in single combat. He had sailed the waters again on board the Seaworm, where he had first met Adzo amidst a blood-soaked retreat. Memories of his dead friend came to Einar every night. He missed Adzo, his strange accent, his belief in the nailed god and his humour.

Einar pulled again, pushing his legs against the bench in front and feeling the muscles across his back and shoulders stretch and strengthen. His wounds stretched, burned and ached, but Einar took the pain, using it to fuel his anger like logs in a burning brazier. Twelve men pulled oars aboard the Seaworm, and another dozen rowed the Windspear. Ivar's ship cut through the water alongside them, water foaming about her prow as men grunted and pulled just like Einar. Only twelve men crewed each ship, just as Ivar had ordered, barely enough to heave the ships toward their destination. Just enough to make Dolgfinnr believe Ivar came for him from the sea, that he attacked again in search of the raven banner in the same way as One Leg Bolti had come to the Dogsblood's beach and died in a river of blood.

Fishing boats, small skiffs, coracles and single-mast faerings came to look at the warships and darted away like minnows whenever they came close. Ivar had made sure that shields hung across both sheerstrakes, and he had ordered every man to surrender his helmet. Ivar had mounted each helmet on a spear stave and lashed them to rowing benches and rigging with stout hemp rope, so that to any onlooker the two ships seemed crammed with warriors.

"There they go," said Styrr, pulling his oar on the bench next to Einar's. "Scuttling away like rats to tell their master of our coming."

"Adzo jumped from such a ship," Einar replied. "When One Leg Bolti died, and we fled on board the Waveslicer."

"Aye, well, at least he died a free man. I'd rather live for one summer as a free carl, than a lifetime in thrall to a fisherman."

"Look, there is the Fjordviper!" said Yngvi. As they rowed towards the bay, a harbour came into view on the settlement's western edge. Four longships rested in the gentle swell, one of which was Ivar's Fjordviper.

"Last time we were here, we lost that ship and her crew," Einar mused.

"I haven't forgotten. Nor has anyone else," said Halvdan. "Dolgfinnr knew we were coming then. He was ready for us."

"What if he's ready for us again?" asked Yngvi. "Bastard might be in the hills waiting to ambush us like fools."

"Only we aren't fools, are we?"

"We were that day."

"Aye, well. He ain't expecting us now. Then he was waiting. He had beaten Bolti and captured Lord Ragnar's standard. Dolgfinnr knew we would come, had King Gudrød at his side to help him win. Now he thinks we're beaten, that we ran away like curs. This time it's us who's springing a trap, not them wolf sons of whores. Dolgfinnr sees two ships and two crews coming to attack him. He has the greater numbers and all he sees in his future is slaughter, our slaughter."

"The beacon's lit," called Halvdan, pointing up to the same clifftop where a fire had once warned Dolgfinnr of Bolti's attack.

Einar could not see as he pulled, rowing with his back to their destination. He rowed in his *brynjar* with his axe and seax in his belt. He wore reddish-brown trews tied about his calves with winingas leg wrappings, and his two arm rings caught the midday sun every time he twisted the oar stave. Last time, One Leg Bolti had charged the beach and lost his head upon the shale and sand, but for all Ivar's madness and unpredictable rage, he would not die so easily.

"Right, lads," Halvdan called as he leapt down from the steerboard platform and stalked along the deck. "Oars in. Prepare to go overboard."

Einar stowed his oar, grabbed a spear and shield, and readied himself. They had hugged the coast, keeping pace with Ivar's march south from Tromoya, tacking with the wind and looping out into the sea so that they did not go too far ahead of the marching column. The ships went far enough out to sea to scout for any sign of King Gudrød's fleet in case the Hunter had stayed in Agder after all, but they found none.

That morning, Ivar had advanced on Dolgfinnr's stronghold whilst his two warships approached from the sea.

"Here they come," breathed Styrr, pointing his spear towards the beach, and so they did.

Dolgfinnr himself pranced along the shore on his resplendently white horse, and his wolf warriors gambolled about him, clashing axes on their shields and blaring war horns. Each of them wore their distinctive wolf pelts about their shoulders over bare torsos, as did Dolgfinnr himself.

"The champion of the North," breathed Halvdan. "Bastard's going to earn that title today. Over the side, lads."

Halvdan went first, one meaty hand on the sheerstrake and then over the side into the grey-green water. Einar followed for the second time that summer, gasping as the chill water took his breath away. The tide slopped against the Seaworm's hull and Einar waded chest-deep through the swell, struggling to keep his footing, boots threatening to slip on the bottom and cast him beneath the murky waters. Seawater stung his wounds, but Einar banished the pain to the back of his mind.

Dolgfinnr lifted his weapon, and Einar's chest tightened as he recognised Likbjorn's double-bladed war axe in his killer's fist. A huge wolf warrior rode beside Dolgfinnr with the captured raven banner flying proud. He howled and cocked his head to the sky, and the wolf warriors on the beach leapt and shrieked with anticipation. They too remembered that day when One Leg Bolti led his men to a slaughter in the shallows, and the day they had surprised Ivar and captured the Fjordviper. As Einar came waist-deep in the swell, he longed to charge them, to avenge the dead women and children of Tromoya.

"Hold," Halvdan growled. He banged his shield against Einar's, overlapping it, edge over edge. "Shield wall."

"Bastard can't wait for it," Einar muttered, eyes fixed on Dolgfinnr. Einar rested his axe on the iron rim of his shield. "No matter what happens, he dies today."

"He will if Ivar has his way. For now, we hold."

Two dozen men made a shield wall as the sea tugged and pushed at their midriffs. Dolgfinnr's horse cantered along the beach, its hooves throwing up sand as he glared at the shield wall in the shallows. A lurid red gash ran across his face, the cut inflicted by Likbjorn's axe. Dolgfinnr waved that same butterfly-bladed axe about his head and his wild wolf warriors hushed to an eerie silence. The wall Einar and Halvdan had climbed together rose beyond the beach, the jagged teeth of its palisade threatening shards of broken bone.

Dolgfinnr watched them carefully. He rode his horse into the surf, leaning forward over the beast's neck, staring at the mere two dozen warriors lined up in the water. His hard face searched the Seaworm and the Windspear as though he waited for more men to come, his clever mind wondering if the trifling shield wall was a ruse, some trick to lure him to his death. He saw helmets and shields on the two ships, but no movement, no warriors shouting threats at him from the waves. He sawed on the horse's reins and wheeled the animal around to stare back at his fortress, and then a horn blared from the hills around Dolgfinnr's fortress.

A lone figure came down from the dense pine tree forest. He leapt onto a moon-coloured rock, drew two swords and held them wide at his sides in challenge. The war horn blared again, and one hundred warriors came from the forest carrying shields and spears. They slipped from the boughs and leaves like the *huldu* folk, just as Dolgfinnr himself had surprised Ivar on the day they captured the Fjordviper and sent Ivar into an inglorious defeat. Ivar lifted his blades and the warriors behind him let out a roar with such fury that it was as though the seabed beneath Einar's boots shook.

"Bersa, Ginnlaug!" Halvdan called, leaning

back towards the ship. The two archers appeared at the Seaworm's prow, both women clutching their bows. "Kill that big bastard with the banner."

No sooner had the words left Halvdan's lips than two white-feathered arrows soared across Einar's head and thumped into the wolf warrior's chest.

"Bloody fool, coming to war without armour," said Styrr as the immense man holding the raven banner swayed in the saddle and then fell with a splash into the shallows. Another man ran from Dolgfinnr's massed ranks and scooped up the raven banner, carrying it away from the water's edge.

The wolf warriors on the beach ceased their capering and banging of weapons. A silence fell over them as their heads snapped back and forth between the men on the hill above them and the warriors in the water. Ivar called something, pointing one of his two swords, Hugin and Munin, down at Dolgfinnr.

"What did he say?" asked Ulfketil Brownlegs, standing four shields down from Einar.

"Don't know, couldn't hear him," said Styrr. Einar couldn't hear either, but he could imagine the threat and challenge Ivar called down to his enemy.

Ivar hopped down from the rock and his warriors followed, charging down towards the beach like an avalanche. Axes, seaxes and spears glinted and Dolgfinnr's wolf warriors looked to their jarl for orders, caught between an enemy at sea and one howling down at them from above. Dolgfinnr ducked as an arrow glided over his head and he dug his ankles into his horse's flanks and cantered towards his men.

"Time to earn our arm rings," Halvdan snarled. "We go together. Keep the shield wall tight until they break. Who do you fight for?"

"Ivar! Ivar! Ivar!" Einar and the warriors in the water roared as one.

"Then let's see you do it."

The shield wall moved with practised efficiency towards shore, and Einar kept pace with Halvdan. His heart thumped in his chest and he ground his teeth. The prospect of facing Dolgfinnr's brutal killers kindled the fire of war in Einar's belly. Einar and Halvdan's left feet moved together, spears poised and shields overlapped even though the tide washed about their legs, threatening to tip Einar off balance. The rest of the shield wall kept that pace, and they shouted together at each left-footed step to help keep time.

Dolgfinnr leapt from his horse and waved his

axe about his head, ordering his men into battle formation. Einar couldn't hear what was said over the crash and slide of waves upon shale, but Dolgfinnr had the greater numbers and so he set fifty men facing towards the sea, and ordered the rest into shield wall formation, facing Ivar's charge.

Arrows whipped into the enemy as Bersa and Ginnlaug loosed shaft after shaft. They had no archers of their own, but waited with spears ready, gathered in a ragged line, wolf pelts iron-grey above their bare chests. Einar and the warriors in the shield wall advanced until the sea lapped at their knees, and then the wolf warriors came. With bloodcurdling howls, they launched their spears and Einar caught one on his shield's iron boss. He tilted the shield upwards and batted another spear over his head to splash harmlessly in the sea.

"Bull's horns!" Halvdan shouted. "Bull's horns!"

The men understood that order, just as they understood the *Svinfylking* and a dozen other shield wall formations. Einar took a step back, as did every other man in the wall, so that they formed two ranks of ten warriors. Fifty battle-hardened enemies awaited them in the shallows, ready to kill them as they struggled in the surf. One Leg Bolti and his men had died in the same way, pulled by the tide, footing unsure as enemy warriors had spliced and carved at them with wickedly sharp blades.

Einar advanced in the second rank, with Styrr beside him and Halvdan in front. More spears came, their blades crunching into linden-wood, and one Windspear warrior out of Einar's line of sight cried out in pain. The enemy warriors charged, surging from the beach in the battle-madness. They came not in a shield wall, but ragged and defiant with axes and shields clutched in their fists.

"Brace yourselves!" Halvdan roared, and then the enemy hit the shield wall with a crunch of iron, wood and bone. The impact drove Halvdan back into Einar's shield, and Einar held him there. He could not push him forward, for it would drive the bull-necked shipmaster onto an enemy blade. So Einar braced him, and Halvdan lunged forward.

Axes and spears rent and chopped at the Hrafnborg men. Another cry peeled out and there was blood in the water. Einar stabbed his spear forward and drove its point into a wolf warrior's eye. Another appeared, beating at Halvdan's shield. Halvdan relinquished his spear, the weapon resting above the lines of battle as men pressed together as close as lovers. Halvdan stabbed beneath the rim of his shield with his long knife and a wolf warrior yelped out in pain and fell away. The long knife tore open the warrior's groin, and blood flowed copiously, staining the water and mixing with the blood of other dying men.

The enemy leapt and jabbed with their weapons, the sheer force of their number beating the Ragnarsson shield wall backwards. Einar shuffled in the shale and sand, trying to hold his ground but pressed backwards by the enemy's ferocity.

"Horns! Horns!" Halvdan ordered, grabbing his spear again and stabbing at enemy throats and faces within reach.

Einar and the second rank broke off from the shield wall. Five ran left and five right so that they came about the wolf warriors' flanks, encircling them like curving bull's horns, and Halvdan's front rank was the head. Einar ran to the left, splashing through the murky seawater until he cleared Halvdan's shield wall and then broke from the water. He came about the wolf warriors, and he and Styrr charged their flank without mercy. Einar banged one wolf man off his feet with a shield thrust and punched his spear point into the unprotected chest of another. An arrow slapped into the thigh of a squat enemy and Styrr tore out his throat with his spear.

"Kill the bastards!" Halvdan bellowed above the battle din, and the wolf enemy began to retreat, their greater numbers suffering as they found themselves under attack on three sides. Halvdan burst out of the shield wall, eyes wide with fury, slashing at the enemy with his knife. Einar followed. He threw his spear at an enemy, dropped his shield and drew his axe and seax. Einar thrust past Styrr's shield, chopped his axe into a wolf warrior's haunch, and opened his guts with his seax. He and Halvdan were amongst them, two giant men in *brynjar*s fighting at close quarters against foes with bare chests and midriffs. A knife scraped across Einar's chainmail and another stabbed at his lower back, but his mail took the blows.

Knives and axes clanged, and it became a blur of rage and skill. Blood sprayed across Einar's face. Men screamed in agony and others died. Einar chopped his axe into a man's chest and then stamped him down onto the sand and continued stamping on his face and throat as he fought the next man. The enemy tried to peel away from Halvdan and Einar's fury, and once their foremost fighters flinched and backed away, the rest ran. A hulking man bawled at Einar, rearing up in front of him, his wolf's fur rank and his breath fetid. He kicked Einar in the midriff, but Einar hooked his seax behind the man's calf and cut across the back of his knee. He staggered, flailing with his axe, and Halvdan hit him so hard with his blade that he cut the enemy's head from his shoulders.

That sickening sight was enough to send the rest of the enemy warriors to flight. Styrr hurled his spear after one and it caught the running man between the shoulders.

"Shitworms should at least wear leather," Styrr commented, his own leather jerkin wet with other men's blood.

Einar wiped sweat from his brow as the enemy ran for their lives. Across the beach, Ivar's men fought Dolgfinnr's main force. Weapons clanged, men shouted, and the din of battle resonated across the bay.

"Odin sees us," Einar gasped, sure that the All-Father would rejoice in such bloodletting in the mortal combat between two foes. "Tonight new warriors shall join his Einherjar, swelling the ranks of Odin's corpse-army."

"Aye, well, let's hope I'm not one of them," said Ulfketil Brownlegs.

"Now we attack their rear," said Halvdan. He sheathed his axe and picked up a dead man's axe, so that he held an axe in each hand. Einar sheathed his seax and stowed his axe in its loop. He picked up a long-hafted war axe and clutched it in two hands. "No shield wall," Halvdan continued. "We just kill the whoresons. Ivar will give an arm ring to the man who retrieves the raven banner."

Einar ran across the beach, with Halvdan on one side and Styrr on the other. They charged at the enemy facing away from them, at enemies focused on facing Ivar's warriors who were now engaged in full battle with Dolgfinnr's men on the beach. The wolf warriors who had run from the water's edge did not join their comrades, but made for the settlement itself, their thirst for war slaked by the blood of their shield brothers.

The rear rankers in Dolgfinnr's force turned once they heard boots pounding towards them. They wore pelts and carried weapons like the rest of Dolgfinnr's men, but these weren't the champions who fought at the front with the hardest men. These were the shirkers, the men who waited for the shield wall to break before they struck a blow at fleeing enemies and wounded men.

Einar let out a bloodcurdling roar, using the memory of the dead women and children of Tromoya to give his arms and shoulders strength. He swung his long-handled war axe about him in a great arc and his blade cut an enemy warrior from navel to neck. Einar kept on swinging, bringing the axe about him so that its blade cut high and then low. The shirkers tried to run, tried to get away from the twenty warriors attacking them from behind, men already mottled with blood and filth from the fight at the sea's edge.

A wolf warrior with a long, braided beard caught the haft of Einar's axe and ripped it from his grip. Einar turned on his heels and seized the seax from the small of his back, and in one fluid motion, he sliced open the man's stomach and rammed him out of the way with his shoulder. Halvdan, Styrr, Ulfketil and the rest tore into them like demons from Niflheim and soon Dolgfinnr's army parted in panic like river water flowing around stone. Einar saw Ivar and Skallagrimr through the melee, then Radbod, Thorkild and others fighting savagely against Dolgfinnr's warriors.

The raven banner flew amongst the press of Dolgfinnr's warriors, and Halvdan made for it, slaughtering any of the enemy who blocked his path. Einar followed, drawing his axe and cutting at an enemy who found themselves attacked in front and behind. A tattooed warrior with a scarred face held the raven banner, and he stabbed at Halvdan with the spear from which the banner flew. The spearhead sliced open Halvdan's shoulder in a spray of bright blood, but then the bull-necked shipmaster set about the tattooed man like a rabid dog. He cut him so many times with his weapons that before the man could react, his face, neck and chest became a tapestry of torn and tattered flesh. The battle standard fell and Halvdan scooped it up, his face twisted with the sheer ecstasy of victory. Einar roared with him, waving his axe in the air, revelling in the unbridled joy of killing men who wished to rip his own life away, of victory where the only alternative was death.

The battle lines suddenly parted. Einar and Halvdan found themselves in a sliver of open space between the two forces. Men lay dead or writhing in pain about them. The sea breeze whipped the iron stench of blood and the acrid smell of sweat and piss about Einar's nose. Halvdan waved the raven banner and grinned at the enemy warriors. Einar turned, standing with his own men facing Dolgfinnr's men, the chests of the latter heaving, their faces drawn taut with fear. More of them lay dead on the sand than Ragnarsson's men, and now Ivar stepped before his warriors, his two swords dripping with gore and his handsome face feral and savage.

Dolgfinnr Dogsblood stood before his men, still wielding Likbjorn's butterfly-bladed axe. His face and forearms bled from multiple cuts and his chest heaved from the exertion of battle.

"I challenge you, champion of the Northmen," Ivar shouted so that every man on the beach could hear him.

"You couldn't challenge an old drunk to a pissing contest," Dolgfinnr spat.

"When you die, I shall bring your head back to

my father and we shall set your skull above our hall so that all men know the price for breaking an oath to Ragnar Lothbrok."

"An oath to a *nithing* is no oath at all. What are you without your father? Nothing but a little whelp with expensive swords. A dwarf who yaps like a pup. Everything I have, I won in battle: my axe, my ships, my men, this land. I had nothing! Nothing! With these hands I won my fair fame. What can you say, Ivar the *slyðra*? That your papa gave you ships and warriors so that you could come and yap at better men? Come then, come and fight with Dolgfinnr Dogsblood."

The smile dropped from Ivar's face, and he lifted his swords in salute. The survivors from both armies stepped back to give their warlords space, and Ivar and Dolgfinnr circled each other. Dolgfinnr held his axe two-handed, crouched, his muscled chest and shoulders bunched and rippling with power. Ivar moved lightly on the balls of his feet, half the size of Dolgfinnr; slim, lustrous and lithe, like a cat. Dolgfinnr bellowed and hurled himself at Ivar, the heavy axe moving in his hands as though it weighed nothing. Ivar swayed away from the first strike, ducked beneath the second, and blocked the third with both swords. The sound of those mighty weapons coming together shuddered Einar's bones, and he gaped at the awesome spectacle of two exceedingly skilled warriors fighting for supremacy.

Ivar and Dolgfinnr sprang apart, then came together in a flurry of steel, blinding speed and impossible skill. Ivar turned, twisted and cut at Dolgfinnr. He sliced at the bigger man's legs, abdomen, and arms. Every time Dolgfinnr attacked, it was in a place Ivar had been a fraction earlier and the champion of the North bellowed in frustrated anger and swung the axe with such force that for a heartbeat, Einar thought he would smite Ivar in two. But in an astonishing feat of warrior agility, Ivar jumped. He leapt high into the air and the butterfly blade swept beneath him. Dolgfinnr stumbled, dragged off balance by the heavy axe he had expected to cut into Ivar's waist. Ivar landed lightly and stabbed the points of both swords into Dolgfinnr's stomach.

The wolf warriors groaned as one, and their lord gaped at the lengths of sharp steep protruding from his body.

"I am the champion of the Northmen," Ivar snarled, his eyes gleaming. He yanked his swords free and swept them about him so that Dolgfinnr's blood spattered across his own men. Ivar strutted with his chest out, daring any other warrior on the beach to face him. Dolgfinnr sagged to his knees, and he dropped his heavy axe. Ivar gestured to the weapon, and Dolgfinnr leant forward to pick it up. As he did, a gout of dark blood slopped from his mouth to stain the battle-churned sand. Dolgfinnr fell onto his side, and Ivar darted toward him. He dropped his Munin sword and grabbed the axe haft, pressing it into Dolgfinnr's dying hand. Ivar bent over him and whispered something into the Dogsblood's ear. Then Ivar rose and, with a sweep of his sword, he sliced off Dolgfinnr's head.

The Ragnarsson army cheered for their lord, and Einar roared with them. The enemy warriors backed away. All willingness to fight slipped away from them with Dolgfinnr's death. Ivar turned, basking in the acclaim, sword raised high above him, pointing towards Asgard and Odin All-Father. He caught Einar's eye and nodded. He had faced the impossible adversary and emerged victorious. They both had.

Ivar let his men sack Dolgfinnr's settlement, but Einar took no part in it. He sat on the beach and thought of Adzo, of Likbjorn, One Leg Bolti and the others who had died that bloody summer. Adzo would never again return home to Frankia. Einar lay back on the sand and stared up at the shifting sky. The pain of his wounds returned as the
heart-pumping thrill of battle subsided. Cuts to his arms and body stung and the bruises to his face ached. He imagined Adzo's family watching for him every morning on a distant Frankish shore, hoping for their son and brother to return.

Nobody in Hrafnborg waited for Einar's return, nobody would grieve his passing when he died beneath an enemy's blade out on the Whale Road. Perhaps he should seek a wife, and have a family? Einar wasn't so sure. Summer would be over soon, and raiding season at an end. Then it would be time to use his share of the plunder to find a house, to keep warm through winter until it was time to set sail again.

Much and more had happened since he had left Hrafnborg. Einar had avenged his father and had killed Vigmarr Svarti. He had started the year as a youth without place or promise and now Einar was a warrior of reputation. Dolgfinnr Dogsblood was dead and the raven banner was recovered. Ivar took oaths from any of Dolgfinnr's men who wanted to join his crews, and he sent men to secure the Fjordviper and the other three ships in Dolgfinnr's harbour. Those who did not swear to become Ivar's men died on the beach.

For as long as he could remember, Einar had dreamed of becoming a warrior. He had dreamt of shining axe blades, glorious swords, champions, and the clash of iron on stout shields. He was a carl now, a warrior who pulled an oar aboard the warship Seaworm, but his adventures had only just begun…

PETER GIBBONS

AUTHOR MAILING LIST

If you enjoyed this book, why not join the authors mailing list and receive updates on new books and exciting news. No spam, just information on books. Every sign up will receive a free download of one of Peter Gibbons' historical fiction novels.

https://petermgibbons.com

ABOUT THE AUTHOR

Peter Gibbons

Peter is the winner of the 2022 Kindle Storyteller Literary Award, and an author based in Kildare in Ireland, with a passion for Historical Fiction, Fantasy, Science Fiction, and of course writing!

Peter was born in Warrington in the UK and studied Law at Liverpool John Moores University, before taking up a career in Financial Services and is now a full time author.

Peter currently lives in Kildare Ireland, and is married with three children. Peter is an avid reader of both Historical Fiction and Fantasy novels, particularly those of Bernard Cornwell, Steven Pressfield, David Gemmell, and Brandon Sanderson.

Peter's books include the Viking Blood and Blade Saga and The Saxon Warrior Series. You can visit

Peter's website at www.petermgibbons.com.

Printed in Great Britain
by Amazon